THE HANGMAN'S HOLD

MICHAEL WOOD

KILLER READS

A division of HarperCollins*Publishers*
www.harpercollins.co.uk

KillerReads
an imprint of HarperCollinsPublishers Ltd
1 London Bridge Street
London SE1 9GF

www.harpercollins.co.uk

This paperback edition 2018

First published in Great Britain in ebook format by HarperCollins*Publishers* 2018

A catalogue record for this book
is available from the British Library

ISBN: 978-0-00-831162-9

This novel is entirely a work of fiction.
The names, characters and incidents portrayed in it are
the work of the author's imagination. Any resemblance to
actual persons, living or dead, events or localities is
entirely coincidental.

Printed and bound by CPI Group (UK) Ltd, Croydon, CR0 4YY

To Christopher Schofield
A genuine life saver, a good friend and a huge supporter.
He doesn't only support me, but The Asses and Donkeys
Trust too. Pomegranate anyone?

Chapter One

Day One
Thursday, 9 March 2017

The pale grey, or the sky-blue tie? The grey one would go with the jacket, but the blue would match the shirt. Maybe no tie at all.

With a sigh, he threw both ties at his reflection in the wardrobe mirror and fell backwards onto the bed behind him. He turned to the alarm clock on the bedside table. The harsh digits in a terrible Day-Glo green, which wouldn't match anything in his wardrobe, told him it was almost six o'clock. He still had time.

He pulled himself up and looked at his tired reflection once more, something he'd been doing quite a lot of in the last couple of weeks.

'Look at the state of you,' he said to himself. 'Forty-five years old and you're panicking over what to wear. It's a few drinks, that's all. Just two people having a drink together. Where's the harm in that?' He gazed deep into himself as if expecting an answer. His face was red. There was a sheen of sweat on his forehead and a gleam in his eyes.

Of course, it was more than just a few drinks. It was a date. An actual date. A trial run to see how two people, who, according to a computer seemed ideal for each other, would get on in reality. It was also his first in more than twenty-five years.

Following his divorce, and a long period of adjustment, Brian Appleby had thought he'd been left with a life of singledom, a life dedicated to himself and the things he enjoyed doing. He'd go on holidays with friends, trips to the theatre, and when he fancied being alone, he could watch a film on the sofa with his feet up and his socks off.

Unfortunately, life hadn't worked out that way. All his friends had abandoned him, as had his family. He could understand that. He would probably have done the same in their position. At first, he'd tried to tell himself he didn't care. Screw them. Yes, he'd made a number of mistakes, but he'd paid his price. Shouldn't he be able to move on and continue with the rest of his life? Why couldn't other people see that? Their loss. If they didn't want him around, he'd find new friends.

That had been easier said than done. New friends were hard to come by; especially when you were a stranger with a past you refused to talk about. Again, he hadn't cared, in the beginning. He enjoyed his own company. But evenings in front of the TV eating pizza and not talking to anyone had soon begun to take its toll. The tipping point had come when he'd walked into Domino's and the young girl with greasy hair serving had looked at him and said: 'Good evening, Brian. What are you in the mood for tonight?' She knew his name. He knew her name. He knew the name of every member of staff. How far had he fallen that he personally knew the people who worked in his local takeaway? He had quickly ordered and made his escape, returning home to examine the pathetic existence his life had become.

His light at the end of the tunnel had come in the form of an advert on late-night television. A new website had been set up for the recently single looking to meet new people 'for socializing, et cetera'. He hadn't been too bothered about the 'et cetera', but he'd missed having someone to share his interests with.

He'd logged on, created a profile and spent a full evening trying to find a decent enough photograph of himself. That had been a task in itself as he hadn't been able to remember the last time he'd had his picture taken. Actually, that wasn't true. He could remember, but a police mugshot wasn't something you used to attract a lady. Eventually, he'd resorted to taking a selfie, his first (and hopefully last) one. He'd surprised himself by how smart he looked in his suit and his neatly combed hair. Fingers crossed he looked completely different from the picture of him that had been slapped all over the tabloids.

After a week, he had chatted to eleven different women. None of them were his type; he didn't have a type as such, but he knew that the ideal woman would jump out of the screen at him. Eventually, she did – a professional single woman named Adele Kean, a few years younger than him, attractive, 'enjoyed the theatre, eating out, and a good film'. She ticked all the right boxes. She was the one.

Brian had spent an hour with a pad and pen drafting the perfect opening message to send to her. He'd wanted to make sure his spelling and punctuation were correct and tried to be funny without seeming desperate. He mentioned his recent trip to the Crucible (though he didn't say it was only to watch the snooker) and how one of his favourite films was *Rebecca* starring Laurence Olivier, even though it was really *Die Hard*. He sent the email and waited impatiently for a reply.

His wait was a long one. It was five days before it arrived with an apology for her tardiness but she had been busy with work. She thanked Brian for his lovely message, said she had seen *Rebecca*, but it was years ago, and promised to look it up online next time she had a free evening. She also complimented him on his photograph and hoped she would hear from him soon. It was a good sign Adele hadn't recognized who he was from his photograph. He had changed over the years, but he was worried he was still identifiable.

She heard from him very soon. Within thirty minutes of her reply landing in his inbox he was hitting the send button on his second message, the content of which seemed to come easier this time.

For a week, messages went back and forth – Brian was itching to suggest a meet but didn't want to scare her off. On the Wednesday, Adele took the first step and offered her telephone number. His heart almost skipped a beat when he read that one.

Brian liked her accent – a mixture of Sheffield and Manchester. She was surprised she couldn't hear any American in his since he'd told her he spent eight years teaching English in the States. He'd forgotten about the accent issue when he came up with that lie. He'd never even been to America. The conversation ran on without any awkwardness or silence and by the end of the chat they had arranged to meet for drinks the following evening outside the City Hall.

So, which was it to be, the pale grey tie or the sky-blue one? Or maybe no tie at all.

'Damn it, Brian!'

Typically, it was raining. Typically, Brian was caught in traffic. Typically, Brian was five minutes late arriving at the City Hall.

He expected to get there and find the steps completely deserted. But was pleasantly surprised when he spotted her standing under the shelter of a large umbrella looking stunning and elegant in a long black coat.

He called out to her and she turned to him and smiled. She was so attractive, with a wonderful smile. She was perfect – exactly what he had been looking for.

'Brian Appleby?' she asked.

'I am so sorry for being late. What is it with traffic when it rains? I was over twenty minutes on Chesterfield Road. I couldn't believe it,' he mumbled.

'You don't need to apologize it's fine, honestly. I was a minute or two late myself.'

He smiled. 'Shall we go into Lloyd's for a drink?'

'I'd like that,' she replied.

The short walk to the pub was made in silence, but it wasn't awkward. Out of the corner of his eye, Brian stole glances at the woman beside him. The slight breeze carried a hint of her scent – a subtle sweet perfume mixed with her natural aroma. He wanted to touch her, to feel her smooth skin on his fingers. No. Not yet.

'What will you have?'

'Gin and tonic, please.'

'OK. Do you want to try and find a table while I get the drinks?'

For early Thursday evening, the pub was busy. Sheffield, undergoing a seemingly never-ending period of regeneration, was trying to get people to stay in the city centre after work rather than head straight home. A council campaign had been launched and a new cinema and several bars had opened. So far it seemed to be working.

Adele found a spot by the window and waited for Brian to return from the bar.

'Don't you drink?' she asked, looking at the orange juice he'd brought for himself.

'I'm driving.'

'Oh.'

'So, you're a pathologist, you were saying on the phone last night? That must be interesting.'

'It is,' Adele beamed. 'It's a great job. Very time-consuming, but I do enjoy it.'

'And you have a grown-up son?'

'Chris. Yes, he's twenty-one. He's not long since left university and started his first job this week.'

'What's he doing?'

'Same line you were in: teacher. It's only temporary, to cover maternity leave, but who knows? It's good experience too.'

'Definitely. How's the training going? I noticed you were limping slightly,' Brian said.

'Oh, that's nothing, it's these shoes,' she smiled. 'A friend of mine and I are training for a half-marathon. We're raising money for a brain tumour charity. I lost someone close to me a couple of years ago. His wife and I are doing the race to raise money in his memory.'

There was a brief pause in the conversation as the topic slowly died and neither knew where to go next. They both took lingering sips of their drinks.

'Do you run?' Adele asked.

'No. Dodgy knee. I walk a lot though. I like to get out into the country when I can.'

'Oh yes, I remember you saying that's why you chose to move to Sheffield.'

'Yes, a large city but right on the doorstep of the countryside. It's ideal.'

'So why did you decide to return to England after eight years in the States?'

'Well I was made redundant and rather than try to find work I thought I'd come home. I never intended to stay out there as long as I did.'

'Why did you go in the first place?' Adele asked, leaning forward. She seemed genuinely interested.

'Well,' he said, blowing out his cheeks. 'I'd just split from the wife and wanted a clean break of things. I thought an ocean between us might help the healing process.'

'Did it?'

'Yes,' he smiled. 'It did.'

'I can still detect a London accent.'

'Oh I'll never lose that,' he grinned. 'Would you like another drink or shall we go for something to eat?'

Adele looked at her watch. It wasn't even eight o'clock yet. There was plenty of time for a meal. They decided on another drink. Adele told him more about her work and her friends. Brian mentioned about his ex-wife and how he found her in bed with another woman. In the toilets he refused to look at his reflection; he genuinely liked this woman; how could he tell her so many lies?

***

By nine o'clock they were sitting at a table by the window in a restaurant in Leopold Square waiting for their starters.

Adele had been in here many times with Matilda and felt relaxed.

Brian looked around him like an excited child on his first trip to a theme park. The delight in his eyes soon disappeared when he noticed a woman staring at him. Her lingering glances were unsettling. Had she recognized him? If he'd taken Adele's seat, his back would have been to the restaurant and he could have concentrated on his date. Shit.

'Go on,' Adele prompted.

'Sorry?'

'You were saying about your surprise visitor.'

'What? Oh … yes.' He tried to ignore the woman across the room, but it wasn't easy. Why did she keep looking at him? 'We were told there was going to be someone important visiting the school. We all thought it would probably be some reality TV so-called celebrity the kids would go crazy over but none of the teachers would recognize. I was halfway through my lesson when there was a knock on the door and in walked Michelle Obama.'

'You're joking!' Adele gasped.

'No word of a lie. It was incredible. She had all these security people with her with their dark glasses.'

'Did you actually talk to her?'

'I did. She sat in on the lesson for a while and watched the kids read then she came over and spoke to me. She asked where I was from and joked about my accent.'

'What was she like?'

'She was lovely. Very warm, welcoming, easy to talk to. She genuinely seemed interested.'

'That's brilliant. I love Michelle Obama,' Adele said. 'I've never met anyone famous. Well, no one alive anyway,' she said, thinking back to a former soap star she once had on her pathology table.

'No one alive? What are you, pathologist to the stars?'

'Something like that.' She smiled.

'I bet you have a few stories to tell.'

'Plenty. And not a single one of them appropriate over dinner,' she said as the waitress arrived with their first course.

He looked over again at the woman. This time, she gave a hint of a smile and nodded her head at him. It was a knowing smile and he didn't like it. Then, the penny dropped. Of course, she'd trimmed his hair this morning. Crisis averted.

'Is this the first time you've used a dating website?' Brian asked once the coffee had arrived at the end of their meal.

'Yes. I was extremely nervous about it, if I'm honest. I'm not used to putting my life on a website like that. It was strange. We put so much of ourselves on the Internet, don't we? I dread to think what will come up if I ever google myself.' She smiled.

Brian googled himself on an almost daily basis. His life was laid bare for everyone to pore over. Fortunately, there wasn't a recent photograph of him. Besides, who would be looking for him in Sheffield?

'I know what you mean. Finding seventy-five words to describe yourself is harder than you expect. And I was suddenly very self-conscious about my height,' he laughed.

'I had a half-hour debate with my son over my eyes. I think they're blue; he thinks they're green.'

Brian leaned forward. 'They're definitely blue. A lovely warm blue.'

Adele blushed.

'So.' Brian sat back, obviously uncomfortable. 'Why decide to do it now?'

'Well, Chris doesn't need looking after anymore. I've got my life back. Unfortunately, the world has changed since I last went on a date. This seems to be the way of doing things now. What about you? Wasn't there anyone in America?'

'No. Well, there were a few dates, but never anything long-lasting.'

'Would you have stayed out there if there had been?'

'I'm not sure. The longer I was there the more I missed England.' He paused, 'I've really enjoyed this evening, Adele. You've made me laugh for the first time in ages.'

Adele blushed as she smiled. 'That's kind of you to say, thank you.'

'Would you like to meet up again?'

'Yes. I'd like that.'

The bill arrived, and they agreed to pay half each without any argument. When they left, the temperature had dropped, and Adele shivered. Brian helped her with her coat and they made eye contact. He leaned in and kissed her on the lips. It lingered for a few seconds before Adele pulled away.

'Sorry,' he said.

'No … I just …'

'That's OK. I understand. Take things slowly.'

'Exactly. You don't mind?'

'No. Of course not. May I walk you to your car?'

'I'm getting a taxi home.'

'I'll walk you to the taxi rank then.'

They shared another brief kiss at the taxi, and Brian closed the door once Adele was safely inside. As it pulled away from the kerb she turned back and waved. Brian waited until the taxi had turned the corner before he headed for the car park. He took out his mobile and opened up the photos app. He scrolled through the pictures he had taken of Adele standing outside the City Hall before they'd met. She smiled at a passer-by. She looked at her watch. She looked left and right, then left again. She paced. She checked the time once more. There was a reason he was a few minutes late. He couldn't take his eyes off her.

Adele sat back in the taxi and found she had a silly smile on her face. She had just had the best date of her life. Brian was charming, funny, intelligent, and he didn't seem to mind that she'd turned away from the kiss when his tongue started to intrude. She took her phone out of her bag and began sending a message.

On my way home. Great night. Brian was lovely.

The reply from her best friend, Matilda Darke, was almost instant.

Is he going home with you?

No he isn't. I'm not that kind of woman.

You used to be, lol.

I've grown up a lot since then.

Will you be seeing him again?

Yes. I liked him a lot.

Any tongue action?

My lips are sealed.

Spoil sport.

We kissed. Twice. No tongue.

Hot! I hope he wore protection, lol.

'I can't park on your road, I'm afraid,' the taxi driver said, interrupting Adele's text conversation.

'Sorry?'

'There's traffic on both sides and if this sodding Audi behind me gets any closer he'll be performing a colonoscopy.'

Adele looked out of the back window but could see nothing but the bright headlights. 'That's fine. Park around the corner. I can walk.'

The taxi turned left and pulled up in front of a shop. The Audi shot round and drove down the road at speed.

'Sorry about that, love. Some people shouldn't be allowed on the road.'

'Tell me about it,' she agreed. Most of the people who came into her lab were the result of car-related deaths.

Adele paid the fare and tipped the driver. She turned her back to the taxi, buttoned her coat up to the neck against the stiff March breeze and headed for home.

Traffic wasn't usually so bad on her street. There were cars parked bumper-to-bumper on both sides. Somebody must be having a party.

As she walked down the poorly lit road she checked her phone, the brightness lighting up her face. It was just after eleven o'clock, not too late then.

It was a quiet night, and a cold one. The stars were shining in their billions as Adele looked to the pitch-black sky. There wasn't a cloud visible. She shivered and pulled the collar up on her designer coat. A dog barked somewhere. Its resounding call set off a chain – a cat meowed, another dog barked, an owl hooted.

Adele stopped dead in her tracks and looked about her. She couldn't make up her mind if she had heard something or if it was her imagination. The loud clacking from her shoes echoed as she took long strides to the safety of her house. For some reason, she wanted to get home, quickly, and lock the door behind her.

As Adele reached her front door the security light came on. She realized her house keys were buried somewhere in her handbag. She grabbed for the keys and struggled to find the Yale to unlock the door. Her fingers were cold and shaking. She pushed it open and almost fell into the house, slamming it closed behind her. She put the safety chain on, locked the top and bottom bolts and came to rest with her back against the solid wood.

'Chris?' she called out to the dark, silent house. 'Chris, are you home?'

She kicked off her expensive but painful shoes and sighed with relief. She headed for the kitchen when a dull thud from the living room caused her to stop in her tracks. There was someone in her house. If Chris was home, he would have made himself known by now.

She turned and studied the door. Her eyes were locked on the handle, as if waiting for it to be pushed down from the other side. She grabbed it, slowly depressed it, and opened the door carefully.

Adele opened it wide enough to put her arm through and flick on the living room light. The yellow glow made her squint. She listened intently but couldn't hear anything from the other side of the door. She pushed it fully open and froze in horror.

'Who the bloody hell are you?' she asked.

Brian Appleby hadn't wanted the evening to end. He had had a wonderful time with Adele. The kiss at the end was beautiful. He thought he'd made a mistake when he tried to go further, but he understood. They had to get to know each other, what they liked, disliked, how quickly they wanted to take this. He was prepared to wait.

He took no notice of his journey home. He drove along Heeley and Woodseats while his mind went over the date and pictured Adele's blushes and smiles. She really was a beautiful woman. Her hair was soft and shiny, she didn't cake herself in too much make-up, her jewellery was understated yet elegant. Everything about her was as close to perfect as it was possible to get.

Brian parked in his usual place right outside his detached home on Linden Avenue. He smiled at a neighbour as she let her cat out for the night, then went inside.

It was ten past eleven. He decided to treat himself to a glass of Jameson's or two in his armchair and go over the date one more time.

He turned on the living room light to find a man sitting in the middle of the sofa.

'Who the bloody hell are you?' Brian asked, his voice filled with anger at the boldness of his intruder.

'Good evening, Brian. How was your date?'

'What the …? Hang on, I know you, don't I?'

'Were you able to control yourself? Or did the old urges come flooding back? On the other hand, this one's a little older than what you usually go for. Are you trying to be a model citizen? It's a bit late for that, isn't it?'

'Have you been following me?'

'Why don't you take a seat, Brian. We've got a lot to talk about.'

'How did you get in?' he asked, not moving from the doorway.

'If you'll sit down, I'll explain everything.'

Tentatively, Brian made his way over to the armchair, not once taking his eyes off his intruder. He sat, perched on the edge. 'Go on then, explain. And if I don't like what I hear I'm calling the police.'

'I don't think you're going to want to do that.'

There was a calmness about his strange visitor that frightened Brian. How did he know so much about him? How long had he been following him?

'Why not?' Brian frowned.

'See that bag on the coffee table? Open it.'

Brian looked down at the small tote bag. 'What is it?'

'It's for you. A present.'

'I don't want it,' he said defiantly.

'Open it,' the intruder said, more forcefully.

Still not taking his eyes from his visitor, Brian edged towards the coffee table and opened the light cotton bag. He frowned, not making sense of what was inside. He reached in and pulled it out.

'Jesus Christ! Who are you?'

Chapter Two

DCI Matilda Darke couldn't get used to her new car. The silver Ford Focus she had driven for years had been written off by the insurance company late last year after she'd swerved to avoid a head-on collision and crashed into a tree. Rather than upgrade to something shiny and modern, Matilda had opted for another silver Ford Focus. The only difference was the licence plate. That wasn't technically true. It felt different. She couldn't pinpoint why, but Matilda wanted her old car back. There was something familiar about it that couldn't be replicated in the newer model.

She turned into Linden Avenue and quickly applied the brakes. Nothing wrong with those. Ahead of her was a crowd of onlookers, neighbours in dressing gowns, carpet slippers and hastily put on jogging bottoms and trainers. People who had left their homes and filled the road at the first sighting of a police car.

She climbed out of the car and had an iPhone thrust into her face.

'DCI Darke, can you tell me what's happened here?'

'As you can see, I've just arrived.'

'You must know something.'

'And you are?'

'Danny Hanson. Senior Crime Reporter on *The Star*.'

'Ah! You're Danny Hanson?'

He beamed at the fact a DCI knew who he was.

Matilda dug into her inside jacket pocket for her own iPhone, selected the camera and took a photo of the young journalist.

'Did you just take my picture?'

'I certainly did.'

'Any reason why?'

'I'd like to show my team who not to talk to when they attend a crime scene.'

Matilda reached the garden gate of the house she had been summoned to. Feeling the warm breath of the journalist on her neck she stopped and turned around. He couldn't have been older than twenty-five, but looked younger. She wondered if he was still asked for ID when he bought a scratchcard. She gave him the once-over – the neatly messed-up dark brown hairstyle, the plain blue tie, the dark blue shirt, the skinny black jeans. He looked like an interviewee for his first Saturday job.

'Is this to do with the Starling House case?' he asked.

'Not entirely. You're the journalist who keeps calling me late at night, aren't you? Where did you get my number?'

'My predecessor,' he said.

'Your predecessor wasn't at *The Star* long enough to get my number.'

'Ah.' He broke eye contact for the first time.

'Ah indeed. You know, I admire ambition. However, there's a fine line between ambition and breaking the law. Right now, you've passed the police tape; you're breaking the law. Don't worry, I'll give you this one. Step out of line again and I'll personally see you locked up. Understand?'

'But I—'

Matilda held her hand up to silence him. 'Trust me, you need to pay attention to what I'm saying. You're young, you're handsome, you'd be very popular in prison. Now, back on the other side of the tape,' she said with a sinister smile.

'You can't just—'

'Are you seriously trying to pick an argument with me? Go.' She pointed. 'And if you're quick, you'll be just in time for your PE lesson.'

Matilda turned away before Danny Hanson could reply. DC Kesinka Rani was waiting in the doorway of the house. She handed her a paper forensic suit, and Matilda flashed her warrant card to the uniformed officer standing guard.

'Morning, Kes. I do enjoy a good quarrel with a journalist first thing.' She slipped into the forensic suit, placed on the overshoes and stepped inside the detached house. 'Make sure he's shifted, won't you?' she said, looking over her shoulder at the lingering journalist.

'Will do. Steve, could you?' Kesinka asked the PC standing on the doorstep.

'No problem.' Steve left his post and grabbed Danny by the elbow. The reporter tried to shrug him off but winced under the grip of the PC.

It was a cold morning, and although there was no heating on inside the house and the front door was wide open, it was good to get out of the bitter spring air.

'Why have I been called out to a suicide?' Matilda asked.

'It's not your regular suicide.'

'Is there such a thing as an irregular suicide?'

Kesinka didn't reply. She pointed to the entrance to the living room and stepped back, inviting Matilda to see for herself.

'Oh,' was all Matilda could say upon entering the room.

The large living room stretched the entire length of the house. Close to the bay window overlooking the road was an oak dining table. On the wall was a display cabinet which housed a collection of silver trinkets. In the middle of the lounge was a cast-iron wood burner. There were a few logs inside but, judging by how clean it was, a fire hadn't been lit in a while. An expensive-looking Chesterfield sofa and matching armchair pointed to a fifty-inch television in the corner. And, right at the back, in front of the patio doors, was a figure hanging by the neck from an exposed beam, a white pillowcase over his head.

Matilda stepped into the cold room. A body of white-suited forensic officers were busily dusting for prints on the patio door handles and taking photographs from every conceivable angle. In the corner, one officer was sketching, and another was laying a sheet directly beneath the swaying body.

'Do we know who he is?' Matilda asked quietly to Kesinka.

'Not confirmed yet. Aaron's upstairs with Ranjeet trying to find some ID.'

'Who called it in?'

'The woman next door was hanging some washing out. She just happened to look up and noticed someone hanging in the window.'

Matilda apologized as she squeezed past a forensic officer to peer through the glass. The border between this house and next door was a privet hedge measuring no more than four-feet high. It wasn't very private, hence why the woman next door was able to make such a gruesome discovery.

'Does she know who is living here?'

'Yes.' Kesinka took out her notebook. 'First name is Brian. She thinks his surname is Appleton, but not one hundred per cent. He lives alone as far as she knows.'

Matilda looked back to the hanging body. 'Has Dr Kean been called?'

'I've no idea, ma'am.'

'She has. There was no answer from her mobile,' one of the forensic officers said.

Matilda frowned. She had no idea who had spoken to her. As she looked around the room she realized she only knew Kesinka.

'Where's my team?' she whispered.

'Aaron's upstairs. Faith is next door with Mrs Fitzgerald. Sian's still on annual leave, and Rory is off today, hospital appointment. Scott isn't in until later. Oh, DI Brady left a message this morning. He's broken a tooth and got an emergency appointment with the dentist.'

'That's a relief. For a moment I thought everyone had deserted me.' She smiled. She walked back to the body and introduced herself to a scene of crime officer.

'Diana Black, nice to meet you,' came the reply in a strong West Country accent. Diana had only been living in South Yorkshire for three weeks, but the confidence in which she went about her work showed she had been doing this for a number of years. 'I've taken plenty of photographs and close-ups of the neck and the fingers.' She lifted up the left hand of the hanging man, which had been placed in a plastic evidence bag. 'If you look closely you can see there's some blood under his nails, possibly skin samples too. We should be able to get a match if there is. Now, I know it's not my job, but I've had a feel of the neck and there is no broken bone. Plenty of bruising and rope burns, which suggests he struggled a lot.'

'So not a suicide?' Matilda asked. She had been lost in Diana's accent. It made a change from the gruff thick Yorkshire she was surrounded with on a daily basis.

'If it is, it's the first case of suicide by hanging I've come across where the person has covered their face and I've been in this job almost thirty years.'

Matilda looked at Diana. Although she was wearing a white forensic suit with the hood up and a face mask on, her eyes were still visible. There didn't appear to be any wrinkles, and her voice sounded light, young. If she had been working for nearly thirty years she had to be in her mid-fifties at least. Matilda wondered what face cream she used.

'Also,' Diana said, picking up an evidence bag from the box by her feet, 'the contents of his pockets – car keys, loose change, parking stub. And he's wearing outdoor shoes. I've never known anyone to hang themselves and look like they've just come home from a day at work.'

'No wallet?'

'There was one in his jacket pocket. I've bagged it but … sorry, can't remember his name: tall bloke, looks miserable.'

'DS Connolly?' Matilda smiled at the perfect description of one of her sergeants.

'That's the one. He took it upstairs with him.'

'Thanks, Diana. Any chance we can get our mystery man cut down and the hood removed?'

'Sure. By the way, it's a good old-fashioned hangman's noose.'

'How can you tell?'

'Thirteen twists in the rope – a proper hangman's knot, or a "forbidden knot" they used to call it. I'm a bit of a geek when it comes to facts about killings. Too gruesome for *Mastermind* probably.'

Matilda walked away while the forensic officers set about carefully cutting the rope to lower the body to the floor. She dug out her mobile phone and rang Adele. It went straight to voicemail.

In the background, she heard Diana Black ask a colleague if he knew the name of the last man to be hanged in Britain. Matilda would have bet her salary Diana knew.

'Adele, it's Matilda. Can you give me a call when you get this message, please?' She hung up and looked at the screen with a frown. It wasn't like Adele to have her phone switched off.

'Ma'am, you're going to want to see this,' Aaron Connolly called. By the sound of the heavy footfalls he was bounding down the stairs. Following him was the incredibly tall and unnecessarily handsome DC Ranjeet Deshwal.

'Morning, Aaron, how's Katrina?' Matilda asked.

Aaron's wife was eight months pregnant. She was suffering with endometriosis and pre-eclampsia and needed careful monitoring. Aaron had been full of excitement upon finding out he and his wife were finally going to become parents after years of trying. When her illnesses had been uncovered the dour expression he usually carried returned. All he needed was a long grey coat and he could be Idris Elba's stand-in on an episode of *Luther*.

'She's at her mother's, in Rhyl, for a couple of weeks, resting. I'll be glad when she's had this sodding baby. I'm going grey.'

Matilda smiled. 'How long does she have left?'

'She's not due until April. I've told her, there's no way we're having a second.' He swallowed and tried to laugh it off, but the stress and strain of an expectant father was etched on his face.

'What am I going to want to see?' Matilda was keen to enquire how Aaron was feeling and show she cared but felt uncomfortable whenever the topic strayed from anything work related. She'd also chosen the wrong time, as usual. Aaron was a very private man; he wasn't going to want to talk about his personal issues surrounded by his colleagues. She wished she could be more like Sian Mills, the surrogate mother of the group who took everyone under her wing, including Matilda.

'I've found a diary. Look at his appointments for yesterday.'

Matilda took the diary from him. Her eyes widened as she read down the page:

12:00 – hairdressers
13:30 – collect jacket from dry cleaners
19:00 – Adele Kean @ City Hall

Matilda turned back to the body, which was carefully being lowered into a body bag. 'Jesus Christ! Who the hell is he?'

Chapter Three

Matilda dialled Adele's number as she sat in traffic on Chesterfield Road, but again it went straight to voicemail. Matilda immediately thought the worst. Once the traffic began to clear, she slammed her foot down on the accelerator and headed for the city centre. She had to pass Adele's office on the way to her house in Hillsborough, so turned off to see if she'd arrived late for some reason.

Matilda was let into the building and ran along the corridor to the post-mortem suite. She pulled open the door and was hit by how bright it was compared to the dull morning outside. There was a woman in the corner of the room she had never seen before.

'Hello,' Matilda called out. 'I'm looking for Dr Kean. Is she in yet?'

'No. Can I give her a message?'

Matilda frowned. 'Who are you?'

'Lucy Dauman. I'm Dr Kean's assistant,' she said, flicking her blonde hair back.

'What happened to Victoria?'

'She left last week. She's moved to Stockport.'

'Oh I see.' *Another* new face. 'If she comes in make sure she rings me straight away, even before she takes her coat off.'

'OK,' Lucy said, looking perplexed. 'And you are?'

'I'm DCI Matilda Darke,' Matilda replied testily.

'And she has your number, does she?'

'Just get her to call me,' Matilda replied with anger, already halfway out of the door.

Now Matilda was panicking. It was unusual for Adele not to be in work. It was almost unheard of for her to be out of work and not answering her phone. Matilda's mind raced ahead and came up with all kinds of scenarios. Did she go to sleep last night and not wake up this morning? They had been training hard for the half-marathon next month. She tried not to think about the worst-case scenario, but it wasn't possible. An image entered her mind of Adele hanging lifelessly from a light fitting, a noose tied around her neck.

As she drove out of the centre of town, Matilda remembered the texts they had sent to each other following Adele's date. They'd had a lovely evening. They'd kissed. They'd gone their separate ways. That was the last she heard from her. She was in the taxi on her way home. What if she hadn't got there? Taxi drivers were at the centre of the Rotherham abuse scandal. What if Adele had been attacked in the back of the taxi and was lying dead in a ditch somewhere?

Matilda knew it was selfish, but all she could think about was what would happen to *her* if Adele was dead? She was all she had. Since Matilda's husband, James, had died she had relied on Adele to keep her sane. She was always there whenever she needed her. Without her, she was completely alone.

'You selfish bitch,' she chastised herself as she ran through a red light.

Matilda turned into Adele's road at speed, almost mounting the kerb. She pulled into the first available parking space without indicating, ignoring the four-letter tirade from the driver of a BMW behind her. She ripped off her seatbelt, slammed the car door behind her and ran to Adele's house. She looked up and saw closed curtains in all the windows. The house seemed to be in silence.

'Shit,' Matilda said to herself.

Matilda had had a copy of Adele's key for as long as she could remember, but, until now, she had never had cause to use it.

Shutting the front door behind her, she stood in the hallway and listened tentatively for some sign of life. There was nothing. All she could hear was a distant clock ticking, the hum from the fridge in the kitchen and the sound of the central heating rattling through the house. And her own heart pounding in her chest. As she stepped along the hallway she dreaded what she was going to find.

'Adele, Adele,' Matilda called out. 'Are you in?'

'Of course I'm in,' Adele replied, stepping out of the kitchen into the hallway.

'Oh my God, what the hell's happened to you?' Matilda asked noticing the black eye on her friend's face.

'I've been burgled.'

'What?'

'I got home last night and there was a man in the living room. I must have disturbed him. He ran past, gave me a backhander, and left.'

'Why didn't you call?' Matilda asked. Her voice was full of concern. She leaned in to get a better look at Adele's face. Her left eye was purple.

'I dialled 999 and was told to report it to my local police station. I called 101 and they gave me an incident number to give to my insurance company.'

Adele made her way into the kitchen, and Matilda followed. She looked around but there was no mess in here, apart from a glass panel missing from the back door. There was a small piece of plywood nailed over the hole.

'Has anything been taken?'

'Fortunately, no. It looks like he came through here and went straight into the living room. He opened some drawers but left empty-handed.'

A tear fell down Adele's face, and Matilda pulled her into a tight hug. 'You should have called.'

'I was going to, but Chris came home not long after me and we started to tidy up. When we realized the police weren't coming out, we made the back door secure. By then it was after two o'clock.'

'Where's Chris now?' Matilda released Adele and walked her to the breakfast table. She sat her down and went to make them both a coffee.

'He's gone to get some locks.' She sniffed hard and wiped her eyes. 'I've never been burgled before.'

'Neither have I.' Matilda filled two mugs from the boiling water tap and took the coffee over to the table. 'How do you feel?'

'Sick. Why do people think they can just come into someone else's house and help themselves?' Adele's voice broke as the emotion got the better of her.

'I don't know, Adele.'

'And why don't you investigate anymore? I've been given an incident number. Nobody's coming out to check for prints or anything.'

Matilda turned to her friend with a blank expression. She had no idea what to say.

'I'm sorry,' Adele said. 'It's like you asking me why people die.'

'Do you want to come and stay with me for a few days?'

'No. Thanks, but I have to carry on as normal. If I went to stay at your house I wouldn't come back. It's a good job my date was last night and not tonight with this shiner.'

Matilda's face dropped as she suddenly remembered the hanging man at a house in Linden Avenue. She looked to the floor, not sure how to proceed.

'What's wrong?' Adele asked.

Matilda and Adele had known each other for twenty years, give or take. They were more than colleagues, they were best friends. Together, they were strong enough to cope with anything. What Matilda was about to say would test that strength.

'Adele, the bloke you went out with last night—'

'Brian,' Adele interrupted.

Matilda took a deep breath. 'He wasn't called Brian Appleby, was he?'

'Yes. How did you …? Oh God. What's happened?'

'Adele, I was called out to a house this morning in Linden Avenue. A man was found hanging in his living room.'

'Hanging? You mean he committed suicide? Jesus! What does that say about me? He went home after our first date and hanged himself?' Tears rolled down Adele's face.

'No. Adele, he didn't kill himself.'

'What?'

'We think he was murdered.'

Adele stood up and went to the counter, tore off a few sheets of kitchen roll and dried her eyes. She loudly blew her nose and rubbed it red with the rough paper. 'Murdered?' she asked. 'I don't …? This doesn't make any sense.'

'Obviously I'll have to wait for the results from Forensics and I'll need to draft in a new pathologist, but I'm pretty certain he was murdered.'

'Oh no. Oh God, no.' Adele moved over to the sofa in the corner of the kitchen and slumped into it. 'He was a lovely man. Why would anyone do such a thing? What was it, a robbery or something?'

'I've no idea yet, Adele.' Matilda frowned. Her mind started working in overdrive. Adele and Brian go out on a date; by the next morning one has been burgled and one has been murdered. Coincidence? 'What can you tell me about him?' Matilda asked, moving over to sit next to her friend.

'I'm not sure really.' Adele composed herself and ran her fingers through her knotted hair. 'He's not been back in England long. He's been living in America. He's from somewhere down south originally. Essex, I think he said.'

'Any family?'

'He didn't say. There's an ex-wife but no kids. I can't believe it. I really liked him.'

Matilda's phone started ringing, and she looked at the display. It was Aaron. 'I'm going to need to take this.'

Matilda waited until she was out in the hallway before she answered, and then she kept her voice low.

'Ma'am, I just want to let you know that I've found some photo ID and shown it to the neighbour. Forensics have removed the hood covering his face and it matches his passport.'

'So it is the man who lives there then?' Matilda asked, not wanting to say Brian's name in case Adele overheard.

'Brian Appleby, yes. The thing is, I've run his name through the PNC – the bloke's a nonce.'

'Sorry?'

'He's on the sex offender's register. He got out of Ashfield Prison, in Gloucestershire, last year after spending eight years in prison for a series of sexual assaults on young girls.'

'Bloody hell!'

Matilda ended the call and turned back to the kitchen. Through the gap in the door she saw Adele sitting on the leather sofa tearing the kitchen roll with shaking fingers. She looked up at Matilda with a tear-stained face and a swollen eye. She had seen her upset and sad in the past but now she seemed vulnerable. How could Matilda go in there and tell her the first date she had been on in more than twenty years was with a convicted sex offender?

Chapter Four

'Why weren't we told there was a sex offender living on our patch?'

DCI Matilda Darke was in her tiny, cluttered office with the door closed. DS Aaron Connolly was in front of her desk with a thick file in his hand.

'I've no idea. According to this, when he was released from prison, he went back to his home in Essex, but was more or less forced out by the neighbours. He decided on a fresh start in Sheffield and informed Essex Police of his intentions. They were fine with him moving, probably just glad to get rid of him. He was in touch with his probation officer on a regular basis and did everything right.'

'Until he came here and didn't even bother informing us.'

'That's what it looks like.'

'How long has he been out of prison?'

'He was released in January last year.'

'So how did he afford such a nice house in Linden Avenue?'

'I've no idea, ma'am.'

Matilda looked past Aaron out into the incident room. The lack of officers was startling. It seemed unnervingly quiet too, though that probably had something to do with the absence of DC Rory Fleming who could frequently be heard above everyone else, even when the room was at full capacity.

'Aaron, go back to his house and give it a thorough going over. I want to know everything about this Brian Appleby. What's he been doing since last January? Why did he choose Sheffield? Talk to the neighbours – don't mention he was a sex offender though – and find out what they know about him. What he did for a living, the usual stuff.'

'Will do.'

'Is that his police file?' Matilda asked as Aaron was about to leave.

'Yes.'

'Leave it with me.'

He handed it to her. 'I was thinking, Brian was a sex offender and his murder looks like an execution. Vigilante?'

'I was thinking that myself,' Matilda said, running her fingers through her hair. 'But who knew he was here when even we didn't?'

'Maybe someone followed him up from Essex.'

'It's possible. I don't like vigilantes,' she said, turning to the window. She rolled her eyes at the uninspiring view. 'They're unpredictable, they're violent, and there's usually more than one victim.'

It was strange looking through the one-way mirror and seeing someone she knew sitting nervously in an interview room. Standing in the observation bay, Matilda watched Adele. Less than twenty-four hours ago she was in a restaurant with a charming man having a delicious meal and a pleasant conversation. Now, that man was dead, murdered, and Adele had been the last person to see him alive.

The door opened and the diminutive Assistant Chief Constable Valerie Masterson entered and joined Matilda. Still dressed in her overcoat and wearing a woollen hat a couple of sizes too big, she had obviously come straight from the car park.

'I've just heard. How is she?' Valerie asked, nodding towards Adele through the glass.

'I don't know.'

'Who gave her that black eye?'

'She surprised a burglar last night.'

'Are the two connected?'

'I don't know. I doubt it. I'll look into it, though.'

'I hope you're not intending on interviewing Dr Kean yourself.' Valerie's concern for Adele didn't last and quickly turned to admonishment.

'Of course not.' *I would have done if you hadn't turned up.*

'Do I need to bring in someone else to run this investigation?' Valerie asked staring intently at her DCI.

'No. I'm more than capable of detaching myself.'

Valerie rolled her eyes, though Matilda didn't see. She was fixed on Adele. 'Matilda, I know the two of you are close. I don't want your friendship getting in the way of a murder investigation.'

'It won't.' Matilda turned to look at her boss. 'I guarantee it.'

Matilda brushed past the ACC and into the corridor, where Chris Kean, Adele's son, was waiting. He'd changed dramatically since finishing university. Gone were the unruly hair and sombre scowl of the modern-day student, the dour expression of a generation with the worry of the entire universe on their shoulders. He had been transformed into a member of the working society. He was smart, neat, tidy, handsome, and had put on a little muscle thanks to the training he'd been doing with his mother and Matilda for the half-marathon.

As soon as he saw Matilda he jumped up from his seat. 'How's my mum?' he asked, the look of worry had returned.

'She's fine, Chris. There's nothing to be concerned about. We just need to talk to her about her date, that's all.'

'Are you going to interview her?'

Matilda looked back at the observation room, wondering if Valerie was listening. She lowered her voice. 'No, Chris. I'm not allowed.'

'Why not? She'd feel more comfortable with you in there.'

'I know, but it's a conflict of interest. We're friends. It would be the same if you were in there. I'm sorry. She's going to be interviewed by Aaron and Scott. She knows them; she's worked alongside them for years. She'll be fine. Trust me.'

'But why are they allowed to interview her if they know her yet you're not?'

'Because they've never held her hair while she's vomited a bottle of Prosecco down a toilet.' Matilda smiled but Chris didn't seem to see the funny side. 'Look, Chris, you shouldn't be here. You'll have to wait in reception.'

Chris sat back down, slumping heavily into the plastic chair. 'It's all my fault.'

'What makes you say that?' Matilda asked sitting next to him.

'I've been badgering her for months to go on the dating sites, meet someone,' he sniffled. 'She's lonely, Mat. I can see it in her eyes. She says she's not, but she is.'

'I know, Chris. I blame myself too.'

'Why?'

'I've been so wrapped up in myself. Your mum is my best friend. She's always been there for me and I should have been a better friend in return.'

'You've been a great friend. You helped her when she first came to Sheffield.'

'That was twenty years ago,' Matilda scoffed. 'It's time I moved on. I need to start embracing life more, going out, enjoying myself. I think me and your mother deserve a holiday.'

'Really?'

'Yes.' Matilda found herself smiling. 'We should go somewhere warm with a beach, plenty of bars, maybe sing karaoke and chat up some blokes.'

Chris smiled but looked embarrassed.

'Chris, you shouldn't worry about your mum. You're just starting out in life, you need to find out who you are, travel, meet new people, move away maybe. Your mum is going to be fine. I'll see to that.'

'You promise?'

'Girl Guide's honour,' Matilda said, raising her right hand and giving the three-fingered salute.

'You were a Girl Guide?' He sniggered.

'Well, not for long, I swore at the Patrol Leader – on more than one occasion. Come on, I'll take you through to reception. If the ACC sees you here we'll both be in trouble.'

DC Scott Andrews had been called in early. With Sian Mills on leave to decorate her house following the aftermath of her home being flooded, Matilda wanted someone alongside DS Aaron Connolly who Adele knew and liked. This would be a formal and recorded interview, but it needed to be as unobtrusive and sensitive as possible.

Matilda met Scott in the hallway in reception. He walked towards her carrying a tray of drinks.

'I've snatched a few chocolate bars from Sian's drawer too. I thought it might make things seem a bit more relaxed.'

Dressed in a dark grey suit with white shirt and grey tie, Scott looked his usual smart and dapper self. His hair had been recently trimmed. He was the embodiment of style. Today, however, his smooth complexion was one of worry. Adele was a regular figure in the station: everyone knew her, liked her, and respected her. Nobody wanted to see her interrogated.

'Are you OK to do this?' Matilda asked, noting his furrowed brow.

'Of course. Who's that?' He lowered his voice and nodded at Chris Kean who was frantically chewing his nails.

‘That’s Adele’s son.’

‘Blimey, she doesn’t look old enough to have a son that age.’

‘Open with that line and you’ll have a friend for life.’ She opened the door for Scott and followed him through towards the interview suites.

‘Aaron!’ Matilda called to DS Connolly, who was talking to DC Easter. He made his excuses and joined Matilda outside interview room one. ‘Just the facts, Aaron. Don’t be too personal. We know Adele, she’s not a suspect,’ Matilda warned.

‘Yes, boss.’

Matilda watched as Scott and Aaron entered the room. She hoped to give Adele a reassuring smile, but she didn’t look up from the table. The door closed, and Matilda was left in the corridor. She went into the observation room. She may not be able to conduct the interview, but there was no way she was going to allow it to be unsupervised.

‘Friday, 10th of March 2017. Interview with Adele Kean. Those present are myself, Detective Constable Scott Andrews—’

‘Detective Sergeant Aaron Connolly.’

Scott nodded at Adele when she didn’t speak.

‘Oh, sorry, Doctor Adele Kean,’ her voice was broken and soft.

‘Dr Kean, you are not under arrest and you haven’t been cautioned. This is a formal interview, as we believe you to be the last person to see Brian Appleby alive. Do you understand?’

Adele nodded.

‘You’re going to have to reply for the benefit of the recording,’ Scott said, leaning forward, his voice gentle and low.

‘I’m sorry. This is all new to me. Yes. I understand.’

‘Adele, can you tell me how you came to meet Brian Appleby?’ Aaron said, sitting back in his chair.

Adele closed her eyes and shook her head. She wasn’t embarrassed about using a website to find a man, everyone did it these days, she just hoped she wasn't asked why she wanted to find a soulmate in the first place. That, she was embarrassed about.

'It was a dating website aimed at people of mature years.'

'Who made contact first?'

'He did.'

'How long after the first message did you arrange to meet?'

'Just over a week, I think.'

'And who chose the date and time to meet?'

'I did.'

'Did he arrive on his own?'

'Yes.'

'Was there anyone watching or following you? Did you see anyone acting suspiciously?'

Adele frowned. 'No. Well, I don't think so. I didn't take much notice of anyone else.'

'Where did you go when you'd met?'

'Lloyd's Bar. We had a couple of drinks then on to Zizzi's for a meal.'

'Was there anyone in Lloyd's Bar who you thought might be watching you or Brian?'

'No. I was just out having a drink, I wasn't looking for anyone watching us. I mean, you don't, do you? I'm not a paranoid person.'

'It's OK, Adele, try and relax,' Scott jumped in.

Adele took a deep breath. She had a sip of her tea, but it tasted foul. 'We had a lovely evening together. We had a meal, a good chat, swapped stories, and then went our separate ways. That was all.'

'What did he tell you about his past?'

Adele shook her head. What he had said had obviously been a lie. She couldn't believe she had been duped. 'He told me he'd been living in America for eight years. He said he was an English teacher.'

'He didn't mention having been in prison?'

She flinched at the word. 'Of course he didn't,' she raised her voice. 'If I knew that I would have walked out of the restaurant.'

'What else did he tell you about himself?' Aaron asked.

'He said he was divorced. His wife had cheated on him with another woman. He'd moved to America to put some distance between them. I felt sorry for him. Can you believe that? I actually felt sorry for him.'

'Adele, you didn't know,' Scott said, taking on the role of a friend. 'There's no way you could have known.'

'Are you going to tell me what he'd done?' she asked. Matilda had only told her the basics in the car on the way to the station: that he had been killed and was known to the police. When pressed further, Matilda claimed she didn't know all the facts herself.

'Do you really want to know?'

'No.' She half-smiled.

'How did Brian seem last night?' Aaron asked, remaining focused and formal.

Adele thought for a while. 'Nervous to begin with, but then so was I. We both soon relaxed. He was chatty, he smiled, he laughed. He came across like any other normal member of the public.'

'How did the date end?'

Adele baulked at the word date. It was like she was reviled for having a date with a criminal. 'He walked me to the taxi rank opposite John Lewis. We kissed and said we'd arrange to go out again. I went home.'

'Did Brian say how he was getting home?'

'He was driving.'

'Did he drink alcohol during your date?' Scott asked.

'No. He had juice.'

'Did you see which direction he headed in after he'd left you at the taxi rank?'

'No. As my taxi pulled away I turned to look through the rear window and he was still stood on the pavement. He waved. I waved back. That was it.'

'Adele,' Scott adjusted himself in his seat, 'when you arrived home, did Brian contact you anymore that night?'

'No.'

'Did anything out of the ordinary happen?'

'You mean apart from being burgled?'

The detectives remained silent, giving Adele a chance to relax and calm down a little before continuing.

'Did you recognize the person burgling your home?'

'No. It all happened so quickly. He was dressed in dark clothing.'

'You're sure it was a man?'

'He was tall, a great big barrel. Yes, he was a man.'

'Did he say anything?'

'No. He looked at me and ran towards me. I just froze. The next thing I know there's this gloved fist in my face and I'm on the floor.'

'Did you lose consciousness?'

'No. I was just a bit dazed.' Adele wiped her nose with a soaked tissue. She took a deep breath. 'I don't want to know what Brian had done, but do you think I was set up? Get me out of the house then burgle me?'

Scott and Aaron exchanged glances. 'I don't think so, Adele,' Scott said.

'It's bad, isn't it? What he did. He didn't spend eight years in prison for being a serial burglar, did he?'

'No.'

'I … No. Don't tell me,' she said before bursting into tears. She eventually stopped enough to speak. She looked up. 'He was a rapist, wasn't he?'

Scott turned away. He had no idea what to say.

Aaron leaned forward and placed his hand over Adele's. 'I'm only telling you this now because you're in such a state. There's no point in you getting better, then finding out afterwards and feeling all shit again. Brian Appleby was on the sex offender's register.'

The tears stopped flowing. 'The bastard,' Adele hissed.

In the observation room, Matilda was slumped into a very uncomfortable chair. She had one hand clamped to her mouth. Her eyes were full of tears. She couldn't imagine the torment Adele was going through right now.

Chapter Five

'In 2008, Brian Appleby was sentenced to sixteen years for sexual offences on three girls under the age of sixteen. He was released from Ashfield Prison, in Gloucestershire, in January last year after serving half of his sentence.'

The briefing room was packed with detectives and uniformed officers. Matilda Darke was perched on the edge of a desk near the front. Her face was a picture of worry. She had just observed her best friend describe her date with a sex offender. It had been a horrible experience. Adele was usually a confident, positive person, but this could damage that.

As soon as the interview had concluded, Adele had been allowed to leave the station. Matilda had said she would go round straight after work and see how she was. She hoped she would be welcomed when she knocked on the door.

'Police first became aware of Brian Appleby when Daisy Bishop, the fourteen-year-old daughter of his next-door neighbour, accused him of putting his hand up her skirt in the summer of 2008,' Aaron continued, reading from the file to the whole room. 'Once that came to light, two other girls made allegations: Allegra Chalmers said he had sex with her on two occasions in 2007, and Bryony Watts accused him of raping her, also in 2007.'

'How old were Allegra and Bryony?' DI Christian Brady said. Having just had a tooth extracted that morning, the left side of his face was slightly swollen, his speech affected.

'Allegra was fifteen and Bryony thirteen.'

'Bastard,' Christian muttered, immediately thinking of his own young children.

'Good riddance to bad rubbish,' Ranjeet said. Nodding from other officers around the room showed they shared his sentiment.

'So he's released from prison in January and goes home to Essex. Why doesn't he stay there?' Scott asked.

'Hate mail, windows broken, spat at in the streets. He was basically run out of town,' Aaron said.

'Why did he choose Sheffield?'

'No idea. His wife divorced him a year after he was sentenced. His parents and two brothers disowned him. He has no connections at all with Sheffield.'

'When did he move up here?' Scott asked.

Aaron flicked through the file. 'He approached Essex Police in the summer. He last visited them in August, telling them he'd found a place to live in Sheffield.'

'Aaron, what did you find in his house?' Matilda asked for the first time.

'Nothing that stands out. He was a very meticulous man though. He kept and filed all his receipts and bank statements. Everything was neat and tidy. There's an address book but I haven't had time to go through it all yet. I had an email from Forensics who have searched his laptop and there's nothing on it. He used it mostly for shopping. There's no pornography on there, no questionable websites visited, a few photos of family, that's it.'

'Could it have been wiped?'

'Maybe, but Forensics would have been able to tell. There is, however, one very creepy piece of evidence we've found.'

'Go on,' Matilda instructed.

'His mobile phone. It was in his inside jacket pocket. While looking through it, Forensics found eighteen photographs of Adele Kean standing outside the City Hall. The timestamp on them matches the time Dr Kean says they met. It looks like he was taking her picture without her realizing before they met.'

'Pervert,' Ranjeet uttered.

Matilda bit her bottom lip. She wondered how close Adele came to being harmed by this man. 'Keep that between us,' she told the room. 'Adele doesn't need to know about that.'

'Agreed,' Christian struggled to say.

Matilda frowned. 'If he was so meticulous and well-organized, why didn't he report himself to South Yorkshire Police when he arrived here?'

There was no reply because nobody could give one.

'I'd like to know how he could afford such a lovely house when he didn't work,' Faith said, opening a fun-size packet of Maltesers from Sian's drawer.

'The house was rented,' Aaron said. 'Private landlord. Brian had the money because he'd sold his home in Essex for over half a million pounds. That was reduced, too, for a quick sale.'

'Didn't his wife get the house in the divorce?'

'According to her witness statement in the file,' Aaron said, flicking through the paperwork, 'she wanted nothing to do with him at all.'

'I can understand that,' Faith said. 'Who would stay married to a pervert?'

'So, who would want him dead?' Scott asked.

'The family of the victims would be high up on the list, I'm guessing,' Faith said.

'But how did they know where to find him? He's hardly likely to leave a forwarding address with the new owners in Essex, is he? Also, if we didn't know he was here, how could anyone else?' Matilda asked.

'We need to speak to Essex Police,' Christian mumbled. There was a slight ripple of laughter at his struggled attempt to pronounce Essex. 'Faith, how did you get on with the neighbours?'

'The standard reply – he kept himself to himself, seemed like a nice man, always said hello when he saw you in the street, quiet, no loud music or parties. The perfect neighbour.'

'People are often quiet and keep themselves to themselves for a reason,' Scott said.

'That's pretty cynical, Scott. People can be quiet because they want to live their life how they want to. Not everyone has to be the life and soul of the neighbourhood,' Faith said.

'I know that. I just meant, people have secrets. We all do. If we don't want those secrets getting out, then we stay in the background.'

'So what's your secret then, Scott?' Faith asked, a mischievous smile on her face.

'I think we're wandering from the point here,' Matilda said before Scott could reply. 'What we need to do next is find out who knew Brian was a sex offender and who knew where he was living. He wasn't working, so we have no colleagues to ask. His neighbours have all been interviewed, so who else is there?'

Again, the room went quiet.

'Maybe the answer lies in his life before he came to Sheffield. Question his family, former neighbours, find out where they were last night.'

'I hope sending officers to Essex isn't coming out of my budget,' Christian said.

'It's not coming out of anyone's budget. We'll get Essex Police to go round and interview them for us. In the meantime, this stays in this room. I don't want anyone talking to the press about a sex offender being murdered. Speaking of which,' Matilda said, pointing to a photograph on the wall, 'you will notice we have a new addition to our wall of shame. That is Danny Hanson. He's a journalist on *The Star* and fancies himself as some kind of maverick reporter. Memorize that face. If you see him, ignore him. Now, ladies, he's young, he's good-looking, don't let him bewitch you with those puppy eyes. Understand?'

There were sniggers from around the room.

'Ma'am,' Faith asked, raising her hand slightly. 'Shouldn't we contact other people on the sex offender's register in the area, see if they've been followed or noticed anything suspicious lately?'

'Not yet. We'll put that on the back burner.'

The door to the CID suite burst open and a flustered DC Kesinka Rani charged into the room. 'Ma'am, you're not going to believe this. I've just had a call from the Northern General. Alec Routledge has been admitted to intensive care in the early hours of this morning. He's been badly beaten and stabbed.'

'Who's Alec Routledge?'

'He's a sex offender.'

Chapter Six

The journey to the Northern General Hospital was conducted in silence. DC Faith Easter had volunteered to drive Matilda, and Kesinka Rani was in the back, reading through Alec Routledge's file that Scott had emailed to her phone.

'Alec Routledge is a paedophile,' Kesinka punctured the silence with the disturbing statement. 'Released from prison in 2013 and has lived in Sheffield ever since. He was a football coach and abused eight boys on his team between 1994 and 1997. Sentenced to twenty years and released after sixteen. Parole was refused three times before eventually convincing a panel he had been rehabilitated.'

'What is so attractive about Sheffield to sex offenders?' Faith asked.

'Have there been any other incidents involving attacks on him recently?' Matilda asked, ignoring Faith. She didn't turn around in her seat to look at Kesinka. She sat facing forward, watching the outside world blur past her at forty miles per hour.

'No. Well, if there have been he hasn't reported them.'

'So why now?'

'No idea. According to uniform, neighbours heard a commotion during the night but, to be fair, when isn't there a commotion on Gleadless? Alec was found by his sister when she came to pick him up this morning. He didn't answer the door, so she let herself in with her key.'

'Pick him up? Where were they going?'

'To visit their mother in a nursing home.'

'Do you have a photograph of Alec Routledge?'

Kesinka handed her phone to Matilda. Alec was in his mid-sixties. He was only five-foot seven inches tall, slight build, grey hair, what was left of it, and a harsh, weather-beaten face.

'Is this a recent photograph?'

'Last couple of years or so.'

'Hmm,' Matilda mused.

'What is it, ma'am? Don't you think it's related?'

'No. Brian Appleby was hanged. He was over six foot, well-built and broad, yet someone managed to hang him. Why couldn't they do the same to Alec Routledge? He wouldn't have taken any time to overpower.'

Standing outside the room in ICU was PC Steve Harrison. He stood tall and cut a dashing figure in his uniform. The impression his face was giving was one of boredom.

'Any news?' Matilda asked.

'None whatsoever. A fine way to spend your birthday.'

'Is it your birthday?' Kesinka asked, a grin on her face. 'Happy birthday. How old are you?'

'Twenty-nine.'

'Are you doing anything to celebrate?'

'I'm going out for a meal with my girlfriend. With any luck,' he said, stealing a sidelong glance at Matilda.

Matilda wasn't listening. She was staring through the window at a comatose Alec Routledge, hooked up to tubes and wires leading to breathing machines and heart rate monitors. His face was a mess of purple bruises, red marks and white padding. His features were unrecognizable. A woman sat by his bed, who

Matilda took to be his sister, looking down at the floor and dabbing her eyes with a crumpled tissue.

'Kes, go and have a word with her. I want to know everything about him, especially who he interacts with. Faith, speak to the nurses, see what his chances are.'

'What about me, ma'am? Do I have to stay here?' PC Harrison asked.

'For the time being, yes,' she replied while walking away to the end of the corridor.

Last November, DC Rory Fleming had been attacked by a convicted killer while he was being interviewed at the station. The teenager had leapt across the table and began senselessly pummelling Rory with his fists, raining down blow after blow. By the time Matilda reached him Rory was unconscious. He was rushed straight to theatre where he underwent an operation to relieve swelling and internal bleeding on his brain. When he eventually woke up, the first thing he was concerned about was his hair, which had been shaved.

He had been signed off work for the rest of the year and returned at the end of January. The bruises had gone, and his hair had grown back. The once well-built and toned detective was now slightly thinner and had a gaunt look about him. He took this as an excuse to raid Sian's snack drawer at every opportunity.

While on her way to the Northern General, Matilda had sent Rory a text asking where he was. She found him in a large waiting room staring up at a silent television screen showing a dull mid-afternoon antiques programme with subtitles. She sat down next to him.

'How's it going?'

'Hello, boss. I'm OK. I had enough of daytime TV when I was at home recovering, now I've got it here too.' He nodded towards the television.

'Just a routine check-up, is it?'

'Yes.'

'Any problems?'

'No.'

Matilda blamed herself for Rory's attack. She should have kept a closer eye on him. He had taken the Starling House case to heart, was eager to know what turned a teenage boy into a killer. His questions had led to him being beaten, and Matilda would never forgive herself.

'Is everything OK?'

'Yes, everything's fine. I'm expecting to get discharged today. If they ever call me in.'

'Running late?'

'Yes. Forty minutes. I've been X-rayed, had my blood pressure checked, and spoken to a psychiatric nurse. I'm just waiting to see the consultant. They don't rush, do they?'

'They don't have to. I had a call yesterday about Callum Nixon.'

Callum Nixon was the teenage killer who had attacked Rory. He had been sentenced to life in prison for murdering two teachers in Liverpool. He had recently been moved to a YOI yet spent most of his days isolated from the rest of the inmates.

'He's had another ten years added to his sentence.'

'Considering he was in prison for life it's hardly going to make any difference, is it?' he shrugged.

'Not really. Are you still living at home?' Matilda asked. Rory had moved back home late last year after splitting with his long-term girlfriend.

'For now. Me and Scott are thinking of getting somewhere together, you know, share the cost. It's doing my head in at home. My mum's treating me like I'm a child again. She keeps saying I should get a safer job in a call centre or something. If I worked in one of those places, I'd go mad and end up going on a shooting spree.'

Matilda smiled. 'She's just worried about you.'

‘I know she is, but … listen, if I kill her, will you help me hide the body?’

Matilda laughed. A hearty laugh from the pit of her stomach, something she hadn’t done for a while. ‘I think I’ll go before you start asking me for the best method in which to do it. I’ll see you back at work tomorrow.’

‘Thanks, boss.’

As Matilda left the hospital she looked at an email on her phone. The post-mortem on Brian Appleby had been delayed. Obviously Adele Kean couldn’t do it, so a pathologist had to be drafted in from another district. Scene of crime officers had finished at Brian’s house. No foreign fingerprints had been found, no fibres, no DNA, nothing that couldn’t be explained. There was no sign of a forced entry, no broken locks, tampered windows. There was a key in the back door, which suggested maybe Brian had hidden a spare outside. The killer hadn’t needed to break in. Whoever murdered Brian Appleby was so skilled and knowledgeable about forensics they knew exactly how to leave no trace. Matilda found that incredibly frightening. She couldn’t help thinking this was going to be a long-running case.

Chapter Seven

'Am I allowed in?' Matilda asked, standing on the doorstep of Adele's home in Hillsborough.

'Of course you are,' Chris laughed. 'She's in the living room. Go on in. Would you like a glass of wine or something?'

'Wine would be perfect, thank you.' She felt as if she could down a whole case of the stuff after the day she'd had.

Matilda made her way into the living room. She peered around the door and saw Adele in the centre of the sofa. Her face was a question mark of confusion. Wearing no make-up, her eyes were red from crying, which made her black eye and worry lines more prominent. She looked older, sadder.

'Do you know what I love about this time of year?' Matilda said, walking in with two heavy plastic bags.

Adele was startled at Matilda's brash entrance and looked up. 'What's that?' She tried to sound like her usual self. She smiled but it was obviously forced.

'All the boxes of chocolates and Easter eggs on the shelves. I was like a child,' Matilda said, raising the bags. 'I've got your favourites, Ferrero Rocher.' She took out a large box of the chocolates and handed them to Adele. 'I couldn't decide on Dairy Box or Milk Tray, so I bought both. I've got us a couple of giant Easter eggs too. Only a fiver.'

'Easter isn't for another month,' Adele laughed.

'That doesn't matter. I thought tonight we could watch a film on Sky, get pissed and give ourselves diabetes with this lot. What do you think?'

Adele's face lit up and she looked ten years younger. 'Don't you have a murder to solve?'

'I do. But my best friend needs a bit of pampering. Brian's still going to be dead in the morning.'

Chris walked in with a fresh bottle of wine and three glasses. His eyes widened at the coffee table laden with treats. 'Ooh, can I join in, or is this girl's night?'

'You're more than welcome, Chris, providing you let me paint your toenails.' Matilda smiled.

'I think I'll give it a miss. I might go round to see Josh. Mum, do you mind if I go out?'

'Chris, you don't need to ask my permission,' Adele scoffed.

'I know. I meant, are you OK, on your own?'

'I'm not on my own, Matilda's here.'

'OK. Well, I won't be long.' He leaned over and kissed his mum on her cheek, said goodbye to Matilda and left the house.

'He's a good kid,' Matilda said.

'He's not a kid, he's a grown man.' Adele had a faraway look in her eye. 'He's not my boy anymore.'

'He'll always be your boy. It's just … he's grown up. That's what we do. We evolve and move on. Blimey, Milk Tray have changed since I last had a box. Apple Crunch? You can have that one,' Matilda said, reading the back of the box.

'I'm not doing much moving on,' Adele said wistfully.

'No. Neither am I. But we're going to change that.'

'Are we?'

'Oh yes.' Matilda smiled. 'It's a bit late for New Year resolutions, but we're going to grab 2017 by the balls and make it a good year for both of us.'

'Are we? How?'

'Well.' Matilda thought for a moment. After a pause, she said, 'We've got the half-marathon next month, we're training for that …'

'Some training,' Adele nodded at the boxes of chocolate.

'We're allowed a night off. Anyway, after the half-marathon and after we've been released from hospital, you and I are going on a holiday.'

'Really?' Adele asked with a hint of a smile on her face. 'Where?'

'I haven't decided yet. Somewhere warm where the sea is blue, the sand is golden, and women in their forties wearing a swimming costume aren't sneered at.'

'Oh. We're going to Worthing?' Adele wrinkled her nose before laughing.

***

'Do you know what I can't get my head around?' Adele asked.

They were on their third bottle of wine, though Adele had drunk most of it. The floor was strewn with screwed-up chocolate wrappers, and Matilda and Adele were slumped on the sofa, balancing a box of chocolates on their laps. *Captain America: The Winter Soldier* was just finishing; the credits were rolling.

'How Bucky managed to survive that fall from the train in the first place?'

'No, about last night.'

'Oh. Go on.'

Their voices were slow and relaxed. Adele's was slightly slurred.

'How charming Brian was. He genuinely seemed like the perfect gentleman, yet he turned out to be a sex offender. How could he put on an act and be so convincing?'

'I don't know, Adele. I've been thinking about that myself all day. Maybe he had atoned for his crimes. Maybe he was moving on from his past and trying to rebuild his life.'

'I understand prison is all about rehabilitation and once they're released they should be able to return to normal society, but … I don't know.'

'Go on,' Matilda urged.

'Say, for example, we went on a second date, and a third, and we started to get close. Would he have eventually sat down and told me what he'd done? If so, how would I have reacted? I like to think I'm a forward-thinking person who could have seen past his crimes to the man he now was, but, what if I wasn't? What if I was a bigot who thought he should have rotted in jail? This has really made me question what kind of a person I am.'

'You know what kind of a person you are. You're kind, gentle, intelligent, honest. You would have approached what he told you with an open mind.'

Adele shook her head. 'I don't know.'

'OK,' Matilda said, sitting up to be more comfortable. 'Pass me the Ferrero Rocher. Now, based on your first date, you said he came across like the perfect gentleman. Keeping that in mind, what if he had visited you this morning and said "Adele, you're a great woman, I had a lovely time, but you should know I served eight years in prison for sex-related crimes". What would you have done?'

Adele thought for a while. She had another sip of her wine, then finished the whole glass. 'Honestly? I would have admired him for telling me the truth. Unfortunately, I wouldn't have felt safe being alone with him. I wouldn't have wanted him touching me. If he's raped someone, how do I know he's not going to rape me?'

'That's a very honest answer.'

'But does that make me a bad person?'

'No. It makes you human.'

'We're taught from an early age to forgive and move on. But there's no way I could have made any kind of life with Brian, knowing he was a sex offender.'

'There are some crimes that are unforgiveable, Adele. Even when they've served their time, criminals can't expect to fully return to a normal life. There is no excuse for what Brian did. He may have been trying to put his past behind him, but that's not always possible. Don't beat yourself up for having a normal, human reaction.'

'He was charming, but he was scum,' Adele said.

'Was that on his dating profile? If so, you've only got yourself to blame.'

For the first time that evening, Adele threw her head back and let out a loud laugh.

'*Captain America: Civil War*?'

'Definitely. Hawkeye's in this one.'

Danny Hanson, only crime reporter on *The Star*, lived in a shared terraced house just off Ecclesall Road overlooking Endcliffe Park. He hated his attic room. It was cold in winter and boiling in the summer. All his possessions were in cardboard boxes and he couldn't move without having to stride over them. His housemates were two trainee nurses he hardly ever saw and a student from China who had very limited English. Unfortunately, this was all Danny could afford, and on his meagre wages, it was all he was likely to be able to afford for years to come.

Sitting on his single bed with his laptop open, he was on a forum page about Sheffield life. He was hoping for some gossip about the dead body found at Linden Avenue this morning, but so far, there was nothing.

His mobile started ringing. He looked at the screen, but the caller's ID had been withheld. He was tempted to ignore it, believing it to be another sales call about his broadband provider.

'Hello,' he answered, sounding bored.

'Danny Hanson?'

'Speaking.'

'I hope you've got a pad and pen to hand.'

'Who is this?' Danny's ears had been pricked.

'The bloke found dead on Linden Avenue this morning was Brian Appleby. He'd been executed by hanging. He was a paedophile from Essex.' The caller hung up.

A smile spread across Danny's face. He looked at his phone. The screen was blank. Had he just dreamed that phone call? He logged on to Google, typed in 'Brian Appleby' and saw stories about a man who had been sentenced for sex offences against underage girls. He opened a blank Word document and began typing, his fingers hammering hard on the keyboard. Once he'd written the basic story, he'd give someone in the police a call, see if they could confirm it. If not, he'd pass it on to his editor. She'd know whether to risk publishing it or not. He could almost smell the print on his first front-page splash.

Chapter Eight

Danny Hanson left work early Saturday afternoon. He'd been busy since first light trying to get confirmation for his story. He'd spoken to a few detectives in CID who had refused to comment, giving him the stock reply that a statement would be released in time. However, Danny wasn't satisfied with that. In the end, he decided to use underhand tactics to get through to someone lowly.

'Hello, my name's Gerald Wiley. I was mugged last week. I spoke to a lovely girl in uniform who said she'd help find whoever it was stole my watch. I didn't get the lass's name. Do you think I could speak to someone, please?' Danny asked into the phone, putting on his best old-man voice.

He was transferred from the switchboard and a young-sounding PC answered who was more than happy to talk to Danny. He quickly launched into his spiel about how he knew who the dead man in Linden Avenue was and just wanted his research efforts confirming. The PC refused to give his name, but his comments would definitely be enough to use in the paper. It helped that Danny had his iPhone held up to the receiver, recording the conversation.

At just after two o'clock in the afternoon, Danny left work. As he made his way for home, he saw a board outside a newsagent's advertising the local paper. There it was, his first ever front-page story.

PAEDOPHILE EXECUTED

It was a simple headline, but it packed a punch. He didn't even attempt to hide his grin upon seeing his byline. He'd post a copy of the paper off to his mum. She'd be very proud.

Matilda and Adele lost the majority of the weekend to a hangover and feeling sick after the amount of sugar they had consumed. It was what they both needed: a chance for them to discuss their futures as two independent, single forty-somethings and for Adele to try and put the whole Brian Appleby incident behind her. Famous last words.

Matilda had called DI Christian Brady and put him in charge of the investigation for the weekend. Fortunately, budget cuts came in handy on occasion and this was the perfect time to blag a couple of days of light duties. Christian kept calling, filling her in on the interviews with neighbours, but nothing dramatic required her attention. She went home on Sunday morning feeling better about herself. She hoped Adele did too.

Matilda woke up early on Monday morning, an hour before her alarm was due to sound. She headed straight for the treadmill in the conservatory and ran 10K in just under one hour. She smiled at the time on the display, happy with how far she had come in the short space of a couple of months. Strangely, she was looking forward to the half-marathon, though she didn't dare say anything as crazy out loud.

She breakfasted on granary toast and a black coffee before showering. This morning, she decided to put on a bit of make-up. While Matilda sat in her dressing gown and applied a touch of eyeliner, she tried to remember the last time she had done this – probably James's funeral. That was almost two years ago. When she was finished, she liked what she saw in the mirror. She had definable cheek bones, her face looked smoother and younger. She should do this more often.

With a spring in her step, Matilda went into the living room, picked up her framed wedding photograph and gave James Darke a big kiss, leaving a lipstick mark behind which she refused to wipe off.

'I love you, James,' she said with confidence. There was no cracking in her voice, no tearful emotion at losing him so early into their marriage, just a determined statement of love from wife to husband.

'Is everything all right, ma'am?' DC Scott Andrews said, entering Matilda's office.

'Yes, fine. Why?'

'You look different. Brighter,' he mused.

'I had a good night's sleep. How's Alec Routledge?' she asked, wanting to get off the subject of her appearance.

'He's still unconscious, but Forensics have found plenty of evidence in his house. DI Brady said neighbours have identified a couple of people who were seen running away from his home. I think he's hopeful on making an arrest within the next few hours.'

'Good. I don't think there's a connection with Brian Appleby, but we'll keep an open mind until it's confirmed. Any news on who spoke to the press over the weekend?'

'No. Nothing yet.'

'I thought not. Any more contact from Danny Hanson?'

'He's called the switchboard a few times. And, yesterday, he accosted me in Graves Park while I was on a run.'

'I hope you didn't tell him anything.'

'Of course not.'

'He's certainly determined. I'll give him that.'

Scott went to leave the room, but hovered in the doorway.

'Do you want to tell me something, Scott?' she asked.

'I do, yes.'

'Go on then.'

'Can I sit down?'

'Of course.'

'Brian Appleby kept a diary and he put all his appointments in it like trips to the dentist and doctors, etc. On Thursday, 15th September last year, there's a note for him to come to South Yorkshire Police and register himself as living in Sheffield.'

'Oh,' Matilda said, her interest suddenly piqued.

'Aaron said yesterday that Brian was a meticulous man. It appears he really was and had intended to come to the station to report his move.'

'And did he?'

'Well we don't have him listed on our register of known sex offenders. Yet there's nothing in his diary to say it didn't happen, or he couldn't make it, or he'd come on a different day.'

'Strange.'

'Very.'

'OK. Leave it with me, Scott. I'll have a think. Good work.'

'Thank you.'

Matilda's phone started to ring. She waited until Scott closed the door to her office before answering. 'DCI Darke.'

'My office, Matilda.' The line went dead. Only ACC Masterson had that kind of control.

'I'd offer you a coffee, but my machine started smoking this morning,' Valerie said, giving a dirty look to the small coffee maker on top of a filing cabinet in the corner of the room. 'I'm guessing you've seen Saturday's edition of *The Star*.'

Matilda hadn't, but she'd read the headlines on her phone. When she saw the physical newspaper in Valerie's hands her heart sank. She hadn't had a good relationship with the local newspaper over the past couple of years. At every turn, they seemed to delight in pointing out her errors and questioning her ability to be leading South Yorkshire's CID.

Valerie slapped the newspaper down in front of Matilda. She leaned forward, refusing to pick it up, as if it was covered with some kind of flesh-eating bacteria. The bottom of the front page said the story was continued on page five. Matilda couldn't resist. She opened the paper and continued reading.

'Who the hell leaked all this?' Valerie fumed. 'Murder hasn't been confirmed yet, and how did they know he was a paedophile? And where did this execution part come from?'

'I have no idea,' Matilda said, reading the rest of the story. 'Is this true?'

'What?'

'This other story at the bottom. Are we getting a Major Crimes Unit?'

'It's being mooted.'

'Why? It's not been a year since the Murder Room was abolished.'

'We have twenty-six unsolved murders on our books at present. We need a team whose sole purpose is major crimes and cold cases. Look, we're deviating from the point. Who leaked this?'

'I don't know. I will find out though, trust me.'

'When you do, I want them handed over to me,' she said. Her wrinkled face was red with fury. 'I will not have any officers on my force spilling information to the press for the price of a few pints.'

As Matilda left the room she started thinking of the new faces she'd seen around the station lately. When the Murder Investigation Team was up and running, she had her own small team of faithful, dedicated officers – Sian, Aaron, Rory and Scott. When it closed and they merged with CID, she had welcomed Faith and Christian into her fold. Now there was Kesinka Rani and Ranjeet Deshwal, who she didn't know at all. And every time she saw a uniformed officer it seemed to be a different face. Then there were a whole new bunch in the forensic team at Brian Appleby's house. It was a fact of life that things changed, people moved on, and new ones arrived. Matilda wasn't well known for allowing many people into her confidence. For the sake of her own sanity, she would need to adapt, trust, and bond. The very thought filled her with dread.

Chapter Nine

Doctor Simon Browes was a man who always had a smile on his face and a mischievous twinkle in his eye. Even during the more disturbing aspects of his job. For a forensic pathologist, he was jovial, sprightly, and full of life. At thirty-five, he was younger than Adele Kean, and he oozed confidence. There wasn't anything special in his appearance. He didn't have film-star good looks, a chiselled jawline or a rippling torso, but his charm made him very attractive to the opposite sex.

Usually working in Nottingham, Simon had received the call to fill in for Adele and arrived in the steel city in record time. He was dedicated to his job and would drop anything if necessary, much to the consternation of his wife and three children.

Lucy Dauman greeted him in the pathology suite and showed him into Adele's impossibly tiny and cluttered office. Lucy had cleared some space on the desk for him to use to write up his reports and had found him a clean mug with no chips or cracks.

'So, Victoria has headed for pastures new?' he asked, taking off his duffel coat and looking around for a hook. He draped it over the back of his chair.

'Yes. Stockport. I think she has family there.'

'And what about you?'

'What about me?' Lucy asked with a frown.

'What's your story?'

'I don't have one.'

'Everyone has a story,' he said, leaning against the desk and folding his arms. At six-foot one he towered over the five-foot five technical assistant. His steely glare was bewitching.

'I don't.' She blushed, tucking her blonde hair behind her ears. 'I'm twenty-six, I live with my sister, have a cat called Odie and student debts that would make Greece look well managed.'

Simon smiled. 'Single?'

'Ye-es,' she said slowly. She had already clocked his wedding ring and wondered where this conversation was going. She didn't want there to be any awkwardness, particularly in such a confined space.

The door to the autopsy suite was pulled open and Matilda Darke entered the room.

'Ah, DCI Darke is here,' Lucy said, quickly. 'Let me introduce you.'

Unfortunately, Lucy didn't get a chance. She was about to open her mouth to speak when Simon overtook her and approached Matilda with large strides, holding his hand out for her to shake.

'Detective Chief Inspector Darke, great name for a detective, pleasure to meet you finally,' he said with a Cheshire cat smile.

Matilda shook his hand. 'Likewise,' she said. 'You are?'

'Sorry, Simon Browes, forensic pathologist. I believe I'm replacing Adele Kean on this particular case. She has a personal connection, I've been informed.'

'Well, she—'

Simon held up his hands. 'You don't need to tell me, none of my business.' He clapped his hands together. 'Shall we begin? I'll go and scrub up. Will you be joining us, DCI Darke?'

Dressed in ill-fitting green theatre scrubs, apron, gloves, wellington boots, hat and face mask, Matilda stepped carefully through the footbath and into the small and dimly lit post-mortem suite.

There was one fixed table in the centre of the room. On it lay Brian Appleby covered in a white sheet. Four other people stood nearby – Simon Browes, Lucy Dauman, and two others who looked identical in their scrubs. One was a Forensic Imaging Specialist, to photograph the post-mortem at every stage; the other was the Crime Scene Manager, there to collect trace evidence. Under their protective layers, Matilda couldn't tell who was who.

In the corner, was a brightly lit anteroom known as the SOCO room. This was where the evidence was passed through to a waiting detective constable. In this case, Faith had made the journey from the police station. Her expression showed that she wasn't happy about being here, but at least there was a wall of glass between her and the gruesome act of an autopsy.

'What did the results of the digital autopsy show?' Matilda asked.

'We haven't done one,' Lucy said.

'Why not?'

'I was told this was death by hanging,' Simon said.

'It is.'

'Then we don't need a digital autopsy. The majority of what we need to know is external. As for internal, bruising won't show up on the scans. It will save time and money for me to perform a straight invasive post-mortem.'

'What about the organs?' Matilda asked.

'What about them?' he asked, getting slightly irate at the delay.

'Don't we need to do a digital autopsy to see their condition?'

'As far as I have been made aware, there are no gunshot or stab wounds. We're not looking for the trajectory of a bullet or a snapped-off point of a knife. May I begin?'

'By all means,' Matilda said, reluctantly stepping back so as not to get in the way. She doubted if radiologist Claire Alexander would be happy.

Lucy removed the sheet and was presented with a body bag lying on the table. She broke the lock and opened the bag revealing a pale Brian Appleby inside.

Matilda angled her head to one side and studied Brian's face. She could understand why Adele had been attracted to him. He had thick, dark brown hair, a firm jawline, smooth skin and just the hint of grey in his stubble, giving him a distinguished look. Matilda had to remind herself this man had sexually assaulted three young girls. There could even have been more. He had used his charms to convince Adele he was an upstanding member of the community, just unlucky in love. What did he need to do to win over a fifteen-year-old girl?

'Did you hear me?'

Matilda looked up to see all eyes on her. 'Sorry?'

'DCI Darke, if you're not comfortable viewing a post-mortem you don't have to stay,' Simon admonished.

Matilda stole a glance at Faith in the SOCO room who was hiding a smile. 'I'm fine. I was … thinking.'

'Well, have a think about this. Your man here was strangled before he was hanged.'

'Really?' she asked. 'He didn't die by hanging?'

'He may well have been unconscious when he was finally strung up but if you look at the rope marks on his neck, they run horizontally.' Simon beckoned her closer to the body. 'As you can see, the rope was tied around his neck, but it's not a firm mark at the back. I think he was subdued in a stranglehold, so the killer would have more control.'

'I don't understand,' Matilda frowned, trying, but failing, to picture the scenario.

Simon let out a heavy sigh. 'Imagine the killer standing behind you. He has his arm wrapped around your neck squeezing hard to render you unconscious, or on the cusp of passing out. He lets go. You fall to the floor, gasping for breath, and he throws the noose over your head and hangs you up with it. The rope cuts into your throat and goes up the side of your neck around the back of your ears. It's a very slow and painful death.'

'Right,' was all Matilda could say. She changed her mind on what type of person could overpower someone of Brian Appleby's build. They needn't be stronger, taller, fitter; the element of surprise was more than enough.

'Do you know the signs of ante-mortem hanging, DCI Darke?' he asked.

'The presence of ecchymosis around the ligature and the dribbling line of dried saliva down the front of his shirt,' Matilda replied with a slight smile on her face.

'Very good,' he said, a slight condescending tone to his voice. 'Not just a pretty face, DCI Darke,' he added, for want of something better to say.

Or maybe I called Adele this morning and she told me what to look for.

'Judging by the crime scene photographs, this is a partial hanging as his toes were found to be touching the floor. Is that correct?'

'They were just touching the ground, yes.'

'The weight of the head, arms and chest provide the fatal pressure on the neck. Mr Appleby was a well-built chap. His own muscle was his killer. I'm going to cut through the rope and leave the knot intact. I'm sure your Forensics are capable of tracing the rope and finding skin samples within the fibres.'

'How long would he have taken to die?' Matilda asked.

'I'm surprised you don't already know the answer to that, DCI Darke,' he smiled at her through his face mask, his eyes twinkled. 'It depends on how long he was struggling with his assailant. The usual time period for death by hanging is three to five minutes. He will have lost consciousness fairly quickly. However, when you're dying, those few minutes can seem like an eternity.'

Dr Browes cut through the rope. 'As I expected, a simple slip knot. A decent enough rope too, not too thick, not brittle. Your hangman wasn't an opportunist. He, for argument's sake let's call him a he, knew the size of his victim and brought along the adequate tools required.'

'Thirteen twists too,' Matilda said, remembering Diana Black's comment from Thursday morning. 'A typical hangman's noose, I believe.' She was enjoying being smug.

Simon Browes ignored her. 'I'm going to cut him open and take a look at his organs now. Not squeamish are you, DCI Darke?'

'Not at all,' she lied.

'Ms Dauman?'

'Of course not,' another lie.

Chapter Ten

'Are you all right now?' Lucy Dauman asked as she stood over DCI Darke with a glass of water.

Matilda looked around her, wondering how she had got from the autopsy suite to Adele's office.

'Yes, I'm fine. It's been years since I've collapsed at a post-mortem.'

'I haven't been doing this job long. I always think I'm going to faint. I get warm and feel sick, but I've managed to control myself so far.' She smiled.

It wasn't the sight of the scalpel cutting into the body, the smell coming from the internal organs or the sounds of ribs being broken: it was Dr Simon Browes's haphazard manner and lack of respect for the man on his table. He ran the scalpel down Brian Appleby's chest like he was opening a parcel from Amazon. He tore back the skin and cracked open the ribcage like a starving cannibal. The fact Matilda hadn't eaten since first thing hadn't helped either.

'Have some more water, you still look a little flushed.' Lucy handed Matilda the glass.

'Is he always like that?'

'I've no idea. Today's the first time I've met him. He's good at his job though, you can't deny that.'

Matilda took another large slug of water and a deep breath. 'Is the post-mortem complete?'

'Yes, it is.'

'I'm guessing Dr Browes is waiting for me to do the post-autopsy briefing.'

'He is.'

'I hope he's changed his clothes,' she said, slowly getting up from the chair. 'I don't think I could stand the sight of any more blood today.'

By the time Matilda saw natural daylight she had been in the Medico-Legal Centre for over six hours. Faith had returned to the station, probably telling everyone how Matilda had fainted during a post-mortem. A DCI collapsing at the sight of blood would be comedy gold among the uniformed officers. They were just getting over the video Rory filmed on his mobile phone last year of Matilda being lifted over floodwater by a hunky fireman.

The post-autopsy briefing was conducted in the windowless family room. The heady smell of different fragrances of air freshener, coupled with Dr Simon Browes delighting in giving Matilda all the details in glorious technicolour, made her want to vomit all over his designer shirt and tight trousers.

In the end, he summed up what Matilda had already surmised: Brian Appleby died by strangulation. The blood and skin samples under his fingernails were evidence he struggled. Unfortunately, the samples belonged to him. He had pulled at the rope as it tightened around his neck and squeezed the life out of him.

As Matilda made her way, delicately, to the car park, she couldn't help but feel sorry for Brian. Then she remembered who he was, how he had fooled Adele, and his victims. She felt sick. She needed something to eat.

A tentative knock on the glass door caused Matilda to look up from her cluttered desk.

'Ma'am, can I have a word?'

'Of course, Ranjeet, come on in.'

DC Ranjeet Deshwal had recently transferred from West Yorkshire Police. He was in his mid-twenties, slim with the shiniest black hair Matilda had ever seen. He wore rimless glasses and a stud in each ear. She wanted to ask him how he managed to get the knot in his tie so big but, when she looked at his neck, all she could picture was the lifeless body of Brian Appleby hanging from his ceiling.

'DI Christian Brady is observing an interview,' he began in a thick West Yorkshire accent. 'He wanted me to tell you that three lads have been arrested in Gleadless for the assault on Alec Routledge. One of them has admitted it and landed his two mates in it too. They don't know anything about Brian Appleby, though.'

'I never thought they were linked. Thanks for telling me, Ranjeet.'

'You're welcome.'

'How are you settling into South Yorkshire Police?' she asked as he was heading for the door.

He stopped in the doorway and turned around. Matilda was pretty sure his smile was fake. 'I'm enjoying it. Great bunch of people.' He nodded several times before leaving the office.

Matilda tried hard not to smile. A great bunch of people? Was that true? She looked through the window at the officers going about their duties. There was only Scott and Faith she knew by first name. The room was packed yet she didn't know a single one of them. *You're to blame for that. Invite them out for a drink.*

'I'll think about it,' she said quietly to herself, before rolling her eyes.

Sitting in Matilda's office, Aaron Connolly and Scott Andrews were squeezed into the small space. All three had a cup of coffee balanced somewhere on Matilda's untidy desk and they'd raided Sian's snack drawer. She was due back tomorrow, so someone was going to have to run to the supermarket to replenish the stolen items.

'It turns out Brian Appleby did have kids,' Scott said, opening a Boost. 'Alicia is twenty-one. She's currently on a gap year in France. George is nineteen, and, get this, he's studying at Sheffield Hallam University.'

'Why am I only learning this now?' Matilda asked.

'I only found out myself this lunchtime. Brian had an address book, but all the names were initials. I've been looking them up, and George Appleby lives in a shared student property on Penrhyn Road.'

'Maybe that's why Brian moved to Sheffield then. To be closer to his son. I think we're going to need a word with this George. Scott, go along with Faith and bring him in.'

'Tonight?'

Matilda looked out of the window and noticed it was dark. A glance at her phone told her it was just past eight o'clock. 'First thing in the morning then. You can go with Sian, Scott.'

'Will do.'

'Who spoke to the wife?'

'Unfortunately, I did,' Aaron said. 'She was very short with me and blamed me for bringing him back into her life. She practically slammed the phone down when I asked where she was on Thursday night.'

'Did you get an answer?'

'Sort of. I've been on to the local police in Southend. They're going to send someone round to have a more in-depth chat with her. I don't think she's a suspect.'

'Did Essex Police go to speak to Brian Appleby's old neighbours?'

'They did. None of the neighbours have been in contact with Brian since he left for Sheffield. They were glad to see him go. I think they were worried house prices would drop.'

'OK. What about his neighbours on Linden Avenue?'

'Faith and Ranjeet are back there with a team of uniforms. They're trying to catch anyone who was out during the day,' Aaron said. 'So far, none of them are aware of Brian's past. They thought he was the ideal neighbour.'

'Jesus, it just shows you we have no idea who lives next door, do we?'

'So where do we go from here?' Aaron asked.

Matilda leaned back in her chair and blew out her cheeks. She had no idea. 'Well let's see if anything comes up once the son and all the neighbours have been questioned. If not, we'll have to rely on Forensics to pull something out of the hat.'

'I thought you might like to know,' Aaron said, 'the phone lines have been ringing off the hook.'

'Oh! Witnesses?'

'No. Since *The Star* printed that story about paedophiles in Sheffield, we've had people calling in and reporting anyone they suspect to be child molesters.'

'Bloody hell. Aren't people lovely?'

'I know. The calls are going to have to be followed up though.'

'Right,' Matilda said. 'I'll have a word with Christian. We'll put a team together. This is all we need.'

Adele Kean was doing something she hadn't done since Chris was a baby – she was watching a soap opera. She recognized the character of Eric Pollard (just), but everyone else was a mystery to her. Wearing tracksuit bottoms and an oversized sweater, her hair uncombed and her face without make-up, she sat on the sofa staring into the distance. How could she have been so naive as to trust a stranger, especially one she had met on the Internet. Never again.

She had spent the afternoon deleting her profile on the three websites she had registered with and the apps from her mobile phone. From now on, her mobile would be just for making calls, sending texts, and playing solitaire between post-mortems. The game for the lonely. How apt.

The landline started to ring. She decided to ignore it. It would only be a company trying to get her to claim for PPI. It stopped ringing and started again almost immediately. She looked at the display – *unknown number*. If the caller couldn't identify themselves, then she didn't see why she should answer. It stopped then started again.

'Jesus Christ,' Adele exclaimed. She picked up the handset and pressed the green button. 'Hello?' she asked, an annoyance in her voice.

'Dr Adele Kean?'

'Yes.'

'My name is Danny Hanson, I'm a reporter on *The Star*. Is it true you were on a date with a known paedophile the night before he was found murdered?'

Adele was struck dumb. She could hear her heart beating loudly in her chest. She gripped the phone tight and pressed it hard against her ear.

'Dr Kean? I've heard you're good friends with DCI Matilda Darke. How do you feel knowing that South Yorkshire Police were not aware there was a paedophile living on their patch? Surely if your best friend had known, she could have saved you all this heartache.'

Adele ended the call. 'Bastard,' she said, throwing her phone onto the seat beside her. She picked up a sofa cushion and hugged it tight to her chest. She wondered how he had managed to find out all that information about her.

Chapter Eleven

'Is your house back to normal then, Sian?' Scott asked from the driver's seat of the pool car.

'Yes, thank goodness, but at the expense of these,' she said, showing off her dry, calloused hands. 'I used to have lovely nails.'

'They'll soon grow back.'

'Yes, I'll just get them nice for the summer and they'll be ruined again. Stuart wants to irrigate the garden, so the house doesn't flood if we get more heavy rain.'

Scott tried to hide his smile.

They parked in the last available space in the small car park near the main entrance to Sheffield Hallam University. Sian stepped out and took her long black coat from the back seat. The stiff breeze whipped her shoulder-length red hair. She shivered and trotted to keep up with Scott who was a good eight inches taller than her.

They were in luck; George Appleby was on campus and currently in a lecture. A heavily pregnant administrator led the way. While Sian was asking questions about the impending birth, Scott was taking in his surroundings. University seemed so long ago to the twenty-six-year-old DC. He enjoyed his time at Nottingham University. It had been liberating. Although, looking at the students now, he was probably better off where he was. He didn't remember being so bloody miserable. Yes, they would be leaving university with three times the debt he left with, but while he was studying he didn't care about that. He had a ball.

Sian and Scott waited in the corridor while the administrator went to collect George from a lecture hall.

'It won't be long until your kids are coming to uni, will it?'

'How old do you think I am?' Sian asked. 'My eldest is studying for his GCSEs. There's plenty of time before he comes here.'

'What does he want to do?'

'I've no idea. I don't think he knows either,' she replied, looking into the distance.

'From an early age I knew I wanted to be a detective. I think it was Sherlock Holmes that got me interested.'

Sian smiled. 'Real-life police work is a bit of an eye-opener, isn't it?'

'Just a tad.' He smiled back. 'Also, I don't play the violin or smoke opium.'

The door opened, and the administrator stepped out followed by a tall skinny George Appleby. His pale pallor, his mound of unruly dull-red hair, his oversized clothes, made him appear in urgent need of a hot meal.

'I'll leave you to it,' the administrator said before she waddled off down the corridor.

'George Appleby?' Sian asked.

'That's right.' He looked nervously at the two detectives.

'I'm DS Sian Mills from South Yorkshire Police. This is DC Andrews. We'd like to ask you a few questions about your father, if that's OK?'

'My father?' he asked in wide-eyed surprise. His eyes darted nervously from side to side to make sure they weren't overheard.

'Yes. When was the last time you saw him?'

The nervous look was replaced with one of disgust. 'I've no idea. It was years ago. Why?'

'Do you know where he lives?'

'Yes. He's in Ashfield Prison,' he said, lowering his voice.

Sian and Scott exchanged glances.

'What's going on?'

'I think it would be better if we continued this conversation back at the station. This isn't really the place.'

George Appleby sat in the interview room, guarded by PC Steve Harrison, looking up at the crime prevention posters. In the observation bay, Sian and Matilda were studying the skinny young man.

'So, he had no idea his father was out of prison?'

'Unless he was a very good liar,' Sian said. 'How do you want me to play this?'

'Break the news that his father's dead first, then mention he's been living in Sheffield for over a year, see what reaction you get.'

'What do you think? Father shows up at his digs wanting to make amends and George snaps?' Sian asked.

'I'm not sure. It does seem strange that Brian Appleby would move to Sheffield and not contact his son.'

'He doesn't look like he's got the strength to string his father up. His arms are like twigs.'

'A lot of students seem to be sporting the emaciated look these days. I don't like it,' Matilda said.

'No. A bloke should have some meat on him. Have you seen my Stuart? Built like a rugby player with thighs to match. Lovely,' Sian said, almost drooling.

'OK, Sian, when you're ready,' Matilda nodded to the interview room.

When Sian broke the news of his father's death, she handed George a tissue. He had his head down, but there were no tears.

'Does my mum know?' he asked, looking up.

'Yes.'

'What about Alicia?'

'I think that's been taken care of. George, we believe your father was murdered.'

'Murdered? Because of what he did?'

'We don't know. George, your father was living here in Sheffield.'

'What?' He seemed more shocked by that than hearing his father had been killed.

'He was living in Linden Avenue. Just off Meadowhead,' Scott said.

He shrugged. 'I've been drinking on Woodseats. That's not far away, is it?'

'No it isn't.'

'George, has your father tried to contact you at all?'

'No. Never. How long has he been living up here?'

'About a year.'

'Bloody hell.'

'George, did your father know you were studying in Sheffield?'

'I'm sorry, but do you mind not calling him my father? What he did … well, he's not my dad. I refuse to have that kind of person as my dad. To answer your question, no, he didn't know I was studying in Sheffield. As far as I'm aware, most of the family washed their hands of him when he was found guilty. My mum, sister, aunts and uncles, nobody went to visit him.'

'From our point of view, it seems strange that you both ended up in Sheffield,' Sian said.

'Well, it's a very popular city for universities. You know, people from all over the country come here.'

'But we don't know why your fa— Brian moved here. Is there any link your family has to Sheffield?'

'No, I don't think so.'

'Why would he choose Sheffield?'

'I have no idea. He was locked up in 2008. I was a child. I don't know him at all,' he said, nervously scratching at his wrists.

'Is there anyone who would know about why he'd moved here?'

He shrugged again. 'You'd need to ask my mum, but I doubt she'd know either. Maybe he made friends with someone in prison who lives here, I'm sorry. I can't help you,' George said, getting agitated.

'George,' Sian said, adjusting herself in her hard plastic seat, 'we found this address book in your father's – Brian's – house. He knew where you lived.'

'What?'

Sian pushed it across the table to George. The book was open at the As with George's details written in neat block capitals.

'Oh my God,' he exclaimed. 'How did he …? I …'

'Did he ever come to see you?'

'No.'

'Did your housemates say you'd had a visitor while you were out, or did they notice someone hanging around?'

'No,' he replied, his face was a map of worry. 'Do you think he was following me?'

'I really don't know, George. I'm sorry.'

'This is a nightmare.' He ran his skinny fingers through his tangled hair.

'OK.' Sian shifted in her seat again. 'George, I'm only asking this for elimination purposes, but where were you on Thursday night?'

'Last Thursday?' he asked quickly. His eyes widened.

'Yes.'

'Is that when he was …?'

'Yes.'

'I was at home.'

'Can anyone verify that?'

'No, I don't think so. I was in my room. I should have been working in the uni bar but there was a balls-up with the rota. I didn't mind. I was shattered after working four nights in a row until the early hours. I decided to have an early night instead.'

'How early?'

'I don't know. About nine o'clock, I think.'

'Alone?'

'Of course alone. I thought you were asking me for elimination purposes? It sounds like you're accusing me of something.'

'Sian,' Matilda said through her earpiece. 'Ask him about his feelings towards his father. Call him his father too.'

'George, how do you feel about your dad?'

His eyes flitted from Sian to Scott and back again. He swallowed hard a couple of times. Eventually, he replied. 'I despise him.' He spoke with such venom and hatred that it seemed to resound off the walls.

'Why is that?'

'Wouldn't you hate your dad if he raped little girls?'

'But he's still your father at the end of the day.'

A wave of emotions swept across George's pale face. 'I despise him. For what he did, I hate him. I physically hate the man. He's not my dad. As far as I'm concerned I don't have a dad.'

'What do you think?' Matilda asked Sian as they stood in the foyer of the station watching through the doors as Scott led George to the car.

'He hates his father. Hate is a very good motive for murder.'

'He was building himself a decent life here in Sheffield. University, new friends, finding out who he really is, and then Brian comes along to ruin it all.'

'Do you think they were in contact?' Sian asked. Neither of them took their eyes from the student.

'It's possible. Look at it from Brian's point of view. You've been released from prison and practically been run out of your home. Your wife, brothers and parents want nothing to do with you. Your son, however, was only nine when you were put away. You've not heard from him or seen him since. Surely, you're going to try to make amends, get him back on side.'

Sian thought for a while. 'I think I would. If it was me. I'd want to contact my children and apologize for what I'd done.'

'Maybe that's what Brian did.'

'And George wanted nothing to do with him. Maybe we should have a quiet chat with George's housemates, when he's not around, obviously.'

'Definitely. He has no alibi either. We'll be speaking to him again.' Matilda walked over to the double doors and pulled one open. George was just getting into the car when he looked up and saw Matilda. He gave her a simple smile. She wasn't going to be fooled. She'd seen smiles like that before.

Chapter Twelve

Day Ten
Saturday, 18 March 2017

He may have been only five years old, but Jason Lacey knew the benefits to having a birthday fall on a weekend rather than a weekday – he didn't have to go to school. He woke up earlier than usual, excited at what his parents had planned for him that day. He ran into their bedroom and jumped on the bed. It was like Christmas morning all over again. At least he'd waited until it was light this time.

After breakfast, which he ate in record time, Jason was allowed to open two presents. His mother ushered him out of the room to get dressed upstairs.

'Right, let's go through the plan one more time,' Karen said to her husband, entering the living room while putting her coat on. She spoke in hushed tones just in case her son was listening.

Joe sighed and lowered his newspaper. 'I'm not thick. I know what I'm doing.'

'You're not even dressed yet.'

He looked down at his cartoon pyjamas and dressing gown.

'Have you been sat there reading the paper while I've got myself and three kids ready?'

'It's the weekend.'

'It's also your son's birthday. Now, are you sure you don't want to take the kids to the cinema and I'll collect everything?'

'You really don't trust me, do you?' He smiled.

'It's not that,' Karen started to flounder. 'It's just … well, organization isn't your strong point, is it?'

Joe dug around in the pocket of his dressing gown and pulled out a tatty sheet of A4 paper. He unfolded it. 'See, I have your instructions with me which I shall carry out to the letter.'

She kissed him on his recently shaved head. 'You know how to make me happy.'

'I thought I did that on *your* birthday last month.' He winked. He grabbed the waistband of her jeans and pulled her towards him.

The sound of three small children thundering down the stairs interrupted them.

'Right, we'll be off now. Don't forget, presents first, cake last. We'll be back by four at the latest.'

'Should we synchronize watches?' he asked, staring intently at the Breitling he'd been given for Christmas.

'Promise me you'll not forget anything.'

'I promise.' He smiled.

Karen leaned forward and kissed him on the lips. 'Make sure you have a shave too.'

'I'll even wash behind my ears.'

Karen rolled her eyes and left the room. The three children, Esme, Victoria, and birthday boy, Jason, were all excitedly waiting in the hallway wrapping themselves up in their coats, scarves, and gloves.

'Are you guys ready?'

'*The Lego Batman Movie*!' Jason almost screamed at the top of his voice.

Joe kissed all of the children in turn and told them to have a great time. He picked Jason up and raised him high in the air.

'You're getting big now, birthday boy.' He kissed him on the cheek. 'Enjoy the film. Tell me all about it when you get back.'

'Ok.'

Karen turned to make sure the kids were out of earshot. 'Remember …'

'I know, presents first, then cake.'

'And don't drop it either or I'll drop you.'

'Such a lovely way with words.' Joe kissed his wife hard on the lips before she could issue any more instructions. He waved them off and closed the door.

The silence, no chattering wife, no excited kids, was deafening. He breathed a sigh of relief and smiled. As much as he loved his family, he appreciated his alone time just as much.

It was an unusually cold morning. The sun was shining in the clear blue sky, but it was bloody freezing. As Joe selected fifth gear, he slammed his foot down on the accelerator and headed into Derbyshire. The rolling landscape was covered with a sparkling layer of frost, bare trees reached into the air, sheep grazed on the steep hillside, and the sound of birds singing was heartwarming. Winter was maintaining its stronghold on 2017 for a little longer than usual. With these stunning views, it didn't matter.

Joe had struck lucky when it came to in-laws. Karen's parents were kind and generous. They welcomed Joe into their family and forgave him his past deeds. As long as Karen and the kids were happy, they were too. They invited Joe in for a hot chocolate to warm him up before presenting him with a sack full of gifts for Jason. It was exactly like the Christmas Eve present run.

'There's a little something in there for Esme and Victoria too. I didn't want them feeling left out,' Karen's mum said.

'You don't need to do that, Alice. You gave them all plenty at Christmas.'

'Well, I just want them to know we think about them all. Give them a big kiss from their grandma and grandad and tell them we'll see them tomorrow.'

Joe headed back to Sheffield. He stopped off to fill up with petrol, then went to the far side of the city to collect the cake from the baker.

'Oh my God, that's brilliant,' he beamed when he opened the box and saw the large cake inside. 'Jason will love it. It's his favourite Minion.'

'Well I hope you all enjoy it.'

'We will.'

The box was secured with the seatbelt and Joe drove carefully back to Meersbrook. He couldn't stop smiling as he imagined the look on Jason's face when he saw the cake. He drove straight into the garage and closed the door behind him.

Before he'd left, Joe had set the dining room up for the mini-party they were having later with a few of Jason's friends from school. The table was clear, and Joe could place the cake in the middle without any hassle. It was heavier than expected.

He took the lid off the box, carefully removed the large yellow cake from it and placed the smiling Minion on the table. He stood back and inspected it. Karen would kill him if there were any damages. He was amazed something so intricate could be made out of sponge and icing.

The attack caught Joe unawares. The wind was knocked out of him from behind, and he fell to the floor, hitting the ground with a loud thud.

Dazed, he shook his head and tried to stand up, but something was pushing down on his back and he fell to the floor once again. He looked up and saw his pained reflection in the patio windows screaming back at him. Above him was a dark figure dressed in black who had one foot on his back, pressing him to the floor. He couldn't breathe as he felt his ribs starting to break.

'I could easily kill you. It wouldn't take much for a broken shard of a rib to pierce your lung and for it to fill with blood.

You'd gag. You'd choke. You'd drown in your own blood, but it wouldn't take long before you lost consciousness.'

The pressure was released from Joe. He was in a great deal of pain, but he managed to turn over onto his back. He coughed as he struggled to regain his breath.

'Who the fuck are you?' he asked.

The man dressed in black took off his backpack, unzipped it and took out a length of rope. He held it aloft, showing Joe the noose swaying at the end of it.

'I'm your executioner.'

Panicking, Joe tried to get away. He didn't get far as he banged the back of his head on the patio window. He turned, reached up for the handle and pulled, but it was locked. He felt the noose go over his head and squeeze into his neck. He tried to get his fingers under the rope, but it was no good, it was too tight. Already his breathing was laboured, and he felt light-headed as he was dragged along the carpet.

'Wake up, Joe,' his attacker shouted, slapping him across his face. 'You need to know why you're being executed. You're taking all the fun out of it.'

'What do you want?'

'Justice. That's all I want.'

'I haven't done anything wrong!'

The man let go of the rope, and Joe fell back, hitting his head once again on the floor.

'How can you say that? How can you deny what you've done? When you're breathing your last breath, think of Rebecca.'

Joe's eyes widened. That was a name he hadn't heard in years. 'No. Please,' he wept. 'I've got a family. Please. Don't kill me.'

At the sight of Joe begging and pleading for his life, the Hangman smiled.

'Mum, I feel sick.'

'I told you not to eat all those fries.'

It was going dark by the time Karen and the children made their way from Meadowhall back home to Meersbrook. They'd had a great day, although when planning it, Karen hadn't taken into account the annoyance of Saturday shoppers. She had felt a headache come on after ten minutes. The volume of *The Lego Batman Movie* hadn't helped either. The burger in Oasis afterwards was tasty, but the wall of noise from those around her took the edge off her appetite. Jason, however, had delighted in finishing off everyone else's fries. Now, he was paying the price. When she'd gone to the toilet and seen her reflection in the mirror she looked as if she'd aged ten years since arriving at Meadowhall. The mall sapped every ounce of energy from the moment you arrived. When the extension opened it would be hell on earth.

'Have you had a good day, Jason?' she asked, trying to distract him from feeling sick.

'It's been brilliant,' he brightened up. 'I can't wait to tell Dad about the film. Do you think he'll take me to see it again next weekend?'

'I'm sure he will,' Karen said smiling, knowing her husband was a big kid at heart and would probably enjoy *The Lego Batman Movie* even more than Jason did, if that was possible.

Karen turned the corner and pulled up in front of the house. She wondered why it was in darkness. Maybe Joe was planning to jump out and shout surprise. Jason would love that.

Jason climbed out of the back seat and ran to the house. The front door was unlocked and he went straight in. Karen could hear the calls for his father from the road. For a tiny child, he had a loud voice. Victoria and Esme helped Karen with the bags of shopping. She had just closed the boot when a glass-shattering scream came from the house. She dropped a bag and a bottle smashed. Red wine spilled out of the torn plastic and ran down the road. She froze as she looked at the open doorway of her home and saw her little boy staring at her. His face was pale, and he was shaking violently. Her mouth opened but she couldn't speak. Her heart seemed to have stopped beating and her world stopped turning.

Chapter Thirteen

Matilda had been waiting for this phone call since last Saturday morning. Something at the back of her mind told her there would be a second victim. Brian Appleby had been hanged in what looked like an execution. Someone had obviously known about his past and decided he needed to pay with his life rather than just eight years in prison. If they had taken the trouble to research Brian, and set up such an elaborate and gruesome murder, they wouldn't stop at one victim; others would be in the planning. One week later, Matilda had been proven correct.

In the car on the way, Aaron filled Matilda in on the details. It sounded frighteningly similar to the Brian Appleby murder. The victim, in this case, was Joe Lacey, who was not on the sex offender's register but was known to the police.

On the 1st of January 1997, following a New Year's Eve party with his girlfriend, Karen, who later became his wife, he dropped off Karen at her flat and drove home. It was nine o'clock in the morning and Joe had been drinking since early afternoon the previous day. He knocked down and killed eight-year-old Rebecca Branson. He didn't stop.

Later that day, the police called to his flat and arrested him for causing death by dangerous driving. He was breathalyzed and found to be five times over the legal limit. He was sentenced to twelve years in prison, but was released in 2004 after seven years, aged only 24.

Since then he had gone on to marry Karen and have three children. His life had returned to normal, which was more than can be said for the parents of Rebecca Branson.

It was pitch-dark by the time the pool car pulled up outside the semi-detached house in Meersbrook. Crime scene tape surrounded the house and a uniformed officer was outside the front door. The usual gawkers were standing on the pavement, arms folded firmly across their chests to stave off the cold, a look of angst and worry on their faces. Secretly, they were enjoying the change from the norm. This beat watching cheap reality shows on television.

DC Faith Easter climbed out of the car from behind the wheel. 'Bloody hell it's freezing. I wish I'd brought my gloves.'

Sian Mills almost slipped on a patch of black ice. 'I'm going to have to get some better grips on these shoes.'

Matilda led the way to the house. She was presented with a white paper suit from PC Harrison and slipped into it with ease.

'What the hell is that?' Matilda asked sticking her head around the corner into the dining room.

'Wow, that's so cool,' Faith said. 'It's a Minion.'

'What's a Minion?'

'It's a PC who stands guard in freezing temperatures,' came the reply from PC Harrison outside.

Both Sian and Faith laughed.

'It's a character from a film,' Sian corrected.

'I'll take your word for it,' Matilda said.

'We're in here,' a call came out from the garage.

It was accessed from a door in the hallway next to the kitchen. Artificial white light from floodlights filled the freezing cold room. An Audi was parked in the middle, shelves full of oddities lined both sides. At the top of the room, three steps made from MDF led down to the garage. From a hook in the ceiling hung the lifeless body of Joe Lacey.

Standing on a stepladder next to the body was a blue-suited Adele Kean. 'Good evening, Matilda.'

'Evening, Adele,' Matilda replied, looking directly at the hanging man. He had a white pillowcase over his head. The rope resembled the one used to hang Brian Appleby, and Matilda counted thirteen turns in the noose. This was definitely no coincidence. She swallowed hard and forced down the bile rising in her stomach. It wasn't the sight of a hanging man that made her feel sick, it was the thought of a killer striking again.

'His feet aren't touching the floor; would the drop be enough to kill him?' Matilda asked, remembering her conversation with Simon Browes at Brian Appleby's post-mortem.

'His feet are only eight inches off the ground. He could have been strung up rather than pushed off the top step. At a guess, I'd say asphyxiation.'

'Who found him?'

Sian entered the garage, took one look at the hanging body, then down to her notepad. 'According to the first responder, it was the victim's son, Jason. He's only five. In fact, today is his fifth birthday.'

'Bloody hell, he's not going to forget this birthday in a long while.'

'The mother, Karen, was out with all three kids. Joe was getting the house ready for a birthday party. They came home, Jason comes rushing in and finds him hanging.'

'What time did they leave this morning?'

'About ten o'clock. Ish.'

'And what about when they came back home?'

'Around five o'clock.'

'Adele?' Matilda asked.

'You know I don't like time of death questions.'

'After ten o'clock this morning?'

'Yes. I'd say anything from noon until the time he was found. That's a guess. Listen to what the neighbours say and go with that,' she warned.

'Thank you, Adele.' Matilda smiled. 'Where are the family now?'

'Karen's sister lives three doors down; they're in there. The kids are distraught,' Sian said.

'How's the mother?'

'Quiet, by all accounts.'

'OK. We'll leave them for tonight. Get an FLO to stay with them. I want them all interviewed first thing in the morning.'

'Are you happy with what you've seen, Matilda? Can we cut him down and take him to the mortuary?' Adele said.

'Yes, sure.'

'Can someone help me take the weight of this man, please, so I can unhook the rope?' Adele called out to anyone who would listen.

'Two seconds,' Lucy Dauman said placing the pillowcase carefully into an evidence bag.

Matilda turned away from her friend. She led Faith by the arm to the other side of the garage. 'Faith, you're good with computers, have a look online for anyone who thinks people like Joe Lacey or Brian Appleby should have served longer sentences.'

'You think they're linked?'

'I do. Keep this to yourself for now, until we find something that connects them.'

'Will do.'

'Aaron,' Matilda called out to the DS as she saw him pass the doorway at the top of the steps. 'Get Kesinka and Ranjeet out here to knock on a few doors. I know it's dark but it's still only early evening. I want to know if anyone saw anything suspicious, not just today either. Has anyone been hanging around lately?'

Aaron nodded and walked away, pulling out his mobile phone. He seemed distracted, probably thinking of his heavily pregnant wife. Matilda had no idea how he was feeling, but even she was starting to wish Katrina would hurry up and have this bloody baby.

Matilda stepped back from the scene of activity and watched as Adele Kean, Lucy Dauman, and a scene of crime officer slowly lowered Joe Lacey to the ground. He was sealed inside a padlocked body bag. Matilda unzipped the forensic suit and took her mobile out of her inside jacket pocket.

'Sian.' She signalled her sergeant over to her as she searched for a number. She lowered her voice. 'Do me a favour, go and visit George Appleby and find out where he was from lunchtime onwards.'

'You don't think …?'

'Right now, I don't know what to think.' She put the phone to her ear and waited for her call to be answered.

Matilda went back into the house and nodded at PC Harrison standing next to the front door, who noted on his clipboard that she'd left the scene. She looked around at the sea of onlookers and neighbours who were standing behind the police tape straining to see any action. *Ghouls.*

'Ma'am, I'm sorry to interrupt you, but I thought you'd like to know we've found a body, another hanging,' she lowered her voice. 'I think we may have a vigilante operating in Sheffield.'

Chapter Fourteen

'Out of everyone in this room, who is the most sympathetic among you?' Matilda asked as the briefing into Joe Lacey's murder began. All eyes turned to look at Sian.

'Why do I get the feeling I'm being set up here?'

'I need someone considerate and sensitive to interview the Lacey children.'

'That leaves out Rory,' Scott said, to much laughter from around the room.

'Thank you, DC Andrews, for volunteering to accompany Sian,' Matilda said.

'You should learn to keep your trap shut,' Rory laughed.

'Rory, you're coming with me to the post-mortem.'

'But I'm still recuperating from my attack,' he said, putting on a sickly voice and, for some reason, a cough.

'Never mind. Adele and Lucy are both highly trained should you have a funny turn. You couldn't be in better hands. Now, Kes, how did you get on with the door to door last night?'

'We're going back this morning to finish off,' she said, tucking her shoulder-length black hair behind her ears. 'A couple of the neighbours said they saw Karen going out with the kids, then Joe left on his own about half an hour or so later. He came back after a couple of hours, but that's it. Nobody seems to have seen anything else.'

'OK. Finish the rest of the street off then start over. After a night's sleep, they may have remembered something else. Do we know the point of entry?' Matilda asked.

'There are scratches on the lock on the back door,' Aaron said. 'It was closed but unlocked when Forensics were going through the house. Maybe a lock-pick of some kind.'

'This is someone who knows what he's doing, then. Rory, get the rope from the Brian Appleby murder. I want to see if it's a match for the one used on Joe Lacey. Also, try and find where it came from.'

'Really? You can buy rope anywhere.'

'It'll keep you nice and busy then, won't it? Faith, any joy with the forums?'

Faith looked tired. Her hair wasn't as neat as usual, and Matilda was sure she was wearing those same clothes yesterday. 'I've only just started, ma'am.'

'What were you doing yesterday evening? It was still only early when we found Joe Lacey.'

'I know, but I didn't think it was worth coming all the way back to the station.'

'I'm sorry?' Matilda looked shocked. 'This is a murder investigation. There's no such thing as regular office hours when a body is discovered. Every minute counts. You should have made a start on the task I'd set you.'

'I'm sorry, ma'am. I'll get right on it.' She lowered her head to her desk. The eyes of everyone else in the room were fixed on her. She blushed with embarrassment.

Matilda's gaze was locked on Faith while she continued talking. 'Aaron, track down Rebecca Branson's family. I want to know where they were yesterday and if they knew where Joe Lacey was living. Now, does anyone have anything to add, any questions?'

‘Are we linking the Brian Appleby murder with Joe Lacey?’ Christian Brady asked.

‘Not officially, but you have to admit, there are similarities. For now, let’s concentrate on finding out who killed Joe Lacey. Once we have a suspect we can try and find a link with Brian Appleby. Right, as you are all aware, the details of Brian’s murder were leaked to the press. If this happens again there will be serious trouble. We only talk about the case in this room. No gossip in the canteen, nothing on social media and don’t say a word to family and friends. Is that clear?’

There were mutterings of agreement from around the room.

Matilda pointed to the photo of Danny Hanson which had been graffitied with a pencil moustache and glasses. ‘Remember this face. If you see him, keep your mouth shut.’

Matilda should be able to trust the people on her team – to do their work diligently and professionally – and to an extent, she could. But how far did their loyalty go? She stood up to go into her office, signalling for Christian Brady to follow her.

‘Close the door, Christian. How’s the family?’

‘Fine thanks. Well, I had the in-laws over last weekend and they’re still bloody here. Apart from that everything is fine.’

Matilda smiled. ‘Christian, is there anything going on with the team?’

‘What do you mean?’

‘I’ve got a sense that not everyone is giving the job their full commitment. Faith seems very distracted. I can understand Rory not being back to his usual self, but Scott’s quiet and even Sian’s a tad withdrawn.’

‘Maybe they don’t like working on a Sunday.’ He smiled.

‘Nobody likes working on a Sunday, Christian.’ She knew exactly what she would be doing if Joe Lacey hadn’t been killed last night. She’d be sitting in her library with a cup of tea, a packet of biscuits and a good book. Sometimes, an entire day would go by and Matilda had done nothing but read. It was relaxing, comforting.

'The winter blues, then,' Christian added. 'Spring seems to be taking a while to show itself.' He shrugged.

'Could you keep an eye on them, maybe have a succinct chat?'

'Sure. If you think it'll help.'

When Christian opened the door to leave, Matilda caught the tail-end of what Kesinka was saying outside '...if you kill someone, you deserve all you get.'

As Matilda made her way to the ACC's office, she almost bumped into Faith Easter coming out of the toilets.

'Sorry, ma'am.' Faith's eyes were red and her hair was slightly wet as if she had tried to flatten the stuck-up parts.

'Faith, is everything all right?'

'Yes, ma'am.'

'You seem a little distracted lately.'

'I'm fine, honestly. I'm sorry I didn't come back to the station last night when you asked. It won't happen again.' She tried to walk away but Matilda stopped her.

'Faith, I know we haven't worked together for long, but you're a very capable detective. I see a bright future for you. However, you need to continue to focus. We can't allow any distractions, especially in a case like this. I know you're young and you probably like going out and drinking like everyone else of your age, but you need to give one hundred per cent every day.'

'I will do. Sorry, ma'am. It won't happen again.'

'Good.' Matilda smiled. 'I'd like to see you make sergeant, at least before Rory.'

'I'd like that too.'

'Excellent.'

Matilda watched as Faith headed back to the incident room. She seemed to have a spring in her step and her hair swished from side to side with each bounce.

That's what you need to do more of, Matilda, encourage your team. Let them in.

'If I see the words vigilante or serial killer appear in the press, I shall not be responsible for my actions. Are you listening to me, DCI Darke?'

Matilda's mind was elsewhere. She was sitting opposite Valerie Masterson's desk nursing a black coffee which was rapidly going cold, but she couldn't help thinking she had missed something at the briefing earlier.

'Sorry?'

'Is everything all right?'

'Yes. Fine. Well, apart from having a potential serial killing vigilante on my patch,' Matilda replied with a sarcastic smile.

Valerie rolled her eyes. 'You don't have proof there is a connection yet. Until you do, they are two separate cases. What's happening with the Brian Appleby investigation, anyway?'

'It's run cold, I'm afraid. Alibis check out with his daughter and ex-wife. His family haven't had anything to do with him since he was locked up. Sian is going to have another word with the son today, just to check on his alibi for last night.'

'You don't think he's responsible for the Joe Lacey murder too, do you?'

'I have no idea. I hope not. He seems like a nice lad, but …' she let the sentence float away. She had been tricked before.

'What about forensics on the Appleby case?'

'Nothing. Whoever killed him did an excellent job not to leave a trace.'

'Who knows enough about trace evidence?'

'Anyone who watches *CSI* or *Silent Witness*,' Matilda said. 'Or with access to the Internet. Let's face it, if you're planning a murder you can find anything you like online. You don't necessarily have to have a degree in forensic science.'

'Someone with a grudge, maybe?'

'Against who?'

'The law. Brian Appleby sexually assaulted three girls. That's something you're going to live with for the rest of your life, yet he's released after eight years.'

'I thought you didn't want to talk about it being a vigilante?'

'So you were listening, then? I said I didn't want it appearing in the press. If this is someone waging a one-man war against the police, then he needs to be found and stopped as soon as possible before he strikes again, because he will,' Valerie warned. 'Would you like me to get a criminal psychologist in, so he can tell you the type of person you're looking for?'

'I don't think it will come to that,' Matilda scoffed. 'I've got Faith checking Internet forums. People like this can't help themselves from announcing to the world from behind the safety of their keyboard how the law needs changing to protect the victim. There was already something on local radio this morning about people wanting to bring back hanging.'

'Yes, but those kinds of people don't usually act on their beliefs.'

'Leave it with me. If I need the services of a psychologist, I'll let you know.'

'Make sure you do. I don't want any more unsolved murders on our books.'

Matilda placed her untouched coffee cup on the desk and rose.

'By the way,' Valerie said as Matilda reached the door. 'I had an email on Friday, we will be getting a Major Crimes Unit at some point this year. Maybe you should think about applying to head it. It could mean promotion too.'

Matilda nodded. 'Maybe.'

'It would look good for you if you went into any promotions interview having solved a very tricky double murder.'

Blackmail? Really? You are desperate.

Chapter Fifteen

'I'm Detective Sergeant Aaron Connolly, this is Detective Constable Faith Easter, South Yorkshire Police. Could we have a word?'

It wasn't difficult to track down Clive and Amanda Branson. They were still living at the same address in Norfolk Park as they were twenty years ago when their only child, Rebecca, was killed in a hit-and-run incident.

Amanda had answered the door. She was overweight with an uncontrollable mound of light grey hair. Her floor-length dress was bright and flowery. Its cheeriness hadn't reached her face, which looked maudlin and sad. Aaron wondered if this was her permanent expression.

'What's it about?' she asked through the gap in the door.

'It would be better if we talked inside, Mrs Branson.'

'I'm not sure. My husband isn't here.' She looked nervous.

'It won't take long.'

She thought about it before closing the door to take off the chain. She let them in and showed the way to the living room.

'I can't offer you a drink, we're out of milk. That's where my husband is now, you know, buying a few bits.'

'That's fine. Do you mind if we sit down?'

‘I suppose not.’

Aaron and Faith sat on the chintz sofa. The decoration was busy and old-fashioned. The threadbare carpet a dull mix of mismatched colours. The wallpaper, cream with large pink flowers running up the walls. The furniture, orange veneer and pre-1980s, was scratched and needed to go to the skip. In fact, the whole living room needed gutting.

‘Mrs Branson, do you know of a Joe Lacey?’ Faith asked.

She flinched at the name. ‘Of course. He’s the man who murdered my little girl.’ Amanda looked uncomfortable, perched on the edge of an armchair. Her fingers were entwined, nervously playing with each other. She glanced to a framed photograph of a young bespectacled girl on the fireplace.

‘Do you know where he lives?’

‘No.’ She frowned. ‘Why should I?’

‘Mrs Branson, Joe Lacey was found dead at his home yesterday evening. We believe he was murdered.’

Amanda Branson remained stoic. She didn’t even blink. ‘Oh. Well, I can’t say I’m sad about that. What goes around, comes around.’

‘Mrs Branson, where were you and your husband yesterday?’

Her eyes widened. ‘What do you want to know that for?’

‘Purely for elimination purposes,’ Aaron said.

‘Elimination? You suspect us of killing him?’

‘At the moment—’ Aaron began.

‘Out,’ she exploded. ‘Get out of my house. It’s bad enough you come in here and bring that man’s name back into my life, but to actually accuse me of killing him. No. I won’t have it. Get out of my house.’ She struggled to pull herself up from the battered armchair.

‘Mrs Branson—’ Faith tried.

‘No. I won’t hear any more of it,’ she thundered to the door. ‘I don’t know how you’ve got the nerve. Don’t you think we’ve been through enough?’

'Fine. We'll leave,' Aaron said. 'I'm sorry to have upset you.'

'*Upset me*? You don't know the half of it. If you must know we were both here all day and all night. We watched television until eleven o'clock, then went to bed. Now go on, out.'

The door slammed behind them. On the doorstep Aaron buttoned up his coat while Faith dug her gloves out of her pocket. The temperature seemed to have dropped.

'Well, that was a display,' Aaron said.

Faith was about to reply when they saw a dishevelled-looking man struggling up the hill under the weight of a heavy shopping bag in each hand. She nudged Aaron. 'Do you think that's Clive Branson?'

'Mr Branson?' Aaron called to him.

'Who wants to know?' he asked, wheezing. He stopped walking. Judging by his laboured breathing, he could talk or walk, but couldn't do both at the same time.

'DS Connolly, DC Easter, South Yorkshire Police. I was wondering if you could tell me where you were yesterday,' Aaron continued, as they walked over to him.

'Why?'

'Joe Lacey has been found dead. We believe he's been murdered. We know of your history with him and we'd like to eliminate you from our enquiries.'

'Joe Lacey's been murdered?' he asked, wiping his mouth with the back of his hand. 'How?'

'We're not sure, yet,' Aaron replied before Faith could answer. 'If you could just tell us where you were.'

'I was out all day yesterday with my brother.'

'Really?'

'Yes. Really.'

'Your brother can confirm that, can he?'

'Of course.'

'What time did you get back?'

'Dunno. It was late.'

'What about your wife?'

'What about her?'

'Was she with you?'

'No. She was at home all day. I went out with my brother. Look, I don't want you hassling my wife, she's not a well woman. Now, if you'll excuse me.'

Clive Branson barged past the detectives and waddled to his house.

'I can smell smoke,' Faith said.

'That'll be because of all the pants on fire around here,' Aaron said, giving her a knowing look.

'There's nothing like a post-mortem to kick-start your working week,' Matilda said as she cleared a few files off a chair and made herself comfortable.

The autopsy on Joe Lacey had taken just over four hours. The pathologist and the DCI, once they had washed and changed, sat in Adele's office with a strong coffee each. The smell of caffeine mixed with soap.

'Have you got anything to eat, I'm starving?' Matilda asked.

Adele opened her bottom drawer and pulled out a couple of packets of crisps.

Since Adele's date with Brian Appleby and his true identity had been revealed, Adele had changed. She said it didn't bother her, and she tried to return to her usual bubbly self, but there was an underlying sadness that had come to the surface. The smile she painted on didn't reach her eyes. The black eye from the burglar had almost faded; there was just the hint of a bruise.

'Is everything all right?' Matilda asked.

'Yes, fine. Now, Joe Lacey,' she said. 'There was no evidence of a hangman's fracture, but there were signs of a lack of oxygen to the brain.'

'Which means the hanging didn't kill him?' Matilda asked.

'Well it did, or I wouldn't have spent four hours with my hands inside him. It means it wasn't a quick death. He was starved of oxygen and died from asphyxiation.'

'The same as Brian Appleby.'

'Exactly.'

'Interestingly, Joe Lacey seemed to have put up a bit more of a struggle than … the first victim,' Adele couldn't bring herself to say Brian's name. 'There is evidence of bruising on his back, carpet burns, which suggest he was dragged, and three of his ribs are cracked.'

'He fought back.'

'Don't get your hopes up. Joe was a nail biter. There's nothing there to collect skin samples from.'

'Shame. Same killers?' Matilda asked.

'I'm no detective. All I can do is read you the results. However, the knots are identical, to the left of the neck, in both cases, and they both died by asphyxiation. The difference in this case is there was a gap of about eight inches between Joe Lacey's feet and the floor. Whereas with … Brian Appleby, his feet were touching the ground.'

'A complete hanging for Joe but a partial one for Brian,' Matilda said. 'I've been reading up.'

'God bless Google.' Adele smiled. 'With a complete hanging, you would expect death to come quickly. As there is evidence of the brain being starved of oxygen, I would say he was strung up slowly rather than dropped from a height.'

'Joe Lacey wasn't a little bloke, though, was he? He's what, five-foot ten?'

'Five-eleven.'

'Five-eleven, and his weight?'

'Fifteen stone, give or take a few pounds.'

'So, in both cases, the killer has had to subdue his victims in some way, which suggests he's not as big as them,' Matilda said thinking aloud, picturing George Appleby and his skinny frame. 'Hmm,' she mused. 'What about the bruising on the neck? Is that similar?'

'Yes. Very. The noose was placed around the neck and tightened. He was incapacitated before he was hanged. You can see the various points of friction on the neck from the rope.'

'It's got to be the same killer,' Matilda said with a deep frown on her face.

'Or two killers who know each other well enough to exchange notes,' Adele said.

'Please don't complicate things more than they already are.' Matilda squeezed the bridge of her nose.

'Are you OK? You look tired,' Adele said.

'I am tired.'

'So am I. I'm not sleeping much lately.'

'Still thinking about Brian?'

Adele nodded. 'I had a dream about him a few nights ago, a really weird and unsettling one.'

'I suppose me saying something basic like try to ignore it won't help.'

'Probably not.' Adele smiled. 'A bottle or two of Prosecco might.'

'Don't go down that road, Adele. Look what happened to me after James died.'

'I know. I don't know why I'm behaving like this. It's not as if we were married or anything; we had one date.'

'But you liked him, didn't you?'

'I did. I really did. He was lovely. But then I remember he was a paedophile and I can feel my flesh crawling.'

'Would a hug help?'

'A hug from Tom Hardy might.'

'I'll see what I can do.'

Matilda's mobile started to vibrate in her pocket. She looked at the screen. It was the ACC calling. 'Shit, sorry, I'm going to have to take this.'

She squeezed past Adele and left the autopsy suite into the cool corridor outside the double doors.

'Yes, ma'am.'

'We appear to have made the front page of the local newspaper again.'

Chapter Sixteen

HIT-AND-RUN KILLER FOUND DEAD

By Danny Hanson

The killer of eight-year-old Rebecca Branson, the victim of a hit-and-run on New Year's Day in 1997, has been found dead at his home in Meersbrook, Sheffield.

Joe Lacey was discovered hanging in the garage of his semi-detached home by his five-year-old son, Jason, yesterday, in this, the twentieth anniversary of the tragedy.

Joe Lacey, 37, was five times over the drink-driving limit when he knocked Rebecca off her bike close to her home in Norfolk Park. She suffered massive head injuries and her parents were advised by doctors to turn off her life support machine five days after the incident.

Mr Lacey, then of Jordanthorpe, was sentenced to twelve years in prison for causing death by dangerous driving. He was released in 2004 – just seven years later.

A neighbour, who did not wish to be named, said yesterday, 'I had no idea he was that Joe Lacey. He seemed like a normal, happy family man. He doted on his kids. He was always taking them out. And you couldn't have wished for a nicer neighbour either; he'd do anything for anyone. He came into my house many times when I had a problem with my washer. This is going to upset a lot of people around here.'

Scene of crime officers and DCI Matilda Darke, formerly of the Murder Investigation Team, were all at the scene late into the night. Neighbours are wondering if there is more behind the apparent suicide by hanging of Joe Lacey.

Mr Lacey's death comes just a week after the killing of sex offender Brian Appleby, who was executed in his own home by hanging. With two victims both known to the police and no sign of an arrest imminent, does Sheffield have a serial killer at work?

The Unsolved Murders of South Yorkshire Police. Pages 4 and 5.

'Who is talking to the press?' asked the stern-faced Valerie Masterson. She slammed the laptop closed, not wanting to see the story anymore and sat back in her oversized chair. As she arched her fingers, she resembled a diminutive Bond villain.

'I have no idea. I certainly haven't. I told everyone in CID this morning to keep it to themselves and not breathe a word to anyone,' Matilda said.

'Then either they ignored you or it's been leaked in some other way.'

'That leaves uniform or SOCO? I doubt it's any of them. Maybe it was one of the neighbours. You know what people are like these days, they all want their moment in the sun, no matter how brief. Someone will have got on the phone to the papers as soon as they saw the first cop car arrive. Probably hoping they'll be on *Celebrity Big Brother* next year,' she said bitterly.

'Yes, I suppose it could have been one of the neighbours,' Valerie mused. 'I don't like this – the press knowing more than they should do. Hang on a minute, no, it can't have been a neighbour: the article says Joe Lacey was hanged. Surely when questioning the neighbours, one of your officers didn't reveal that information.'

Matilda thought about who was conducting door-to-door enquiries – Ranjeet and Kesinka.

'I don't believe it was any of my officers, but I will have another word.'

'Yes, you will. I will not have anyone working in this station who is in the pocket of the press. Do you understand?'

'Perfectly.'

'Good. Make sure your team do too.'

Matilda knew when she'd been berated, and if she was going to be on the wrong side of a dressing-down from the ACC then so were her team. She left Valerie's office and marched for the CID incident room.

Sian Mills and Scott Andrews left the family interview suite and headed straight for the canteen. They were both physically exhausted, having questioned a tearful and numb Karen Lacey, as well as her three heartbroken children.

'I think that was one of the hardest interviews I've ever had to conduct,' Scott said when he arrived at the table with a tray laden with hot drinks and slices of chocolate cake. He slumped into his seat and released a heavy sigh.

Sian helped herself to the largest slice. 'That poor boy. Finding his father hanging like that. I don't think he'll ever get over it.'

'When you get cases like this, Sian, involving children, do you think of your own kids?'

'All the time,' she said with a mouthful.

'How do you switch off?'

'Years of practice. The trick is, when you get home and lock the front door behind you, you stop being a detective and become a mother. My kids are my kids and I involve myself in their lives. I don't want them knowing what I've done during the day, so I don't take it home with me.'

'That can't be easy.'

'It's not, especially when it's a particularly disturbing case, or, like you said, involving kids. Just keep your eyes open and you'll be fine. And make sure you have plenty to do outside of work too.'

'I have. Has Rory told you, we're looking for a flat to share. Get us both out from our parents' clutches.'

'That's a good idea. Have a look at the ones on the Riverside Exchange.'

'I hadn't thought of there. Close to town and work. Thanks, Sian.'

'Well I didn't make sergeant on just my looks.' She smiled, tossing back her shoulder-length red hair.

'Ma'am, I've had *The Star* on the phone—' Faith began before Matilda cut her off.

'I don't want to hear it,' she said without stopping, marching through the incident room to her office.

'They want to know if there's a connection between Joe Lacey and Brian Appleby.'

'OK everyone, listen up,' Matilda raised her voice to the whole room. 'Phones down. Rory, come out of Facebook.'

Looking sheepish, Rory closed the lid of his laptop.

'Someone is leaking information to the press. I'm not singling any of you out, but they're getting their information somehow. They're already linking Appleby and Lacey. Now, let me know if you hear anything; it can be in the strictest confidence and I won't name you. We cannot allow the press to jeopardize our work. Do you understand?'

There were nods and mutterings from around the room.

She stared at the blank faces, studying each of them. 'Good. Now, back to it.'

Matilda turned from her team and went into her office. She closed the door behind her. She usually liked her team to know she operated an open-door policy. They could walk in and discuss anything, personal or professional, whenever they wanted to. However, right now, she needed time to think.

Through the glass walls she looked at the CID incident team, the detectives from the old MIT she knew so well, the new members of her team, the uniformed officers and civilian support staff. One of them was leaking information to the press. Who, and how was she going to be able to find out?

Chapter Seventeen

'Not at university today?'

Sian and Scott were standing in the communal living room in the terraced house George Appleby shared with four other students. There was an underlying smell of burnt food and body odour, mixed with cheap perfume. The laminate flooring was dirty and sticky, and the furniture mass-produced.

'No. I don't feel well.' George was wearing boxer shorts, a tight white T-shirt and a dressing gown over the top. He didn't look well, but he was pale and skinny – not the picture of health at the best of times.

'Hangover?' Scott asked with a smile.

'No,' he replied, falling into the uncomfortable sofa. 'Do you want a cup of tea or something?'

Sian leaned back and peered into the adjoining kitchen. The sink was filthy and piled high with dishes. The kettle was grimy and covered with fingerprints.

'I've not long since had one, thanks,' she lied.

'Is this about, you know, my dad? Have you found anything out?'

'Not as such, no. George, can you tell us where you were on Saturday from midday onwards?'

'Why?'

'Humour me.'

He looked away. If it was possible, his face appeared even paler. 'I was here,' he eventually replied.

'All day?'

'Yes.'

'You didn't go out?'

'No.'

'Not at all? Not to the shops or anything?' Scott asked.

He looked Scott in the eye but turned away before answering. 'No.'

'Can anyone verify that?'

'Well, not until late on when Cassie came home around seven. Why?'

'Do you know a man called Joe Lacey?' Sian asked.

He shook his head. 'Who's he?' George asked quickly.

'Or Rebecca Branson?'

'Oh my God, please don't tell me more victims have come forward saying my dad … you know.'

'No. Nothing like that.'

'Then why are you asking?'

'Just curious. You've never heard of these people?'

'No.'

'Right, well, we'll leave you to it then. I hope you feel better soon. Come along, Scott.'

Sian and Scott headed for the front door.

'Hang on a minute,' George called out. 'Aren't you going to tell me what all this is about?'

Sian slammed the door behind them. 'Thank God for that,' she exhaled. 'Jesus it was rank in there.'

'It took me back to my student days,' Scott said with a smile.

'Please don't tell me you were as untidy as that.'

'Well, first time away from home, you let yourself go a bit, don't you?'

'No, you bloody do not. It's called having some self-respect. And did you see his boxer shorts? They didn't leave much to the imagination, did they?' She turned on her heel and headed down the gennel to the car. Scott followed, smiling to himself.

George Appleby sat with a heavy frown on his pale face. He was going over the questions the sergeant had asked him. Why was she asking them? It made no sense. He swiped a pile of newspapers and magazines off the coffee table and found his iMac underneath. Balancing it on his lap, he turned it on. He tried to remember one of the names the female detective said, Rebecca something. He'd heard it before but couldn't think where. Rebecca. Rebecca. He smiled to himself. Branston pickles. Rebecca Branston. Google asked him if he was looking for Rebecca Branson, he clicked on the correct spelling and up came her life story, her cut-short life story.

He clicked on a link for the site of the local newspaper and read a story by Danny Hanson all about Joe Lacey's death on Saturday. Towards the bottom of the page was a list of other stories the reader may be interested in. George's father's name was mentioned. He clicked on the first story and his father's face popped up on the screen. It was an old picture taken before he was sent to prison. All the raw emotions came flooding back. His father was a paedo, how was that possible?

George logged on to Facebook and typed in Danny Hanson's name. He planned on messaging him, asking him how he slept at night when he was putting people through hell with his sensationalism, when a message popped up. He didn't recognize the sender:

George, I hear your dad was a nonce. Is that why no one's ever seen you with a girlfriend? Like kids yourself, do you?

George recoiled. So the vitriol had started. He had expected it to be sooner than this. He deleted the message. Internet trolls were cowards anyway; too scared to say what they thought in real life, so they hid behind their computers.

He noticed he had several notifications, more than usual. He clicked on the icon.

You have been tagged in a post.

You have been tagged in a photograph.

Martin Baker and eight others have mentioned you in a post.

Sally Klein and twenty others have tagged you in a post.

'Jesus,' he said to himself, once again running his bony fingers through his hair. Should he read what everybody seemed to be saying about him, or should he ignore them, hoping they'll stop eventually when something better comes along? 'Fuck it,' he said, looking at some of the comments.

***Becky Wainwright**: I went out with **George Appleby** a few times. I wondered why he kept wanting to go to parks and push me on the swings. His idea of a romantic date was a kid's happy meal at Maccy D's. Like father like son. LOL.*

George shook his head. He'd never even heard of a Becky Wainwright before. Looking at her photograph, he'd never seen her either. Just that one comment was enough for him to slam his laptop closed. He heard the sound of a key in the lock: one of his housemates coming home. He didn't want them to see him crying so ran upstairs, laptop under his arm, cursing Danny fucking Hanson for starting all this in the first place.

'The Bransons are hiding something. They both gave different alibis for where they were on Saturday,' Aaron Connolly said.

'Let them stew for the rest of the day then bring them both in tomorrow morning.'

Normally, Matilda would take the softly-softly approach, maybe send Sian around to have a friendly chat, but with the press seemingly leading this investigation, she wanted to get the upper hand.

The evening briefing had failed to reveal any new leads. Kesinka and Ranjeet had been back to Meersbrook to interview the remaining neighbours. Typically, nobody had seen anything suspicious at all on Saturday. Just when you want the neighbours to be nosey they turn a blind eye.

Forensics hadn't found anything of interest at the Lacey house. Once again, the killer had managed to gain access and not leave a single trace of himself behind. The similarities between the Joe Lacey and Brian Appleby murders were startling, but there was nothing to link the two victims. Brian had only been in Sheffield a matter of months, before that he lived in Essex and never visited Yorkshire. Joe was Sheffield born and bred and had only left the county to go on holiday, and that was always abroad. The furthest south he'd ever travelled in England was Nottingham. They had nothing in common; they didn't belong to the same bank or gym; they didn't shop in the same supermarket. The only thing they shared was the fact they had criminal records.

Matilda left the station early. It was only six o'clock, but it was pitch-black. The heavy clouds over Sheffield were releasing a fine drizzle turning the steel city grey and dank.

While sitting in traffic, Matilda looked out into the dark Sheffield night. She saw people heading home after a hard day's work. They were wrapped up against the elements and held themselves stiff as the wind cut through them. Their faces all had the same expression – harsh, defeated, tired, sad.

This winter had been a long one. It seemed never-ending. November and December were fine because there was Christmas to look forward to – the parties, the presents, the get-togethers. Once New Year was out of the way, all you had left were three months of dark nights, freezing temperatures and bad weather. Add to that the fact you were fatter from the excesses of Christmas, the dreaded credit-card bill arriving through the post, and a sense of emptiness, you could understand why people walked around looking like members of a funeral procession.

Matilda opened the garage door with the remote she kept in the glove compartment. It closed behind her and plunged her into a cavernous black. She gingerly made her way into the main part of the house. It was cold. The heating hadn't come on. The doorbell rang and she went to answer it.

'Hello, I saw you come home. A parcel arrived for you this morning,' Mrs Wilson from two doors down said, handing over a heavy Amazon box.

'Oh, thank you.'

'You're welcome. Any time.'

Mrs Wilson stood on the doorstep longer than was necessary, looking over Matilda's shoulder into the house.

Matilda closed the door and carried the box into the kitchen. She couldn't remember ordering anything from Amazon. Using a knife from the block, she cut into the cardboard and recognized the smell of new books before she even pulled back the flaps. The latest hardbacks by some of her favourite authors, plus a few paperbacks she'd seen on sale were carefully packed.

A smile spread on her lips. Since she had inherited a huge collection of crime fiction novels from Jonathan Harkness, a killer with emotional problems Matilda had been unable to save, she had become hooked. Adele thought she was hiding her feelings and emotions behind reading and building the collection. She'd promised her friend she wouldn't allow it to take over her life. However, there wasn't a week that didn't go by without at least two deliveries from Amazon or the Book Depository.

Matilda took the box upstairs to her library. She always smiled when she walked into the room and saw the books waiting for her like faithful old friends. She understood why Jonathan

Harkness had immersed himself in fiction. The world was a dark and dangerous place, especially the one Matilda inhabited. Why not close the door and hide behind books? Yes, they were all crime fiction, but by the end of the novel, the balance of power had been restored.

Matilda unpacked the box and added them to her to-be-read pile in the corner. It was threatening to take over the whole room. She looked at the shelves surrounding her. All of them were full to capacity. She placed her hand on the spines of the hardbacks and stroked them. She felt safe in this room. She felt happy.

'A few more to add to the collection, Jonathan.'

***

Sitting in the living room with a plate of an oven-ready lasagne on her lap, she called Adele.

'How are you doing?' Matilda asked.

'I'm fine,' she lied.

'It's OK not to be fine.'

'It's also OK to be just fine.'

'That's fine then,' Matilda smiled. 'Are you still sworn off men?'

'Absolutely. They can all take a running jump as far as I'm concerned.'

Matilda glared at the mantelpiece and the framed photograph of her and James on her wedding day. She had now reached the stage where looking at him no longer opened the floodgates, but she still felt sad.

'Chris and I are going out for a run in a bit if you fancy it?' Adele asked, quickly changing the subject.

'No thanks. I did ten kilometres on the treadmill this morning. Oh, did I tell you, Scott has asked to join us for the half-marathon. He was doing it anyway but said he'd help us raise more money.'

'That's kind of him. Can he run?'

'Yes. He spent half an hour at lunchtime showing me photos

of all his races. I had no idea he had such muscular legs under those suits.'

'Ooh,' Adele said, a hint of flirtation in her voice.

'I thought you said all men can piss off?'

'It depends on how hunky their thighs are.'

Matilda could be clinging on the railings of the Titanic as it plunged into the cold Atlantic Ocean and Adele would still be able to make her smile. Following the Brian Appleby incident, Matilda had thought Adele would withdraw. In a way, she had. However, her sense of humour was too strong to stay hidden and there were warming glimpses of it trying to reappear. It made Matilda smile.

Good for her. Now why can't I move on?

She looked back at the wedding photo. She knew why she couldn't move on – because she didn't want to.

***

The disappointing lasagne had given Matilda indigestion. She took a swig of Gaviscon from the bottle and headed upstairs to her library. She made herself comfortable in the Eames chair, put her feet up on the matching footstool and wrapped a knitted blanket around her. She picked up the hardback by Peter James. She was over halfway through. After an hour of reading, her eyes were becoming heavy. Her mobile, sitting on the coffee table next to her, beeped and vibrated, making her jump. She placed the bookmark neatly among the pages and put the book carefully on the table. The message wasn't from a number she had stored in her phone. She opened the text message:

2 down.

Chapter Eighteen

'Has the number been traced?'

'Yes. It's a pay-as-you-go and no longer in service, as I expected.'

Matilda was sitting at her desk with a uniformed Valerie Masterson standing in front of it, her arms tightly folded across her chest.

'I don't like this.'

'I'm not so keen on it myself,' Matilda said, trying to be flippant. *If in doubt, make a joke.*

'The killer knows you're working on the case. How?'

'Well anyone who reads *The Star* would know I was leading it. It's on the Internet, too, and Rory told me it was trending on Twitter last night.'

'I bloody hate social media,' Valerie said to herself. 'Who has your number?'

'I've no idea. I've had it for years.'

'Anything else comes through, I don't care if it's three o'clock in the morning, I want you to tell me straight away. Is that understood?'

'Sure.'

'And I don't want you replying to him without clearing it with me.'

'Of course.'

'I mean it, Matilda. You start a conversation with him without my say-so and I'll suspend you.' A look of worry was etched on Valerie's face.

'He's taunting us, isn't he?' Matilda said, after a silence.

'It would appear so. I'm going to call the university to get a criminal psychologist to have a look at the case.'

Matilda rolled her eyes. 'I don't think that's necessary just yet, ma'am.'

'Well I do. I want this solved before this bastard picks his next victim.'

'Ma'am,' was all Matilda could say. Once Valerie Masterson had made up her mind about something, it was very difficult to get her to change it.

'So we're getting a profiler?' Sian asked.

'I'm afraid so.'

'I've got a fiver on him being a loner who still lives at home with his parents,' Rory mocked.

'I'll go with him having a menial job and low intelligence,' Aaron said, putting his hand up.

'Sexually inadequate, possibly still a virgin, and unable to perform,' Faith said.

They all started laughing as the clichés went around the room. Even Matilda raised a smile.

'OK everyone, calm down. Let's get on. It's obvious the Brian Appleby and Joe Lacey cases are linked. We need to find out why. I know there's no connection between the two victims, but the killer has targeted them for a reason. Any suggestions?'

'They're both criminals,' Christian Brady said, struggling with the wrapper on a BLT from the canteen.

'Sticking with Brian Appleby for a moment, who knew he had moved to Sheffield?' Matilda asked.

'Apparently nobody; but me and Sian still aren't convinced about the son,' Scott said.

'What's his alibi for the Lacey murder?'

'He doesn't have one.'

'We need to keep a watch on him. Christian, can you organize a few plain clothes to tab him?'

'For how long? I've already had a roasting this week about overtime.'

'Well fingers crossed George kills his next victim in working hours. Just trail him. I'll deal with the overtime.' *No wonder I have a permanent headache with all this eye-rolling.*

'You do realize you've just said that in front of a room full of witnesses, don't you?' he said with a smile.

'Yes. Just get it sorted, Christian.'

'Will do.'

'Thank you. Now, let me just check one more time, none of his neighbours knew he was a registered sex offender?'

'No,' Faith said.

'So who the bloody hell knew he was here?' Matilda said, the frustration evident in her voice.

'We could already know who the killer is,' Christian said, looking at the inside of his sandwich with contempt. He removed a gristly piece of bacon and flicked it into his bin. 'Maybe we've already interviewed them and they're lying to us.'

'Someone lying to the police? Madness!' Rory said, heavy with sarcasm. A laughter rippled around the room.

'You really think we've already met the killer?' Matilda asked Christian.

'I wouldn't be surprised. He sent you a text. In my eyes, he's taunting you. He's probably watching how the case progresses.'

Matilda looked up at the two large whiteboards on the wall. One for each victim. She sighed. 'In that case, we need to start again. Interview the Lacey family, especially the wife, Karen, get her to tell us everything about her husband. All the neighbours too, friends, colleagues, go through their entire lives. With Joe Lacey being a Sheffield resident and committing his crime here it would have been easy to find him, but not Brian Appleby. He obviously kept himself to himself, so he wouldn't have interacted with many people. Once we find out who Brian Appleby knew, it shouldn't take us long to find the connection with Joe Lacey.'

'What if there is no connection?' Scott asked.

'You're not helping, Scott,' Sian said.

Matilda turned back to the murder boards. *What if there was no connection?* The very thought made her blood run cold.

'Danny Hanson,' Danny said as he answered his mobile. He was sitting at his desk in the cluttered newsroom of *The Star*. He had been going through his emails, hoping to find a reply from a university criminologist he'd emailed, when his phone rang.

'I've got some information on your killer,' the caller's voice was low and deep.

'I'm sorry?' Danny asked, he ducked so nobody around him could see his face.

'I know who the killer is. Nine o'clock tonight. Weston Park, by the bandstand.'

'How do I …?' Danny was speaking to the dialling tone. He looked at his phone. The caller hadn't left their number.

Danny sat up straight. He didn't think of the worry or the dangers of going to a park at night to meet a complete stranger. As nonchalantly as he could, he glanced over the top of his computer screen at the other reporters in the newsroom. Had they overheard his conversation? No, they were busy on their own stories. Should he tell anyone? Better not. He returned his attention back to his keyboard and began typing. He couldn't fail to hide his grin. All he thought about was who he was going to thank in his acceptance speech when he won the Journalist of the Year award.

'Meet the Bransons.'

Matilda joined Rory in the observation bay overlooking interviews one and two.

'In room one we have the lovely Amanda Branson, who called me a young upstart. I have no idea what that means, but I don't think she was being pleasant. In room two we have Clive Branson. He's monosyllabic and he smells. Would you like to conduct the interviews, ma'am?'

'And rob you of the pleasure, Rory? No, you go ahead.'

Rory tutted and left the room.

Neither of the Bransons had been arrested. At first they had resisted going to the police station for a formal chat, but when Aaron told them they could be charged with obstructing an investigation, they exchanged glances and waddled to the waiting police cars. Both had declined to have a solicitor present.

Rory's face soured as he entered the room and was hit with whatever odour emanated from Clive Branson. He sat down beside Scott who wore a similar expression. This was an interview they would both want to get through quickly. Rory turned on the recording equipment and stated the preliminaries.

'Clive, you told us you were out with your brother on Saturday and didn't get back until late. Your wife told us you were both at home all day. Which one of you is lying?' Rory asked.

Clive Branson was slumped in his chair, head down, studying the badly stained and scratched table. Rory and Scott were looking at the top of his head. His hair was thick and wavy and dark grey. There were flecks of dandruff on the shoulders of his wax jacket and he gave off a musty smell, as if his clothes hadn't been washed for weeks. He slowly lifted his head up and stared at his interviewers. His face was weather-beaten. Since the death of his only child, he'd obviously found very little to smile about.

'I did,' he eventually surrendered. 'Well, we both did really. I wasn't at home and I wasn't with my brother. I told Amanda I was with my brother, but I wasn't.'

'Where were you?' Scott asked.

'I'm going to get into so much trouble.'

Rory leaned forward, breathed in a lungful of Clive Branson's rancid odour then quickly sat back. 'Look, Mr Branson, if you're having an affair that's nothing to do with us. It's not a police matter and we have no need to tell your wife.'

'I'm not having a bloody affair,' he called out. 'Me and Amanda, we don't have much money.' He swallowed hard. He was obviously finding it difficult to tell his story. 'After Rebecca died, we both sort of fell apart. We were on medication for years. I started drinking and we split up for a while but managed to sort ourselves out. Unfortunately, trying to get a job when you've a gap on your CV of a decade isn't easy. Getting any kind of benefits is a joke too. I've worked since I was sixteen, I've paid my taxes and national insurance and I couldn't get a penny. Bloody council. They'd have given me everything if I'd been a sixteen-year-old girl with two kids by different blokes and a drug habit.'

'Mr Branson,' Scott interrupted, getting him back on track.

'Sorry,' he said. 'It's just this country drives me mad sometimes.' He paused while he composed himself. He took a deep breath. 'I nick food.'

'Pardon?' Scott asked.

'I nick food, and other things that they throw away, from the back of supermarkets. It's perfectly safe to eat. They just can't sell it to the public when it's past it's gone-off date. It's their own faults anyway. If their prices weren't so high in the first place there wouldn't be so much waste. Are you going to do me for it?'

Rory looked to the two-way mirror. He couldn't see Matilda, but he knew she could see him. He raised his eyebrows for her to answer Clive's question.

Matilda stared through the glass at the sad and desperate Clive Branson. 'They've suffered enough over the years. Give them the details of the local food banks and tell him to cut back on the stealing and be more vigilant. Give them both a lift home, too.'

Matilda sighed and left the room, heading to her office. Rebecca had been killed more than twenty years ago. Joe Lacey had been swiftly caught and served seven years in prison. Once released he had continued with his life, got a job and a family. The Bransons had been in limbo since 1997. Matilda felt sorry for them. She wondered how she would be after twenty years without James. She might have stopped crying every time she thought of him, but she would still miss him, she would always miss him.

Chapter Nineteen

'Matilda, I'd like you to meet Dr Dalziel.'

'Where's Pascoe?' *Shit, did I say that out loud?* 'Sorry.'

ACC Valerie Masterson had called Matilda and politely summoned her to her office to meet the criminal psychologist.

'I get that all the time, no need to apologize.' Dr Dalziel stood up from the seat in front of Valerie's desk and turned to face Matilda, holding his hand out for her to shake.

Matilda froze. The intensely ice-blue eyes were reminiscent of her dead husband, James. She always thought James's were his best feature and they were what had first drawn her to him. She had not seen any like that on anyone else before or since. Now she was standing opposite a tall man in a tailored black suit with neatly cut blond hair, who was looking at her with her husband's eyes.

'Matilda.' Valerie brought her back to reality.

'Sorry.' Matilda closed her eyes tightly shut. 'Sorry, just thinking about something.'

She looked at Dr Dalziel and realized he still held his hand out. She shook it and felt a frisson as his warm right hand gripped hers. Her gaze dropped to the pale skin and the manicured nails.

'Nice to meet you, Dr Dalziel,' Matilda said with a dry mouth.

'Please, call me James.'

Matilda's eyes widened and she took a deep breath. The room around her began to blur. She held out for the chair in front of her and went to sit down, hoping the doctor and her boss hadn't noticed her odd behaviour.

'Coffee, Matilda?' Valerie asked.

I think I need a large brandy.

'No, thank you, ma'am.'

From the corner of her eye, Matilda saw James Dalziel take the seat next to her. She didn't dare look at him. Was she imagining this? Dr Dalziel (she couldn't bring herself to call him James, not yet) didn't resemble her husband, the colouring was all wrong, but those eyes. Had he filled in a donor card?

'Matilda, are you with us?' Valerie asked.

'Yes, of course.'

'Then you agree then?'

'Oh yes, absolutely … to what?'

Valerie let out an audible sigh. 'To Dr Dalziel taking a look at the murder case and trying to identify a potential suspect.'

Shit! No I do not agree to that.

'While I'm sure Dr Dalziel is perfectly qualified, I don't think we are quite at that stage yet. We have had a link between the victims confirmed in the text I received last night, but we need to look closer at the victims and see what connects the two of them.' Matilda was floundering. Her hands were firmly pressed together, and she played with her wedding ring.

'DCI Darke, it is early days in your investigation,' James Dalziel began. Matilda noticed his accent had a hint of Scottish, along with something else. It was deep and strong, yet smooth and relaxing. 'I have only worked on two cases of serial murder in the past and I'm usually brought in at a much later stage in the investigation. However, I was told it was of paramount importance that a suspect be identified as soon as possible to avoid a third victim. If I can help in any way, I am more than prepared to do so.'

Matilda hadn't heard a word. She had turned in her seat and was fixed on those eyes and that accent.

'Well, Matilda …?' Valerie asked.

'Yes. Absolutely. I'm open … to any advice Dr Dalziel can offer,' she waffled. 'Would you both excuse me? Call of nature.'

Matilda charged into the nearest ladies' toilets she could find and made her way to the furthest stall. She slammed the door closed and sat on the toilet seat lid. She was reminded of the days of her panic attacks when she first returned to work – any slightest upset would set her off.

She took her iPhone out of her jacket pocket and swiped to unlock it. Touching the photos app she opened a folder containing her fifty favourite pictures of James Darke. They were the photos that made her smile, brought back memories of the good times, and took her to a time when she was last truly happy. When she looked at them now, her eyes filled with tears. There was no denying the fact that James Dalziel was a handsome man. He was tall, well built, and took care of his appearance. The fact he was called James made Matilda wonder if he was some kind of sign. Was her James up there looking down on her, disappointed with the amount of grief and heartache she was carrying around? Was this his way of telling her to get on with her own life, maybe meet someone else?

'I don't want anybody else,' she choked.

She swiped across the screen of her phone – James on the beach on their honeymoon wearing just a pair of shorts. He didn't have the body of an Olympic gymnast, but he was trim and there was clear definition. He gave a cheeky grin to the camera. The next photo was one of him in their back garden at home standing in three feet of snow. He looked bulky in his winter coat, waterproof trousers and wellington boots. Again, he was smiling directly into the camera as the flakes of snow fell down on him. The next picture was of James in bed. Matilda couldn't remember when this one was taken, but he looked as if he had recently woken up. His wavy hair was a tangled mess, he was sleepy, warm, and cuddly. Another swipe and there was a cheeky shot Matilda had taken as he stepped out of the shower. He was all wet, glistening, steaming, and naked. Matilda would give up everything in the world if she could spend just one more day in those arms.

The sound of someone entering the toilets brought Matilda out of her past. She put her phone away, wiped her eyes and blew her nose. As she washed her hands in the sink, she wondered if she would be able to work with James Dalziel.

Matilda was sitting at her messy desk in her office. James and Christian on the opposite side. A knock on the glass door made Matilda look up. She waved Sian in.

'I thought you'd all like a cup of tea,' Sian said, carrying a tray of mugs. 'I didn't know how you took it, Dr Dalziel, so I've brought a few little tubs of milk and sachets of sugar. Would you like anything from the snack drawer?'

'We're fine thanks, Sian,' Matilda said before James could reply.

'OK. I'll leave you in peace then.' As Sian left, she turned to look at Matilda and with wide eyes she mouthed 'Oh my God' and nodded at James. Matilda struggled to stifle a smile.

'So, James, what can you tell us about the killer?'

'What do you want to know?'

'A name and address would be handy.' She smiled.

James smiled back, and Matilda felt a flutter in her stomach. 'If I could, I would. I don't mean to sound disrespectful or callous but, if we had a third victim, I would have more to work on.'

'Fingers crossed he's stalking one right now,' Christian said, rolling his eyes.

'Can we confirm if we're looking for a man?' Matilda asked.

'Most definitely.'

'Why most definitely?'

'For a start, the majority of serial murderers are male. Also, your suspect will be white. The first two victims are white and serial murderers rarely kill outside their own ethnic group. However, take a closer look at Brian Appleby,' he said, pulling up a photograph of Brian from the desk. The picture was of Brian hanging from his living-room ceiling. James hadn't even flinched. 'He's well over six-foot tall, he's a big bloke, and there were no signs of him being drugged. Someone overpowered him. No offence to women, but I can't see the average woman being able to do this.'

'You've obviously not seen Sian when she's in a mood.' Christian smiled.

'If it was a woman,' James continued, 'she would have had to pounce on him unawares. That kind of makes sense when you see what Brian is wearing. According to the witness statement of Adele Kean, Brian is wearing in the photograph exactly what he was wearing on their date. A woman could have been lying in wait for him to come home, but then where's the mess? Where's the evidence of a struggle? The house is perfectly neat and tidy.'

'There was evidence Joe Lacey had put up a struggle,' Christian said.

'Yes he did. But from the evidence before me, I'm seeing a male-inflicted crime,' James replied with conviction.

'OK,' Matilda chimed in, sensing the hostility between both men. 'We all know that why plus how equals who. We know the how. What about the why?'

'They both had criminal records. They were strung up like they'd been led to the gallows. This smacks of a vigilante,' Christian said.

'But they'd served their time,' Matilda commented.

'That's not always enough for some people,' James began. 'You read stories in the newspapers all the time about soft sentencing and judges being out of touch with reality. Maybe he thought Brian Appleby and Joe Lacey hadn't served long enough.'

'If that's the case, then it's going to make the third victim a lot harder to find,' Matilda said with a sly smile. 'We didn't know

Brian Appleby was in Sheffield. He was on the sex offender's register and should have contacted us when he arrived, but he didn't. Now, who would know who he was?'

'The local police where he lived, his probation officer, his neighbours, and whoever they all talked to. Unfortunately, with the Internet, news spreads like wildfire. Have there been any cases of break-ins with his probation officer, or the police station? Anything going missing?'

'I'm not sure,' Matilda said, looking to Christian.

'I'll check that out.'

'What about the killer as a person?' Matilda asked. 'What kind of person are we looking for?'

'Somebody tall, strong, intelligent, quiet.'

'Why quiet?'

'Like you said, nobody knew Brian Appleby was in Sheffield. There is going to have been a lot of research involved to find him. The killer will have been very busy keeping all of this information to himself, and he won't want to slip up and reveal it until he's ready. He's surrounded by people, we all are in this day and age, but he'll be in the shadows.'

'You're not making it easier for us to find him.' Christian laughed.

'Sorry.' James smiled.

'That description doesn't match George Appleby, Brian's son. He has no alibi for the time of both murders. He denies knowing his father was in Sheffield,' Matilda said.

'If George was going to kill his father, it wouldn't have been like this,' James said, pointing at the photographs of the victims. 'There would either have been a struggle in Brian's home, or George would have just hit him from behind, struck when he saw the chance. This is not the work of a child killing his disgraced father.'

'So, I can rule George out?' Matilda asked.

'If he has no alibi, by all means keep your eye on him, but

from my point of view, I'd say you can definitely rule him out.' He smiled.

Matilda had to turn away. She couldn't look at that smile or those twinkling eyes without feeling she was betraying her James.

'Why did he text me?' she asked after a long silence.

'A large number of serial murderers can't help but involve themselves in the investigation. He's confident he has done everything right, so you'll never catch him. He's contacting you to tell you he's out there. My best guess is that you, Matilda, personally know him.'

Matilda's eyes went wide in shock. 'You think I know the killer?'

'I'd stake my reputation on it.'

Chapter Twenty

It was 7 p.m. and it was as black as midnight. Matilda pulled into the car park of Ecclesall Woods. Adele and Chris were already waiting for her. Adele flashed her headlights to identify herself.

'Are we mad, or what?' Adele said, climbing out slowly from behind the wheel.

The temperature hadn't been much above freezing all day. Now darkness had fallen, it was rapidly dropping away and was already two degrees below.

'Of course we're mad. No sane person would be out at this time of year. Chris, how's the new job going, still enjoying it?'

'Yes. Some of the kids are a bit scary. I think I know which ones to keep an eye on, but it is going well so far.'

'I'm pleased,' Matilda beamed. She had known Chris all his life. She had looked after him when Adele was studying to become a pathologist, or if she had been called out. She'd changed his nappy, wiped his face, pushed him on the swings. She was like a second mother to him. She worried for his future almost as much as Adele did.

'Are we just standing around here to see which one of us loses a body part to the cold first, or are we actually going running?' Adele asked.

'We're waiting for Scott. Here he is now,' Matilda said, recognizing the black Peugeot 508.

Scott parked in the bay in front of Adele and turned off the ignition. Unlike Matilda, Adele, and Chris, Scott leapt out of his car, full of zest and vigour. He was dressed for the occasion – Thermax long-sleeved top and pants, a lightweight fleece and a zipped Gore-Tex over-top.

'Why are you wearing that?' Matilda asked.

'Because we're running and it's cold.'

Matilda, Adele, and Chris all looked at each other with guilty expressions. They stood in the poorly lit car park in battered trainers, old jogging trousers and coats. Mo Farah would have been horrified.

'You have to look after your body when you're exercising, especially in extreme weather conditions,' Scott said.

'We're running around a park in Sheffield, not trekking the Andes. I'd hardly call this extreme weather conditions,' Matilda said with a shiver.

'I thought you were serious.'

'We are.'

'You don't look it.'

'OK,' Adele stepped in. 'I think we should elect Scott to be our official coach, agreed? He can tell us what to wear, how to run, and what to eat. What do you say?'

Matilda and Chris both nodded.

'Well you all need someone,' he said. 'After this session, I'll look online and send you all links to what you need to buy. Matilda, you're going to have to dump those shoes as soon as you get home.'

It was strange for Matilda to hear a DC call her by her first name. Scott didn't seem to hesitate or have any qualms about being so familiar.

'What's wrong with my shoes?'

Scott raised an eyebrow.

'Scott, this is my son, Chris. He's an English teacher. Chris, this is Scott. He's a DC on Matilda's team.'

They shook hands and exchanged pleasantries. Scott offered Chris a spare bandana to keep warm.

'It's nice seeing co-workers out of office hours, isn't it?' Adele said as an aside to Matilda. 'I always imagine Scott to be quite shy and withdrawn. Look how passionate he is being about running.'

'Down girl, you're old enough to be his mother.'

'Matilda, don't be so disgusting, the thought never crossed my mind. Although, if I was twenty years younger ...'

'You said you were giving up on men after the whole Brian Appleby episode.'

'I did. That was until I saw Scott's bum. Just look at it,' she said as Scott opened the boot of his car and bent inside. 'I'd gladly sink my teeth into that.'

'Do you have to?' Matilda said. 'I have to work with him on a daily basis. I don't want his bum popping into my head every time I look at him.'

'I wouldn't mind his bum popping into my head.'

'You're a pervert, Adele, do you know that?' Matilda said, walking off, leaving her best friend standing alone.

Matilda, Adele, and Chris were ready to set off until Scott called them back to warm up. He laughed when Matilda told them their usual routine – trot around the park chatting until they were knackered, then to the coffee shop for a latte and a chocolate twist.

They began at a steady pace: Scott and Chris in front with Matilda and Adele behind. Adele was smiling, her eyes focused on Scott's backside, while Matilda's mind wandered as she thought about the Joe Lacey murder. Why had the killer chosen to strike on his victim's son's fifth birthday? How long had he spent tracking down his victims? Was he, right at this moment, stalking his third, planning everything in the minutest of details?

Matilda looked around her. Everything was shrouded in darkness, yet she couldn't help feeling the killer was lurking, watching her.

'What are you thinking about?' Adele said, breathlessly.

'Nothing,' Matilda struggled to reply.

'Yes, you are. You seem distant … pensive.'

'I always … look like this … when I'm running … it's called … being knackered.'

Matilda stopped, causing Adele to stop.

'What's wrong?'

'I need to ask you something,' Matilda said, bent over, hands on knees, trying to get her breath back.

'Is everything all right?' Scott called out from further up the path. He'd stopped running but was jogging on the spot.

'Yes. Fine. You two go on ahead,' Adele said, waving them away.

'After Robson left you,' Matilda began, referring to Adele's former partner and Chris's father, 'how long before you started thinking about going with another man?'

Adele blushed, though it could have been the biting wind. 'A week after he left I slept with the bloke who lived in the flat next door.'

'Oh my God, Adele, you didn't,' Matilda couldn't hide her shock. 'You never mentioned this before.'

'I'm not proud of what I did, but I was so angry and pissed off. He'd popped round for some reason and we got chatting. The next thing I know we were in bed.'

'Adele Kean, you dirty girl.'

'Why do you ask?' Adele quickly asked to change the angle of the subject.

Matilda took a deep breath. 'Valerie's brought in a profiler to help with the Appleby and Lacey murders. Adele, he's bloody gorgeous. As soon as I looked at him I fancied him.'

'There's nothing wrong with that,' she shrugged.

'But James hasn't been gone two years yet.'

'So. You're a woman. You have emotions and feelings. It's perfectly natural to find someone handsome.'

'I didn't just find him handsome. If I'd been alone with him, I'd have probably jumped him.'

Adele laughed. 'And you call me a tart for lusting after Scott's bum.'

'I don't want to forget James,' she said. There was a catch in her throat.

'You won't forget him. He's your husband and you love him. It's about moving on with your life. Isn't that what we said we'd do this year?'

'Yes,' Matilda grudgingly admitted.

'There you go then. See what happens with this bloke. If he asks you out for dinner, then go. You don't need to sleep with him. Take it slowly.'

'True. I'm not you,' she grinned.

'Cheeky cow.'

'He's probably married with kids anyway.'

'Maybe.' Adele smiled.

'What are you smiling at?'

'You.'

'Why?'

'Nothing. It's just … you've got a sparkle in your eyes. It's good to see the happy Matilda coming back to the surface.'

'Happy? I don't think I know the meaning of the word anymore.'

Chris jogged back over to them. 'I thought you two were catching us up,' he said, panting for breath.

'We did. We were running so fast we passed you and you didn't even notice,' Matilda said. 'Come on, let's go and have a coffee.' She had suddenly lost interest in training. It didn't help that the cold wind had chilled her to the bone.

Scott and Chris set off ahead. Behind, Matilda put her arm around Adele and led her away.

9 p.m.

Danny Hanson was shivering with cold. His coat was buttoned up to the collar, his scarf was wrapped several times around his neck and he had his beanie hat pulled down low, yet he was still bloody freezing. He hopped from foot to foot, trying to get the blood circulating and thaw his frozen veins.

He looked around the bandstand. He was alone in the park, alone in the pitch-dark. He must be absolutely crazy. Weston Park Museum in front of him had been closed for hours. The sound of the busy main road was muffled by his hat. The Children's Hospital on the opposite side of the road was lit up. It didn't seem to matter what time of day it was in a hospital, they were always busy, always working.

He struggled to take his mobile phone out of his inside pocket with his thick woollen gloves on. He squinted at the brightness of the screen. It was almost 9.15. This was obviously a prank, or maybe it was one of his colleagues, jealous that he was getting the lead stories. Danny was about to head off for home when he heard his name being called. He turned around but there was nobody there.

He stood, staring into the distance, taking in as much of the park as he could in the darkness. He was completely alone, but he was sure he'd heard his name. He let out an audible sigh. This had been a waste of time. He had taken two long strides to the gates when he felt someone approach from behind. His reflexes weren't fast enough and, whoever it was, had grabbed Danny's scarf and begun to pull on both ends, tightening it around his neck.

Danny choked. He grabbed for the scarf, but it was no good. His woollen gloves were useless for getting any kind of purchase. He tried to scream but no sound came out. He grabbed at his neck, scratching, pulling at the scarf, desperate to breathe.

Danny fell forward onto the cold, hard ground. He ripped at the scarf, pulled it off his neck and began gasping for air. He turned onto his back and looked up at his attacker as a tall figure loomed over him.

'You should be careful who you meet in the dark, Danny. You never know what kind of trouble you're going to get into.' The voice was low and deep, menacing.

'Who are you?'

'You should realize your actions are going to have consequences. Think of that the next time you write your shite in the paper.'

'Who the hell are you?' Danny said, louder this time as his breathing began to return.

His attacker said nothing. He turned on his heel and ran off into the darkness, leaving Danny Hanson behind in the cold. As he looked up at the retreating figure running under a lamp post, he caught a glimpse of dark red hair.

After a hot shower, which thawed Matilda and set the blood flowing freely throughout her body again, she made herself a large cup of tea and went into the living room. Usually she would sit with a book and a packet of biscuits, but with Scott's words ringing in her ears, she decided to leave the cookie jar alone.

'I'm doing this for you, James,' she said to the wedding photo on the mantelpiece. She was looking at her husband, but as soon as she said his name she immediately pictured James Dalziel. She closed her eyes and shook the image from her head. There was no comparison to James Darke. Her husband was tall, good-looking, intelligent, funny, romantic, an excellent kisser, great in bed, useless in the kitchen, always chose the best restaurants, struggled to pronounce the word 'prepared', which was very sweet, and made a wonderful cup of tea. He was the perfect man. Well, maybe ninety-five per cent, there's no such thing as the perfect man. Ninety-eight per cent.

Matilda's mobile vibrated on the sofa next to her. A text message had come through from someone not saved in her phone book.

Have you done anything you haven't paid the price for?

It was the killer. So maybe she was right: he had killed Brian Appleby and Joe Lacey because he believed they hadn't paid correctly for their crimes.

Matilda stared at the message for so long the screen went blank. She turned the phone back on and looked at it again. She shouldn't reply. Valerie told her to call her at any time of the day or night should she receive another message from the killer. The clock on the mantelpiece told her it was almost midnight. She should phone Valerie.

Although, Valerie would want to see the message for herself, and she would probably want James Dalziel to take a look before deciding what to do about it. The killer obviously wanted to chat now, to open up a dialogue between himself and the police. By the time she'd gone through the rigmarole of contacting her boss and the criminal psychologist, he could have changed his mind. No, Matilda needed to use her initiative. She needed to reply now.

No. I haven't.

Matilda sent the reply and sat back in the sofa. She waited. The screen on the iPhone went black. She didn't move. She didn't dare leave the sofa in case she missed the beep of an incoming text.

Matilda contemplated going to bed. She was starting to get cold, but there wasn't a great signal on her phone in her bedroom. In the living room, it was on five dots. She should wait.

Ten minutes later, the phone beeped and she quickly picked it up.

Two words: Carl Meagan.

Chapter Twenty-One

'What did I tell you?'

Valerie Masterson was fuming. It wasn't the first time Matilda had defied her orders, and it wouldn't be the last either.

Matilda had called her boss first thing in the morning. She had had a sleepless night wondering if she should reply and start a conversation with the killer who was obviously delighting in taunting Matilda. In the end, she had turned her phone off. Before going to Valerie's office, she had the killer's number traced. Once again it was from a burner phone.

'Who's Carl Meagan?' James Dalziel asked.

Matilda and Valerie both looked at him as if he'd just asked who The Beatles were.

'What? I'm Scottish,' he replied, as if his nationality was an excuse.

'Carl Meagan was a seven-year-old boy who was kidnapped from his home a couple of years ago …'

'March 25th 2015,' Matilda interrupted.

'A ransom demand was sent to his parents. They own a chain of organic restaurants throughout South Yorkshire. Matilda was leading the case and was the point of contact for the exchange.

Unfortunately, a series of errors led the kidnappers to flee, and Carl hasn't been heard from since.'

'I vaguely remember the case.' James nodded. He noticed Matilda's painful expression. 'I'm guessing you blame yourself.'

'On the day of the exchange, my husband died,' she began, looking off into the middle distance. 'He'd been ill for a while and I was constantly running from the hospital to work and back again. I didn't sleep or eat. In hindsight, I should have handed the case over, but I didn't. My husband died, and I went straight to the drop-off point with a quarter of a million pounds. I went to the wrong car park and the kidnappers panicked.'

'Wow. I can see why you'd blame yourself. You've not heard from the kidnappers since?'

'No,' Valerie replied.

'When they knew you were at the wrong car park, what happened?'

'I said I'd go to the right one. I ran but when I got there, they'd gone.'

James took a lingering sip of his coffee. 'I think it's safe to say Carl Meagan was dead long before you went to the drop off.'

'What?' Matilda was shocked at his nonchalance. She had assumed Carl was dead, but she would never say it out loud, and not in company.

'If Carl was alive, the kidnappers would have made contact again. It was a business transaction, they wanted the money. There is only one reason why they didn't call and that's simply because Carl was dead.'

Simply? 'Maybe they killed Carl after I ballsed-up,' Matilda said.

'No. You were prepared to go to them. They panicked as they assumed they'd be found out for having already killed Carl. They were chancing their arm in asking for a ransom, and it didn't work. They got scared and ran.'

'So you think Carl Meagan is dead?' Matilda asked slowly.

'I do. Obviously I don't know how. Maybe it was an accident, who knows? I don't think you should beat yourself up about it, though.'

Matilda let go of the breath she was holding and visibly slumped in her chair.

'Getting back to the point,' Valerie said. 'The killer seems to think Matilda should pay for what happened to Carl Meagan.'

'Who knows about Matilda's involvement with the Carl Meagan case?'

'Any of the thousands of people who have read the book,' Matilda said, looking at the floor. Her body may have been in Valerie's office, but her mind was elsewhere, always the case whenever Carl Meagan was mentioned.

'There's a book?'

Valerie went over to a cabinet on the far side of the room. She unlocked the top drawer and took out her own personal hardback copy of *Carl* written by his mother, Sally Meagan. She handed it to James. 'DCI Darke and South Yorkshire Police are the bad guys.'

'It was in the *Sunday Times* top ten for seven weeks. It will have sold thousands,' Matilda said flatly.

James flicked through the pages. 'May I borrow this?'

'Of course.'

'Matilda, can you think of anyone who has a grudge against you? I don't just mean in the Carl Meagan case; that could be a smokescreen. Is there anyone in your work or personal life who could taunt you like this?'

Matilda took a deep breath. She looked at Valerie, but her face was expressionless. Matilda could only think of one name, and she didn't want to say it out loud.

Chapter Twenty-Two

'Are you going home?' Sian Mills said as she entered Matilda's small office. Everybody else had left for the day.

'Soon. I was just thinking.'

'You've been in a very thoughtful mood all afternoon. Anything I can help you with?'

'No. You get off home to your family.'

'Are you sure?'

'Yes. Go on.'

'OK. I'll see you tomorrow.'

'Goodnight, Sian. Sian,' Matilda said, calling her back, 'as far as I'm concerned you know this team better than anyone. Who do you think could be talking to the press?'

She blew out her cheeks. 'I've no idea. I have thought about it and I can't see any of them going behind our backs to the papers. Either that or I don't want to see it.'

'I know what you mean. This is going to split the team, isn't it?'

'Only if we allow it.'

'Go home, Sian. Take the night off. Put your brain into sleep mode and relax.'

'I'll certainly try, but Stuart's wallpapering the dining room at the moment. See you tomorrow.'

Matilda watched while Sian gathered her things and left the office. There was something at the back of her mind niggling away, gnawing at her brain. She couldn't pinpoint what it was, but she had a frightening feeling she knew exactly what was going on.

Matilda didn't drive straight home. Out of the station car park, she turned left and headed to the opposite side of town from where she lived. Fortunately, she had missed the rush-hour traffic.

She found the road in Worrall easily, despite never having driven here before. She slowed to a crawl and looked out of the side window for the right house number. Eventually, she applied the brake and turned off the engine. She had arrived.

Matilda didn't intend to get out of the car. She sat looking at the detached house. There was a light on behind heavy-looking curtains in what Matilda guessed was the living room. Someone was obviously home. Should she walk down the drive and knock on the door? The thought of what would happen when her call was answered filled her with dread. She couldn't face the barrage of abuse she knew she'd receive.

'Go home, Matilda,' she berated herself.

She didn't. She remained still, her eyes fixed on that barely lit window, waiting for something, anything, to prove there really was someone home. She had a long wait. It was seven minutes (though it felt longer) before there was a glimmer of life. A shadow moved across the window. A light came on in the room on the other side of the front door. The curtains were open, and the kitchen was lit up in a brilliant white light. She saw clearly what she had come to see: the sad face of the occupant.

Surprisingly, Matilda breathed a sigh of relief. She felt relaxed. There was someone there, where they should be. She turned on the engine and performed a five-point turn on the narrow road before heading for home.

***

Matilda kicked the door to the dining room closed behind her and slammed a large pile of files down on the table.

'I'm sorry, James, but this is a matter of importance.'

As usual, Matilda was alone in the house. With the television off, no radio, no background noise apart from the sound of clocks ticking and the fridge humming, Matilda spoke to James to stave off the suffocating silence.

'I told you at the time we didn't need a six-seater dining table. We were hardly the dinner-party type. I think the most we've had around this table is that time Adele and Chris came over, and then it was only for fish and chips. Although,' she said with a grin spreading across her face, 'I seem to remember us celebrating our third wedding anniversary in this room.' She blushed and was thankful, for once, she was alone.

She spread the files on the table and took out several photographs from the top one. Blown-up images of Brian Appleby and Joe Lacey hanging, their heads covered with white pillowcases. She had stolen a packet of Blu-Tac from the stationery cupboard at work and began to stick the photographs on the wall of the dining room. An hour later it resembled the briefing room back at the station. She pulled out one of the oak chairs and sat down, looking at the wall adorned with crime scene and post-mortem photographs, close-ups of rope burns on necks, fingernails with blood and skin samples beneath them.

'So, Brian Appleby was a paedophile and Joe Lacey caused death by drink-driving. They served their sentences and were released from prison to become members of society once again. Something, or someone, links these two men. Who or what? I've been told I can rule out George Appleby,' she said to herself sticking up a photo of George she'd managed to get from the student union. 'But do I want to? This doesn't feel like a son killing his father and I haven't even met him, so why is he texting me?'

Matilda's phone beeped an incoming text message. She looked

for her bag among the stacks of files and paperwork. Again, it was from a number she didn't recognize:

According to the news, Sheffield appears to have a serial killer on its hands.

Matilda ran into the living room and turned on the television to the BBC News channel. A man wearing a ridiculous tie was talking about football. At the bottom of the screen, the ticker gave the latest headlines:

BREAKING: TWO PEOPLE MURDERED IN SHEFFIELD LINKED TO ONE KILLER.

'Shit,' Matilda said quietly.

She wondered if ACC Masterson was at home watching the news right now. Whoever was leaking this information to the media, Matilda hoped it was worth it, because when Valerie found them, she would crucify them.

Matilda waited for the main headlines, but nothing more was mentioned. They probably didn't have all the information yet. She went into the kitchen and flicked the kettle on. As it boiled she wondered what was worse: having someone on her team leaking secrets or the panic on the streets of Sheffield when people woke up tomorrow morning to find news of a serial killer on the front pages.

The kettle boiled, but Matilda, in her own reverie, leaned against the kitchen counter staring into space as her mind went through the members of her team. *Let's start with Faith…* The security light from outside came on. A brilliant white seeped into the kitchen from the side of the curtains. Matilda looked up. Someone was in her garden. The house next door was still empty. On the other side were an elderly couple. Their Jack Russell used to come through to her garden, but Mr Selby had blocked the gap in the fence.

She stood still, waiting, hoping for the light to go out. From the living room, her mobile phone signalled an incoming text message. She ignored it, her eyes fixed on the window. The sensor should have turned off by now if it had just been a passing cat or a low-flying bird. Eventually, it went out and Matilda visibly relaxed. She had been holding her breath. Her mobile burst into life once more. She was about to leave the kitchen when the security light came on again. There was definitely someone in her garden.

Shit!

She picked up a marble rolling pin from the counter and made her way slowly to the door. The roller blind was down. She peeled back the edge enough to peek round and see into the garden. There was nothing there. The security light went out, and she moved away from the door. Maybe it was a fox.

Matilda returned to the counter to make her cup of tea. Again, she heard her phone once more from the living room. She ignored it. The security light came on. This time, Matilda acted fast. She grabbed the rolling pin and the key from the hook on the wall and ran to the back door. She unlocked it, swung it open and stepped out into the pitch-dark, freezing cold night. The security light went out and immediately came back on again. She went around to the side of the conservatory and stopped. She dropped the rolling pin onto the paving slab opened her mouth and screamed.

Chapter Twenty-Three

The Land Rover pulled up. The front passenger door was opened before it came to a complete stop. Valerie Masterson jumped down and slammed it closed behind her. She had been in bed when the call came through and dressed quickly in the dark. It was unlike her to leave the house looking dishevelled in skinny jeans, a baggy sweater and wellington boots. Her overcoat was full of muddy splashes from long walks with her dogs near her home in the Derbyshire countryside.

She walked down the driveway and looked at the uniformed officer standing on the doorstep. He didn't need to ask to see her ID. He knew who she was. He nodded and said good evening. She smiled and walked past him into the warm house. Without taking off her boots, she turned into the living room where Matilda was sitting on one of the sofas with DS Sian Mills next to her, both were holding mugs of strong tea.

'Matilda, how are you?' Valerie asked.

'I'm fine, ma'am. Thank you.'

'You're not hurt?'

'No. Just shaken up a bit.'

'Is it still there in your garden?'

'Yes, ma'am.'

'Right.'

Valerie made her way through the living room and kitchen and out into the back garden. Floodlights had been erected and a team of scene of crime officers were scouring the area, looking in bushes and hedges for traces of the intruder. In the middle of the garden, swinging from a barren oak tree, was a mannequin, hanging by the neck as if it had been executed. The wig was identical to Matilda's hairstyle and the clothes were similar to an outfit she had worn recently.

'Same rope as the others,' a forensic officer on a stepladder next to the mannequin shouted. 'Hangman's noose again, too.'

'Get it cut down as soon as you can,' Valerie said. She turned and went back into the house, shaking her head. The killer was playing games, using her officers for their own sick pleasure.

'Are you sure you're all right?' Valerie asked for the third time.

'I'm fine. Just shocked that's all.'

'That's understandable. I don't want you staying here tonight. Do you have somewhere to go?'

'I've phoned Adele,' Sian said. 'She's on her way over.'

'Good. Tell me about the text messages.'

Matilda picked up her iPhone from the coffee table and selected the messages. While she had been in the kitchen and making her gruesome discovery, she had received twelve texts, all from the same sender – the killer. She handed the phone to the ACC who scanned the screen. He was taunting her about the serial killer news story. He seemed to be relishing the attention. He alerted her to a third victim in her garden.

'I'm guessing you disturbed him. You were probably meant to get the messages and look out of your window and see the mannequin hanging. It makes me wonder what else he had planned,' Valerie said, not taking her eyes from the phone.

'What are you talking about?'

'He was texting you while he was setting up his display. He wanted you outside. Why?'

'To see my expression, I'm guessing. If he wanted to attack me he could have done.'

'When you went around to the back of the house, did you leave the door open?'

Matilda thought. 'I'm not sure. I … probably.'

'Has anything been taken?' Valerie asked, looking around.

'No. Nobody came into my house. I wasn't out for more than a couple of minutes. I saw the thing hanging from the tree, screamed, then ran in.'

'Matilda?' Adele's worried voice was heard from the entrance of the house.

'In the living room,' Matilda said.

'Oh my God,' she said, charging into the lounge and pulling her best friend into a bear hug. 'Are you all right?'

'Yes, I'm fine. Just a bit shaken.'

'Go and pack a bag. You're coming home with me.'

'Matilda,' Valerie stopped the DCI. 'Tomorrow morning, I want you in my office first thing. This has gone too far. You can't solve this on your own.'

'I'm—'

'This is not open for debate, Matilda.'

'Ma'am.'

Matilda had stayed over at Adele's on many occasions in the past and had enjoyed a comfortable sleep in the spare room. Last night, however, she couldn't sleep at all. The thought of someone watching her, being so close to her and not knowing who it was, frightened her. She eventually fell asleep just after three o'clock and was woken at six by Adele.

Matilda knocked on Valerie's door and was asked to enter straight away. Wearing yesterday's clothes, Matilda saw the ACC and James Dalziel waiting for her. The strong smell of coffee, mixed with whatever fragrance James had liberally sprayed, filled the room. Valerie was back in her regular uniform. It had been strange seeing her in casual clothing last night, she'd almost looked taller.

'Matilda, how are you? Did you sleep well?' James said, just as Valerie opened her mouth to ask the same questions.

'Yes. Fine thanks,' she lied.

'Take a seat,' Valerie said as she went to pour a coffee for Matilda.

James offered a sympathetic smile to Matilda. She smiled back but looked away quickly. Every night she wished her husband was back with her. Now it was like her wish had come true, but in a twisted David Lynch kind of way.

'I don't think we need to worry about a member of your team leaking information to the press,' James said. 'It's more likely to be the killer. I don't know why I didn't see it before.'

'That is a relief,' Matilda said. 'I didn't think any of my officers would have spoken to the press, but I was certainly looking at one or two of them differently, and I didn't like that.'

'I can understand. Now, about last night …' James said, leaving the rest of his comment unsaid.

'I appreciate you're both concerned, I am, too. However, I'm not going to fall apart. I'm stronger than you realize,' she said, directing the final comment to the ACC.

'James was questioning his original profile before you arrived, Matilda.'

'I didn't actually create a profile,' James corrected her. 'I'm in two minds as to whether the killer is being a vigilante and targeting the law, or if he's targeting you directly, Matilda.'

'W-why would he do that?' she stuttered, taking a long sip of coffee. She had refused breakfast at Adele's. Sitting in the office, strong caffeine on an empty stomach, she was starting to get the shakes.

'You've arrested a large number of people in your career, some of them you're going to piss off. Who has a grudge against you?'

'I've put away many murderers in my time, most are still behind bars – I hope so anyway. I don't think anyone hates me enough to kill two people.'

'Matilda.' Valerie leaned forward on her desk and glanced at James. They had obviously been talking at length about her. 'The killer is communicating with you. He's taunting you. From his point of view, he has a very good reason for doing this. I need you to think about who that might be.'

Matilda thought. She didn't like where this was going – back to the sad detached house in Worrall. Then she wondered if this had something to do with Carl Meagan, then dismissed it. Not everything was about Carl Meagan, no matter what her disturbed mind assumed.

'What are we doing about finding this killer?' Matilda asked, louder than she had expected. She could feel a rage beginning to boil inside her.

'Like I said, I'm wondering if the killer is targeting you for a specific reason. What I cannot put together is the victims and you. Why these victims? Do you know any of them?'

'No.'

'Did you work on any of their cases?'

'No.'

'So, what could the killer be trying to say to you by these particular victims?'

'Isn't that a question we should be asking you?' Matilda asked James. She looked to Valerie and raised her eyebrows. *I said we didn't need a bloody profiler*.

'I'm going to need more time,' he replied.

'Of course you do. More time and maybe another victim or two. Meanwhile the press is out there saying there's a serial killer on the loose and you've got more than half a million people living in Sheffield scared. Not to mention me being spied on in my own home. No rush, you take your time.'

Matilda slammed her coffee cup down on Valerie's desk and stormed out of the room, leaving the door open.

'Walpole, Compton, Pelham, Pelham-Holles, Cavendish, Pelham-Holles, Stuart, Grenville, Wentworth …'

Matilda uttered the names of the British prime ministers under her breath then stopped herself.

'Shit!' she called out, kicking a vending machine. She had been told to recite the names of prime ministers by her former therapist, Sheila Warminster, whenever she was having an anxiety attack in order to regain control of her breathing. She thought she was better. She thought she was past this. Now her anxiety had reared its ugly head once again and she was back to a time when her husband had recently died and the whole country was blaming her for Carl Meagan going missing. *So much for fucking therapy.*

Chapter Twenty-Four

Following a thousand and one questions by people asking how she was, Matilda went into her untidy office and closed the door firmly behind her. She didn't know whether to burst into tears or scream. By the end of the day she expected to do one of them in front of her team and that would lose all the respect she had spent years building up.

'Any chance of a word?' Christian asked, knocking on the glass door.

'Of course, Christian. Come on in.'

'There are rumours you're being targeted by the killer. Are you still in charge of this investigation or is someone else being drafted in?'

Matilda blew out her cheeks. 'Until I'm told otherwise I'm still leading this. Why?'

'Well,' he began, sitting down, 'I've spoken to Kate Stephenson, she's the editor of *The Star*. Apparently one of her journalists has had a phone call from someone claiming to be the killer and wants to come in for a chat. She's phoned several times already this morning.'

'Will you do me a favour?' Matilda eventually asked.

'Sure.'

'I haven't eaten since last night. Could you get me a bacon sandwich and a strong cup of tea? Then give me ten minutes and I'll be fighting fit.' She wondered if she was trying to convince Christian or herself.

Christian smiled. 'Coming right up.' He left the office, closing the door carefully behind him.

Matilda turned in her chair to look out of the window at the uninspiring view of the Sheffield landscape. *Bloody hell the steel city had some ugly buildings.* With her back to the main incident room she started to cry. They weren't tears of sadness or fear, they were tears of anger.

Aaron and Faith once more pulled up outside the depressing-looking house in Norfolk Park, home to Clive and Amanda Branson. Neither of the detectives were looking forward to this interview. They had received a frosty reception last time and after Clive's revelation that he and his wife were living on what he could steal from the back of supermarkets, a great deal of sympathy was felt for the parents who were still grieving for the loss of their only child twenty years ago. Nobody wished to put them under more stress.

'What do you want?' Clive Branson asked when he opened the door. His greeting was cold and laced with tension.

'I'm sorry to bother you again, Mr Branson, would it be possible for us to have another quick word?' Aaron asked, putting on his most placatory voice.

It was obvious from his taut facial expression that Clive was on the brink of erupting. He shook his head and eventually relented, stepping back from the doorway and allowing both detectives to enter.

It was colder inside than it was outside, and Faith shivered. The hallway was dark and dingy. There was a filthy mirror on the wall, peeling wallpaper, and the surrounds of door handles and light switches were dark with years of dirty fingerprints. The

Bransons had no pride left. They didn't seem to care how they lived. It was as if they were merely existing.

Amanda Branson was sitting in an armchair by the fire. She was knitting and didn't drop a stitch as she looked up and rolled her eyes at the unwanted visitors.

Clive sat in his usual armchair. There was no other seating left for the detectives. They were not being encouraged to stay long.

'I'm sorry to call unannounced but I was wondering if I could ask you some more questions about the murder of Joe Lacey?'

'I don't know how you have the nerve to mention that man's name in my home,' Amanda said, almost under her breath. The speed of her knitting had increased.

'Just say what you want to say then leave us in peace,' Clive said.

'I'm not here to accuse you of his murder, Mrs Branson. I want to know if you are aware of anyone who may have wanted him dead; someone connected to your daughter, perhaps.'

Amanda stopped knitting.

'What?' Clive asked, struggling to keep hold of his pent-up aggression.

Aaron struggled. 'Is there anyone, apart from yourselves, who took Rebecca's death particularly badly who you think may be seeking retribution?'

'There is no one else,' Clive said slowly and clearly. 'There's just me and Amanda. It's always been just me and Amanda for twenty years. What are you getting at?'

'We're trying to find a motive for Joe's death and—'

'And you want our help,' Clive finished Aaron's sentence. There was a smirk on his face. 'You've got a bloody nerve. Where were you when Rebecca was killed, eh? Where were you when it came to the aftercare? What kind of support do you think we got from South Yorkshire Police? None. Absolutely none. You were fucking useless. If you think I'm going to do your work for you, you've another thing coming. Now, go on, get out. I don't want you bothering me or my wife ever again. Go on. OUT!'

‘I’m sorry,’ Aaron said quickly. ‘I’m sorry to have caused—’

‘Just go,’ Amanda said.

Aaron and Faith backed out of the living room. They hurried to the front door and were soon in the cold fresh air of a March afternoon. They both took deep breaths.

‘That poor couple,’ Faith said.

Aaron remained silent, his face a map of worry.

‘Aaron, you OK?’

‘Me and Katrina have taken years to conceive. What if anything happens to our child? Will we turn into the Bransons?’

‘Oh Aaron,’ Faith said, reaching up and putting a comforting arm around his broad shoulders. ‘You can’t think like that or you’ll end up a nervous wreck.’

‘You want to protect your kids, to look after them and keep them safe, but eventually you have to give them some freedom to go out into the world on their own. What happens if they don’t come back?’

‘Aaron, I’m sure every new parent thinks that at some point. It’s called being responsible. You and Katrina are going to love your baby and he or she will grow up knowing what’s right and wrong. You’ll be great parents. I know it.’

Faith gave Aaron her most sympathetic smile. He smiled back, though he looked more painful than reassured.

‘Do you ever think about having kids?’

‘Eventually. One day. Come on, let’s get back to work and you can buy me a coffee.’ She quickly headed to the car.

As they drove away, Faith looked at the Branson’s house and saw Clive staring at them from the living room.

‘I knew it would have been a waste of time coming here,’ she said. ‘Why are we putting so much effort into this? A paedophile and a drunk driver have been killed. Whoever did it has done the world a favour.’ She folded her arms and turned to look out of the window at the depressing Sheffield suburb.

Chapter Twenty-Five

Valerie Masterson had stepped out from behind her desk and rearranged the small seating area to accommodate the editor of the local newspaper, Kate Stephenson, Danny Hanson, James Dalziel, Matilda and herself. As Valerie approached carrying a small tray of coffees, she noticed how uncomfortable they all seemed.

Matilda looked tired sitting in the middle. To her left was James Dalziel who was wearing a very expensive black suit. Matilda kept stealing glances at him, but she always appeared awkward in his presence. Was there something going on between them? Surely not, Valerie thought. She knew how devoted Matilda was to her dead husband. To Matilda's right was the painfully young Danny Hanson. He seemed uncomfortable being among people higher up the chain of command than he was. He probably never thought he'd be having coffee with the editor, the ACC and DCI of South Yorkshire Police, and a highly respected criminal psychologist – not so early in his career anyway. Then there was Kate Stephenson – a tall, stylish woman in her late thirties. She was wearing a long black coat and had shoulder-length flowing dark brown hair and bright red power heels. She didn't look uncomfortable at all. She had no reason to be; there was a serial killer in Sheffield and he was telling his story direct to one of her journalists.

'Kate, Danny, thank you for coming in to see us,' Valerie said, placing the tray on the coffee table in front of them and telling them to help themselves. She took a seat. 'You could so easily have just published the stories and made life very difficult for us, but I appreciate you being so open.'

'You're very welcome, Valerie. As you know *The Star* is a great supporter of the police. If there is any way in which we can help your investigation, we will do so.'

Matilda bit her tongue hard. The placatory sentiment was almost embarrassing.

'Now, Danny, tell the ACC what's been happening,' Kate said.

At the mention of his name, the nerves struck Danny. He was about to take a sip from his coffee and looked up. He placed the cup down on the saucer, his shaking hand causing the china to rattle and spill some of its contents.

He cleared his throat. When he spoke, his voice was hoarse. 'Right, OK. Well, I received the first call the night after Brian Appleby was found dead—'

'*First call*? How many of them have there been?' Matilda interrupted.

'Four,' Danny said quietly.

'What?' Matilda almost screamed. 'You've had four phone calls and you're only coming to us with this now?'

'DCI Darke,' Kate began. 'I only found out about the calls yesterday. I don't think you can apportion any blame here. Danny is a young and very ambitious reporter. Any of us in his position would have kept this a secret.'

'I don't believe it,' Matilda said, fuming. 'You do realize we could charge you with obstructing a murder investigation.'

'OK. Let's calm down. Nobody is going to be charging anyone,' Valerie said, placing a hand on Matilda's arm. 'Now, Danny, tell us what happened.'

'OK.' He cleared his throat again. 'Well, the killer called and told me that Brian Appleby was a paedophile from Essex and that he'd been hanged. There was a bloke on my journalism course who was from Southend. It turns out he knew someone in Essex Police. I gave them a ring and asked if they could confirm Brian Appleby was a known paedophile, and they did,' he said, not looking at any of the other four.

'The second occasion?' Matilda asked. Her voice was loud. It was obvious from her facial twitching that she was struggling to control her emotions. She had been blaming members of her own team, looking at each and every one of them and wondering which one was a betrayer.

'The day the story was printed,' Danny said quietly, his head still lowered. 'He called to congratulate me.'

'What did you say to him in return?'

'Nothing. I didn't get a chance. He hung up.'

'What number was he calling you from?'

'It was an unknown number.'

'Did he call you on your mobile?'

'Yes.'

'A work phone?'

'No. My own personal one.'

'How long have you had that number for?'

Danny flustered as he tried to think under the quick-fire barrage of Matilda's questions. 'I don't know. Years.'

'Who has your number?'

He shrugged. 'A lot of people. It's on my Facebook page.'

'Oh, for God's sake.'

'That will do, Matilda,' Valerie chastised.

'Danny, tell them about the third call,' Kate said.

'The third was similar to the first. He told me Joe Lacey was a murderer who was involved in a hit-and-run. He supplied all the details. I just listened.'

'And the fourth conversation,' Kate prompted.

'Conversation?' Matilda asked, aghast. 'You mean you spoke to him?'

'He called me yesterday. He told me he's going after a child killer.'

'What? He's told you his next victim?' Matilda almost cried out.

'No. He didn't give me a name.'

'What does this person sound like? Does he have a local accent? Does he sound old or young?'

'Matilda,' Valerie gave her DCI a dark look, as if chastising a small child.

Danny struggled. 'I don't know. It's a low, deep voice. The last call seemed different from the others. It may not have been the same person. It could be someone pissing about.'

'We have had a few hoaxes,' Kate interjected.

'How do you know they were hoaxes?' Matilda asked.

'Over twenty years' experience,' Kate smiled.

'We'll need your phone,' Matilda said, turning to Danny.

'Now steady on,' Kate said.

Valerie held up her hands. 'Can we all just calm down one second, please? I think we're letting our emotions get the better of us. Danny, you said you had a conversation with the killer. What did you talk about?'

'He, er, he said he was going to murder a child killer. I asked him why.'

'What was his answer?'

'He said she was a criminal. He said the police weren't doing anything about it, so he was going to instead, because someone had to make a stand.'

'He definitely said *she*?'

'Yes.'

There was a silence.

'Tell them everything, Danny,' Kate instructed.

Danny cleared his throat and licked his lips nervously. 'He said that murderers were being allowed to go free and Matilda Darke wasn't doing anything to stop them.'

The silence in the room intensified and all eyes turned to Matilda.

'He actually mentioned DCI Darke by name?' Valerie asked.

Danny nodded.

'Go on,' prompted Kate.

'I asked him how he knew she wasn't doing anything about it. He said that she was a murderer herself, so she had sympathy for the killers.'

Valerie almost fell back into her seat, her mouth wide with shock. Matilda went white.

'Who have you killed, DCI Darke?' Kate asked, her voice loud and clear.

Matilda scoffed at the ridiculousness of the question. 'I haven't killed anyone.'

'The murderer seems to think so. Who do you think he has in mind?'

'I really don't think this line of questioning is necessary,' Valerie said, still reeling from the shock of Danny's admission.

'You see, I think it is. I'm sure the readers of *The Star* will too. Matilda is a highly respected detective. She was in charge of the Murder Investigation Team and is now head of CID with a very large team of detectives beneath her. If she is a killer, people have a right to know.'

'Kate, do you honestly believe I would allow a known killer to be in charge of CID? A murderer to serve as a detective? This is obviously a slander to detract from the killer's own motive, enabling him to continue while all eyes are on Matilda and this force.'

James cleared his throat. He sat back in his seat and watched the drama play out, his eyes batting back and forth like a spectator on Centre Court at Wimbledon.

Kate was relishing having the upper hand. 'Matilda, if this

killer is going after people who he feels haven't fully paid their debt to society, aren't you nervous of being caught by the Hangman?'

'I sincerely hope you're not going to be using that nickname in your papers,' Valerie said.

'Too late for that, I'm afraid,' she smiled. 'The afternoon edition is already rolling as we speak. So, Matilda, the name of your victim …?'

'I can only assume,' Matilda began, her voice shaking, 'the killer was talking about Carl Meagan. Nobody knows what has happened to him. However, from my point of view, if he is discovered dead, I will consider myself to be a contributor to his murder.' A tear slid down Matilda's face. She didn't wipe it away.

'I think we should perhaps leave it there, for now, don't you?' Valerie said, looking nervously at every one in turn.

'Fear is spreading through Sheffield like the plague, Valerie. They want to know they're safe and that South Yorkshire Police is committed to catching this killer before he strikes again. From what I've witnessed here, I'd say they've every reason to be concerned. I know I won't be sleeping safely in my bed tonight.'

'Every single officer working for South Yorkshire Police is committed to keeping the people of this county safe,' Valerie said, standing up. She straightened her uniform, something to do to hide the shaking of her hands.

Valerie ushered Kate and Danny to the door. Kate, however, wasn't finished.

'DCI Darke, don't you think it's about time you stepped down?' she asked. 'Allow someone with a stronger personality to take control, perhaps.'

Matilda jumped up out of her seat. 'Well, if you hadn't withheld crucial evidence from the police, while two people were being murdered, maybe we would have already caught the killer. I hope you think of that when you're sleeping in your bed tonight.'

Chapter Twenty-Six

Valerie had followed Kate and Danny out of the office, slamming the door behind her. Matilda and James were left alone in the awkward silence.

'You just played right into her hands,' James said.

'I know. I'm sorry. I couldn't help it, though. Did you see the way she kept grinning at me? Bitch.'

'She's a journalist. It's what she does. Your job is to rise above it.'

Valerie came back in. Her face like thunder. She didn't take her eyes off Matilda until she had sat back down. She was breathing heavily, fuming at the outcome of the meeting.

'What the hell were you thinking of?' she eventually said. 'I think I've managed to persuade them not to print any of that. I've had to promise them exclusives if any further victims are discovered. I simply cannot conceive …' she stopped when she saw the look on James's face. She turned to Matilda, the broken DCI to her left. The anger she felt faded away. 'Matilda, how are you feeling?'

'Sick,' she said quietly.

'James, I notice you didn't contribute to the meeting. I'm hoping you have drawn some conclusions,' Valerie said.

James adjusted himself in his seat and smoothed down his tie. 'It's safe to say your team are in the clear when it comes to someone leaking information to the press. I can't help thinking that the killer's motives changed after his first victim.'

'What do you mean?'

'Well, Brian Appleby isn't from Sheffield, so nobody within South Yorkshire Police worked on his case. Not one single officer, including Matilda, knew he was living here until he was killed. However, the killer is targeting Matilda now, but couldn't have been at the time he murdered his first victim.'

Valerie looked perplexed as she thought. 'Maybe he was waiting to see which detective was going to oversee the case.'

'No. If the killer had knowledge of who Brian Appleby was, then he's going to know who is working in South Yorkshire Police and who will be in charge of the investigation. He will have already known there was a high chance it would be Matilda.'

'So you think that something happened *after* Brian Appleby was found to force him to switch his, anger, shall we say, towards Matilda?'

'Yes, I do.'

'But what?'

'I've no idea. Maybe Matilda has already met the killer and he's become fixated on her for whatever reason.'

Both Valerie and James turned to look at Matilda who was still staring into the distance.

'Matilda, I'm going to need a list of all the people you've come into contact with since all this began.'

Matilda shook her head. 'That isn't going to be a long list. It's not me who interviews the suspects. It's not me who goes knocking on doors. The only people I see are the members of my team, the scene of crime officers and the pathologists.'

'If it's not someone Matilda already knows, James, who could the killer be?'

James was uncomfortable. He looked briefly at Matilda before going back to Valerie. 'If Matilda doesn't know the killer, then she obviously has a stalker who is very good at what he does.'

Valerie asked James to leave them both. He offered a few words of comfort to Matilda, but they fell on deaf ears.

Valerie moved seats, so she was sitting next to the DCI.

'Matilda, you spent more time with Philip and Sally Meagan than anyone else. Do you think one of them could be targeting you?' Valerie asked, her tone was gentle.

Matilda shook her head.

'They will need to be interviewed,' Valerie said. 'I'll send Sian round. Matilda, I want you to go home.'

'I can't turn my back on this. It's one of the biggest cases I've had in years.'

'It's also the most personal. I'm not asking you to turn your back on it, but you've had a shock. We all have. I want you to take a couple of days off, have a good long think about who, in your past, is capable of doing something like this.'

'No. I need to be here.'

'No, you don't.'

Matilda started crying. 'Shit!' She tried to hide her tears, but it was too late. 'I don't want to be home on my own.' She could barely control her emotions as the tears took over.

'I'll give Adele a ring, get her to come and collect you. I'm sure she won't mind you spending more time at hers. I'll also get someone to go over your house, check the security.'

Matilda smiled through the sniffles. 'The security's fine. James made sure of that before he died. He knew I was going to be on my own in that big house, so he had everything alarmed.'

'It can't hurt giving it an inspection, can it?'

Matilda wiped her eyes and composed herself. 'Carl Meagan is going to haunt me forever, isn't he?'

'I'd be lying if I said no,' Valerie said. She pulled her chair closer to Matilda and sat down. 'When I was first made a DI, I was in Brighton. There was a young girl called Charlotte Knowles.

She was only seventeen and so beautiful. Tall, slim, long blonde hair. She was found murdered on Boxing Day, strangled and dumped in woodland. Her parents were inconsolable. We interviewed her boyfriend, an ex-boyfriend, both of whom had alibis. We spoke to friends, tutors at her college, neighbours, family members, but nobody stood out as a suspect. We tested over a thousand volunteers for the DNA, but we came up with nothing. To this day, I have no idea who killed Charlotte Knowles, and she is constantly on my mind. I remember her birthday, the day she went missing, the day she was found, the day of the funeral. Even now, twenty-six years later, I still think of her, and her family. I have an excellent record for the cases I worked on, but I can never, and will never, forget Charlotte. Charlotte Knowles is my Carl Meagan. You'll never forget him, and for that, I'm sorry.'

Matilda had stopped crying. She looked at her boss. She had never seen her so thoughtful, so human, before. 'We can't find them all, can we?'

'Unfortunately, no, we can't.'

The ACC and the DCI sat in silent contemplation for a while. People often thought about the families of the victims who didn't have justice, but nobody thought of the police officers, the detectives investigating and doing everything in their power, and more, to find those responsible. They too carried the burden for the rest of their lives, but nobody gave them a second thought. They're supposed to be above emotional involvement, but a good detective cares. Valerie cared about Charlotte Knowles, and still does. Matilda cared about Carl Meagan and will do until the day she dies.

'Help yourself to another coffee. I'll give Adele a ring,' Valerie said, breaking the silence.

'Are you sure you don't mind me staying?' Matilda asked again, standing in Adele's hallway.

'For the eight hundredth time, no, I do not mind. Matilda,

you're my friend. My house is your house. Now, make yourself comfortable in the living room while I get us a drink. Not there, that's my spot,' she said as Matilda was about to sit on the sofa. 'I'm joking, sit where you like.'

Matilda perched on the edge of the sofa and looked around. Adele's house was lived-in. It was a proper cosy family home full of gifts and items bought from holidays, with photos on the wall of Chris growing up. Matilda smiled at a framed one on the mantelpiece that she remembered taking at Halloween about ten years ago. Adele was dressed as Morticia Addams with Chris as Pugsley. Everything in Matilda's home was sterile. There was the odd photograph of her and James, but she wanted to keep the majority of her memories private to her bedroom.

'Here you go.' Adele entered carrying two empty glasses in one hand and a bottle of white wine in the other. 'Now, tell me everything that's going on.'

'I can't.'

'You can. You know I'm not going to tell anyone.'

'No. I mean, I can't tell you because I've no idea myself.'

'Oh, Mat.'

'Someone is targeting me. Someone hates me so much that they've killed two people so far, and I know there are going to be more, I know it. Why would anyone do something like this? If they hate me then just come for me.'

'Don't say that.'

'Why not? What kind of an egotistical power trip are they on?'

'I don't know, Mat, but if this person is on some kind of a power trip then that makes them incredibly dangerous. I don't like the thought of them just coming for you. I don't want you to end up dead.'

'So what do I do? Go into hiding?'

'No. You fight. You fight hard. Whoever he is, he's a coward. He doesn't have the balls to face what he thinks is so important, so he's committing his murders to make up for his own shortcomings. But you do have the balls. You need to find him and show him you're not going away.'

'He's killed two people, Adele, he's got balls.'

'But he doesn't have them where it counts. Say he is targeting you, why doesn't he just come up to you? Because he's scared. He's hiding behind some kind of macho bravado he's invented to make himself look good. Beneath it all, he's nothing more than a schoolyard bully.'

Adele's words seemed to make sense. *Why hadn't James Dalziel come up with this?*

'Do you think so?'

'I do. Don't hide and don't be on your own. Stand up, rally your army, and come out fighting.'

'I'm not much of a fighter,' Matilda said.

'You don't have to be. You have people on your side – Christian, Aaron, Sian, Rory, Scott, Faith, me and Chris. We're your army.'

Adele noticed Matilda's face soften. She had got through to her. She put her arms around her and pulled her into a friendly hug.

Chapter Twenty-Seven

Sian looked through the closed iron gates at the large five-bedroom house. There were lights on, obviously someone at home. She had no reason to turn around and go back to her car, though that's what she wanted to do. She took a deep breath and pressed the button on the intercom.

'Hello,' came the reply.

Sian cleared her throat. 'My name is Detective Sergeant Sian Mills from South Yorkshire Police. I'd like a word with either Sally or Philip Meagan please.'

'Hold your identification up to the camera, please, above the speaker.'

Sian wrestled with her warrant card and pulled it out of her inside pocket. She held it to the small lens. There was no reply, no more comment, just the gates starting to open.

Pocketing the warrant card, Sian made her way up the gravel drive. She felt she was being watched from the house and tried to be confident and professional. With her shoulders back and her head high, she took long strides. At the solid wooden front door she raised a gloved fist to knock, but it was opened before she had a chance.

'DS Mills, I'm Sally Meagan, please, come on in.'

Sally Meagan was five-foot nine in heels. She was dressed elegantly in flowing black trousers and a white shirt with frilly collar. Her naturally wavy hair was dyed blonde and rested on her shoulders. Her understated make-up was a cover to add life to her painful face. The unknown, the grief, the worry was a permanent feature.

She stepped to one side and closed the door behind Sian, who looked in awe at the tastefully decorated hallway.

'Do you have any news?' Sally asked, a glimmer of hope in her eyes.

Before she could answer, a large golden Labrador bounded into the hallway from the living room. With tail wagging and tongue lolling, he came to a stop by Sian and started sniffing her.

'Woody, stop that. Sorry. He'll calm down in a minute. He's the nosiest dog in the world.'

'That's OK.' Sian smiled, bending to stroke the dog. 'I remember him from … well, when we first met. He was just a puppy then.'

'Yes. We got him for Carl when he was six. They were inseparable. Woody hasn't barked since the day Carl disappeared. He still pines for him in the evenings.'

Woody had lain down and rolled onto his back for Sian to scratch his tummy. He seemed to be enjoying the attention.

'Is it about Carl, why you've come here?' Sally asked, a hint of hope in her voice.

'No, I'm sorry, I haven't,' Sian quickly replied.

'Oh.' Her face fell. Another knife in the heart. 'Would you like to go through to the lounge?' she asked, pointing the way. Her voice suddenly cold.

'Thank you.'

Sian walked to the living room which was almost as big as her house. The first thing her eyes fell on wasn't the oversized expensive sofa, the thick Chinese rug, the large marble fireplace or the tastefully simple chandeliers, but the photograph of Carl Meagan on the mantelpiece. It wasn't big, but it was in a beautiful solid-silver frame. The smiling child, the spitting image of his mother, on a Christmas morning, surrounded by presents, a large tree in the background.

'Please, sit down,' Sally instructed.

The silence was awkward while both women made themselves comfortable. Woody gave an audible sigh and curled up on the floor beside Sally.

'Can I get you a drink or something?' The offer was made for the sake of being polite. It wasn't genuine. The icy stare and the arms firmly folded told Sian that.

'No, I'm fine, thank you. Is your husband home?'

'No. He's at one of our restaurants in Barnsley. If it's not Carl, what is this about?'

'Mrs Meagan—'

'Sally.'

'Sally. I'm really sorry to have to ask you this, but, have you had any contact with Matilda Darke recently?'

Sally's face twitched at the mention of the DCI's name. 'Contact? What do you mean?'

'DCI Darke is currently receiving some negative attention and we're contacting people who may have a grudge against her …'

'You think I'm stalking her?' Sally said, slapping a hand on her chest. She raised her voice in what could have been shock or anger. Woody lifted his head.

'No, I don't. I've been asked to cover all bases. I wouldn't be doing my job properly if I didn't ask,' Sian tried to be placatory.

'If you're doing your job properly, then you're the only one in South Yorkshire Police who does. Why don't you try to find my son? You think I've got time to piss about stalking Matilda Darke? Come with me.'

Sally jumped up, grabbed Sian's arm and pulled her to her feet. Sally headed for the door, her right hand firmly gripping Sian's wrist.

They went down the corridor, past the dining room, through

the kitchen and down a few steps. Woody trotted closely behind them. There were two closed doors. Taking a key from her pocket, Sally unlocked one and pushed it open. She practically threw Sian inside.

Standing in the middle of the makeshift office Sian looked around. The walls were covered in photographs of Carl, maps of South Yorkshire and the UK with pins scattered at various locations. The desk had a bank of three computer monitors and a large printer on it. A stack of posters, with Carl's face and the word MISSING at the top, were ready to be distributed. In the corner was a large pile of the hardback book Sally had written. This was a nerve centre in trying to find a child who had been missing for two years.

'This is what I spend my days doing. I'm scouring the Internet for any mention of Carl. I'm updating the website. Emailing missing persons charities offering my services to help find other children. Talking to other parents who have lost their children. Posting on message boards and forums asking for people to keep searching for my Carl. I'm updating Facebook and Twitter. I spend about sixteen hours a day in this room. Do you think I've got time to go hassling Matilda Darke?'

Sian looked at Sally. It was obvious she wasn't living, merely existing, until she knew the fate of her child. This was not a woman capable of killing two people and stalking a DCI.

'This is what I do every day.' Sally went over to the desk and picked up a mailing list. 'Here's all the people around the country who are also searching for missing relatives. We help each other out. I send them posters of Carl to add to their own collection.' She moved over to the tower of hardback books and picked one up. 'The paperback comes out in the autumn. I've been asked to write a couple of extra chapters, updates on the investigation. I've nothing to say. It's like he's just disappeared off the face of the earth, as if he never existed in the first place. This is my life now,' she said, looking around the small room.

'I'm sorry,' Sian said for want of something better to say. It sounded pathetic as soon as she opened her mouth.

'I blame Matilda. I hate the fact she was allowed back to work, that she can just get on with her life as if nothing happened. I hate her.'

'Sally, there isn't a day goes by without Matilda beating herself up for not being able to bring your son home. She thinks about him all the time. She isn't getting on with her life as if nothing happened; she's a changed woman. She will never forget him, and she will always be looking for him.'

'I don't want to hear this.'

'Sally …'

'Please, go,' she said quietly. 'There are only two things that keep me going – trying to find Carl and hating Matilda. If you can't give me Carl back, then please don't take away my hatred.'

'I'm sorry,' Sian said. She stepped around her and left the room. 'I'll see myself out.'

Sian was halfway down the corridor before Sally called to her. 'I'm sorry. I didn't mean to take it out on you. I hate Matilda. But I have more important things to do than make her life a misery.'

Sian offered a sympathetic smile then turned to leave. Once she was outside, she leaned back against the closed door and took a deep breath of cold air. It was stifling in the house, not due to heat, but the atmosphere, the depressive shroud that weighed heavy in every room.

Sian walked quickly down the drive. She couldn't leave fast enough. She wanted to go straight home and hug her children.

Chapter Twenty-Eight

CITY IN FEAR AS THE HANGMAN NAMES THIRD VICTIM

By Danny Hanson

The people of Sheffield are living in fear. The Hangman has already claimed two lives and plans to murder more victims.

The Hangman has contacted *The Star* and, in a cryptic message, stated that he will be targeting a child killer next. In a meeting between our editor and the Assistant Chief Constable of South Yorkshire Police, it is clear the police are out of their depth and DCI Matilda Darke and her team are clueless as to who is holding the city to ransom.

Cont. Pages 4 & 5.

Danny Hanson couldn't park in his usual spot. It was always a race to get the best spaces and, as he was late home from work, he'd missed his opportunity. He parked around the corner and walked back to the house.

Since his attack, he'd withdrawn into himself. He was no longer interested in seeing his byline on the front page. He didn't care about getting a scoop. He just wanted to survive.

Danny hadn't told anyone about the attack in Weston Park. He didn't care if it was the killer and he was the first person to get a good look at him, he didn't want anyone to know. He wore a high-neck jumper to hide the marks left by his scarf and he blamed his gruff voice on a cold.

It was dark, and a stiff wind was blowing. To his left was Endcliffe Park. Was his attacker watching him, ready to pounce? There were plenty of trees he could hide behind. He heard a noise coming from the park. He stopped in his tracks and turned around. It was a man walking his dog, coughing as he sucked on a cigarette. Danny sighed and continued to the house that seemed like a million miles away. It wasn't the most secure property in the world, but right now, it seemed like the perfect haven to hide in.

As he approached the turning onto his road, there was a huddled figure sitting by the road sign. A thick blanket around their shoulders, a gloved hand stretched out. Danny passed this person most days, a beggar asking for spare change. Or was it?

'Jesus!' he muttered to himself. He was turning into a nervous wreck.

He picked up his pace until he was up the gennel and opening the back door. He slammed it closed and rested against it.

'That was good timing,' Gina, one of the nurses said. 'I've made enough pasta to feed an army, you're welcome to help yourself, if you're hungry.'

'I'm not,' he said, heading for the stairs and taking them two at a time.

Once he was in his attic room, he closed the door and placed a couple of boxes of books in front of it, so nobody could enter while he was asleep, if he went to sleep.

Matilda hardly slept. Her mind refused to switch off. It was the second night she had spent away from her home since James had died.

Before she'd gone to bed last night she received many texts

from Sian, Rory, Scott and Aaron asking how she was. Valerie had called and left a voicemail, even James Dalziel had emailed. She didn't reply to a single one of them. She wanted to be on her own with her thoughts. Unfortunately, Matilda's thoughts were not rational. When she lay back in bed and tried to think of who could be targeting her, she just thought of Carl Meagan, his parents who were going to have to face another grilling by police; hadn't they suffered enough? Then James Dalziel popped into her mind. Did she really have feelings for him, or was she just surprised by the similarities between him and her husband?

Eventually, Matilda fell asleep just after three o'clock.

She was awake by five thirty and was in the kitchen drinking a black coffee and eating a Bounty when Adele walked in.

'I thought I heard someone moving around down here. I assumed it was Chris going for a run until I heard the kettle going.'

'Sorry, I didn't mean to wake you. Hang on, Chris goes out for runs at this time of the morning?'

'Yes. He said we were slowing him down. He meets Scott in the park and they do about five miles.'

'Bloody hell, they're putting us to shame.' She looked at the Bounty she was about to put in her mouth then slammed it down on the table.

'Can't you sleep?' Adele asked, flicking the kettle on and spooning a large amount of coffee into a mug.

'No. My mind just kept spinning. I've never faced anything like this before, Adele. I don't know how to cope with it.'

'I think the best thing for you to do is to surround yourself with people who are there to help you – me and Chris, Valerie, Sian and the rest of your team. We all care for you and will do everything we can to make sure this killer is caught.'

'What if he's never caught? He's been very clever so far.'

'He'll slip up somewhere. He'll get too cocky.'

'But how many more people are going to have to die before he makes a mistake?'

'Mat, don't do this to yourself,' Adele said, moving to the other side of the table and putting an arm around her. 'You've taught your team well. They'll find him.'

With Adele and Chris both at work, Matilda had the house to herself. She stood at the living room window looking at the busy street, wondering if there was anyone out there watching her. Had someone followed her from work yesterday, and tracked her every movement until she ended up back at Adele's? Were they now watching from a distance, spying on her, waiting for that perfect moment to strike?

Matilda shivered and went to sit back on the sofa. She picked up her mobile and made a call.

'Good morning, Sian. How are things going?'

'Not too bad. Me and Scott paid another visit to George Appleby this morning to see if he can vouch for his whereabouts for the time that mannequin was placed in your garden.'

'And can he?'

'This time he can. He was at home with his housemates. Two of them were there when we questioned him. They all agree they were home watching TV.'

'Do you believe them?' Matilda asked.

Sian hesitated. 'I really have no idea.'

'Oh. That's not what I wanted to hear.'

'It's not what I wanted to say. His housemates were treating this like a game. One of them was flirting with Scott and the other kept giggling.'

'And this is the next generation of surgeons and politicians, is it?'

'No wonder the country's in a mess,' Sian sniggered.

'How is the team getting on with trying to find any local child killers?'

'Oh that's all been sorted. There aren't any in Sheffield.'

'Really?'

'Everyone out on licence within South Yorkshire is accounted for. Not one of them killed a child.'

'If the killer goes into a different area then we really are screwed. Keep an eye on the news. If there's a similar murder in a different county, I want to know about it.'

'Other forces don't always like sharing intelligence,' Sian said.

'Let's hope he sticks to South Yorkshire then. Has anyone been to see Carl Meagan's parents yet?'

Sian sighed. 'Yes. I did, unfortunately.'

'Oh.' Matilda didn't like the sound of that. 'And?'

'Trust me, Matilda, you really don't want to know.'

Matilda thought for a while. Sian was probably right. If she heard Sally was happy and getting on with life, Matilda would wonder why she wasn't. If she heard Sally was a complete mess, popping antidepressants and swigging vodka morning, noon, and night, she'd blame herself. Sometimes, ignorance was bliss.

'Anything else going on?'

'Not so far. How are things with you?'

'They're OK,' she lied.

'I was thinking,' Sian began. 'Shall I have a word with that psychologist bloke, see if he can come up with anything?'

'Oh yes? I'm guessing it'll have to be a quiet chat in a cosy corner of the pub,' Matilda said, teasing Sian.

'I'm shocked. What do you take me for? I'm a happily married woman.'

Matilda went quiet.

'Is everything all right?' Sian asked.

'Yes. Fine,' she sighed. 'Anything else happened I should know about?'

'Not really. We've had three stabbings overnight. Two in the city centre and one in Worrall. No life-threatening injuries and three suspects already in custody.'

Worrall.

Matilda quickly said goodbye to Sian and hung up. It was time to pay another visit to Worrall. This time, she would definitely be knocking on the door. Who was the one person who hated

Matilda so much they would move heaven and earth to see her destroyed? Ben Hales.

Ben Hales was a former detective inspector at South Yorkshire Police. In 2010 when the Murder Investigation Team was planned, both Ben and Matilda were in the running to head the unit. Unfortunately for Ben, Matilda was given the job and promotion to detective chief inspector. To say Ben took the news badly was an understatement.

Following the death of James Darke and the collapse of the Carl Meagan case, Matilda was given an enforced period of leave, and Ben Hales was made acting-detective chief inspector and interim head of the Murder Investigation Team. He had hoped Matilda would never return and he would be given the role permanently. Nine short months later and Matilda was back at South Yorkshire Police.

To be eased into work gently, Matilda was assigned to a cold case before being allowed on front-line duty – the twenty-year-old Harkness double-murder case. Hales hoped Matilda would be unable to solve it and her reputation would be irreparable. In order to seal her fate, Ben decided to solve the cold case himself, and he went to any lengths to do so.

Ben was consumed with the desire to discredit Matilda and was eventually fired for assaulting a witness and deliberately misleading an investigation. His fall from grace was very painful and very public.

His wife left him, and his two daughters wanted nothing more to do with him. He allowed his loathing for Matilda to eat away at him, and when the pressure became too much he broke into her house in order to confront her. By then he was a shadow of his former self and he could have snapped at any moment. When he had Matilda pinned against a wall in her own home, he pulled himself back from the brink just in time. He had come within minutes of raping her.

Fleeing her home, he drove at speed into heavy traffic and deliberately crashed his car. However, he couldn't even take his own life. While recovering from his injuries, he resigned himself to the fact he was to spend the rest of his days a ruined man, slowly fading away while Matilda continued to rise.

This was madness.

While Matilda drove through the streets of Sheffield she doubted her reasons for making the journey. Was she really contemplating the notion that former DI Ben Hales was a serial killer? Yes, he may hate her. Yes, he probably blamed her for his career failing, but would he go to such extreme lengths to prove his point?

'Ben Hales is a serial killer,' Matilda said the words out loud, then snorted. It was preposterous.

She pulled over without indicating and heard an overtaking driver call her a stupid bitch. She turned off the engine and rested her head on the steering wheel.

What am I doing?

Matilda rang the doorbell on Ben's door and stood back, waiting for it to be answered. She was about to turn away when it eventually opened. What she saw took her by surprise.

'What do you want?'

Matilda couldn't reply.

When she had last seen Ben Hales it was when he'd broken into her house last year. Then he was thin and gaunt. Now, he had piled on the weight. His hair was overgrown and matted. He had a full beard he did not look after and brown teeth. There was a smell coming from inside the house, or was it from his clothing? It was a mixture of discarded food, stale alcohol and sweat.

'I'd like a word,' Matilda eventually said.

'I've nothing to say to you.' He started to close the door.

'Please,' she pleaded.

He left the door ajar and walked away leaving the decision up to her whether to enter or bugger off back to where she came from. The fetid smell from inside told her to run but, as much as she knew Ben Hales wasn't a killer, she needed to have it confirmed by the man himself. Reluctantly, she stepped inside.

The once clean, bright house, beautifully decorated and lovingly cared for, was now an abandoned wreck. The carpet was sticky underfoot from spilt food and drink. Broken bulbs hadn't been replaced giving the house a dark and depressing atmosphere. The surfaces were cluttered with empty pizza boxes and curry containers; squashed cans of cheap lager lay strewn where they had landed. Dark, black cobwebs hung from the ceiling and dust covered the tops of doors and cabinets. This could have been the home of a latter-day Miss Havisham.

Matilda took slow steps into the living room. Ben was in the armchair, feet up on a matching footstool. Both items had seen better days. The widescreen television on the wall was showing a horse race with the volume muted.

'Say what you have to say, then go,' Ben said without turning around.

'I thought you and Sara got back together again after you …' she tailed off, not wanting to mention his attempted suicide.

'After I tried to kill myself?' he finished for her.

'Well, yes.'

'We did. She didn't stay long, just long enough so that she wouldn't feel guilty if I tried and succeeded a second time.'

'Oh. I'm sorry.'

He looked up at her. 'Are you?'

'Yes. Can I sit down?'

Ben shrugged. Matilda went over to the sofa and tried to find a space among the newspapers and discarded clothing.

'Ben, what's happened to you?' she asked with genuine concern.

Ben took in the room as if seeing the mess for the first time. 'This is what happens when everything in your life turns to shit.

I have no job, no wife, no family. I couldn't even kill myself properly. What do I have to look forward to? Who do I have to look after myself for?' His voice was full of resentment.

'For yourself. Ben, you used to be so well turned out. You had haircuts and wore nice clothes. You took care of your appearance.'

'And then you came along and destroyed everything.'

'No. That's not true. I didn't do anything. All I did was my job. When I became DCI I made it clear that we could work together. I was prepared to make our relationship work. It was you who refused to adapt. I'm not taking the blame for all this.'

'No. I didn't think you would. When you went on leave I thought that would be it. The MIT would be mine. It should have been, too. When you returned you should have been back as a DI, with me in charge, but oh no, there were too many men at the top already. There had to be a woman running things somewhere. So Queen Matilda is given back her throne and I'm tossed aside once again.'

'My God, you're still bitter after all this time.'

'I'm not bitter. I'm just angry. I'm angry at you being able to get away with fucking murder and not face the consequences.'

'What did you say?' Matilda asked. Like the killer, Ben had accused her of murder.

'What?' he asked, genuinely perplexed.

'You said I was able to get away with murder. Is that what you believe?'

'Well, yes. When you came back, you weren't in a fit state to run the MIT. You were popping pills and running into the toilets to cry every five minutes. You were unstable. But you were also Valerie Masterson's blue-eyed girl. Like I said, you could have walked into her office with a body over your shoulder and slammed it down on her desk and she would have let you off with it.'

'Ben, you need to get over this. If you let all this resentment eat away at you then it's going to kill you,' she warned.

'I don't exactly have a lot to live for.'

'Yes, you do. You have two daughters. You're not even fifty yet. You can start again.'

'And do what?'

'Anything you want to do. Go travelling, get a new career—'

'Become a security guard at Tesco,' he finished her sentence. 'A very tempting offer. Look, just say what you came here to say and then go. I really don't want to have a long conversation with you about the future.'

Matilda sighed. On the drive over she had not expected to see the house and Ben in this state. It was a shock. It was incredibly sad. Despite their differences, Matilda knew Ben Hales was a brilliant detective. To see him wasting away in his own filth was heartbreaking.

'Ben, I know you don't like me, but, would you do anything to hurt me?' she asked carefully.

He looked up at her. 'What are you talking about?'

'Would you ever do something that could lead to me losing my job?'

'Like what?'

'I don't know.'

'Matilda, you're not making any sense. Stop pussyfooting around and just come out with it.'

'OK, let me ask you another way. Where were you on Thursday, the 9th of March?'

Matilda knew his reply was going to be laced heavily with sarcasm just by the twinkle in his usually dull eyes.

'Oh, that's easy, Thursday night is opera night. Yes, I was with a few friends all dressed up in top hat and tails. I can't recall without looking in my incredibly packed diary, but I think it may have been *Don Giovanni*.' He rolled his eyes. 'What do you think I was doing? I was probably sitting here drinking until I passed out like I do every night. Now are you going to tell me what is going on or are we going to play twenty questions? What's the significance of the 9th of March?'

Matilda shook her head. She was growing tired of Ben's self-pitying. Why should she go for the softly-softly approach? 'Ben, did you kill Brian Appleby?'

'What? Who the hell's ...?' The penny dropped. 'What?' He almost yelled. Matilda recoiled. 'You think I'm the killer, don't you? You think I've been going around killing people who have committed crimes and given light sentences in order to shame the police? Matilda, I really do dislike you. In fact, I loathe you with a passion; but do you honestly think I spend my days sitting here wondering how I can get back at you?' He stood up. Matilda did too and started to back away slowly. 'You are some piece of work,' he seethed. 'Do you honestly think I could have killed two people?'

Matilda didn't say anything. She couldn't. She was struck mute by the rage emanating from him.

'Well? Do you?'

'No. I'm sorry—'

'Oh, that's OK then, if you're *sorry*. Let's all go back to being friends and we can get on with the rest of our lives. How do you feel every time you pick up a newspaper and see Carl Meagan's face staring at you? I bet you feel sick, I bet you feel guilty, like you want the ground to open up and swallow you whole. It's the worst feeling in the world, isn't it?'

'Yes,' she whimpered.

'So why would you come around here and make me feel exactly the same way?'

'Ben, I'm sorry. I really am.'

'Do me a favour, Matilda. Fuck off and leave me alone.'

He'd backed Matilda into a corner against the front door. It was almost like a year ago when he'd trapped her in her own house. This time it was much worse.

Ben leaned into her, grabbing her by the throat with a strong and dirty hand. He squeezed hard. She tried to pull him off, but he was too strong.

With his face almost touching her he said, 'If you ever come back to my house again I swear to God I will fucking kill you, do you understand me?'

She tried to answer, but she couldn't. She made a squeaky, whimpering noise. That seemed to be enough, as Ben released his hold and Matilda almost dropped to the floor. He pushed her out of the way and pulled open the front door. A cold blast of fresh air rushed into the hallway. She ran to her car, one hand on her throat, the other searching in her pockets for her keys.

Matilda climbed in behind the steering wheel, closed the door and locked it from the inside. She looked out of the side window, half expecting to see Ben threatening her from the pavement or glaring at her from his doorstep, but he wasn't. She suddenly felt incredibly guilty. What was she thinking of, coming here, accusing him of two murders? She took a deep breath and started the ignition. She could still feel Ben on her. She could still smell him. Matilda opened the windows and allowed the cold air in. There was no doubt in her mind that Ben Hales had the potential to kill, but he wasn't the killer of Brian Appleby and Joe Lacey.

Chapter Twenty-Nine

Day Twenty-Two
Thursday, 30 March 2017

Katie Reaney had two small travel cases open on her bed. Next to them were two piles of tiny clothes. She gently began packing, smoothing each item as she delicately placed them in the cases.

'Erm, you do realize they're only going away for two nights,' her husband, Andy, said as he entered the bedroom.

Katie muttered in agreement and nodded. She didn't turn around.

'Don't you think you're packing too much?'

Katie shook her head, still not saying anything, still not turning around.

'What's wrong?' He went over to her and saw she was crying. 'You silly cow, Katie, come here.' He took the small T-shirts from her hands and pulled her into a hug. 'Is that why you don't want to come with me to drop them off?'

'Yes,' she cried into his shoulder.

He pushed her out of the hug and held her at arm's length. Her mascara had run slightly.

'You have nothing to worry about.'

'I know.'

'They're spending two nights with my mum. I'll be with them tonight, and we'll both go and pick them up on Sunday morning. You'll be pulling your hair out again in no time.'

'I know. I'm being silly,' she said, sniffling.

'No, you're not. It's natural.'

'Then why aren't you upset?'

'Well, according to my mother I'm a heartless sod, and in our last argument you called me insensitive.'

Katie laughed through the tears. She heard the sound of tiny feet thundering up the stairs. 'Don't let them see me crying, and change your T-shirt.'

'Why?'

'I've snotted on your shoulder, sorry.'

Katie looked at her reflection in the mirror to make sure her mascara hadn't run. Her eyes were red and puffy; there was nothing she could do about that. She neatened her dyed blonde hair and tried various smiles before she found the most convincing one.

'Right kids, give your mum a big hug and tell her you love her,' Andy instructed the well-wrapped children in the hallway of their semi-detached home.

In turn the two children hugged Katie. She gave them both a big kiss, told them to behave, not to eat everything Grandma had in her pantry, to go to bed on time and not to traumatize the cat too much. She also gave Andy the same instructions.

She helped Andy secure them into the back seat of the Audi then stood in the doorway of the house, waving them off, smiling through the pain of her two children spending the night away from home without her for the first time. As soon as the car turned right at the end of the cul-de-sac, the floodgates opened. Katie closed the front door and rested against it.

'Andy was right, you are a silly cow,' Katie told herself.

She splashed her face with cold water in the bathroom and looked at her blotchy reflection in the mirror. Tomorrow she would be thirty years old. How did that happen? Where had these dark lines under her eyes come from? And the crow's feet?

Katie opened the bathroom cabinet and took out a face pack. She had her evening all planned out – her favourite film on DVD, a big pack of peanut M&Ms, manicure, pedicure and face mask and she would look amazing for her birthday meal out on Friday. Before she went downstairs she smiled at the black dress hanging on her wardrobe door. She couldn't believe she was back to being a size ten.

The house was eerily quiet without a five-year-old and three-year-old running around the place, screaming at full volume. Katie would have access to the remote controls for an entire night – that almost never happened. Suddenly, she wasn't so sad Jenson and Bobbi were away for a couple of nights.

Katie had just sat down on the sofa, *This Means War* was starting, and the wine was poured, when her mobile started to ring. It was probably Debbie, seeing how she was coping without the kids. She stood up to get her phone from the table and didn't look at the display. She muted the volume on the TV.

'Hello?' she asked.

'Hello,' it was a man's voice. 'Can I speak to Naomi Parish, please?'

Katie froze. That was a name she hadn't heard for almost twenty years…

Naomi Parish stood in the doorway of the small bedroom. A soft night light gave the room a warm, comforting glow. She stepped in quietly so as not to wake the sleeping child. She could hear the deep breathing coming from the cot, the little whimpering sounds. She smiled. She looked down and saw Alistair on his back, mouth slightly open. His dummy had fallen out. His eyelids fluttered, and she wondered what he was dreaming about. She reached into the cot and picked him up.

She picked him up.

She should never have picked him up.

He opened his eyes, but it was obvious he was still half asleep.

'Hello, Alistair,' she said in a high-pitched sweet voice. 'You're a lovely boy, aren't you? Lovely big blue eyes. Just like your daddy. I like your daddy, Alistair. Do you think he likes me? I bet he does. The thing is, your daddy used to look at me a lot at one point, but then you came along. And now he only has time for his precious little boy …'

'What!' Katie said quietly. Her mouth had dried. She gripped the phone firmly in her left hand and pressed it hard against her ear. Had she heard correctly?

'Naomi Parish. I'd like to speak to Naomi Parish, please.'

Katie was visibly shaking now. Sweat was trickling down her back and it felt like her heart was trying to break out of her chest.

'I … I … There's nobody here by that name,' she stumbled.

'Are you sure?' he asked, his voice calm and steady.

'Yes. Sorry.' She hung up and slumped onto the sofa before her legs gave way.

The sounds of the house faded, and she was cocooned in a heavy silence. Her breathing was very restricted and laboured. Her vision blurred as she stared into a past she thought was long forgotten and deeply buried. She looked at a small framed photograph on the television unit – Jenson and Bobbi in a paddling pool in the back garden last summer, all smiling and happy…

'Mr Macintosh, I'm so sorry for your loss. My mum sent these flowers round,' Naomi said, standing shyly on the doorstep.

Naomi had spent all morning anxiously watching the house until Mrs Macintosh had left before visiting. She wanted to get Mr Macintosh alone, all to herself. While waiting for the door to open she had undone a couple more buttons on her shirt. She didn't have much of a bosom to show off yet, but it was getting there.

'Thank you. Come on in.' He stepped back from the door and headed for the kitchen. Naomi followed.

'Is Mrs Macintosh in?' she asked.

'No. She's gone over to her mum's.' He slumped down on a chair. He looked like he'd aged in the three days since his son had died. He hadn't shaved and had hardly slept, but it gave him a rugged edge that Naomi liked even more.

Naomi bent down in front of him, placed her hands on his knees and looked up with her big sad eyes. 'If there's anything I can do for you, Mr Macintosh, you only need to ask,' she said in a low and breathy voice. She stroked his legs, his huge muscular legs.

'That's very kind of you, Naomi. Thank you,' he said robotically. His body may have been there, but his mind was elsewhere. He couldn't take in the horrific reality of his son dying.

'Mr Macintosh.' Naomi leaned in towards him and kissed him firmly on the lips.

That brought him back to reality. He jumped up in disgust.

'What the hell are you doing?'

She began opening the remaining buttons on her top. 'Would you like to take me to bed, Mr Macintosh?'

The mobile rang again.

It was still in her left hand. The number was withheld. Was it the same caller? She refused to answer and watched the display until it stopped ringing and faded to black. It started up again almost immediately.

'Shit,' she said under her breath.

Katie threw the mobile onto the armchair. It landed under a cushion, the ringtone muffled. When it stopped ringing the sound of an incoming text message lit up the phone again. She reached across for it, hoping it was Andy or Debbie.

I'd like to talk to Naomi Parish.

As she glared at the phone, the doorbell rang.

Katie looked up. Her heart missed a beat as the sound echoed throughout the house. Andy had a key, he had no need to ring the bell. It wouldn't be Debbie, she was housebound.

The doorbell rang again.

The curtains were closed in the living room. It felt smaller. Claustrophobic. She listened intently for any sound outside the house. She couldn't hear anything.

The doorbell rang for a third time, and she slapped a hand to her mouth to stop herself from screaming.

Katie went out into the hallway and looked at the solid oak door. There were no window panes, so she couldn't see who her caller was. She edged closer, her legs shaking, barely able to hold herself up. With sweaty palms pressing against the door she leaned forward and looked through the spyhole – there was nobody there.

She breathed a sigh of relief and felt her heart rate begin to slow. It was probably just a coincidence: those twins two doors along messing about.

Katie turned around to go back into the living room when she stopped dead in her tracks. Ahead of her, in the doorway to the kitchen, stood a man. He was tall, dressed from head to toe in black. He wore a hooded sweater, the hood pulled right down, concealing his face. Katie tried to scream but nothing would come out, her mouth had dried up in fear.

'Naomi Parish,' the man said.

'Oh my God,' her voice shook with fear. 'I knew you'd come for me.' Tears ran down her face. 'Who are you?'

From behind his back he revealed a thick rope with a noose on the end. 'I'm the Hangman. I'm your executioner.'

'Shit!'

Katie screamed and turned to the front door. She grabbed at

the handle, but it slipped out of her sweaty palms. The chain was on and it was double-locked. She fumbled to unhook it with shaking fingers, but it was hopeless. She felt the noose go over her head and press into her neck. She tried to pull at it, to get her fingers beneath the rope to stop it from strangling her, but the man was too quick.

The Hangman kicked the back of Katie's legs, and she collapsed to the floor. Katie felt her body lighten as the oxygen was cut off from her brain. Her vision blurred, and her breathing became more erratic. Her false fingernails broke as she scratched hard at her neck. The man wrapped the rope around his hands and dragged her backwards. He slowly walked up the stairs, pulling Katie behind him like a dog on a lead. With each step, the rope seemed to get tighter. Her gasps were short and sharp. She was losing her grip on life and colours were beginning to fade.

At the top of the landing, the man tied the rope on the bannister. He lifted Katie up and looked deep into her bulging eyes. Behind him on the wall was a framed photograph of her two young children playing in the sand on a beach in Cornwall, taken a couple of years ago. She loved that picture and smiled at it every time she came upstairs.

From his back pocket he pulled out a white pillowcase and forced it down over her head. 'Any last words?'

She tried to speak. She opened her mouth for something, anything, to come out and save her.

'I thought not,' the Hangman grinned.

The man pushed her over the edge of the bannister and heard her neck snap as the rope tensed.

His work here was done.

Chapter Thirty

'Can I speak to DCI Matilda Darke, please?'

'I'm afraid she's in a meeting at the moment. Can I take a message?'

'It's very important.'

'Who's calling?'

'Danny Hanson. I'm a journalist on *The Star*.'

'All press enquiries should be—'

'I'm sorry, but I need to speak to DCI Darke immediately. Tell her I've spoken to the killer again.'

Danny was sitting behind the wheel of his blue Fiat Punto, impatiently waiting for Matilda to take his call. It was a cold morning and he was dressed in layers. He was parked outside a semi-detached house on Westwick Road. It was in darkness, the curtains drawn and no lights on. It was still early, maybe everyone was in bed. He hoped so, although the journalist in him hoped not.

'Mr Hanson, what can I do for you?' Matilda's voice was frosty. Was she annoyed at being called out of her meeting, or that Danny Hanson knew more about the killer than she did?

'I'm sorry to interrupt you, DCI Darke. I had a call from the killer in the early hours of this morning. He told me the address of his next victim.'

'Shit,' Matilda said under her breath. 'Where are you?'

'I'm outside the house right now. Don't worry, I haven't left the car. I thought you'd want to know.'

'Where are you?' she asked again firmly.

'Westwick Road. It's at Greenhill.' He was talking to a dial tone.

Fifteen minutes later two cars turned the corner and drove at speed up Westwick Road. It was fully light now, and the residents of the quiet cul-de-sac were starting to leave for work and school. They paid no attention to the Fiat Punto that had been parked outside the Reaney house for more than half an hour. They did notice the two screaming cars and the people who jumped out.

Matilda was in the front passenger seat of the first car. She was on the pavement before it had fully come to a stop. From the back Sian and Rory followed. Faith was driving. In the second car was Scott and Aaron.

Danny stumbled out of his car and began talking to Matilda, but she cut him off.

'Danny, I need you to go back to the station with my officers and give a full statement. I also want your phone looked at by Forensics.'

She walked past him and straight up the garden path.

'Hang on a minute,' Danny said. 'I didn't have to call you. I could easily have knocked on the door myself, or tried to gain entry, but I didn't. I'm playing by the rules here, like we agreed. You can't just send me packing.'

'I can, and I will.'

'Fine. But I'm not giving up my phone and you can't make me.'

'I can have you arrested for obstructing an investigation.'

'If you do that, I'll get Kate Stephenson to print everything we have so far.'

'Shit,' Matilda muttered. 'Stay by your car. I'll come and speak to you when I'm ready. Understand?'

'Perfectly,' he said with a smile.

'Is it wrong that I want to give him a backhander?' Matilda said quietly to Sian.

'I'll hold him for you, if you like.'

Matilda knocked on the door and waited. 'He's got one of those annoying smiles I could slap off his face.'

Matilda banged on the solid wood and rang the doorbell. 'Crime reporter at his age! He should be doing vox pops and interviewing old ladies who have worked in chip shops for seventy years.'

Matilda thumped louder this time. She waited impatiently for a few more seconds before bending down to look through the letterbox.

'Oh my God.'

'What is it?'

'I hate to say this, but Danny Hanson was right. We have a third victim.'

One swift hit with the battering ram was all PC Harrison needed to force the front door open. The sound reverberated around the cul-de-sac. Neighbours were out on the street wondering what was going on at the Reaney house. As soon as the door was open, Matilda and Sian stepped inside. They both stopped in the doorway and looked up – hanging by the neck from the bannister with a white pillowcase over her head was Katie Reaney.

'Close the door,' Matilda said.

Sian quickly complied.

'He's changed his MO,' Sian said. 'Our first female victim.'

Matilda remained silent as she glared at the still body. All she could think about was whether Ben Hales was capable of doing this. He was fragile, but when someone is in a rage, the strength they have is immense. Anything is possible. Matilda realized Sian was talking.

'Sorry, Sian, what did you say?'

'She's got kids: two of them.' Sian was upstairs on the landing, looking at a framed photograph of a happy, smiling family.

'Check the bedrooms.'

'Ma'am?' Aaron asked from the doorway, informing her of his presence.

'Aaron, get a full forensic team here. I want every inch of this house covered. Phone Adele Kean too. Seal off the road and interview all of the neighbours. I want to know everything about this family.'

Aaron walked away, pulling his phone out of his pocket.

'The beds are empty. They haven't been slept in,' Sian said, coming back onto the landing.

'Shit! Where the hell are the rest of the family? Look, we can't do anything until Forensics have been. Sian, sort out door to door, let's get a clearer picture of who this family is, and where they are, too.'

'Ma'am, Danny Hanson would like a word,' Rory said from the doorstep.

'I bet he would,' she sighed.

An hour later and the team of forensic officers was in full flow. Sitting in the car with the heaters on and watching through the windscreen, Matilda could see figures moving around in the brightly lit living room. She kept checking at her watch, but time seemed to be slowing down. She wanted to get in there and find out who the victim was, and what she had done that was seemingly a hangable offence.

The front passenger door opened and in climbed Rory Fleming, bringing with him a blast of cold air.

'Jesus, it's perishing out there.' He shivered. 'I'm going to have to start wearing thermals for door-to-door enquiries. You all right, boss?'

'Yes, I'm fine. Just thinking. You found anything out?'

'Yes. They've been named as the Reaney family. Andy and Katie are the parents with two children, Jenson and Bobbi. The woman at the end of the road in number 27 is Debbie Ashmore. She and Katie have been friends since they were at school together. Debbie is in a wheelchair and is virtually housebound. Now, she says Andy took the two children away late yesterday evening to spend a couple of days with his parents. It's Katie's thirtieth birthday today and they were going out tonight to celebrate. His parents live in Ripon. He was spending last night with them then coming back home this morning.'

'So Katie was alone in the house all night?'

'Yes.'

'Who knew about that?'

'Well, Debbie did, obviously. According to Debbie, the rest of the neighbours are friendly, but only to a point. It's not the kind of neighbourhood where everyone gets together for a coffee morning.'

'So only Katie's close friends would have known she'd be home alone?'

'I'm guessing so, yes.'

'Have you looked her up, see if she's known to us?'

'Scott's doing that now. He's on the phone to Kesinka.'

'You didn't tell Debbie what had happened to Katie?'

'No. I said I hadn't even been in the house, so I've no idea what's gone on.'

'Good.' Matilda smiled.

Matilda looked out of the windscreen and saw a forensic officer at the doorway. She signalled Matilda to come to the house.

'Keep going with the rest of the neighbours, Rory. Find out as much as you can about the family – any arguments, raised voices, that kind of thing,' Matilda said, climbing out of the car.

'You think the husband could have done it?'

'Never rule anything out, Rory, until you have the facts.'

Matilda walked back to the house in the corner of the cul-de-sac. She could feel eyes burning into her – neighbours and colleagues alike, all eager to know if anything had been discovered. Danny Hanson stepped out of his Punto. He caught Matilda's eye. He wanted to let her know he was still here, waiting. He was annoying her more and more by the hour.

'It's Diana, isn't it?' Matilda asked the forensic officer in the doorway.

'It certainly is,' she said in her thick West Country burr. 'We all look alike when trussed up in these white suits, don't we?' She handed Matilda one then went into the living room, leaving Matilda alone in the hallway.

The body of Katie Reaney was still hanging from the bannister. The pillowcase was still covering the head. Adele gave Matilda a sympathetic smile from the landing. Why did this scene have a more sombre tone about it? Was it because the victim was female or because wherever you looked there were framed photographs of a happy, smiling family that had been destroyed?

'What can you tell me, Diana?' Matilda asked on entering the living room.

'It looks like the victim was planning an evening in front of the TV. We have a bottle of wine, only one glass, some snacks and a DVD. There's a face pack, nail polish; she was having a girly night in to pamper herself.'

'A friend down the road said it's her thirtieth birthday today. She was supposed to be going out with her husband, so perhaps that's why she was giving herself a treat.'

'There's an iPad and her purse on the coffee table, but what's missing?'

Matilda cast her eye over the glass-topped table. 'Mobile phone.'

'Exactly. I've searched all over the ground floor and haven't found it yet. There's a team upstairs but they haven't come across anything. I'll let you know.'

'Thanks, Diana.'

Matilda walked from the room as Adele was coming down the stairs.

'I'm afraid to say it seems she suffered,' Adele said. They moved over to the body where the hands and feet had already been covered in plastic evidence bags. 'Both of her heels are covered with carpet burns. She's been dragged, either up the stairs if she was down, or along the landing if she was up. Look at the fingernails.' Adele lifted one of the hands to show Matilda. 'They're either chipped or broken. There are plenty of skin samples and blood.'

'Let's hope she fought back.'

'I doubt it. Look.' Adele flicked on a torch and pointed it underneath the pillowcase. They both saw where the rope was cutting into Katie's neck. 'It's tight; it's caused some serious burning and there are scratches deep enough to break the skin. She was scrambling to get the rope off.'

'How did she die? Asphyxia again?'

'No. I've had a feel of the neck, and the second and third cervical vertebrae have been fractured. That would have happened after she'd dropped and the rope had tensed. If you look, the knot is beneath the chin. This is the most effective position for it to be in for a hanging.'

'Is death instant in this case?'

'She would have been rendered unconscious almost straight away. The heart can continue beating for up to fifteen minutes afterwards, that's what makes the body jerk. It's the muscles going into spasm.'

'Ma'am?' Scott called from the doorway.

Matilda looked around to see the young DC's eyes fixed on the hanging woman.

'Yes, Scott. What is it?'

'I've just got off the phone to Kes. We've tried as many different spellings of Katie and Reaney as we can but she's not on the computer at all.'

'What?'

'She doesn't have a criminal record. She hasn't done anything wrong.'

'Then why has she been executed?'

All Scott could do was shrug.

Chapter Thirty-One

With Katie Reaney having been cut down and taken to the mortuary and the scene of crime officers finished, Matilda and her team searched the house for something, anything, that could lead them to why an innocent woman had been executed in her own home.

It was quieter without the mass of white-suited SOCOs going about their business. Matilda felt like she was intruding on someone's private life as she searched through drawers and cupboards. If this was the work of the same killer, and everything was pointing in that direction, what was the reason behind it?

'He's still out there,' Sian said from the bay window.

'Who is?'

'Danny Hanson. In his car. He keeps looking up and then down at his phone.'

'I'm dreading what's going to be in this evening's edition,' Matilda said.

'He's dedicated, I'll give him that.'

'Wouldn't you be? This is a wet dream to him. He's having front-page news delivered to him on a silver platter every day. If this doesn't get him a job on a national, I don't know what will.'

'He wants to be careful; I've seen those movies where the killer contacts the press. He's more than likely to be one of the victims. Did you just smirk?' Sian asked.

'No.'

'You did. Matilda Darke, I'm shocked. You almost smiled at the thought of Danny Hanson hanging from a rope,' Sian said, playfully.

'If he's going to talk to a killer then he needs to accept the consequences.'

'Don't forget the killer has contacted you a few times, too. You could be on his hit list.'

'Don't worry, next time he rings, I'll give him your number.' She smiled and walked away.

'Ma'am, I've found an address book in the bedside table,' Scott said, entering the room. 'It's got the mobile number of an Andy Reaney in it.'

'Jesus,' Matilda said under her breath. She hated making this kind of phone call. 'Give it to me,' she said, taking out her own mobile from somewhere beneath her white suit.

***

'Is this Andy Reaney?' Matilda asked. She was in the kitchen of the three-bedroom house with the door closed, to give her as much privacy as possible. She could feel her mouth going dry already. Delivering the death message never got any easier.

'Speaking,' came the reply. There was heavy traffic in the background. Matilda guessed Andy was driving and (hopefully) using a hands-free device.

'Mr Reaney, my name is Detective Chief Inspector Matilda Darke from South Yorkshire Police. I'm afraid there has been an incident at your home. Is there any chance you could meet me there as soon as possible?'

'An incident? What kind of incident?' Andy's voice had

increased in volume and pitch as all kinds of scenarios ran through his mind. 'Is Katie there? Is she all right?'

'Mr Reaney, I don't want to have this conversation with you over the phone, especially as you're driving. How long do you think it would take you to get home?'

'I'm on my way now. I've just entered Sheffield. I'll be about twenty minutes or so. Can you just tell me what's going on?'

'I'd rather wait until you were here, Mr Reaney.'

'Shit,' Andy said.

***

'I'm guessing this is him,' Sian said as she looked through the living room window and saw a black Audi come charging up the road.

Matilda and her team had removed their forensic suits. The house was a mess of fingerprint powder, items had been taken out of drawers and frames removed from walls. It wasn't the same home Andy Reaney had left last night, and it would never feel like the same home again.

As soon as the Audi screeched to a stop, Andy jumped out. So did Danny Hanson.

'Shit,' Sian said. 'Steve, you're needed.'

PC Steve Harrison pulled the front door open and charged out. He surprised Andy, who stopped dead in his tracks. Steve grabbed Danny by the shoulder and pushed him away, ushering him back to his car. He was leaning down and whispering something into his ear. Matilda couldn't hear what but judging by the frightened look on the young reporter's face it was working. Steve may have been a tad heavy-handed, but she couldn't help but smile.

'Mr Reaney, I'm DS Sian Mills, would you like to come inside?'

The shock of seeing his home taken over by police and the realization that something bad had happened behind the front door suddenly hit him. Once he crossed the threshold, the truth would be revealed and his life, and the life of his children, would never be the same again. He stood stock still halfway up the garden path. His face deathly pale and his eyes wide. His breathing was erratic as Sian put her arm around him and gently coaxed him into the house.

Andy was a tall, solidly built man in his mid-thirties, but he looked older due to the shaved head and the greying stubble on his chin. The worry on his pale face didn't help either. He was wearing loose-fitting jeans and battered Converse trainers. His thick jacket was relatively new.

He could sense a change the second he stepped into the hallway. There was a smell he couldn't put his finger on. Items were missing or had been moved. It was like walking into a stranger's house.

In the living room, Matilda Darke stood waiting for him. She offered him a sympathetic smile that he didn't return. She told him to sit down but it didn't seem to register. His face was fixed in a horrified expression. Sian had to guide him to the sofa.

'Mr Reaney, I'm afraid I have some bad news,' Matilda began as she sat down on the armchair next to him.

That seemed to be the trigger. Tears fell from his eyes without warning. He knew what was coming.

'We found your wife dead this morning, Mr Reaney. We had to break in. She was hanging in the hallway.'

The effect of Matilda's words was evident by his collapse. It was as if his spine had been torn from his body as he slumped into the sofa with a sound Matilda had heard only once before – she had made a similar noise when her husband took his final breath.

'Hanging?' Andy managed to say through the tears. 'No. She wouldn't … she wouldn't … we're happy …'

'Mr Reaney, we don't believe Katie took her own life. We believe she was killed,' Matilda said slowly so Andy could take it all in.

It didn't work. Matilda's words made no sense to him at all.

There was a gentle knock on the living room door. It opened, and Scott popped his head through the small gap.

'I'm sorry to interrupt, ma'am,' he said quietly. 'We've found something. You really need to see this.'

Sian nodded for Matilda to go. She stood up and looked down at the wreck of a man whose life she had just ruined.

'Scott, I have never been more pleased to be interrupted in my life,' Matilda said with relief once she was out in the hallway. She leaned against the closed door and took a deep breath.

'What have you found?'

'It's upstairs.'

As they went upstairs, Matilda looked at the photographs on the wall of a young family enjoying life together. Grinning children and smiling parents – days out in the park, at the beach, celebrating Christmas. This was how life was meant to be. Why had someone felt the need to destroy it all?

Scott led Matilda into the master bedroom where Rory and Aaron were waiting. It was tastefully decorated in pastel colours. The large bed looked comfortable. The floor was polished with an expensive rug in the middle.

'There's a loose floorboard,' Aaron said. 'We prised it open and found this.'

Wearing latex gloves, Aaron handed Matilda a padded envelope. She fished some gloves out of her back pocket and struggled to put them on sweaty hands. Lifting the flap of the envelope, she pulled out a stack of papers and newspaper clippings.

'What is all this?' she asked, flicking through them.

'It's Katie Reaney. Her real name is Naomi Parish,' Aaron said.

'Remind me.'

'In 1998, when Katie – Naomi – was just eleven years old, she murdered one-year-old Alistair Macintosh.'

Chapter Thirty-Two

The briefing room was packed to capacity, and the atmosphere was heavy and sombre. A woman who had killed at the age of eleven had changed her name and identity to live a quiet and peaceful life below the radar. She had succeeded in never drawing attention to herself. She had a menial job and kept her social life to a minimum. Yet someone had found her. Someone had gone to great lengths to identify her, track her down, and execute her. This was an intelligent killer who would stop at nothing to make his chosen victims pay for their crimes. Suddenly, the game had been raised. Every person in the briefing room knew this killer was virtually unstoppable.

Matilda explained who, on the surface, Katie Reaney was. She then handed over to Sian to fill in the gaps on her past.

'Katie Reaney was born Naomi Parish in 1987. She lived in Hastings, in Kent, on the south coast. In 1998, when she was eleven years old, she was babysitting one-year-old Alistair Macintosh when she shook him to death.' Silence gripped the room, and Sian paused.

On the whiteboard was a photograph of a smiling Katie Reaney. Her husband had told them it had been taken on New Year's Eve last year. She was dressed up for a night out, freshly dyed blonde hair perfectly styled, make-up understated yet glamorous, and she smiled into the centre of the camera, showing off her dazzling white teeth. She looked happy, content with the world. Behind the sparkling eyes was the soul of a child killer. Had she managed to put her past behind her, forget all about her crime, or was she simply a very talented actress?

Sian continued. 'Her defence was that Alistair wouldn't stop crying, and she was trying to get him to go to sleep. However, in a statement from Alistair's mother, he wasn't a crying baby. He rarely made a noise and was a peaceful sleeper. He wasn't ill, didn't have a cold or anything, so there was no reason why he would have been crying to the extent Naomi said he was. The jury took less than one hour to find her guilty of murder.'

'What was she sentenced to?' Faith asked without looking up from her desk.

'She was sentenced to life in prison to serve a minimum of seven years. She was released in 2005 from a Young Offenders Institute in Birmingham and refused lifelong anonymity by the Home Office. Now, according to the paperwork found by Aaron in Katie's bedroom, she changed her name by deed poll in 2008 to Katie Simpson. She met Andy Reaney in 2010 and they married within the year, when she became Katie Reaney.'

'So there we have it,' Matilda said, standing up. 'Naomi Parish became Katie Simpson who became Katie Reaney. What we need to find out is who the hell knew?'

'Did she tell her husband any of this?'

'Andy isn't in a fit state to be fully interviewed at the moment,' Christian Brady said. 'He's told us the bare bones of their life together, and he hasn't mentioned anything about her past. He either doesn't know, or he's protecting her.'

'Christian, I want you and Sian to interview him when he's ready. If he *really* doesn't know, then you'll need to break it to him,' Matilda said.

'Is the husband a likely suspect?' Faith asked.

'No. He was in Ripon last night and didn't leave until after eight o'clock this morning,' Scott said flicking through his notebook. 'I've already called Andy's parents and they've confirmed this.'

'Thank you, Scott.'

'So, who is a suspect then?'

'Someone with a great deal of time on their hands,' Rory said. 'I've been online and there's no mention of Katie Reaney anywhere. She's not on Facebook, Twitter, Instagram or any of the other social networking sites.'

'Hardly surprising really, if she's wanting to live in the shadows,' Scott said.

'Naomi Parish is all over the Internet. There's articles about the court case and being sentenced, even when she was released. After that, nothing. There is no way Naomi Parish and Katie Reaney can be linked just by looking online,' Rory said.

'What about photographs of Naomi Parish? Can you see a resemblance between Naomi the child and Katie the adult?' Sian asked.

'No,' Rory answered. 'She was quite a chubby child, and she's got dark brown hair. Katie is slim with dyed blonde hair. It seems like she went to great lengths to avoid any connection to her former life.'

'So it's somebody with access to more sophisticated files,' Matilda said. 'Sian, throw us a Mars bar, will you?' Scott cleared his throat, and Matilda looked up at him. 'Actually, don't bother. I've got a high-energy protein bar in my desk.'

'Should we contact the parents of Alistair Macintosh?' Faith asked.

'I think so. Sian, can you deal with that?'

Faith rolled her eyes but quickly turned away when she saw Matilda had noticed.

'We need to know who was in Katie's life, who trusted her,' Christian said. 'What about that housebound neighbour, Debbie?'

'They've been friends since college,' Scott said. 'They were on the same night school course. Debbie missed most of her education due to being in hospital. She took A-levels at night school, as did Katie when she was released from prison.'

'Could Katie have confided in Debbie?'

'We didn't go into too many details about Katie's past, I didn't know myself then, but she just said Katie was a lovely, quiet woman who lived for her husband and children.'

'She's going to need interviewing again too. Right,' Matilda said going over to the whiteboards. 'The one connection two of our victims have is probation officers. Katie Reaney and Brian Appleby will both have had probation officers. I want them identified. I want their alibis for all the murders. Christian!'

'Leave it with me.'

Matilda ran her fingers through her hair; they came away feeling greasy. 'I want statements from neighbours, colleagues and family members. How close were Katie and Andy? Don't reveal Katie's past to anyone. This is where we have the upper hand over the press. The only people who know are us and the killer. I know we've found out the killer is giving information to Danny Hanson, but if I do find out anyone in here has been talking, I will hang you myself. Understand?'

She left the question unanswered and strode from the briefing room, slamming the door behind her.

On her way to the ACC's office for another meeting with Valerie, and James Dalziel, Matilda dug out her phone and searched for a number. She hoped it was still the right one. It rang and was still ringing when Matilda arrived at Valerie's office. Eventually it went to voicemail, but she decided against leaving a message. As much as she wanted to believe Ben Hales was innocent, she needed to know his movements for last night.

Chapter Thirty-Three

The meeting with Valerie and James was more succinct than previous ones. Valerie was concerned this was spiralling out of control, but James leapt to Matilda's defence. He said because Katie Reaney had kept herself under the radar, very few people would know who she really was. It improved the police's chances of catching the murderer.

This made Matilda smile, and she looked across at the psychologist, who smiled back. It seemed strange to be sitting so close to someone who looked like her dead husband. First, it was just the eyes, now it seemed to be more of him; the smile, the way he sat, held a pen, the warm feeling he gave Matilda every time she was in the same room as him. *What are you doing?* She hated the fact she was looking at another man and thinking such thoughts. She picked up her coffee cup from Valerie's desk and placed it firmly on the back of her hand. The burning sensation ran up her arm. She was punishing herself.

'Thank you,' Matilda said as she and James stood in the corridor outside Valerie's office. Fortunately, the meeting hadn't gone on for too long. 'For what you said in there.'

'My pleasure.'

It was almost seven o'clock and the station was quiet as the majority of staff had gone home for the day. They walked along the dark corridor in silence.

'It must be difficult having a case that runs on. I'm assuming most murders get solved fairly quickly.'

'The domestic ones can do. Luckily, cases like this are very few and far between. They do tend to consume you.'

'Not much free time for other things.'

'No.'

'Can I buy you a drink?'

Matilda stopped walking. 'Yes. Sure. I'd like that,' she smiled.

What the hell am I doing?

James Dalziel was at the bar waiting to be served. Sitting at a small table in the corner of All Bar One, Matilda felt anxious. The evening crowd in polyester jackets, sensible shoes, and lanyards around their necks were enjoying an after-work drink with colleagues to go over the events of the day. After the second or third, they began to loosen up, their body language relaxed and their talk moved away from the office to more private matters. The façade they kept up from nine until five was gone.

'Oh my God, if I'd been there I think I would have wet myself,' said one of the women. She leaned back and laughed, nudged the man sitting next to her and placed her hand on his knee to balance herself.

Were they a couple or just co-workers who were great friends? Matilda couldn't imagine herself being so comfortable with Christian Brady or Rory Fleming, as funny and as sweet as they were.

'Are you sure you don't want anything stronger?' James asked, placing an orange juice down in front of Matilda.

'No thanks. I don't drink on weekdays,' she lied.

'Very restrained of you. I always like a pint to round off a difficult day,' he said, taking a lingering sip of his lager. 'Lovely.'

'You don't deal with murders often?'

'I've consulted on a few cases, but I mostly teach psychology. This is a whole new ball game for me.'

'I'd like to say you get used to it, but I don't think people being murdered is something we should get used to.'

'So what drove you to murder?' James asked rather too loudly. The party at the next table turned to look at them, and Matilda almost choked on her drink. 'Shit! I don't mean what drove you to kill someone. I'm not saying you're a killer or anything. I meant … what I meant was …'

Jesus! He even blushes like James.

'It's OK. I know what you mean.' She smiled. She turned to the group sitting next to them. 'Don't worry, I'm not dangerous.' They gave nervous smiles and went back to their drinks, although they soon left. 'People fascinate me. I know not everyone in the world is a killer, but I'm interested in why people do what they do, why they behave in a particular way, what drives them to the extreme.'

'Depressing,' James said with a hint of a smile.

'It can be. It depends if you allow it to get to you.'

'Do you?'

'Sometimes.' Another lie. *Always.*

'How do you unwind?'

'Well right now, I'm training to run the Sheffield half-marathon. Me and Adele, her son and Scott are raising money for charity.'

'Oh wow, excellent. What's the charity?'

Oh God, I'm going to have to go through the whole story of James dying again. I don't want to cry in public.

'It's a cancer charity. My husband died from a brain tumour,' she quickly said.

'Oh yes, you said that he died around the time Carl Meagan went missing. I'm so sorry. That must have been a difficult time for you.'

'It was. What about you? Are you married?' The words almost

fell out of her mouth as she tried to change the subject of conversation.

'I was. My ex-wife is still in Scotland.'

'Any children?'

'Two,' he beamed. 'I see them as often as I can but it's not easy.'

'I can imagine. Why did you move to Sheffield?'

'The job came up. It was the right time, so I took it. I wish I'd waited for something closer to home, but … I didn't think I'd miss the girls as much as I do. What about you? Any children?'

'No,' Matilda replied quickly. She never wanted children. James hadn't either. However, now he was dead she wished they'd had one: a reminder of the man she loved. 'Will you re-marry?' she asked.

'I'm not sure. If someone special came along, maybe, but I'm not actively looking. What about you?'

Yes, what about me?

Matilda swallowed hard. Before she had met James, she would have said a determined no straight away. Why was she hesitating? Surely just because he looked like her husband didn't mean he would be a near-perfect match. That wasn't healthy, anyway.

Answer him, you stupid woman.

'No. I don't think so,' she eventually replied. She took a long drink of the acidic orange that tasted bitter on her tongue. Over the top of her glass she looked across the table at James, who smiled at her.

'Would you like something to eat?' he asked, leaning forward.

'Yes. I'd like that.'

It was almost midnight by the time the taxi pulled up outside Adele's house. Despite having to pass where James Dalziel lived to get to Adele's, he insisted on staying in the cab, so he knew she arrived home safely. She thanked him for a lovely evening, and genuinely meant it. She couldn't get out of the taxi fast enough though, to avoid any awkwardness over whether to kiss him or not. She watched as the cab drove away. James turned around and waved at her through the window. She smiled. She took her key out of her coat pocket and walked down the short path to the front door.

'Matilda.'

At the sound of her name being whispered she turned around quickly, but there was nobody there. She was sure someone had called out to her.

Across the road was a row of houses then a patch of green land with a few trees, branches swaying in the breeze. Was someone there, hiding behind the trees, watching her, tormenting her?

Plucking courage from somewhere, she put the key back in her pocket and headed for the road. The door behind her opened, bathing her in a soothing yellow glow.

'I thought I heard a car pull up. Forgot your key?' Adele said.

'What?' Matilda kept looking back at the trees. 'Erm … yes … no.'

'Come on, you're letting all the warmth out.'

Matilda entered the house and closed the door behind her, making sure all the locks were secure. She looked through the spyhole, waiting for some kind of movement. She had heard her name being called. There was definitely somebody out there watching her.

'I thought you'd have been in bed by now,' Matilda said to Adele, who was sitting in the living room in her dressing gown, a hardback open face down on the coffee table in front of her.

'I would have been but, when you sent me that text saying you were going out for dinner with the handsome psychologist, I couldn't wait until morning to get all the sexy details.' She grinned.

'There are no sexy details. And who said he was handsome?'

'Sian did.'

'Please don't tell me you've called her to ask about him.'

'No, I did not call her,' Adele said, looking down at the floor.

'You texted her though, didn't you?'

'Yes, sorry. I couldn't resist. Sian said he was gorgeous. She's going to try and get a photo of him tomorrow and send it to me. Or did you take a selfie with him tonight?'

Matilda turned and went into the kitchen. 'You're incorrigible, do you know that?' She switched the kettle on.

'I'm just interested,' Adele said, trotting in behind her. 'I think it's great you're out dating again.'

'I'm not dating him, Adele,' Matilda said, almost ratty. 'I just went for a meal, that's all.'

'But you're out there, that's the main thing. You're not wallowing at home like you have been doing lately. Matilda, come and sit down.'

Adele grabbed Matilda's arms and walked her to the breakfast table. They both sat.

Matilda felt her eyes filling. There was a lump in her throat.

'Matilda, I love you, you know I do. I loved James too. You were the perfect couple. Sometimes, sickeningly so.' She smiled. 'When James died I worried that you'd withdraw into yourself and wither away. To an extent, you have done, but now you're out there having meals with handsome men—'

'It's one man,' she interrupted.

'But it's a start. You've come a long way, Matilda, you should be proud of that.'

'I haven't come a long way at all.' Matilda slumped, a tear fell from her eye.

'Do you think you're betraying James by going out with another man?'

Matilda shook her head, wiped her eyes with the back of her sleeve. 'It's not that. Adele, he's the spitting image of James. You should see him, he could be his clone. I only agreed to go for a drink and have a meal with him because it would be like having one final dinner with my husband. Now, tell me that's an improvement on spending my evenings alone?'

'Oh, Matilda.' Adele stood up and put her arms around her, pulling her into a tight embrace. 'James would want you to move on. He'd want you to be happy.'

'I know he would, but I don't.'

'Don't what?'

'I don't want to be happy without James. If I can't have a future with him I don't want one at all,' she managed to say before the torrent of tears came.

Chapter Thirty-Four

'Mr Reaney, what can you tell us about your wife?'

Andy Reaney looked marginally healthier than yesterday when his entire world had come tumbling down around him. He was still pale and there were dried tear tracks on his face, but he was coherent and able to be questioned.

Sitting in the interview room was Sian and Christian, with Andy on the opposite side of the table. They all had a mug of tea and Sian had brought in a Blue Riband for each of them, not that anyone had taken one yet. Before they began, Andy told them the children were staying in Ripon for a few days longer with his parents until he found the courage to break the news about their mother. He had no idea how he was going to do it.

'Katie was a wonderful mum. She was warm, caring, loved her kids. She'd do anything for them. She'd do anything for anyone.' He smiled through his tears.

'She worked as a doctor's receptionist. Is that right?'

'Yes. She could have done anything she wanted to, she was very intelligent, but she wanted to be there for the kids.'

'Where did you and Katie meet?'

'It was years ago. I'm an electrician. I've got my own business.

I was just starting out when we met. She called me to give her a quote on some rewiring, and we just hit it off straight away. Why are you asking me about that? What's it got to do with anything? Do you think Katie was killed like those others in the newspaper? That she was hanged for something she's done?'

'Mr Reaney—' Christian began.

'No, wait a minute, she's dead. My Katie is dead. My kids have lost their mother. I'm not having you lot accusing her of doing something, just so it fits into what you're investigating. I read the papers. I know you've got dozens of unsolved murders on your books. You're not putting my Katie in with a load of scum just to improve your figures.' Andy was almost out of his chair. His face was flushed with anger.

'Mr Reaney, please, sit down,' Christian said calmly.

Andy looked at Christian's and Sian's blank faces before he retook his seat. He calmed himself with a few deep breaths.

'Mr Reaney, we have some information about your wife that may come as a surprise,' Sian said. 'It's not going to be easy to hear, I'm afraid.'

From inside the cardboard file in front of her, Sian pulled out several evidence bags that contained the information found under the floorboards in Katie and Andy's bedroom.

'Do you know what this is?' Sian asked, laying the first exhibit in front of him.

'No,' he said, barely looking.

'It's a deed poll from a solicitor's office in Birmingham dated 2008. It states that a Naomi Parish legally changed her name to Katie Simpson.'

Andy shrugged. 'OK. So what? She changed her name. Loads of people do that. It doesn't mean anything.'

'Could you tell me who the girl in this photograph is, please?' Sian asked, taking out a newspaper clipping from the folder.

Andy read the headline, 'CHILD KILLER FREED', then looked at the photo. Tears were forming in his eyes once again.

'I don't know,' he said quietly, his emotions making lies of his words.

'Take a good look, Mr Reaney,' Sian said. 'It's Katie, isn't it?'

'No,' he said, swallowing hard. 'No. It can't be.'

'Mr Reaney.' Sian sighed. 'I hate to say this, but when Katie was eleven, she was called Naomi Parish. She shook a one-year-old baby to death and served seven years in a youth prison. When she was released, she changed her name to Katie Simpson.'

'No. You've got it all wrong. This is someone else.'

'We found this under floorboards in your bedroom, Mr Reaney.'

He looked up from the newspaper clipping. His eyes were red. Tears were streaming down his face. Sian handed him a tissue, and he blew his nose loudly.

'But we've got kids,' he struggled to say. 'Why would she have kids if she'd …' he pointed to the newspaper cutting.

'We can only guess by the evidence we have, but I think Katie was genuinely sorry for what she had done in the past.'

Andy nodded. 'She loved Jenson and Bobbi. She loved them more than me, more than herself. She would never, ever, hurt them. I know it. She was a good woman. Oh God! What am I going to tell my mum and dad? This is going to kill them,' he said as he collapsed into himself. His cries were loud and echoed around the room.

'I've just got off the phone to Forensics,' Sian said as she followed Matilda into her small office. 'There are no foreign prints anywhere in the Reaney house, and the only fingerprints on the documents found under the floorboards belong to Katie Reaney.'

'I can't say I'm surprised,' Matilda said, taking off her coat and slumping into her chair with a heavy sigh. 'Where is everybody?' she asked looking out into the almost empty incident room.

'It's lunchtime,' Sian said.

'Is it?' Matilda's mobile started ringing.

'Do you want to get that?'

She looked at the screen. She didn't recognize the number. 'No. They'll leave a message.'

'Well, Aaron's popped home to see Katrina, and Scott and Rory are viewing a flat on the Riverside Exchange.'

'The original odd couple.' Matilda smiled.

'Absolutely. Now, Andy Reaney gave us his wife's mobile number. I've got onto EE and they're going to email across details of the phone records. We're trying to triangulate it now to see where it was last switched on.'

'OK. Keep me updated.'

'Will do. We've also had a call from a Mrs Pickering. She lives next door to the Reaneys, and she said she heard someone in the back garden last night. I've sent Faith round to interview her.'

'What about Alistair Macintosh's parents?'

'I've called twice this morning but had no reply. I'm guessing they're at work. If I don't get any joy later, I'll contact local police and ask someone to pop round.'

'You don't need me here at all, do you?' Matilda asked with a smile.

'Not really. I'm sure Christian and I could cope without you. We could share your massive salary.' She grinned.

Matilda laughed as her mobile started to ring again. 'Very funny, Sian. Hello, DCI Darke,' she said into the phone as Sian left the office, closing the door behind her.

'Katie Reaney was quite the find.' It was the killer.

'What?' Matilda asked.

'Who knew there were so many sinful people living in Sheffield? What sins do you need to atone for, Matilda?'

She listened intently. According to James Dalziel, the killer knew her, that must mean she knew him. She didn't recognize the voice, but he could have been using voice distortion software.

'Who are you?'

'Who am I?' The caller laughed. 'Dig a little deeper, Matilda. You already know who I am.'

'Ben?' she asked quietly, but the caller had already hung up.

Chapter Thirty-Five

Matilda drove as fast as she could through rush-hour traffic. She was soon out of the city centre and heading for Ben Hales's home. Unfortunately, the lights were against her and she had to stop at almost every set. She stared impatiently, drumming her fingers on the steering wheel. The second they changed to amber, she slammed her foot down and broke the speed limit.

The banging on the door was loud enough to wake the dead. Neighbours came to their windows to see who was making such a racket.

'Ben, open the door. Come on, I know you're in there,' Matilda called out as she slammed a gloved fist onto the dirty front door.

'What the hell do you think you're doing?' An elderly woman shouted from next door.

Matilda glanced up. 'I'm looking for Ben Hales.'

'Well he's obviously not in if he's not answering the door.'

'He is in. I know he is,' she said, looking back at Ben's house. She could almost feel him at the other side of the front door, sneering at her. She thumped again, louder.

'Will you stop that?' the old woman shouted. 'I've got a husband in here with Alzheimer's. He's trying to get some rest. He doesn't need you banging the door down.'

Matilda ignored her. She went over to the window of the living room and tried to see inside. She squinted and made a visor out of her hands to get a better view. The television was off, but the place was still a mess.

'I'm ringing the police,' the woman said.

'I am the bloody police,' Matilda called out.

'Yes. And I'm Meryl Streep,' she replied with sarcasm.

Matilda dug in her jacket pocket for her warrant card. 'DCI Matilda Darke. South Yorkshire Police.'

'Oh. You're Matilda Darke are you?' She folded her arms. 'He's told me all about you.'

'I'm sure he has.'

'I don't know how you've got the nerve coming round here, pestering him like this. Why don't you leave the poor man alone? Haven't you done enough already?'

'Me pestering him? That's rich! I don't know what kind of lies he's been telling you—'

The door slammed closed leaving Matilda talking to herself.

She stepped back and looked up at the house. There were no curtains drawn and no lights on. The house seemed abandoned, but she couldn't help feeling Ben was in there, and had heard every word.

'I didn't expect you home just yet,' Adele walked into her kitchen to find Matilda sitting at the breakfast table. There was an open bottle of wine in front of her and an empty glass. 'Is everything all right?' she asked, her eyes on the glass and not Matilda.

Matilda rolled her eyes. 'I've had one drink.'

'I just … I didn't think you drank alone.'

'I don't. Usually. But you have wine here.'

'What's happened?'

'Nothing. Why?'

Adele sat down opposite her. 'You seem tense. Like you're going to explode at any moment.'

Matilda took a deep breath. 'I think I know who the killer is.'

'Well that's great – isn't it?' Adele asked, slightly confused.

'Not really.'

'I don't follow.'

Matilda bit the inside of her cheek, stalling for time, trying to find the courage to voice her views. Unfortunately, once they were out in the open she couldn't take them back. 'I think it might be Ben.'

'Ben? Who's Ben?'

'Ben. Ben Hales. Former Detective Inspector Ben Hales.'

'What? Seriously?'

Adele looked down at the empty glass then back up at Matilda again.

She either thinks I'm pissed or I've finally gone mad.

'I know it sounds, you know, a bit far-fetched, but, the phone calls. It's exactly the kind of thing he'd do – taunt me.'

'Oh God,' Adele sighed. 'Matilda, are you sure about this?'

'Yes. Well, no, but. Shit! I don't know.' She pushed the glass away.

'OK. Matilda, you have three dead bodies. Do you honestly think Ben Hales is capable of killing three people?'

Matilda looked at her hands and saw they were shaking – fear, dread, anxiety? She hid them under the table. 'The killer is somebody who knows about the victim's past, knows information that could only be found by someone who knows where to look. How else could the killer have found Brian Appleby and who he really was? And Katie Reaney. There is nothing online or anywhere to give away her real identity.'

'Matilda, Ben doesn't work on the force anymore. He hasn't done for a long time. How could he get that kind of information?'

Adele tried to be as sympathetic as possible to Matilda, but it was sounding patronizing and placatory.

'There are ways,' Matilda said, less convinced than she had been a few minutes ago.

'After what he did, I doubt he'd have someone on the inside helping him.'

'You don't know how convincing, how manipulative, he can be. His father-in-law used to be a chief constable. He could still have connections.'

'Have you spoken to anyone else about this?'

'No. Not yet.'

'OK. You need to be really convinced about what you're saying before you take it to Valerie.'

'I know that,' she almost snapped. 'Why do you think I've had a drink?'

'Look, run through everything with me and we'll see what fits and what doesn't.'

Matilda slumped in her seat. She had been through it all dozens of times in her head. Would it make sense saying it out loud? 'No. Not tonight. I'm tired. I think I'm going to go back home.'

'Really?'

'Yes. I've overstayed my welcome.'

'Don't be silly, of course you haven't,' Adele scoffed.

'I have. If I stay here any longer, then I won't go home at all.'

'Why don't we go for a run? That'll clear your head. We could join Chris and Scott in the park.'

'What? Are they out running again? Jesus, they're going to leave us for dead on race day.'

Matilda had now been staying at Adele's for a couple of weeks. However, she had only packed for a maximum of three days. Instead of returning back to the house to collect a few more pairs of knickers or clothes for work, she either quickly washed through what she had or went out to buy more items. There was a fear stopping her from going home.

Home. Home is where the heart is, apparently. Her heart was wherever James Darke was, and he certainly wasn't at home right now. She was only desperate to go back there because her memories were there. She needed to feel James around her, his clothes, his belongings, his smell. That had faded months ago, but if she concentrated hard, she could still smell him, or so she thought.

It was only nine o'clock yet there was a silence surrounding her as she drove through the dark and gloomy streets of Sheffield. Where was the traffic? Where were the people who couldn't be bothered to cook so had eaten out?

She turned left into her road and there was her house up ahead. It looked cold and lonely, not inviting at all. It wasn't welcoming her home. It wasn't beckoning her. She dug in the glove box for the tiny garage remote and pressed the button. Slowly, the door began to lift, and Matilda drove inside.

The door closed behind her. She turned off the engine and was plunged into darkness.

Carefully, Matilda made her way around her cooling car to the connecting door to the house. She opened it and stepped inside. It was cold. It was freezing cold. It was also quiet. Why hadn't the alarm sounded? Feeling along the wall next to the door, she found the light switch. She flicked it on, but nothing happened.

Shit.

Had there been a power cut? Matilda tried to remember if her neighbours' homes were in darkness, but she thought she saw a light on next door. Had the electricity been cut off?

She went back into the garage and, after walking around with her arms stretched out like a bewildered zombie, she found a torch. The fuse box was under the stairs.

Back into the house she pointed the torch to the ground, lighting up the mound of post at the front door, mostly brown envelopes, probably bills. There were a few items from Amazon, small enough to be posted through the letterbox. She walked around the other side of the staircase.

Matilda pointed the torch upwards and stopped in her tracks. It took a while for her brain to register what her eyes were seeing. It didn't make sense. It wasn't possible, surely. Then it sunk in. She was looking at the back of a dead man hanging by the neck from her bannister.

Chapter Thirty-Six

WHO IS KILLING THE KILLERS?
By Danny Hanson

A third person has been murdered as a serial killer continues his reign of terror in Sheffield.

Katie Reaney, 29, a mum of two, was found hanging in her home in a quiet cul-de-sac in Greenhill. Her husband and children were not there at the time. Police believe this first female victim is the work of the Hangman, who murdered Brian Appleby and Joe Lacey in the past month.

In a chilling twist, the killer has been contacting *The Star* and informing us of his actions in order to gain maximum publicity for his crimes. In his last call, he revealed Katie Reaney was really Naomi Parish, who, at the age of eleven, was convicted of murdering one-year-old Alistair Macintosh while she was babysitting. Upon release, she changed her name hoping to avoid detection.

According to South Yorkshire Police sources, the killer is very forensically aware and has left no trace of himself at any of the crime scenes.

Detective Chief Inspector Matilda Darke is leading the inquiry, which, so far, hasn't identified any viable suspects.

Selina Bridger, sister-in-law of Joe Lacey, who lives three doors away from the Laceys, said yesterday: 'This is unbelievable. Joe paid for his crime years ago. He was a good man who loved his family. He just got on with his life, went to work, came home, and that's it. The family don't deserve any of this.'

Debbie Ashmore, a close friend of Katie Reaney said: 'Katie was a loving and private person. She didn't confide in me about what she had done as a child, but if she had, it would not have altered the way I thought of her. She was a good friend to me. She must have been genuinely sorry and wanted to live as peaceful a life as possible. I am so incredibly sad.'

Assistant Chief Constable Valerie Masterson said in a statement: 'What is happening in Sheffield at the moment is, of course, very worrying. However, I have every faith in my officers. I advise the people of Sheffield to go about their business as usual, but to be more vigilant. Not all crimes can be solved overnight, but we will catch this killer. I can assure you of that.'

Despite ACC Masterson's statement, confidence in the police from the public is at an all-time low. See the results in our online poll on page six.

Danny Hanson read his handiwork once again. He had a copy of the newspaper on his bed and his laptop open on *The Star* website. His byline had appeared more than ever before in the newspaper since these murders began, but he still felt a tingle when he saw it. This was why he had become a journalist.

He glanced down at his fingers, poised over the keyboard to write an email, and noticed they were shaking. A dark thought came to mind; would this latest front-page story lead to another attack? He closed the laptop and leaned back on his bed. He wasn't strong enough for this level of intensity. Not yet.

At only twenty-four years old, Danny had originally moved from Bristol to Sheffield to study at Sheffield Hallam University. He'd loved the city straight away. From the eyesore of Park Hill flats overlooking the train station and dominating the Sheffield skyline to the 'kettle drums' of the student union, and the locally loathed but strangely bewitching Meadowhall (aptly nicknamed Meadowhell). He had fallen in love with the fish cake you could only get in Sheffield and he liberally poured Henderson's Relish on everything. Sheffield was his new home. He had no desire to leave.

Fortunately, *The Star* were looking for new reporters just as he was qualifying. He didn't even have to interview for the job. That's how impressed they were with his work.

Danny had spent the first six months as a fully paid reporter, covering the courts and minor stories throughout the steel city. It had been a learning curve, not very interesting, but he was improving his skills and learning from the more experienced journalists. He found the courts fascinating and often relished sitting in on a trial at Sheffield Crown Court. He made detailed notes, not just on the case, but on procedure. Who was who? What role did they play? How were witnesses called? One day, with this bank of information, he would put it to good use, he'd write a book, a great courtroom thriller to rival John Grisham.

Until now, journalism had seemed like an adventure. He popped into people's lives, interviewed them, used his soft West Country accent and smiling eyes to charm them into revealing everything. Then he'd write it up and forget about them, move on to the next story.

The current spate of murders in the steel city had changed all that. At first, it was a thrill, there was a serial killer in Sheffield. It was unheard of. It was unbelievable. It was brilliant. When the killer first made contact, it was a wet dream come true. Now, it wasn't as much fun as it was frightening.

Sitting in the attic room, cross-legged on his bed, Danny looked out of the Velux window at the darkened sky. The black nothingness that stretched on forever seemed to be pushing down on him, squeezing him, trapping him. Danny was worried. If the killer was calling him, feeding him information, was he also watching him? He'd lured him to Weston Park. Had he followed him home? Did he know his every move, and if so, was he a potential victim?

Danny's job wasn't just to get the best story possible, it was to uncover information nobody else could; that included finding the identity of the killer, even before the police did. It would be a front-page splash to go down in history. However, what price would Danny have to pay to get that story?

His iPhone started to ring. He looked at the display, but the caller had withheld their ID. It was the killer. It had to be. For the first time, Danny didn't want to know what he had to say. He let the phone continue ringing until the voicemail kicked in. He waited in silence, but there was no notification of a new message. He breathed a sigh of relief.

Jumping off the bed, he went over to the door and locked it. He pushed a heavy cardboard box full of books in front of the door as extra security.

Suddenly, being a journalist wasn't as much fun as it used to be.

It was unusual for George Appleby to arrive home from university to an empty house, but since his father's identity had been revealed, he found he was seeing less and less of his housemates. His so-called friends had stopped texting, and he was losing virtual followers on Facebook and Twitter on a daily basis. Anyone would think *he* was the paedophile, not his father.

He opened the fridge in the shared kitchen and took a bottle of lager from his shelf. He opened it and drank half in a single swig. Just what he needed after a day of lingering glances from fellow students and voices dropping whenever he was near.

He slumped down in the sofa and rested his feet on the coffee table with a heavy thud. There was a note there he hadn't seen earlier. It was in a sealed envelope with his name written in block capitals on the front. Frowning, he picked it up and opened it. He recognized the handwriting straight away: it was Sophie, one of his housemates. She was often leaving people notes. 'Please wash up your dishes, don't leave them in the sink'; 'Please tidy the bathroom after you've had a shower'; 'Please do not use my toothpaste.' He wondered what villainous act he had committed this time.

George,

We've had a house meeting and we wondered if you would consider moving out. We know you haven't done anything wrong, but some of us have started receiving threats at university and Cassie's boyfriend has broken up with her. We've supported you at uni, but it's affecting our lives too. There's no rush, but if you could consider how we're feeling in all of this, we'd really appreciate it.

Sophie, Cassie and Anil.

So much for solidarity. So much for a student union where everyone was in this together. George screwed up the note and threw it to the other side of the room. He finished his beer and lobbed the bottle towards the note. Surprisingly, the bottle didn't break. He needed another drink.

Chapter Thirty-Seven

Matilda stared at the hanging figure. Black shoes. Black trousers. White shirt. Dark hair. Hair. She could see his hair. There was no pillowcase covering his head. Why? Forget why. Who? She wanted to know who it was, who the hanging dead man was in her hallway, but the body had its back to her and was blocking her from walking around to see the face.

Matilda stopped breathing. With a hand clamped to her mouth and the other brandishing the torch, she slowly made her way along the tiled floor. As she came to the hanging figure she pointed the torch up to the head. It was blue and bruised. This was not a fresh body. There was a rancid, rotting smell that assaulted her nostrils. She'd had a hint of something when she first came in but put it down to fruit left in the bowl to rot. She could see the tongue protruding from the mouth but nothing else. With the torch directly pointed at his face it was too bright to make out any features, off to one side and it was too dark to see. She needed to be standing right in front of him.

With her back pressed firmly against the wall, Matilda edged herself slowly around the hanging corpse. The legs brushed against her cheek as she turned to one side. She felt the cold material of the trousers. She could smell the contents of the released bowels.

She looked down and saw a pool of brown liquid on the floor. She stopped moving. She couldn't go any further.

Matilda closed her eyes and took a deep breath. This was a nightmare. This couldn't be happening. This was hers and James's home. James had built it from the foundations up for them to be together in, to grow old together in. It should be a place of comfort, sanctuary. It was already a house of sadness following James's early death, now this.

Matilda braced herself.

'Sir Robert Walpole,' she whispered. 'Spencer Compton, Henry Pelham, Thomas Pelham-Holles, William Cavendish.'

Her anxiety levels were through the roof. She could feel her legs shaking as fear coursed through her veins and chilled her to the bone.

'Thomas Pelham-Holles, John Stuart, George Grenville, Charles Wentworth, William Pitt the Elder.'

Matilda opened her eyes.

She edged further along the hallway; the sound of her body scraping on the wall echoed through the empty house. She pointed the torch up, not directly into the dead man's face, but to one side.

'Oh my God,' Matilda said, her voice shaking. It was all she could say before the torrent of vomit exploded from her mouth.

Fear quickly turned to panic. Matilda pushed past the corpse, heard it banging against the wall, and scrambled with the front door but it wouldn't open. Her palms were sweating, and she kept losing her grip on the handle. She dug in her jacket pocket for her keys, fumbled with the lock and dragged the door open. It stuck on one of the boxes from Amazon. She yanked hard, but it still wouldn't open. She kicked the parcel hard to the other side of the hallway and almost fell out of her house into the cold night air. She took deep breaths. She felt dizzy and dropped to the ground.

With shaking fingers, Matilda grabbed for her iPhone. The

screen wouldn't unlock as she couldn't control her hands. She wrongly entered the passcode twice but got it on the third try. She selected Adele's number and pressed the call button. It seemed to take an age for the call to be answered.

'Matilda, changed your mind about the run?' Adele asked in her usual sing-song voice.

'Adele, you've got to come over quick,' she gasped.

'Jesus Matilda, what's happened?'

'It's Ben,' she gasped. 'It's Ben. Hales. Ben Hales.'

'Oh my God. Matilda, what's he done?'

'He's dead. He's dead. He's in my hallway and he's dead.'

'What? Shit. Where are you?'

'I'm outside. Adele, he's hanging in my fucking hallway. He's hanging.'

Matilda was barely audible. She was struggling to control her emotions. She looked up and saw an elderly man she vaguely recognized as a neighbour walking his labradoodle on a lead. He glared at her with a confused face. He quickly turned away, obviously not wanting to get involved in someone else's drama, and crossed over the road.

'Matilda, stay where you are. I'll be right over.'

'Adele … Adele …' The call had ended.

Matilda looked up into the black sky, opened her mouth and released the loudest and longest scream she could manage, until her body felt drained of energy and she collapsed into a heap on the cold concrete.

Chapter Thirty-Eight

Nobody could believe what they were seeing. The message from their eyes didn't seem to be connecting with their brain. It made no sense at all.

ACC Valerie Masterson, DI Christian Brady, DSs Sian Mills and Aaron Connolly and DCs Rory Fleming, Scott Andrews and Faith Easter all stood in Matilda Darke's hallway and looked up at the lifeless body of former DI Ben Hales. Their faces were blank in disbelief.

'Where's Adele?' Valerie asked, breaking the silence, but not breaking eye contact with the body.

Sian had to swallow before she answered. Her mouth had dried up. 'She's with Matilda in her car.'

'Get her in here. This needs processing. Now.'

'Yes, ma'am,' Sian said quietly. She couldn't leave the house fast enough. She ran up the drive to where Adele had haphazardly parked when she arrived and pulled open the door.

Adele was sitting in the back with her best friend. There was a red cellular blanket wrapped around Matilda, who was shivering. She looked younger, yet her eyes darted from left to right and she seemed to be in a state of shock.

'Adele, Valerie wants you to …' she tailed off.

'OK.'

'I'll stay with Matilda.'

'Thanks.'

They swapped places. Adele grabbed her bag from the boot and made her way down the drive.

'How's the boss?' Rory asked Adele as soon as she stepped into the house.

'I don't know. She hasn't said a word since I got here.'

'An ambulance is on its way,' Valerie said. 'She's probably in shock.'

'I think that's an understatement,' Scott said.

'Adele, I want you to tell me if Ben has been murdered or if he's done this to himself,' Valerie said, her voice returning to something like her normal authoritative tone.

'Sure.'

'Christian, you're in charge. Organize a house-to-house, someone must have seen something.'

'Will do.'

'Is everyone all right?'

'No,' Faith said before turning away and running out of the house.

'OK. I think we should probably take a step back. We've all had a shock. Adele, if you could make a start on the crime scene. I'll get a forensics team out. Christian, I think it would be best if we started the investigation in the morning.'

'Sure. Come on,' he said to the rest of the team, who were all still fixed on their former colleague's dead body.

Christian ushered them out of the house. They slowly walked up the driveway to their waiting cars. Their footfalls were heavy as they had to drag themselves away. In turn, they all looked into Adele's car at a distraught Matilda being comforted by Sian. It would take more than Sian's motherly nature and her bottomless snack drawer to bring Matilda back from whatever state of flux she was currently residing in.

By the time Adele Kean and Lucy Dauman had finished their preliminary investigations, the team had gone home. Only Valerie and Sian remained. Medics had come for Matilda, shone a light in her unresponsive eyes, then patiently transported her to the ambulance, all under the watchful gaze of her nosey neighbours.

'Ben Hales wasn't murdered,' Adele said to them both.

Ben had been cut down and zipped up in a body bag on the cold tiled floor of Matilda's hallway.

'How do you know?' Sian asked.

'Unlike the previous three victims, there is no sign of a struggle. There are no broken fingernails, no skin samples, no blood under his nails, nothing. There is no pillowcase over the head and no evidence he was drugged. Though, obviously I'll have to send a blood sample off for analysis to make doubly certain. However, this looks like a case of suicide by hanging.'

'You're sure?' Valerie asked.

'Almost one hundred per cent.'

'But it makes no sense,' Sian began. 'Why would he kill himself, and here, in Matilda's home?'

'Before I answer that,' Adele said. 'I think we're all going to need a drink.'

It was almost midnight by the time Valerie, Adele and Sian were sitting in the ACC's office back at the police station. For emergencies such as this, Valerie kept a bottle of whiskey and four glasses in the bottom drawer of her filing cabinet. She blew away the dust on three of the glasses, poured them all a good measure, then left the opened bottle on the table with instructions to help themselves.

Sian took a small sip and shivered. She hated spirits. She was a wine drinker, but after the shock of the evening, it would take a whole case of Prosecco to do what a glass of whiskey could do. She choked down a long gulp and felt herself begin to relax.

Adele drank anything that had a percentage mark on the label.

She had never tasted a whiskey this good, however. It was smooth, rich, and made her feel warm inside. The odour tickled her senses. She'd give everything she owned to dive into that bottle.

'So, Adele, what were you going to tell us?' Valerie asked, bringing Adele back from her reverie.

Adele filled them in on the conversation she'd had with Matilda earlier in the evening. Matilda thought Ben Hales had killed three people within the last month. Valerie scoffed at the idea straight away, though Sian looked like she was seriously contemplating it.

'The only snag in the theory,' Adele concluded, 'is that Ben Hales has been dead for several days, whereas Katie Reaney has only been dead for one.'

'How do you know Ben's been dead for days?' Sian asked.

'Rigor mortis had been and gone. He was flaccid and cold. There's not a chance he could have killed Katie Reaney, which means he didn't kill the others.'

'But why take his own life now and in Matilda's house?' Valerie asked.

Sian shrugged. 'He's always blamed Matilda for his lack of promotion. Remember when the MIT was first introduced? He said the only reason Matilda was given the job was because she was a woman. When she came back from her time off after James died, he completely fell to pieces. Again, from his point of view, it was all Matilda's fault.'

'So, he kills himself and does it in Matilda's house because he knows it will screw her up for years to come,' Valerie suggested.

'That's what I'd put my money on,' Adele agreed.

'That is …' Valerie struggled to find the words. 'That's seriously messed up.'

All three filled their glasses in turn as they contemplated what Ben Hales had turned into and the lengths he had gone to make Matilda's life a misery. They sat in silence, listening to the sound of the ticking clock on Valerie's desk and the distant hum of a police station continuing to work during the early hours. A siren faded into the distance; somewhere in the building, a phone rang. Life was continuing as normal.

'So where do we go from here?' Sian asked, taking another sip of the drink she hated the taste of but couldn't resist.

Valerie leaned back in her seat and pinched the bridge of her nose. 'To be perfectly honest with you Sian, I haven't the foggiest idea.'

Chapter Thirty-Nine

Valerie Masterson was facing a logistical nightmare. As much as she hated the term, there was no denying that a serial killer was on the streets of Sheffield. Her star player, DCI Matilda Darke, had been signed off by a doctor, and Valerie had nobody with Matilda's level of experience to take her place.

Since the death of Katie Reaney had hit the local press, the nationals had picked up on it. A female victim was more palatable for the front pages. It added a level of sexiness. A killer ridding the world of a paedophile was, in the eyes of the public, doing everyone a favour. Although Katie Reaney was a murderer, she was a woman and she was attractive – two unique selling points to the red tops. It wasn't even nine o'clock yet and already Valerie had been asked for comments from *The Sun*, *The Mirror*, *The Star* and the *Daily Mail*. As a *Guardian* reader, Valerie had taken pleasure in telling them all to politely piss off.

'You wanted to see me, ma'am?' Christian asked, poking his head around Valerie's already open door.

'Yes. DI Brady, please, come in. Coffee?'

'No thanks, ma'am, I've had several this morning.'

'Yes. I'm afraid I've exceeded my daily quota too,' she said, rubbing her head to try and soothe the hangover. 'Have a seat. How are you feeling after last night?'

Christian sat down and took a deep breath. He looked tired. 'I'm OK.' His reply was strong and convincing. Maybe he was built of sterner stuff than she realized.

'Christian, DCI Darke has been signed off work for a few weeks, which, I'm sure you'll agree, is understandable.'

'Of course.'

'However, that does leave us in a bit of a jam. I could have a DCI drafted in, but this current case would take a great deal of time for someone to get brought up to speed on. You know the case, you know the victims and the team. Are you prepared to step up to the plate as acting DCI?'

Christian's eyes widened with excitement. 'Erm … yes, absolutely. If you think I'm capable.'

'I wouldn't have asked if I didn't think you were up to the task.' That wasn't technically true. Valerie had very few options open to her.

'I won't let you down,' he beamed.

'You can have Sian as acting-DI. I want you to keep me informed on a regular basis and anything you need, just ask. Don't be afraid to knock on my door.'

'I won't. I promise. Thank you,' he said trying, but failing, not to look absolutely thrilled at the opportunity. 'I'll get straight to it then.' He practically jumped out of his seat and headed for the door with a spring in his step.

Valerie guessed he would text his wife the good news before he reached the end of the corridor. She hoped, with fingers firmly crossed, she had made the right decision.

Matilda had spent Saturday night and the whole of Sunday in hospital under sedation. After breakfast on Monday morning, once she had been seen by a doctor, Adele had arrived to take her back to her home. With Sian supervising, Adele had packed clothes and toiletries, added a few books and the wedding photo from the mantelpiece in the living room to the heavy suitcase.

'How is she?' Sian asked. They were standing in the hallway of the house, the front door open. Sian could see a blank-looking Matilda sitting in the front passenger seat of Adele's car.

'I've no idea,' Adele replied.

'Didn't she want to come in?'

'Would you?'

'Probably not. Do you need a hand?' she asked when she saw Adele struggle with the case.

'Please.'

They loaded it into the back of the car. Sian went to the front passenger window and told Matilda to call her any time she needed to chat, then headed for her own car to return to the station. Duty called.

As Adele drove away, she wondered if Matilda would ever be back living there. If she was Matilda, there would be a for sale sign in the front garden before the police had even finished dusting for prints.

'No arguments either. You're moving in with me and Chris for as long as possible,' Adele said from behind the wheel of her car. 'I don't want none of this "I've outstayed my welcome" crap. You just stay until you're ready. There's no rush.'

Staring out of the window, Matilda watched as Sheffield went by in a blur. The clouds were grey and hanging low over the steel city. People went about their business with long faces in heavy winter coats, dull greys and browns, not a single hint of brightness. Shop windows advertised huge discounts to make their sad winter sales seem healthier at the end of the month. Travel agents invited people to get away from the grim Northern winter for a couple of weeks of exotic sunshine, with up to seventy per cent off. Maybe that's what Matilda needed – a break from reality. She had never really been a beach person, but she could choose a city holiday. Apparently, Prague was beautiful. James had often talked about it. He'd been several times before they met. Maybe she could go now. But who with? Matilda couldn't even eat in a restaurant on her own without feeling sad and pathetic; how would she feel in a foreign country walking around with a guide book, talking to herself?

'Why did he do it, Adele?' Matilda eventually asked, turning away from the depressing view.

'Sorry?'

'Ben. Why did he kill himself?'

'He obviously thought his life wasn't worth living anymore.'

'But why did he have to do it in my house? Did he really hate me that much?'

Adele shook her head.

Matilda continued to look at Adele until she realized her question was to remain unanswered. She went back to looking out of the window at Sheffield's dreary landscape.

The afternoon dragged on. Adele had taken the morning off to collect Matilda from the hospital but, at lunchtime, she had left Matilda to her own devices and returned to perform the post-mortem on Ben Hales.

Matilda was alone. At the best of times it was not good for Matilda to be allowed to sit down with her thoughts, as they invariably turned to James, which led her on to the disappearance of Carl Meagan. She tried to shake them out of her head.

Matilda turned the television on and flicked through the hundreds of channels. There was nothing worth watching in the afternoons; repeats of old sitcoms and house-hunting shows. Maybe she could apply to go on one of those. There was no way she could live back in her dream house. The dream had been shattered.

Her phone rang. She looked at the display. The caller was unknown, so she didn't answer. The phone had been ringing most of the day. Even when she knew the identity of the caller, she didn't answer. Sian had sent several texts to see how she was, if she needed anything, someone to talk to. Matilda hadn't replied. Rory had sent a text with a piece of gossip – Faith Easter had been spotted kissing PC Steve Harrison in the corridor. He hadn't had it confirmed yet, but he'd get back to her the minute he had solid evidence.

Matilda sank into the seat and smiled. She was pleased Faith seemed to have found someone. She didn't know much about the DC's private life, but she had heard from Sian that she'd had a run of bad luck with previous boyfriends. She hoped Faith was happy.

The smile faded. Happy? She didn't even know what that word meant anymore.

Acting DCI Christian Brady had set Aaron the unenviable task of informing Ben Hales's estranged wife of her husband's death. With Faith in tow, they gained access to Ben's home and set about trying to find contact details for Sara Hales.

'It smells,' Faith said upon entering. 'Jesus, look at the state of the place.'

They stood in the doorway of the living room and took in their surroundings. Mouldy plates and coffee cups, squashed empty lager cans, empty vodka bottles. This was not the home of the Ben Hales they knew. It was more like a squat.

'This is incredibly sad,' Faith said as she stepped carefully through the debris. She went over to the window and pulled open the curtains, letting in a flood of natural light. She turned back to the pathetic scene of loneliness behind her. 'I think I prefer it with the curtains closed.'

'There are a couple of letters here,' Aaron said, holding up some envelopes. He scanned the envelopes. One to his wife and daughters, and one to Matilda.

'Oh God. Should we open them?'

'No. They're not for us. We need to find his mobile or an address book or something.'

They both set about opening drawers and rifling among newspapers and books.

'I know what Ben did was wrong when he was a DI, but he was good to me,' Faith said as she looked at an old family photograph of Ben, his now ex-wife, and two daughters. 'He gave me an opportunity in the Murder Investigation Team. I mean, I know I messed up, a specialized unit isn't for me, but he gave me confidence. I never thanked him.'

Aaron smiled and went back to looking through the untidy drawers, most of them jammed with old bills and receipts.

'Aaron, do you ever worry about being on your own?'

'Sorry?'

'I know you've got Katrina, but, this job, it's not nine-to-five, is it? We work a lot of hours. Look at the DCI, there are some nights I'm sure she hasn't even gone home. Is that what it does to you? Are we all destined to end up like Matilda and Ben?'

'Faith, I think you're reading too much into this. Matilda and Ben are exceptional cases. Since her husband died, all Matilda has is work. Ben created his own downfall. Now, I'd like promotion. In a few years' time, I hope to be a DI, then who knows. I've also got Katrina, and a baby on the way. They'll keep me sane. I know they will.'

'What about my sanity?'

'I didn't know you had any.' He smiled.

'Oh, you're a very funny man,' Faith replied sarcastically.

After a moment, he resumed his search. He found a battered address book in the top drawer of a sideboard and flicked through it. Most of the pages were empty, evidence of a lack of people in Ben's life. He eventually found what he was looking for. 'Come on, I've found an address.'

Breaking the news to Sara Hales that her husband had died was easier than Aaron and Faith had guessed it would be. They knocked on the door and waited for a reply. Sara was wiping her hands on a towel when she greeted them. Straight away she knew they were police officers.

'You've come to tell me Ben's dead, haven't you?' It wasn't really a question.

Aaron and Faith looked at each other.

'I suppose you'd better come in. I don't intend having this conversation on the doorstep.'

She walked down the hall and left the front door open for the detectives to follow her. She was baking a cake in the kitchen and went back to mixing the ingredients. 'Let's hear it then,' she said, weighing out flour. 'He's either choked on his own vomit or killed himself. Which is it?' She methodically continued her task. 'If I don't get this cake in the oven it won't be ready. So come on, out with it.'

'We found him hanged last night.'

'Hanged?' She looked up. 'I'd have guessed a bottle of vodka and a hundred paracetamols. He's surprised me.' Not a glimmer of emotion in sight.

'We found this letter addressed to you and your daughters in his house.' Faith held out the white envelope.

Sara glanced up again then back down at her cake. 'Throw it on the side, I'll read it later.'

'When was the last time you saw your husband?' Aaron asked.

Sara frowned as she thought, still mixing the ingredients vigorously in the bowl. 'Between Christmas and New Year. My youngest still lives at home. He came round to bring her a present. Late, obviously.'

'How did he seem?'

'I couldn't tell if he was hungover or pissed.'

'How were things between the two of you?'

'The man threatened me with a knife. I'm hardly likely to be his best friend, am I? We were going through a drawn-out divorce and I couldn't stand the sight of him.'

'Mrs Hales—' Aaron began.

'Monroe. I've gone back to my maiden name.'

'Mrs Monroe—'

'Ms.'

'Sorry, Ms Monroe. We found your … Mr Hales, hanging in DCI Matilda Darke's house. It appears he'd broken in and killed himself there.'

Sara paused. 'Did Matilda find him?'

'Yes she did.'

Sara suddenly burst into laughter. 'Oh my God! That's the funniest thing I've heard in ages. I hope the bitch is in therapy for the rest of her life.'

Chapter Forty

'I've got something,' Rory said, slamming the phone down and jumping up.

'Well don't go spreading it around the office,' Sian said without looking up from her desk.

'No, listen. I've spoken to Elizabeth Ward. Katie Reaney's probation officer. A few months ago, her car was broken into and, among other things, her laptop was stolen. It had encrypted files of her clients on it.'

Suddenly everyone in the room was paying attention.

'Go on,' Sian said.

'That's it.'

Sian sighed. 'If the files are encrypted they won't be able to be opened by someone who doesn't have the password. They should be able to tell if they've been accessed, and where. Didn't you find that out?'

'Erm ...'

'That's a no, I'm guessing.'

'I said I'd pop round and see her later this afternoon.'

'Ask the right questions this time, Rory. Also, find out where the car was when it was broken into. There could still be a chance of CCTV footage.'

***

'You'd think in this day and age CCTV footage would be clearer than that,' Sian moaned as, an hour later, she and Rory were watching a grainy image on an iPad. 'My Stuart's colonoscopy was clearer.'

'Eww, you've seen your husband's colonoscopy?' Rory wrinkled his face in disgust.

'We have no secrets.'

The car park where the laptop was stolen no longer had the footage. However, as it was a reported crime, and the case was still active, the video was still in the hands of the police. It was obvious Elizabeth's Alfa Romeo had been the target. The hooded figure on the film entered the open-air car park, walked past several more expensive cars, then chose the 2004 Romeo. He hovered by the back of the car for a few minutes, head almost down at the ground, before swiftly smashing the back window, grabbing a briefcase, a coat, and a carrier bag of shopping, and running off into the distance.

'Replay it,' Sian said.

Rory started the short film again.

'What's in the carrier bag?' Sian asked.

'A few items she'd bought from Marks & Spencer. Apparently, she'd been to do a bit of shopping, then when she got back to her car, she realized she hadn't been to the bank. She was gone less than ten minutes.'

'Is there any chance we can zoom in on the bloke?'

'We can, but it won't be any clearer. Just a bigger blur.'

They both squinted at the robber.

'What do you think?' Sian asked.

'Well he's slim, and tall-ish. White, I'd say. I really don't know.'

'Me neither.'

'Any other cars broken into in the vicinity?' Sian said, stepping away from the iPad and rubbing her eyes.

'No. None. Well, not that day, anyway.'

'So Elizabeth Ward could have been followed and the robber struck when he found the best opportunity. Any joy on the encryption?'

'Unfortunately, yes. It turns out encryption was a polite way of saying she had a password on her laptop. As it was Ward1962, I don't think the killer would have taken long to access her files.'

'Bloody hell, should she be working as a probation officer?'

'I thought that too.'

Scott came bounding into the room with a grin on his face like an excitable puppy. 'Rory, Rory, grab your phone.'

'Why, what's up?'

'Just do it, come on.' He beckoned Rory over.

'Whatever it is you two are doing, I don't want to know about it,' Sian said, putting her arms up and walking away.

Rory ran to the door, snatching his phone from his desk. Scott stopped him as they reached the corridor and held him back.

'Just look around the corner, carefully,' he said, almost whispering.

Rory did as he was told. He held up his phone and took a picture. 'Brilliant. We've got it.'

'Got what?' Sian asked.

'I didn't think you were interested.'

'I'm not,' she replied, lips pursed.

'Yes, you are,' Rory teased.

'Oh, all right,' she relented, too easily.

'Look, it's Faith kissing Steve Harrison,' Rory said, showing her his phone.

'Aww, that's quite sweet.' Sian smiled.

'I'm texting this to the boss. It'll cheer her up.'

'You wouldn't have put them two together, would you?' Scott asked, taking a Snickers from Sian's snack drawer.

'Why not?' Sian asked.

'I don't mean it in a negative way. I just always thought Faith would go for a DI or something.'

Sian sat back in her chair. A small smile appeared on her lips. 'When I was a PC, well, we were called WPCs in those days, I went out with a DS for a while. It was the talk of the station. DS Clive Maybury. He was a handsome bloke, gorgeous eyes.' Suddenly remembering where she was she looked at Rory and Scott, who seemed to be hanging on her every word. She cleared her throat and went back to her work.

'You can't just leave it like that. What happened? Did you get married?' Rory asked.

'Yes, Rory, we got married. Only don't tell my husband and four kids,' she replied with heavy sarcasm. 'Of course we didn't get married, Rory. It was just a fling, eventually, it, you know, flung.'

'What happened to this DS Maybury?' Scott asked.

Sian's face dropped. 'He was gunned down in an armed robbery, just off the Wicker. Sawn-off shotgun. He got both barrels in the chest and was dead before he hit the ground.'

'Oh, Sian, I'm so sorry,' Scott said.

'We'd broken up long before then, but, well, it took a while to get over.'

A silence descended on the two DCs while they took in the tragic turn of Sian's story. She looked at them both; their faces were aimed at the floor. 'Anyway, there's nothing wrong with PC Harrison. He's a good copper. He's always the first to volunteer when it comes to going into schools to talk to young kids about the dangers of drugs and staying safe online. Better-looking than you two, as well.' Sian smiled.

'Fancy him yourself, do you?' Rory teased.

'I'm old enough to be his mother. Get on with your work.'

They went back to their desks as Faith came into the office. She had just passed Rory's desk when he stopped her.

'What?' she asked.

He stared intently at her face, as if studying her. 'There's something different about you.'

'Is there?' She frowned. 'In what way?'

'I don't know.' He squinted and leaned close to her. Suddenly, he sat back and smiled. 'No, nothing, it's OK. I thought you had a PC on your lips.'

Rory and Scott started laughing. Even Sian lowered her head to hide her smirk. Faith blushed.

'Who told you?' Faith asked.

'Nobody,' Rory replied with a huge grin on his face.

'It was Kesinka, wasn't it? She promised. Well, if you're looking for gossip, Rory, here's something for you – Kesinka has been dating Ranjeet since Christmas.'

'What?' Scott gasped.

'You're joking!' Sian called out.

As if her name had summoned her, Kesinka entered the room. She stopped when she saw all eyes turned to her. 'What's going on?' she asked, a look of worry on her face.

'You never mentioned you were going out with Ranjeet,' Scott said.

'You told!' she admonished, glaring directly at Faith. 'You said you wouldn't.'

'You told Rory about me and Steve.'

'No, I didn't.'

'Rory saw you in the corridor, Faith,' Sian said. 'Just now. He and Scott were behaving like schoolgirls.'

'Oh. I'm so sorry, Kes.'

'So we've got two romances going on,' Rory said, rubbing his hands together.

'Yes. All we need is for you and Scott to admit you're dating and everyone's hooked up and happy,' Faith said.

Kesinka laughed. 'I think we should get a hashtag trending on Twitter. What do you think Faith, #Scory or #Rorott?'

'Definitely #Scory. I'm on it,' she said, walking to her desk with a spring in her step.

Rory and Scott both blushed and turned away. Sian smiled. She loved working with this team so much.

Danny Hanson's mobile phone was ringing. As his hand's free still wasn't working, he pulled over before answering. The last thing he wanted was to be arrested for using his phone while driving. He guessed the police would like nothing better than to get him off the streets for a few hours, especially if Kate Stephenson ran the story she was planning about Matilda Darke.

The caller had withheld their number. Danny guessed it was the Hangman. He made sure the doors were locked and took a deep breath before answering.

'Hello,' he'd tried to sound confident and brash, but his shaking voice betrayed him.

'Another bit of news for you; a man has been found hanging in Matilda Darke's house. As much as I would love to claim this one, I'm afraid I can't. Shame.'

The call ended.

Danny sat in silence as he absorbed this latest piece of information. Was it correct? Why wasn't the killer taking the credit? Did that mean there was a copycat? A second killer on the loose? Blood seemed to be flowing on the streets of Sheffield. Danny kept wondering why the killer hadn't called one of the national newspapers and got instant fame. He shook his worries from his mind and dialled Kate's mobile. By the time she answered he had forgotten his doubts and was back in journalist mode again.

'Boss, it's happened again. I've got some front-page news for you.'

Chapter Forty-One

Sian had called in on Adele at the post-mortem suite as she was getting ready to leave at the end of the day. She told her about the letters Aaron and Faith had found in Ben's house.

'What do I do with Matilda's? Is she in a fit state to read it?' Sian asked.

'I don't know, Sian. She's hardly said two words to me since I picked her up from hospital this morning. I cannot believe Ben would have done that. I know he was a shit, but to … it beggars belief.'

'Why don't you take the letter, and give it to her when you think she's OK to read it?' Sian asked. She placed the envelope on Adele's desk. She was just happy to have it out of her possession.

Adele picked it up and looked at Ben's untidy scrawl. 'Matilda' had been scratched in thick biro. Real anger had gone into that seven-letter word. It wasn't written, it was etched. She placed it in her coat pocket. The responsibility was weighing her down already.

Adele arrived home to find Matilda exactly where she had left her – on the sofa, staring into space. Adele looked at her through the glass in the door. She needed to sound positive and happy around Matilda; hopefully it would rub off on her and she would be back to her normal self – whatever that was. Was she normal before she found Ben hanging from her bannister, or before James died?

'Hi honey, I'm home,' she said, breezing into the living room. 'Good news, I clinched the Carter account,' she quipped in a poor attempt at an American accent.

'What?' Matilda looked up from the sofa. She was hugging her knees and had recently been crying.

'Nothing, it doesn't matter. Cup of tea?'

'Yes, please.'

'Have you eaten?'

'Erm … I'm not sure. I don't think so.' Matilda frowned. She couldn't remember the last time she'd had anything to eat. A large nurse had brought her something on a plate this morning, but she couldn't remember what had happened to it.

'How about I make us a quick snack now, and then we can order a pizza later?'

'Yes, sure.'

Adele headed into the kitchen leaving Matilda on the sofa, hugging a pillow.

'I thought you were going into work?' Matilda called out.

'I did.'

Matilda looked at the clock on the wall. It was just after seven o'clock. It was dark outside. How long had she been sitting staring out of the window?

'Did you do the autopsy on …?' She allowed the question to fade away. She didn't want to say the man's name.

'I did, yes.'

'And?'

Adele came to the entrance of the living room and looked Matilda in the eye. 'He wasn't murdered, Mat.'

'Suicide?'

Adele nodded.

There it was – confirmation of the man who hated her and his final act to destroy her.

Adele disappeared into the hallway then came straight back in carrying the letter. 'Matilda, Sian came to the mortuary as I was leaving. They found this in Ben's house, addressed to you.'

'Oh God!'

'What do you want me to do with it?'

'I don't know. Should I read it?' She couldn't take her eyes off the envelope.

'That's up to you.'

'What would you do?'

'I don't know.'

'It's going to be full of blame, anger, his final dig at me, isn't it?'

'Shall I throw it away then?'

'No, I'll read it.' Matilda prepared herself for more character assassination and held her hand out.

'Do you want me to be here with you while … or shall I just? … I'll go and make …' Adele floundered, then walked into the kitchen.

Matilda gripped the envelope firmly in both hands, looking at her name written in block capitals. Did she really want to read the final ramblings of a man who hated her so much he wanted to destroy her mentally?

'Screw it,' she said, running her thumb through the flap and pulling out the handwritten letter.

Dear Matilda,

I'd like to thank you for coming to see me the other day. I've been mulling things over recently, wondering where my life is heading, what I want to do with my future, and I couldn't think of any way out of the slump I was in. Sara didn't want to know me. Neither do my kids. That's not technically true; Rosie messages me when she wants some money. Natalie asks how I am from time to time but I think that's just out of duty. When I reply that I'm fine, I never get anything more from her.

So, you coming to see me was the catalyst. I was in a quagmire with no way out. I think the rest of my life was going to be spent in the armchair watching my bank balance slowly dwindle down to zero as I lost bet after bet and transferred money to my ungrateful daughters.

Once you'd left I decided to end my life, but I wasn't going to go quietly. That would have been too easy. I blame you for everything. You fucked up the Carl Meagan case, you should have been sacked and shamed. I don't know how you can continue knowing what you've done to the Meagan family. How many more lives are you going to ruin before you realize you're poison?

You're probably thinking I'm bitter and jealous. I'm bitter, yes, but not jealous, because I know what is going to happen to you. You've fucked up my life and you're going to fuck up your own. I'm just sorry I'm not going to be around to see it. However, I can rest easy knowing I'm going to be a large factor in you going completely mental.

I know how precious your house is to you. I also know you're going to see me in it every time you walk into the hallway. So, you're going to have a big decision to make – move and let the memories of James fade, or see me every second you're in that house.

One more thing, don't think my death will be the last time you hear from me. You may have caught me at a low point when you visited, but I've not spent the last few months eating takeaways and watching daytime television. I'm a detective. I'm a bloody good detective. Remember that.

DI Ben Hales.

Adele waited outside the living room until she heard movement and decided it was safe to go back in. She entered with a tray carrying two mugs of tea and a packet of dark chocolate digestives.

'Is everything OK?' she asked, noticing Matilda's tear-stained face.

Matilda couldn't speak. The tears came as soon as she saw her friend come into the room. She shook her head.

Adele placed the tray down on the coffee table and saw the handwritten note. 'Can I?' she asked, pointing to it.

Matilda nodded and put her head in the pillow again. Adele sat in the armchair and read the letter.

'Bloody hell,' was all she could say when she'd finished.

'If there is a serial killer out there going after people who haven't been punished fully for their crimes, then I'm definitely high up on his list of potential victims. First Carl Meagan and now Ben Hales. I'm a sitting duck.'

Chapter Forty-Two

'Did you see the newspaper last night?' Rory asked as he entered the incident room.

'No. My eldest is doing his GCSE mocks. He's panicking, so I spent the evening going through his maths. What was in it?' Sian asked.

'They got the story of Hales hanging himself in the boss's house. It was front page.'

'Bloody hell. How did they get that?'

'I've no idea.'

'But Adele said it was suicide,' Scott added. 'The killer couldn't have contacted the paper, so who did?'

The three sat in silence, pained expressions on their faces as they all tried to work out what was happening.

'Right then,' acting DCI Christian Brady said as he came out of his office. He clapped his hands together. 'Let's start from the beginning …'

Last night, on the sofa with his wife, he had been beaming at the prospect of being acting DCI while Matilda was on leave. It may only be for a few weeks at the most, but it didn't matter. This was his chance to shine, to prove to Valerie and the others in charge that he was made of pure Sheffield steel. His wife gave him all the encouragement he needed. This morning, his alarm woke him an hour earlier than usual, and he'd sat at the breakfast table in his T-shirt and boxer shorts making a list of what he wanted to bring up in the morning briefing. A hearty breakfast, a hot shower, and a clean suit, and he went out of the front door with a spring in his step.

'We have no forensics from Brian Appleby,' Sian said, reading from her notebook. 'There are no foreign prints anywhere in his house. From what we can gather, nothing was stolen, despite there being one or two expensive items on display. None of his neighbours had ever been in his house and the extent of the conversations they had with him were of the "good morning, how are you?" variety. Nobody knew him, or his past.'

'Any visitors to his house?'

'No. Nothing.'

'Lucky our killer decided to carry on,' Rory said. 'With just the one victim we'd have been screwed.'

'What about his son, George?'

'I don't think he's a viable suspect,' Sian said. 'There's something about him niggling away at me but I can't for the life of me think what. We're keeping an eye on him though.'

'OK. Victim number two: Joe Lacey. Aaron?' Christian instructed.

'The Lacey house is a complete contrast to Brian Appleby's. For a start, it's a family home. It's lived-in. The place was full of prints. We've checked them against the mother and three children and there are a few we can't identify. Unfortunately, they're not full prints so, even if we did get a suspect, it wouldn't be easy to match anything up. Outside in the back garden, there's a stray footprint from a size ten shoe. Nobody in the house is a size ten. We've asked the neighbours and only one bloke is that size and he doesn't have any shoes matching the print. He also has an alibi for the time Joe Lacey was killed,' Aaron said.

Scott picked up the baton. 'Interestingly, a neighbour of the Lacey's, Mrs Hilde Fargars… sorry, I can't pronounce her name, I think she's Swedish or Danish or something. Anyway, she doesn't sleep much and spends the early hours of the morning sitting at her living room window watching the world go by, as she called it. She said over the past few weeks she's noticed a man slowly walking up and down the street at about four o'clock in the morning. She saw him three days in a row one week.'

'God bless the nosey neighbour.' Rory smiled.

'Description?' Christian asked.

'Tall and slim.'

'Is that it?'

'I'm afraid so. It was dark and she can't see much out of her window as she's in a low seat and her windowsill is covered with crap ornaments.'

'Not a reliable witness then, if she made it to the stand?' Rory asked.

'I doubt it.' Scott smiled.

'The man in the footage from the car park where Elizabeth Ward's car was broken into was tall and slim. If we got a photo of him, do you think this woman would recognize him?' Sian asked.

'I doubt it, but I can give it a go.'

Christian rolled his eyes. 'Anything else?'

'No. Sorry.'

'Victim number three: Katie Reaney.'

Sian began. 'Again, it's the same as the Lacey house. It's full of prints from the family and kids. No sign of a break-in, no foreign forensic evidence.'

'Faith, didn't you go to interview a neighbour?' Christian asked.

'Mrs Pickering? Yes, I did. A sweet old lady, bless her. She called to say she heard someone in the garden on the night Katie was killed. She was in bed at the time and didn't get up to take a look.'

‘What time?’

‘She didn’t say, but it was after ten, because that’s when she goes to bed. Unfortunately, the longer I spoke to her, the more she started to doubt her own statement. At first, she said it was from the back garden, then she said it could have been the front. By the time I left, she was beginning to wonder if she’d dreamed the whole thing.’

‘Completely useless then,’ Rory said.

‘I’m afraid so.’

‘What about the parents of Katie’s victim, Alistair Macintosh?’

‘I had a call from uniformed officers in Hastings. They went round and the house is locked up. According to a neighbour, they’re on holiday in Florida for a few weeks,’ Sian said. ‘They’ve had a couple of more kids since Katie was in their life. A happy ending for them, sort of.’

‘Another dead end,’ Christian said, wiping his brow.

‘I’m afraid so.’

‘So, how do we find the killer?’ Christian asked, slightly flustered.

‘I don’t think you do,’ James Dalziel said for the first time from the back of the room.

There was a noise of scraping chairs as everyone turned to look at him. He felt his collar tighten as all eyes in the room burned into him.

‘What? You’re saying we’re never going to catch this killer?’ Christian put his hands on his hips. ‘That he’s just going to continue killing and killing until he gets bored or dies of old age?’

‘No, I’m not saying that at all,’ James quickly jumped in. ‘I’m not having a go at your policing skills here. I’m saying the killer is very meticulous. He hasn’t left a single fingerprint, and I doubt the footprint in the Lacey’s garden will have anything to do with him either. When you identify him, it will be in one of three ways. One: he’ll make a silly, schoolboy error. Two: he’ll hand himself in. Three: he'll make himself known to either Matilda Darke or Danny Hanson.'

'OK, let's focus on that,' Christian said, loosening his tie. 'I can understand a killer targeting Matilda: she's leading the investigation, she's known in the media etc., but why Danny Hanson? He's just a junior reporter on a local paper.'

'I've been wondering that myself,' James said. 'I wish I could tell you.'

'What if Danny has interviewed the killer in any of his previous stories?' Rory asked.

'The DCI asked me to look into his past,' Sian said, pausing from throwing three Maltesers in her mouth. 'Before this started, most of his stories were court reporting and the odd feature about crime figures and troubled neighbourhoods. He hasn't written anything controversial.'

'He was hanging around Starling House last year,' Scott said. 'I saw him several times.'

'But he didn't get anything front page, nothing to stand out. He was basically used as a filler for background information on Starling House,' Sian said.

'So why Danny Hanson?' Christian almost shouted in frustration.

'I can think of two options,' James Dalziel said. 'The killer, for whatever reason, has latched onto Danny and decided to use him, or, Danny Hanson is your killer.'

Christian blew out his cheeks. 'Shit.'

When the briefing was over, James Dalziel asked if he could have a word with Christian in private. They disappeared into Christian's office and closed the door behind them. Judging by the expression on both of their faces, the conversation was a heavy one.

Rory went over to Sian's desk. 'Sian, I've finally got the information from Katie Reaney's missing mobile phone from EE.'

'About time. They don't rush, do they? Go on.'

'We can see who called and texted her in the run up to being killed. If she was contacted through WhatsApp, though, we've hit a wall as none of that is recorded.'

'Can we see the text messages?'

'No. We can see the number texting, but not the actual message. Now the phone was turned off at 22.07. The last text was from her husband's number in Ripon. He texted at 22.03. I've spoken to Andy and he said he sent her a message saying he loved her. He wasn't worried when he didn't get a reply, as she had told him she was going to have an early night. He's sent me a screen-shot of the message. There are thirteen texts before that one, all from the same number; her housebound friend, Debbie, who lives a few doors away. She's shown me her phone and they're all perfectly innocent texts. Katie didn't say anything about being scared in the house on her own or being watched or receiving any dodgy phone calls.'

'When was the last call to her phone?' Sian asked. She took a sip of coffee and winced at the cold liquid. Time for a fresh brew.

'Two o'clock that afternoon. It was from her mother-in-law double-checking the arrangements for that night. It lasted less than five minutes.' Rory went back to his desk, picked up his empty mug and handed it to Sian with his trademark sweet smile.

'Cheeky sod. By the way, you haven't put anything in the snack drawer for almost a fortnight. Is the phone switched on now?'

'No. All these texts came from a mast close to where Katie lived. It's not picked up again anywhere else. It looks like it was turned off in her house and has remained off since. The killer's probably dumped it somewhere.'

'Why would he steal her phone, if he hadn't contacted her on it?' Sian asked. She had moved over to the drinks station where she went about making her and Rory a coffee.

Rory, bent down, rummaging through the snack drawer for something chocolatey said, 'I can only guess that he messaged or called her through an app like WhatsApp and he took the phone, so we couldn't find out.'

'It would appear James is right then: this killer really does know his stuff.'

'I was going to mention this to Matilda the other day, but the whole business with Ben Hales happened and everything sort of got pushed to one side.' James Dalziel sat down at Christian's desk.

Christian had taken his jacket off and rolled his shirt sleeves up. The enjoyment of the temporary promotion was very short-lived. He began to understand why Matilda looked so harassed when she had the weight of the whole team on her shoulders.

'The thing is, Matilda has been wondering from the beginning how the killer managed to track down Brian Appleby. Then, when Katie Reaney was killed, nobody knew about her past either. She'd even changed her name to hide her true identity. There was only one person who could link Katie Reaney and Naomi Parish and that was her parole officer. So, who knows about parole officers?'

'Everyone.' Christian shrugged.

'But who knows how to get in touch with them? Who knows which officer is assigned to who?'

'I've no idea.'

'A police officer. Perhaps?'

'What? You think the killer is a police officer?'

'With every victim you find, yes I do,' James said.

'But you said you thought Danny Hanson was a possible?'

'And he could still be. If it's not him, then you're looking at someone on the force, possibly someone on your team.'

Christian stared past James's head and out into the incident room. His team were going about their work, following up witness statements, making calls – plotting their next murder, perhaps. His eyes widened. He knew them all. If one of them was a killer, what did that say about his judgement as a detective?

'There is also another possibility.'

'Go on,' Christian prompted, steeling himself for more bad news.

'Danny Hanson and the killer are working together.'

Danny Hanson sat cross-legged on his bed, pen in hand, a thoughtful expression on his face as he wondered what to write next. He'd read a few of the letters members of the public had sent in to the newspaper, and they'd all been full of fear that a serial killer was stalking the streets of Sheffield. The more he read, the more he picked up on the sense of horror people were feeling. He couldn't help but smile.

He should have been working. He should have been writing his next article. Perhaps something about the hard-working residents of Sheffield worrying about having a killer living in their midst, but he had other projects in mind. He went over to one of the boxes around his bedroom. He opened it and was faced with a pile of books, all of them well-thumbed, all of them with Post-It tabs sticking out of various pages. *Mindhunter*, *Journey into Darkness*, and *The Anatomy of Motive*, by John Douglas and Mark Olshaker. *The Serial Killers*, by Colin Wilson and Donald Seaman. *My Life Among the Serial Killers*, by Helen Morrison and Harold Goldberg. All of these were true-crime books written by experts in the field of criminal psychology who had worked for the FBI and helped to catch some of the most dangerous killers in history.

These were what interested Danny more than the panic and fear the people of Sheffield were feeling. Within these pages, lie the structure and the making of what made a killer. This is who the Hangman was.

Chapter Forty-Three

Matilda was expected. She pulled up outside the cottage and the front door opened. Frank Doyle stepped out, his expression mixed. He welcomed his daughter, but he was worried for her too. He went around to the driver's side and opened her door.

'Hello, sweetheart. Are you all right?'

'Yes, fine thanks, Dad,' she replied. She couldn't help but smile at her father's concern. Although Adele cared for her, and so did Sian, there was something comforting about having her dad still wanting to protect his child.

'Come on in. Your mum's made you a big lunch.'

'I'm not that hungry, Dad,' she said, climbing out of the car.

'Don't tell her that. Besides, you've lost weight. I can tell.'

'I'm in training for the half-marathon, I'm supposed to have lost weight.'

'You look gaunt.'

'You're starting to sound like Mum.'

'Come on, let's get in,' Frank said, noticing his wife staring at them through the kitchen window.

Penny Doyle (she hated being called Penelope) stood in the entrance to her kitchen, her arms wide open, ready to greet her daughter. Matilda had no choice. She stepped forward and was pulled into a tight embrace, her head firmly pressed against her mother's ample bosom. Matilda could smell her comforting perfume, one she had been using for decades. It brought back memories of being hugged as a child when she'd fallen and hurt herself.

Penny was a formidable woman. At only five-foot tall, she was dwarfed by almost everyone around her, yet she had the biggest personality in the room. She was warm, caring, and welcomed every visitor as if they were family. However, get on the wrong side of her, and she never forgot.

'I like your hair,' Matilda said as she pulled away.

'Thank you. Renee did it for me in the village,' she replied with a smile. 'Come and sit down. I've made us a light lunch, just a quiche and salad. I did some Scotch eggs last night too. I know how you like them.'

'I'm not really that hungry,' she said, stealing a glance at her father as he took her coat off her.

'Don't be silly. You're wasting away.'

'She's training for the marathon,' Frank said.

'Half-marathon,' Matilda corrected him.

Penny studied her daughter. 'I don't like it. You'll lose your boobs. Look at those Olympic gymnasts. They've nothing up top.'

Matilda couldn't help but smile.

***

'I can't believe he would do something so selfish, so hurtful,' Penny said as they were sitting around the table in the kitchen.

Matilda was sitting in the middle, her parents flanked either side. With her back firmly against the kitchen wall, there was no escape.

'We'll come and clean your house from top to bottom, won't we, Frank?'

'Of course. I'll redecorate it for you as well, if you like? I'll get Jeremy's lad to help out. He's a professional decorator.'

With a mouthful of homemade quiche, Penny said, 'Good thinking. I'll give Renee a call. Her sister made those curtains we've got in the spare bedroom. She'll come and measure up for you. You'll not recognize the place when we've finished.'

'But I want to recognize it,' Matilda said loudly. 'It's James's home. It's our home.'

'Just the hallway, love, nothing else,' Frank said, placing a hand on Matilda's. 'You don't want to be reminded of that every time you come home, do you?'

'No,' she conceded.

'There we are then,' Penny said. 'Oh, I had your sister on the phone for an hour last night. She's going to ring you at the weekend. She says you can go and stay with her any time you like.'

Matilda almost shivered. The thought of staying in her sister's house with her annoying husband and two boisterous children was the stuff of nightmares.

'That's kind of her but I need to be close to work.'

'I thought you'd been signed off?' Penny asked.

'I have been signed off, but I don't intend on staying off. There's a killer out there that needs to be caught.'

'Matilda, you know I don't like you talking about murder and death at the meal table.'

'We've just been talking about Ben Hales hanging himself in my house.'

'That's different. That's circumstances.'

Matilda frowned and looked to her father, who shrugged.

'I don't know why you don't leave the police. You've not been happy since James died.'

'That's got nothing to do with the job,' Matilda scoffed. 'I wouldn't be happy wherever I worked.'

Frank placed his hand on top of Matilda's again. 'I don't like the thought of you being unhappy.'

‘I’m not unhappy, I’m just … well, you know … I’m getting there,’ she lied. ‘Running is helping too.’

‘You want to be careful,’ Penny began. ‘Look what happened to Felicity’s daughter when she lost her husband – she cut her wrists in the bath.’

‘Penny!’ Frank admonished.

‘Mum, I don’t plan on killing myself.’

‘All I’m saying is if you keep things to yourself, if you don’t move on, you’ll end up like she did. I think we’ve had enough suicide in this family, haven’t we Frank?’

Frank turned away. His brother’s suicide more than twenty years ago was still raw at times.

‘Mum, can we change the subject to something brighter, please?’

‘Of course we can, sweetheart,’ she replied through a sickly smile. Penny ate quickly, her eyes darting from side to side as she struggled to think of something to say. She hated being quiet. ‘Oh, Frank, did I tell you?’ Penny suddenly said. ‘Renee’s husband’s been given Viagra for his heart. She says it’s given him a whole new lease of life.’

Matilda burst out laughing and spat her quiche all over the kitchen table.

Chapter Forty-Four

Day Thirty-Two
Sunday, 9 April 2017

'Oh my God. I never thought I'd be this nervous,' Adele said.

'Me neither. Is it too late to pull out, do you think?' Matilda asked.

'Yes it is. Come on,' Chris said with a beaming smile.

'I shouldn't be here,' Matilda said. 'We've got a serial killer on the loose and I'm taking time off to run a half-marathon. The press will love that.'

'You don't run South Yorkshire Police single-handed,' Adele said. 'You've got Christian and Aaron there today. And Ranjeet and Kesinka. The city won't burn to the ground just because you've taken a few hours off.'

Matilda, Adele and Chris stepped out of the taxi in Sheffield city centre and looked around them. Thousands of people had descended on the steel city to run the famous half-marathon.

They made their way to the Winter Gardens where they were to meet Scott. He spotted them first and called out, giving them a huge wave. He was relishing this.

'Is Scott some kind of masochist?' Adele asked Matilda quietly. 'Look at him, I've never seen him look so happy.'

'Good morning, Matilda, Adele. Are you ready for this?' Scott said, jumping up and down.

'No,' Matilda said through a painful smile.

'Don't worry about it. You'll be fine. Both of you. Look, just stay together, don't push off too soon, go at a pace that suits you. OK?'

They both nodded.

'Will you be staying with us?' Adele asked.

Scott and Chris exchanged glances.

'Actually, Mum,' Chris said, looking at his feet. 'We were thinking of running on ahead.'

'You're going to leave us?'

'We want a good time.'

'No offence,' Scott said, 'but I've been running this race for a few years, now, and I want to try and beat last year's time.'

'Oh, right. Well, no offence taken,' Adele said.

'Oh, look, there's Sian and Rory,' Scott said, thankful for a distraction.

'Hello, you two, I didn't know you were going to cheer us on,' Matilda said.

'Yes. We're going to pop up to Ringinglow and wave at you from there. Apparently, there aren't many people around that part and Ringinglow is a real bastard to run up, according to Scott,' Rory said with a smile.

The runners took off their jackets and changed into their running shoes. In her concealed pocket, Matilda had some jelly beans and Jelly Babies to give her an energy boost. Adele tied her hair back and put a sweatband around her forehead. They were all ready to take their place in the middle of the second wave of runners due to start the 2017 Sheffield half-marathon.

'Nice of them to give up their Sunday to cheer us on,' Adele said.

'Is that Faith?' Matilda asked, pointing towards the front of the pack.

'I think it is, yes,' Scott answered.

'Is she looking for us?'

'I'm not sure. Faith! FAITH!' Scott shouted.

The young DC eventually heard him and trotted over. She was dressed in jeans and a padded coat to keep her warm. She looked different in casual clothes.

'Hello, Faith,' Matilda said. 'Nice of you to come down and see us.'

Faith smiled awkwardly. 'Well, Steve's running.'

'Is he?' Scott asked. 'Where is he?'

'At the front. You should see the medals he's got for running. He's run the London marathon twice,' she beamed proudly.

'He never said.'

'He doesn't like to brag,' she smiled. 'Well, good luck to you all.' She grinned before heading back to the front to be with Steve.

'She's certainly smitten with him, isn't she?' Matilda asked.

'Not surprising. Have you seen his legs?' Adele said, looking around and spotting him.

'I wonder why he didn't say anything,' Scott said, almost to himself.

The wait to get started seemed to drag on. Matilda bounced from foot to foot, partly to keep warm, but partly to control her nerves.

At just after 9.30, they were off. They hadn't even got to the end of the road before Scott and Chris had ploughed on ahead leaving Matilda and Adele behind.

'How are you doing?' Adele asked.

'We've only just started.'

'I know, but, how are you doing?'

'I'm OK. You?'

'Dying for a latte.'

Further up the road, Matilda registered the sound of applauding from the public on both sides of the road. She looked at them, complete strangers, cheering her on. It made her smile. People had given up their Sunday morning to stand in the cold for several hours to support people they didn't know. Matilda smiled at an elderly couple as the man poured the woman a cup of tea from a flask. Two young children waved Union Jacks. One child had an annoying vuvuzela, and on his own, just aside from the crowd, was Danny Hanson. He took her photo with his mobile.

What was he doing here?

Matilda spotted him, and their eyes met. She was soon past him but she couldn't tear herself away from him. She continued running but looked back. She almost collided with a runner, but Adele managed to keep her friend on her feet.

'You OK?' Adele panted.

'Yes. Fine.'

Was he smirking?

***

Ecclesall Road was a very long road on a steady incline. It took the runners right to the edge of the city and onto the famous 'King of the Hill' known as Ringinglow Road. Ahead of Matilda and Adele, was Scott with Chris a few paces behind. This was Chris's first race and although Scott wanted to keep checking up on him, he couldn't take his eyes off PC Steve Harrison ahead of him. He was way out in front and didn't seem to have broken a sweat at all. There were a couple of times Scott had tried to catch up with him, but it was as if Steve had sensed Scott approaching and had increased his speed. This seemed like a race between uniform and plain-clothed officers. Scott needed to beat him.

One hour, nineteen minutes, and twelve seconds later, Scott crossed the finishing line. He stopped the watch on his wrist and fell to the floor beside the road. A woman came over to him and gave him a bottle of water, which he took a long drink from and then poured the rest over his head. He leaned back against the railings and looked up to see Steve across the way, smiling at him. If Scott hadn't been watching him all the way, he wouldn't have guessed he had run just over thirteen miles. He was fresh. Not a hair out of place and only slightly panting. Scott smiled.

'How are you feeling?' Steve asked, coming over and squatting by Scott. He handed him his race finisher's pack which contained a T-shirt, medal and a few energy treats.

'I'm OK,' he panted. 'You?'

'I'm good. Beat last year's time by more than thirty seconds.'

'Good for you,' he said between breaths. 'I didn't know you ran.'

'I used to do it competitively, but just for fun now.'

'You wouldn't think this was fun, would you?'

'Oh, I don't know. I love it.'

Steve strolled away, hands on hips. Scott watched him as he headed into the crowd and was greeted by Faith, who threw her arms around him and planted a huge kiss on his lips. He didn't notice Chris Kean fall at his feet.

'You all right?' Scott asked, looking down. Chris was red-faced and breathing heavily, sweat was pouring off him.

'I think I've died.'

Scott laughed. 'Sit up. Have a drink.'

'I don't think I can.'

Scott grabbed Chris and pulled him into his lap. He held his head while he fed him water from a bottle. 'Take small sips.'

'Just leave me. Save yourself.'

Two hours, forty-three minutes and nine seconds after leaving the Winter Gardens, Matilda and Adele crossed the finishing line together, arm in arm. They immediately collapsed to the ground in a heap by the side of the road.

'Are we mad?' Adele asked.

'I think so.'

'Never again.'

'Agreed.'

'We've done it though.'

'Have we? Now I know how people feel on the mortuary slab.'

They both laughed, but it was weak and bordering on hysterical.

Matilda opened her eyes to see Sian, Rory, Scott and Chris standing over her. Their faces were blank as they looked down on a worn-out wreck of a human.

'Congratulations,' Sian said. 'I'm so proud of you.'

Sitting at the side of the road, Steve handed Matilda and Adele their finisher's packs.

'There'd better be some alcohol in here,' Adele said as she tore into it.

Matilda pulled open the drawstring bag, put her hand in and pulled out a hangman's noose. She held it aloft. Everyone turned to look at her, yet nobody knew what to say.

Chapter Forty-Five

'Are you sure about this?'

'Perfectly.'

'But the doctor signed you off for a couple of weeks. And he said if you still didn't feel up to it, you could have a sick note for a bit longer.'

Adele was perched on the end of the double bed in the room Matilda had moved in to. Matilda sat at the table in her best working suit, applying a small amount of eye make-up.

'I don't want to take any more time off. I'm fine.'

'You know, you really should have that tattooed on your forehead.'

'What?'

'I'm fine. It's your reply to everything.'

'That's because it's true.'

'Really? So you were fine when you found Ben Hales hanging in your hallway?'

'Well, no, not then, but you didn't ask.' She grinned at her through the mirror. 'Now, however, I'm fine.'

'Aren't you still knackered from the half-marathon? I am,' she said, rubbing her left calf.

'Nope. I'm fine.'

'There's that f-word again.'

'Adele.' Matilda turned in the seat to face her best friend. 'Do you want to know why I'm fine? It's because of you. If it hadn't been for you welcoming me into your home and looking after me I would have probably joined Ben Hales on the end of his rope. However, I'm still here. I'm alive, and that's thanks to you.'

Adele was just about to smile when suspicion took over. 'Flattery isn't going to convince me, you know.'

'Blimey, I can't say anything, can I?'

'Matilda, take the rest of the week off, at least.'

'And do what? No offence but staring at your living room walls all day isn't exactly stimulating.'

'Go out.'

'Where?'

'I don't know. Into town. Shopping at Meadowhall. Go and see your parents.'

Matilda rolled her eyes. 'You've just given me three perfectly good reasons for returning to work.'

'What about that noose in your runner's pack?'

'Probably a sick joke. You know what people are like.'

'Matilda,' Adele called out as Matilda passed her friend and headed out of the room. 'I doubt Valerie will allow you back on the case.'

'I called her last night and we're going to have a chat when I get in. I need to see this through, Adele,' Matilda said as she made her way down the stairs.

'But what about this business with Ben Hales? Won't you need to be questioned? That's not going to do you any good.'

'You said yourself it was a suicide. There's not going to be a hearing or anything.'

'Matilda—'

'Look, Adele.' Matilda stopped in the hallway and turned to her worried friend. 'I have so many questions running around my head and I need to get them answered before I go completely insane. The only way I can do that is by returning to work.'

'Can't you do it over the phone? Give Sian a ring, or Christian. They're more than capable. Ask them what you want, and they'll look into it for you.'

'I know you're thinking of me, but trust me, I'm absolutely fine.'

Matilda could feel Adele studying her, glaring into her eyes trying to find evidence that she was far from fine. Matilda quickly turned away. 'Besides, Rory texted yesterday telling me Faith and Kesinka went on a double date with their boyfriends. I need all the gossip.' She gave an exaggerated laugh.

'You hate station gossip.'

Matilda sighed.

'OK,' Adele conceded. 'Personally, I think you should take more time off, but I know it doesn't matter what I, or anyone else, says. Just, take care, won't you?'

'You make it sound like I go running around with guns. I'm not in the Counter Terrorism Unit.'

'Just promise me you won't work too hard.'

'I have no intention of working too hard.'

'Are you limping?' Valerie asked as Matilda entered the office.

'I think I've got a blister on my right foot from the half-marathon.'

'Oh yes. Congratulations,' she said, though the tone of her voice suggested she didn't mean it. 'Scott said you made good time.'

Matilda smiled. 'He has to say that, doesn't he?'

'Did you know you made the newspaper?' Valerie slapped down a copy on the desk.

The front page had a picture of Matilda running. It wasn't a flattering picture; her hair was stuck to her red face and sweat was dripping down her forehead. The headline next to it wasn't flattering either:

'DARKE RUNS FROM SERIAL KILLER DUTIES.'

'I expected something like this. Danny Hanson was at the race. He took this picture on his phone.'

'I've called Kate. I told her you were running for charity. I mentioned your husband. She's going to run an article in this evening's edition stating that. A quote from you will go a long way to appease the people of Sheffield.'

'What?' Matilda's face went as red as when she was running. 'You want me to give an interview about my dead husband? No bloody way.'

'Just a few lines. It won't take five minutes.'

'Absolutely not. I'm proud of running the half-marathon. I trained long and hard for it. We all did. I'm not justifying my actions to anyone.'

'Matilda, public trust in us is at an all-time low at present. If they see you as some kind of charity runner that will help.'

'No. You can tell Kate anything you want, but I'm not giving an interview. She can piss off. Let her write whatever she likes. We're not on duty 24/7, you know. We're entitled to some time off.'

Matilda stood up and left the room before she said something to her boss she would definitely regret.

Before Matilda could be welcomed by everyone in the briefing room, Christian ushered her into her tiny office and closed the door behind them.

'You look like you've aged five years,' Matilda said with a smile. 'In-laws still with you?'

'What? No, they went home last weekend, thank God. It's about the case. It's something James Dalziel said while you were away. I was going to call you but decided not to. Unfortunately, my mind has been thinking of nothing else and the thought's mutated and I just …'

'Christian, try breathing,' she said, calming him down.

He took a deep breath and slowly lowered himself into the chair opposite Matilda's desk. 'We got talking about Danny Hanson and we wondered if he was the killer. I mean, nobody could understand why a junior reporter was being contacted when there are so many other journalists he could call. Then, James Dalziel said due to how the killer was able to locate Brian Appleby and Katie Reaney that maybe the killer was a police officer, maybe even someone on this team,' he said quietly.

'Blimey, he's certainly hedging his bets, isn't he?' Matilda smiled. 'One minute it's a journalist, the other it's a police officer. What do you believe?'

'I don't know,' Christian said, scratching the worry on his forehead. 'I honestly can't see it being Danny Hanson, but the alternative is one of us, or worse, both. I've been going out of my mind.'

'You should have called me.'

'I know. It's like when you thought one of the team was talking to the press. You didn't want to believe it, but you couldn't help it. I was the same. Is one of them, out there, a serial killer?' he whispered.

'You know more of the team better than I do. What do you think?' Matilda asked.

'I really don't know. I mean, look at Rory, look at Scott. Can you honestly see one of them killing someone? I certainly can't.'

'No. Me neither,' Matilda mused.

They both fell silent.

'You know I said my mind has mutated things?' Christian broke the silence.

'Yes.'

'What if the killer isn't someone on the team. What if the killer is James Dalziel?'

'What?'

'He could be saying all this to detract suspicion from himself.

We've only got him telling us what to look for and we're taking what he says as gospel.'

'Jesus, Christian.' Matilda blew out her cheeks. 'Maybe *you* should take some time off.'

'I know. What are we going to do?'

'We need to bring someone else on board with this; someone a bit more level-headed.'

At the same time, Matilda and Christian both said, 'Sian.'

Chapter Forty-Six

Day Thirty-Four
Tuesday, 11 April 2017

The second the clock struck six, the workers of KKE Engineering downed tools and headed for the changing rooms. Overalls were removed, coats and bags collected, and they were out of the door before five past the hour.

There was a reason most of them were in a hurry to leave tonight and that was to celebrate Gordon Berry's forty-seventh birthday.

'God, I need a drink,' Suzanne Marr said. 'I purposely came on the bus today, so I could have a few drinks tonight. I know it's a week night but screw it, I'm getting pissed.'

'As if you need an excuse to drink,' teased Alicia Richardson, who worked on the same bench as her. 'Will you be buying the birthday boy a drink?'

'Of course, it's only fair.'

'I bet you'd like to be doing other things to him, as well.' She smiled.

'Bugger off, Alicia. He's in the middle of a divorce and it's not that long since his mother died. The last thing on his mind is going to be finding someone new.'

'He's a bloke, Suze. Undo your top couple of buttons, get a few lagers down him and invite him back to your place.'

'Alicia, don't be filthy. I'm in my forties for crying out loud. That kind of behaviour may be acceptable to people like you in your twenties, but when you get older you're a bit more refined.'

'Refined? Do I have to remind you of the Christmas party 2015?'

'Shut up, he's coming.'

Gordon Berry, tall and slim, with dark hair greying slightly at the temples and a rugged face, trotted across the car park to catch them up. 'Good evening, ladies. Have you had a good day at work?'

'Yes, fine thanks, Gordon.'

'Good. Well, that's work chatter out of the way. Let's get to the pub and get seriously slammed.' He placed both arms around Suzanne's and Alicia's shoulders and frog-marched them in the direction of the pub.

By the time Gordon, Suzanne and Alicia were on their second drink, the rest of their friends from KKE had arrived. There were around fifteen of them in total, either at the bar or sitting around three tables pushed together in the Banker's Draft pub in Sheffield city centre. It was a large, dark pub in urgent need of a revamp. It didn't give out a welcoming vibe, but the birthday well-wishers were doing their best to lighten the dank atmosphere with their loud talking and exaggerated laughter.

'Gordon, have you heard from the wife on your birthday?' Rupert Molone, the line manager asked.

'You're joking, surely,' he scoffed. 'For the last three years I barely got a word out of her, let alone a birthday card. Anyway, she's in Malta with her new fella at the moment. Good luck to him, I say.'

'You're not bitter then?'

'No. Best thing that could have happened to us was splitting up. We'll still see each other. I mean, our Tony's getting married later this year, but we just drifted apart.'

'You're on the prowl again, then?' Rupert smiled, nodding in Suzanne's direction who was playing on the quiz machine with Alicia.

'If the right woman came along, I wouldn't turn her down.'

'Who's the right woman for you then, Gordon?' Alicia shouted out without turning away from the screen.

'Well it would have been you, Alicia, if that Ryan of yours hadn't put a ring on your finger.'

'Rings can come off, Gordon,' she said as she slowly began to ease the engagement ring up her finger. It was almost off, before she pushed it back down. 'On second thoughts, my Ryan's ripped and has a bum you could sink your teeth into.'

'The only thing that's ripped about Gordon are his kecks.' Rupert laughed.

'Why don't you ask our Suzanne out?' Alicia said.

'Alicia!' Suzanne hissed.

'What? I want everyone to be happy.'

'If Suzanne was up for it, I'd be happy to take her out for a meal one night.'

The group quietened while they waited for Suzanne's reaction. Her back was to the majority of them, still facing the quiz machine. Alicia nudged her and eventually she turned around. She was red with embarrassment and a sweet smile spread across her face.

'Well, if you asked, I wouldn't say no.'

'You fancy it then? This Friday?' Gordon asked.

'All right,' she replied, coyly.

Gordon was on cloud nine as he walked home. It was close to midnight when he left the pub and headed for Attercliffe. It took him longer than usual because he was staggering and zig-zagging from one side of the road to the other. He didn't care how long it took him though. Today was his birthday (well, for the next six minutes), and on Friday night he was going out for a meal with Suzanne Marr.

The house was cold when he opened the front door. He slammed the door behind him and placed his hand on the radiator. He made a mental note to have a word with one of the engineers at work tomorrow. He emptied his pockets and placed the detritus of coins, screwed-up notes, mobile phone and keys on the hall table with an echoing clatter.

'Good evening, Gordon.'

Gordon jumped. He'd gone into the living room and hadn't noticed a shadowy figure waiting in the dark.

'Who the bleeding hell are you?' Gordon slurred.

Standing in front of the window, a man stood tall with his arms folded. There was an air of danger about him. His stance was powerful. The head slightly lowered. The glint from the light through a small gap in the curtains danced in his dark eyes. Gordon shivered.

The figure leaned over to the standard lamp next to the sofa and flicked it on, lighting up the room. Gordon took a step back. He was looking into the face of a complete stranger. He glanced over to the patio doors which were locked from the inside.

'What the hell do you think you're doing in my house?' Suddenly Gordon was sober.

'I've come for a little chat.' The intruder stepped forward.

'I've got nowt to say. Get out of my house.'

'Why don't you sit down, Gordon?'

'Don't tell me what I can and can't do in my own home. Now go on, fuck off. How did you get in, anyway?'

'I've been watching you for a while, Gordon. Key under the mat. Not very original.'

'You bastard.'

'Do I detect a slight slurring to your words there? Have you been drinking?'

'What's it got to do with you?'

'You've always had a problem with alcohol, haven't you?'

'What?'

'Remember what happened to Darren Price?'

That was a name Gordon hadn't heard for years. It was a name he'd never forget. A name he tried not to think about too often.

'Who the fuck are you?'

'Don't you feel guilty? Don't you feel pain over what you did to Darren Price?'

'I didn't do anything to Darren Price. It was an accident. The inquest ruled it to be an accident. Look, why am I even justifying myself to you? Get out now or I'll call the police.'

'I'm not going anywhere, Gordon.'

'What do you want?'

'I'm glad you asked that.'

The intruder leaned down to a rucksack on the floor beside his feet. He unzipped it and took out a length of rope with a noose tied at the end.

'What the fuck? You're him, aren't you? The Hangman.'

'The penny's finally dropped, has it?'

'Fuck you,' Gordon said, turning and running out of the living room.

At the front door, Gordon was struggling to take the security chain off, his fingers shaking in panic. The intruder, a much younger and more sober man than Gordon, grabbed hold of him by the shoulders, pulled him back then slammed him hard into the door. The sound of Gordon's head banging on the solid wood resounded around the hallway.

Gordon's home blurred before him.

The Hangman pushed Gordon hard onto the living room floor.

'You really need to listen to your conscience,' he said, looking down on the stricken Gordon.

'Fuck you,' he spat.

'You're not sorry about what you did to Darren Price at all, are you?'

'I didn't *do* anything,' he replied, saying every word like it was its own individual sentence.

'You were drinking at lunchtime; your reflexes were impaired. Your ineptitude caused a twenty-two-year-old man to lose his life. Don't you think you should pay for that?'

'Who made you judge, jury, and executioner?'

The Hangman reached for his rope and held up the noose. 'I did.'

He leaned down to place the hoop over Gordon's neck, but he wriggled on the carpet. He kicked his arms and legs wildly and, with his left leg, caught his attacker on the back of his knee. The Hangman lost his balance slightly and fell forward. Gordon saw his opportunity and managed to crawl free. He stood up and headed for the hallway. He was almost there when the attacker reached him again. He threw the noose over Gordon's head and pulled him back, tightening the rope.

'You bastard,' Gordon hissed as the life was strangled out of him. He managed to get a couple of fingers under the rope, but it was no use.

The intruder dragged Gordon into the living room.

With one hand under the rope, Gordon reached back to try and hit his attacker.

The intruder stepped forward. Gordon was on the floor on his front, kicking with his legs and his one free arm. Gordon flipped himself over, so he was on his back. His movement was so swift the Hangman let go of the rope, freeing Gordon just long enough for him to headbutt his potential killer in the crotch.

The attacker screamed out in pain and doubled over. Gordon pulled the noose off and stood up. He was gasping for breath but needed to act fast. He pushed his intruder into the coffee table, breaking it into dozens of pieces.

Gordon headed for the front door and managed to get it open. The cold air felt wonderful as it bit into his face. Rubbing his throat, he ran to the car. He fumbled in his pocket for the keys, but they weren't there. Then he remembered throwing them down on the table in the hallway. Shit.

Behind him, he could hear the sound of the intruder running into the hallway. Gordon turned and sprinted up the road as fast as he could. He had no idea where he was going, but the fact he was free and still alive was all that mattered. He ran, pumping his legs harder and harder. Gordon had never been a fit man, and right now he needed to find the energy from somewhere to stay safe for a few hours until daylight. Then he'd go to the police and tell them he'd had a good look at the person who had been terrorizing the people of Sheffield.

Chapter Forty-Seven

Matilda had phoned Sian at home last night and brought her up to speed on what she and Christian had been talking about. Sian received the news in the same way Matilda had done – with shock and disbelief. An hour later, they were still talking, more rationally now, and Matilda had left her DS with the task of going through the entire team and asking herself if any of them had changed recently. Was their behaviour giving cause for concern; were there any secret phone calls or unexplained absences?

The next morning, as arranged, Matilda and Sian met up in her office at seven o'clock, before anyone else had arrived.

'I've hardly slept a wink,' Sian said, slumping down in the seat opposite Matilda.

'I didn't get much sleep either.'

'Do you honestly think one of us is a killer?' Sian said. They had discussed this question over the phone last night, but Sian preferred face to face so she could get a true reaction from the DCI.

'No I don't,' Matilda replied honestly.

'Neither do I. So then why are we doing this?'

'To put our minds at rest.' She shrugged.

'My mind is at rest. Well, it was until you called last night.'

'I'm sorry.'

'No. Don't apologize. We need to cover every angle.' Sian dug in her oversized handbag for her notebook. 'I wrote down everyone's name last night and started to go through them. I immediately crossed off Rory, Scott and Aaron, as I've known them for years. But then I thought, should I *really* cross them off? What do you think?'

Matilda put her head in her hands and let out an audible sigh. 'If one of those three ended up being a killer I'd … well … I couldn't continue in this work anymore. It would just destroy everything.'

'I know what you mean. Now, based on the assumption that the killer is the same person who broke into Elizabeth Ward's car, we're looking for someone white, tall, and slim. I know that's not much to go on, but it's a start. I've crossed off the majority of the women, especially the smaller ones. Also, based on general consensus, I've stuck to the men, as they are more likely to be serial killers.'

'OK. And?'

'I've come up with nothing.'

'Sorry?'

'We're left with four DCs, three DSs and one DI, and that's Christian. Out of those eight, I can't see any of them being the killer.'

'To be honest with you, Sian, I don't think it's one of the team either. However, when you look at the evidence: who would have known Brian Appleby was living in Sheffield? That Katie Reaney was really Naomi Parish? Only a police officer.'

'I don't like this,' Sian said, on the verge of tears.

'I shouldn't have asked you, I'm sorry. Look, why don't I go out and get us a couple of lattes before we start the day proper?'

'I'd like that.' She tried to smile.

As Matilda was leaving the office, she placed a reassuring arm on Sian's shoulder, squeezing it tight. This really was a nightmare.

Walking towards the car park, she past uniformed officers and plain-clothed detectives, all of whom she had seen at crime scenes and in the canteen. They smiled at her, some said hello, a new recruit asked her where the toilets were. Before, she wouldn't have given any of them a second thought. Now, she registered them all, cataloguing their height, build, skin colour.

Gordon Berry had spent the night shivering in a bus shelter. He hadn't slept. He couldn't call anyone because his mobile was at home. It was on the table in the hallway, along with his car keys and his wallet. The only change he had in his back pocket amounted to less than a pound. He had thought of going to a colleague's house, but that would have led to questions. He didn't want to have to start lying again. So, once he'd felt a safe distance away from the Hangman, he found a bus shelter off a main road, and curled up in a corner, out of sight.

Throughout the night, Gordon had gone over every little detail of the man who had broken into his home and tried to kill him. When he closed his eyes tight he pictured his hair, the colour and style, the paleness of his skin, his small ears (the left one had been pierced at some point). The small scar above his left eyebrow, his slightly crooked teeth, his smell (a designer fragrance he had smelled before but couldn't remember where). He would be able to describe the Hangman perfectly to the police.

It seemed to take ages for darkness to fade into light. The low cloud didn't help. Just after six o'clock, when the traffic began to build, people came out to walk their dogs, deliver newspapers and set off early to work, Gordon left the bus shelter. He wondered if people were staring at him. He must look a mess. He could feel two days' worth of stubble, his mouth tasted foul and stale. He could smell himself too, and it wasn't pleasant. Although, there was a hint of the fragrance his attacker had been wearing clinging to his shirt. Maybe somebody at the police station would be able to identify it.

Gordon was shattered. He tried to walk quickly into town, but his legs wouldn't allow it. They felt heavy. He dragged his feet with as much energy as he could muster, all the while looking around, wondering if the killer was searching for him. He tried to remember the other victims from the newspaper. He'd killed them in their own homes, hanged them. Last night, he had failed for the first time. Would he give up on him and go for his next victim, or were his sights still firmly fixed on Gordon? After all, the killer hadn't been wearing a mask. Surely he knew that. Surely he wouldn't want Gordon going to the police. So, where was he?

Carrying a large latte in each hand, a flapjack in one pocket and a brownie in the other, Matilda made her way towards the police station. It was almost eight o'clock and traffic was building up on the roads. Matilda had been up for hours. It seemed like the working day should already be underway.

Matilda climbed the few steps and was about to pull open the door to the main entrance, when it was flung open from the other side with force. It hit her in the face and she fell backwards, down the steps and on to the cold concrete, landing with a thud. The cardboard Costa cups splattered beside her, spilling their contents.

The man coming out of the station ignored Matilda. He jumped down the steps, over Matilda and ran at speed across the forecourt.

'Ma'am, are you all right?'

Matilda looked up to see a blurred uniformed officer standing over her.

'What the hell?'

'I've no idea, ma'am. He just shot out of the station, before I had time to say anything to him.'

The PC slowly helped Matilda up. They both turned in the direction of the fleeing man, who, in his haste, didn't check for any traffic and ran straight into the path of a red Fiat Punto.

Fortunately, the car wasn't speeding. He was hit a glancing blow and thrown onto the pavement.

'Get after him,' Matilda instructed the PC.

'What's going on?' DC Rory Fleming asked, coming out of the main entrance. 'Ma'am, are you all right? Have you fallen?'

'No I haven't bloody fallen, Rory. Get me up, will you?' She held out her hand.

'Are you injured?'

'I don't know. I don't think so,' she said. She was dazed from the fall and hitting her head. Her hands were grazed and her pride dented.

'Who was that?' Rory asked PC Harrison.

'I've no idea. He just got up and ran, well, limped, off.'

Rory and Steve made their way back into the station. Matilda heard Rory mention something about a first aid kit and an accident book. She remained in the doorway looking out over the traffic.

In the distance, the man stopped and turned back to the station. He and Matilda made eye contact over the sea of passing cars. She tried to read something from his facial expression, but he just appeared to be exhausted and confused.

Gordon Berry turned away first and hobbled off.

Matilda put her hand to the back of her head. It came away covered in blood.

Chapter Forty-Eight

'How are you feeling?'

'I'm fine.'

'Are you sure?'

'Yes.'

Sitting in Valerie's office with heavy padding taped to the back of her head, Matilda picked at the pieces of gravel in the palms of her hands.

Valerie brought her a coffee and went to her chair. 'Why are things never simple around you?' Valerie asked with a hint of a smile in her voice.

'I must ooze bad luck.' Matilda tried to smile.

'Are you sure you shouldn't go to the hospital?'

'No. It's just a flesh wound. No stitches needed and there is no sign of concussion.'

'Good. Who was that man?'

'I've no idea. I've got Rory and Steve going through CCTV of the foyer. See if we can get a look at him.'

'And you've never seen him before?'

'No. I don't think so.'

'Bizarre.'

'Very.'

'Anyway,' Valerie said, pulling out a file from her top drawer, 'I've got some good news and some not-so-good news for you.'

'I don't like the sound of this.'

'The good news is we will be getting a Major Crimes Unit at some point this year. The chief constable has said I can put forward any ideal candidate for the role.' She smiled.

'Me?' Matilda looked shocked.

'No. Rory Fleming. Of course, you.'

'Wow, I don't know what to say.'

'Don't say anything yet. It's still very early days and there will be other candidates too.'

'Thank you. So, what's the not-so-good news?'

'I've had Kate Stephenson on the phone almost every day since Ben Hales was found dead in your house. Apparently, the killer called Danny Hanson and said he wished he could take credit for this one, but he couldn't. At least we know he didn't kill Ben Hales.'

'Adele told me it was a suicide. Ben left me a note too. He blames me for everything that's happened to him.' She shook her head. 'I know he wanted my job, but it wasn't my fault I was promoted ahead of him, was it?'

'Are you saying he should have hanged himself in my hallway?' Valerie smiled.

Matilda stifled a laugh. 'I've never known anyone with so much hatred in them.'

'Well, the inquest is still ongoing, obviously. And I get the feeling the press will be sniffing around this for a while. It won't be the last we hear from him.'

Matilda froze. She thought of what Ben had written in his note to her. Even after the inquest, after his funeral, after years of him being buried, Matilda doubted she would ever be free of former DI Ben Hales.

Acting DCI Christian Brady had finished the morning briefing and the incident room was dispersing when Matilda entered.

‘I thought you’d have gone home. How are you feeling?’

‘I don’t have a home at the moment, Christian,’ she said, walking into her office and closing the door behind her. He was going to follow her in, but the door closed in his face.

Valerie had instructed her to go home and take a few days to come to terms with everything, before even thinking about taking over the case again. How could she assume Matilda would be able to live in her home after a man had taken his own life in her hallway?

She slumped into her chair and stared through the glass door into the incident room. Valerie may have a skin like an elephant where the turmoil of someone blaming you for their suicide didn’t penetrate, but Matilda wasn’t like that. She soaked everything up like an emotional sponge. Rory walked past her door, glanced in and smiled. He’d almost been beaten to death last November. He seemed to have made a full recovery, physically and mentally. Sian had been a detective longer than anyone on the team. She’d faced all kinds of horrors over the years yet there was always a smile on her face and a bounce in her step. James had always told her she was a good detective because she cared. Maybe that was the problem: she cared too much.

A knock on the door made her jump. Sian entered.

‘Sorry, I didn’t mean to startle you. Rory told me what happened outside the station. I thought you might like a cup of tea.’

‘Thanks, Sian. I’m afraid I spilt our coffees.’ She took the tea and had a lingering sip. It tasted good. She placed her hands in her jacket pockets and pulled out some damaged snacks. ‘Would you like a squashed flapjack or a battered brownie?’

‘I’ll pass, thanks.’ Sian smiled. ‘I thought you’d like to know, I’ve had a call from Aaron. Katrina’s been rushed into hospital. She’s bleeding. He thinks she’s losing the baby.’

‘Oh God, no. She’s not far off her due date, is she?’

‘No. I saw her at the weekend. She looked ready to burst.’

'Does anybody have any good news?' Matilda asked.

'Scott and Rory have found an apartment they're going to share. They're signing for it this week, apparently, and I won ten pounds on a scratchcard a few nights ago.'

'And you came into work this morning? Fool.' Matilda grinned.

The door burst open and Rory and Steve entered. 'We've got the CCTV footage from the foyer if you're interested,' Rory said.

'I certainly am.'

Rory tapped his iPad a few times and passed it to Matilda. All four huddled around the tablet as they watched a nervous-looking man, whose appearance suggested he had spent last night sleeping rough, enter the station. The camera was above the reception desk pointing down into the foyer. There was nobody in the waiting area. He walked up to the desk and waited, impatiently drumming his dirty fingernails on the desk. A few seconds later, he suddenly turned and ran out of the station as if his life depended on it. He pushed the door wide and disappeared.

Matilda put her hand to the back of her head. It was this moment where she'd been floored and landed on the concrete.

'What was that all about?' Matilda asked once the video had come to an end. She took the padding from her head and felt the small wound. Her fingers came away clean. She threw the padding away.

'I've no idea,' Rory said.

'Maybe he was going to report something, then changed his mind,' Steve suggested.

'But why would you run out so fast like that?' Rory asked. 'It's like he'd seen a ghost or something.'

'Can you play it again?' Sian asked.

'Why?'

'He looks familiar.'

Matilda handed Sian the tablet so she could have the best viewing angle.

'I know him. I'm sure I do,' Sian said with a heavy frown.

'Professionally or personally?' Matilda asked.

'Professionally. It's going to really bug me now.'

'Don't we have any facial recognition software?' Steve asked.

'You've been watching too many James Bond movies, mate,' Rory said.

'Not any more, I bloody won't. Did you see *Spectre*? What a load of shit!'

'Do you think so? I liked it.'

'It wasn't a patch on *Skyfall*.'

'Well, no, but—'

'Excuse me, Mark Kermode and Simon Mayo! Any chance we could save the film review for the lunch break?' Matilda said.

'Rory, can you send me this link?' Sian said. 'Let me watch it a few more times and I'll get back to you.'

Matilda waited until the three were making their way out of her office before she called after Rory.

'Is James Darke in the building, do you know?'

Rory's eyes widened. He waited for her to realize her mistake. She didn't, and he wasn't going to point it out.

'Erm, I don't think James Dalziel is in, no.'

'Right. No problem.'

Rory closed the door quickly behind him, and Matilda sat back down in her chair. Her error suddenly came to her. *Shit*!

Chapter Forty-Nine

'Christian, do me a favour – come and have a look at this CCTV footage and see if you recognize this bloke,' Sian said. 'I've watched it more than a dozen times, but I can't put a name to his face. Ooh, you smell like a cheap tart,' she added when he got closer.

'I was foolishly walking through reception just as Trisha Abbott came in.'

'Blimey, is she still going?'

'She certainly is. Fifty years old and still working the streets.'

'What did she want?'

'Apparently, she hasn't seen one of her fellow street workers for a few weeks and she's worried.'

'Oh. She's probably moved on somewhere else.'

'That's what I said.'

'Anyway, take a look at this for me,' Sian said.

Christian pulled a chair up to Sian's desk and made himself comfortable. He opened her snack drawer and rummaged through the delights wondering what he was in the mood for. In the end, he grabbed for a Snowball and carefully opened the wrapper, so as not to spill any coconut.

'Let me know when you're ready,' Sian said.

'Sorry, go on,' he replied with a mouthful of chocolate and marshmallow.

Sian ran the ninety-second footage. Christian frowned and asked her to replay it. And a third time. The fourth time he pressed pause and zoomed in on a close-up of the man standing at the reception desk.

'That's Gordon Berry,' he said eventually. 'Remember? That business with the mechanic. We interviewed him after that bloke was—'

'Of course it is. Gordon Berry. Christian, you're a star.' She quickly wrote his name down on a Post-It note before she forgot. 'Help yourself to a … well, maybe not,' she said, looking at the mess he'd made of her desk. She decided not to tell him about the bits of marshmallow around his mouth. She needed to get her kicks from somewhere.

'Do you remember Super Saturday?' Sian asked Matilda.

'Is that the day after Black Friday?'

'No. Super Saturday 2012 was when Team GB won all those gold medals in the space of less than an hour at the London Olympics.'

'I'll take your word for it,' Matilda said, wondering where this was leading.

'Anyway, on Super Saturday, Gordon Berry was working for a garage on Queens Road. There was only him and a colleague, Darren Price, working. Gordon went to the pub for lunch at one o'clock and came back at half past two.'

'Long lunch.'

'Liquid lunch too by the sound of it. Not long after his return, there's an incident and Darren Price is crushed to death by a car falling on him. Gordon was arrested at the scene because police officers attending could smell alcohol on his breath and he was slurring his words. However, he was never charged with manslaughter or being drunk while operating heavy machinery.'

'Why not?'

'Because during his investigations, the coroner claimed the equipment in the garage was so out of date that it was only a matter of time before an incident of this nature occurred. Albie Finkle who owned the garage was charged with negligence and found guilty of manslaughter.'

'What happened to Finkle?'

Sian flicked through the thick file in her hands. 'He was fined and banned from owning a business for ten years. He gassed himself three weeks later.'

'Bloody hell. And what about Gordon Berry?'

'Nothing.'

'So the coroner's report blamed the equipment in the garage for Price's death?'

'Yes.'

'But surely Berry should have taken some of the blame for being drunk.'

'You'd have thought so, wouldn't you?'

'We need to pay this Gordon Berry a visit. He sounds like a prime target for our serial killer.'

'Do you think he was coming into the station to ask for protection?'

'It's possible. It doesn't explain why he did a runner though. Come on, Sian, let's go and see what Gordon has to say for himself. You can buy me lunch with your scratchcard winnings afterwards.'

'Mum, it's me,' George Appleby said. He was sitting on his bed in the shared house he refused to move out of. Since the taunting had begun, he had stopped going to university and stayed in his room. He looked a mess. His hair was overgrown, his beard was patchy, and he stank of sweat. For days George had been contemplating calling his mother. Eventually, he worked up the courage.

'George, what do you want? I'm just about to go out,' she said in her usual icy monotone.

'It's about Dad.'

'George, I'm not interested,' she cut him off.

'Mum, listen.'

'No, George, you listen. I had no idea your father had moved up to Sheffield, and I really don't want to talk about him.'

'People *are* talking,' he said quietly, his voice breaking.

'Of course they are, it's what they do.'

'But people are talking about me, looking at me.' His voice was soft. He was on the brink of tears.

'George, you're nineteen years old, sort it out for yourself.'

George took a deep breath. 'There's something else, Mum.'

'I can't have this conversation now, I'm running late for work. I'm sorry, George.'

'Mum, can I come down to visit this weekend?' he asked before his mother could end the call.

'I don't think so, George. I have to go,' she said. She didn't say goodbye, just hung up.

George sat on the edge of his bed, the phone still pressed against his ear. He looked out of the window at the view of the steel city. He hated Sheffield. He hated the university. He wished he'd never come here.

While he'd been on the phone to his mother, he'd felt it vibrate a few times. He looked at the screen and saw he'd received more notifications on social media, more taunts, more people making fun of him. Even complete strangers were getting in on the act.

He leaned down and pulled open the drawer underneath his bed. He took out a length of polyhemp rope. The victims of the Hangman were realizing there were consequences for their actions. It was about time others learned that lesson too.

Chapter Fifty

It took longer for Matilda and Sian to find somewhere to park than it did to find Gordon Berry's house. Eventually, they found a space in the next street and walked back.

'How are your legs?' Sian said.

'Fine now they've stopped throbbing. You should have seen my thighs on Sunday night, Sian. They looked like someone had been at them with a cheese grater.'

'It was worth it though, surely.'

'Oh God, yes, absolutely. And it was lovely of Scott to come on board too. You know, he got his sister to hand around his sponsor form at the school where she works. He raised over a grand on his own, bless him.'

'He's a good lad, Scott. He thinks the world of you, too.'

'Does he?' Matilda asked, looking surprised.

'Yes. Him, Rory and Faith, they won't hear a word said against you. All three of them see you as a career template.'

'Oh. I'm not sure if I like being seen as a role model. I certainly don't feel like one.'

'Well they have a lot of respect for you. The whole team does. Don't let it go to your head though. For every Scott, Rory and Faith, I'm sure there are a dozen who can't stand you.'

‘Ah, thanks, Sian. I can always trust you to keep me grounded.’

They reached Gordon Berry’s house. It was in darkness, curtains closed, no sign of anyone.

‘You wouldn’t think anyone lived here,’ Sian said. ‘Look at the state of those windows. They haven’t been cleaned in months.’

‘Probably why he keeps his curtains closed.’

When Matilda knocked on the door it swung open slightly. They looked at each other with blank faces. Sian took her telescopic truncheon out of her back pocket and extended it to its full length with a flick of her wrist. Matilda pushed the door wide.

‘Hello!’ she called out. ‘Mr Berry.’

There was no reply. Matilda poked her head into the house. It was dark. There were no sounds of movement.

‘Mr Berry? I’m DCI Darke from South Yorkshire Police.’ When she didn’t hear anything, she raised an eyebrow to Sian and stepped into the house.

The first thing Matilda noticed was the freezing cold. Two rooms led off from the dark hallway – a kitchen and a living room. She chose the lounge first. Sian stayed behind, baton held aloft.

Matilda walked inside and turned on the light switch next to the door. There was an obvious sign of a disturbance – broken coffee table, armchair pushed into a bookcase, sofa cushions on the floor.

‘I don’t like this,’ Matilda turned to Sian.

‘No. Me neither. Shall I check upstairs?’

‘Sure. Be careful.’

Sian left Matilda alone in the lounge. Matilda made sure she didn’t touch anything. On the mantelpiece, there were an array of framed photographs. She leaned in to get a good look at them. They were the standard school pictures of young children, holiday snaps. One of the men she recognized from outside the police station, presumably Gordon Berry, in a holiday pose – his arm around another man on a sun-kissed pub terrace.

'There's nobody upstairs,' Sian said, entering the room, baton now firmly back in her pocket. 'The main bedroom is very untidy, and the bed hasn't been made. It doesn't look like there's been a burglary because there's some expensive music equipment up there.'

'So whatever happened was isolated to the living room then?'

'It would appear so.'

'OK, Sian. Get onto Forensics. I want a full team here to give this house a serious going over.'

'Will do.'

Sian pulled her mobile out of an inside pocket and moved over to the window to make a call. 'Matilda, you're going to want to see this,' she said, looking down at something behind the sofa.

'What?'

Sian pointed.

'Is that what I think it is?' Matilda asked following Sian's gaze and seeing a thick rope with a noose tied at the end.

***

'Who was working on where the rope came from?' Matilda asked. She and Sian were back in the car while a forensics team made a full sweep of Gordon Berry's home. Sian had splashed her lottery winnings on two takeaway medium lattes and two muffins.

'Rory.'

'And?'

'Hang on, I've got it on my phone somewhere,' Sian said, searching through her emails. 'Here we are. It's a twelve-millimetre polyhemp rope. It has the look and feel of natural fibres, but it isn't. It's fully weatherproof and doesn't shrink when wet.'

'Where can it be bought from?'

'Absolutely everywhere. Rory looked online and there are more than a thousand stockists in South Yorkshire alone. It's also sold on Amazon. You know when you buy something from Amazon you can ask other buyers a question about the product?'

'Yes.'

'Well, quite a few people asked if it's a good enough rope to hang yourself with.'

'Blimey. And what were the replies?'

'They all said it was. What's more surprising is that not one person tried to talk the buyer out of hanging themselves. They just told them it was fine for the job, and that's it.'

'Nothing surprises me anymore,' Matilda said, looking out of the window.

Sian sipped at her drink, all the while not taking her eyes from her boss. 'Can I ask you a question?'

'Of course.'

'Are you scared?'

Matilda looked at her. 'Of what?'

'Whoever the killer is has obviously got you in their sights for whatever reason. He could be watching you right now. Doesn't that frighten you?'

Matilda took a while to answer. It wasn't that she didn't know how to answer, she didn't want to admit it to herself. She took a deep breath. 'I'm petrified, Sian.'

Chapter Fifty-One

By the time Forensics had finished at Gordon Berry's house it was getting late, and dark. Matilda and Sian searched the house looking for clues as to where Gordon Berry might be. They found a wage slip in a drawer which gave his employer as KKE Engineering in the Wicker. It wasn't far from Attercliffe, but it was almost seven o'clock and the place would be closed. Sian drove Matilda back to the station. Matilda told Sian to go straight home.

Matilda didn't usually mind entering the incident room alone after office hours. She stood in the doorway and turned on the lights. They buzzed and blinked into life. She looked around the open-plan room. Tonight, she felt apprehensive. It had been a long time since she had hunted down a serial killer. In this case, the killer was targeting her personally, for some reason. Why?

She made her way into her small office and closed the door behind her. It was just how she left it, even the computer was still on, but in sleep mode. She hit the keyboard and the screen lit up. Her homepage was the BBC News website. The main headline was of a terrorist attack in Turkey which had left twelve people dead.

Matilda checked her emails. There was nothing of interest. She didn't open a single one of them. She knew what they would contain by looking at the sender's name.

She picked up her phone and saw five text messages, all from Adele. Matilda sent a quick reply to pacify her friend, before throwing the phone down on the table and leaning back in her chair.

What Sian had said had unsettled her. Why was he contacting her? Was it just because she was leading the investigation? But he was contacting Danny Hanson at *The Star* too. Maybe she wasn't being targeted. Maybe this was just a killer who enjoyed being the centre of attention. A narcissist. A sick, twisted, narcissist. There was one person who could put her mind at rest. She looked at her watch. It was almost eight o'clock. It wasn't too late to make a house call.

'I hope you don't mind me coming around unannounced,' Matilda asked, shivering on the doorstep.

'Of course not, come on in.'

James Dalziel stepped back so Matilda could enter. She smiled and stepped into the warmth. A stiff wind had picked up, and, as usual, Matilda wasn't dressed for the weather.

She stood in the hallway and looked around at the tasteful decoration. The floor had the original Victorian tiles, the wood of the bannister on the stairs was stripped oak. The Tiffany lightshade heavy and expensive. James Dalziel was a man of taste.

'Has another body been found?' he asked.

'No. Well, not as such. I was wondering if I could pick your brains.'

He smiled. 'I've been lecturing teenagers all day, there may not be much left, but you're more than welcome to try.'

He ushered her into the living room.

When Matilda saw the thick pile cream carpet, she stopped in the hallway and kicked off her shoes before entering. The heat from the wood burner wrapped itself around her and she felt relaxed. The room was as tastefully decorated as the hallway: large leather sofas, tall, oak bookcases filled with academia and research – not a single crime fiction book in sight. She picked up a framed photograph of two young girls from a small table next to the door.

'Cute girls. Yours?'

'Yes. Martha and Karen.'

'Twins?'

'No.' He laughed. 'They went through a stage where they wanted to dress alike. Martha's eight now. Karen's six.'

'You must really miss them.'

'I do,' he said, taking the frame from her and looking longingly at his daughters before putting it in exactly the same place on the table. 'I'd love to have them living with me, but it wouldn't be fair to take them away from school, and their friends.'

'Couldn't you move back up to Scotland?'

'Can I get you a drink?' James asked, pointing at his own glass of whiskey on the coffee table to change the subject.

'Better not, I'm driving. I'll have a coffee, if it's not any trouble.'

'Sure. How do you take it?'

'Black, no sugar, thanks.'

'OK. Well, make yourself at home.'

Matilda sat down and looked at the paperwork on the coffee table James had obviously been engrossed in before she interrupted. Judging by the title, it wasn't anything to do with the case. Although, Matilda couldn't make sense of the title, so she had no idea what it was about.

In the background, the sound of smooth classical music was pumping out of the speakers. He was so much like her husband, it was frightening. She wasn't sure if she should mention that – probably not. He entered the living room carrying a small tray with two matching cups and saucers. Villeroy & Boch – they weren't cheap either.

'Would you like anything to eat? I could whip up an omelette if you're hungry.'

Matilda tried to remember the last time she'd eaten – a muffin with Sian while they were waiting for Forensics to finish in Gordon Berry's house. How many hours ago was that?

'I'm fine, thank you.'

'Are you sure? Anything to go with the coffee? I've got some biscuits somewhere.'

'No, I'm fine, thank you.'

'So, what can I do for you?' he asked, sitting on the armchair opposite and crossing his legs.

He reminded Matilda of her former therapist, Sheila Warminster. She used to sit with her legs crossed and stare at her with a questioning look made up of forty per cent genuine interest, forty per cent concern, and twenty per cent condescension. It must be a psychologist thing. Maybe they learned that expression on their first day at therapy school.

'The killer is personally targeting me and, well, I'm worried about what's going to happen. How it's going to end. About the people around me; my team. I'd like your advice.'

'OK. Well, why do you think he's targeting you?'

Typical answer from a psychologist. Never directly answer a question but answer with a question.

'Well, he's calling me. He left the mannequin in my garden and he clearly wants my attention. Is he actually targeting me?'

'If it was just you getting the phone calls, I'd say yes, but he's also phoning Danny Hanson.'

'So what does that mean?'

'He's proud of what he's doing. He's killed and he is keen for his name to be attached to his crime, a bit like an artist who signs their paintings.'

'But we don't know his name.'

'It's "the Hangman" as far as he's concerned. You know he's killed three people. Once you have his real name you'll catch him and the element of surprise, the shock factor, will vanish. However, he will have a legacy of being the Hangman, the person who killed three people. Until that time, the whole country is waiting with bated breath for him to strike again. He's got Sheffield scared and he's loving it.'

Matilda leaned forward and carefully picked up her coffee cup. She breathed in the aroma. It was strong, just how she liked it. 'So he's not purposely targeting me?'

'I don't think so. He's targeting you because you're in charge of the case. I mean, you haven't heard from him in over a week, have you?'

How did he know that? 'No. But, well, I have been off for a week.'

'True. But you're back now. Nothing's happened, has it?'

'Sort of.' She swallowed and banished her doubts about James. 'I think the killer has made his first mistake.'

'Go on,' he instructed.

Matilda filled him in on Gordon Berry, who he was, what he'd done and the noose they had found in his living room.

'It sounds like the killer met his match. Where is this Gordon Berry now?'

'I've no idea. We'll start a full search for him in the morning.'

'And you've had no contact with the killer?'

'No. Well, I'm not likely to, am I? He's messed up. He's not going to call me to brag about it, is he?'

'Hmm.' James thought.

'What?'

'Well, you've been off work for a week. The day you're back, he goes after his next victim.'

'So he *is* targeting me for some reason?'

'It's possible he wants you on the case. He sees you as his intellectual match. Only you can investigate what he's doing.'

'Why me?'

'I've no idea. There are two people who can answer that – the killer, and you.'

'Me?'

'I keep going back to this. I really do think you know the killer, Matilda. You've had dealings with him before. To him, every day that passes where you don't identify him, you're failing, and he's winning.'

'He's delighting in watching me fail?'

'I think so. From his point of view, he's got the upper hand because you have no idea who he is. There is a chance the Hangman is enjoying himself so much that he'll become complacent and slip up. However, if you sit around and wait for that to happen, the body count will increase.'

'How do I find out who he is?'

'You look into your own past. Who have you put away? Who have you pissed off so much they want to see you in such torment?'

'Before he killed himself, I would have said Ben Hales,' Matilda said. She drained the last of the coffee and placed it on the table. 'I can't think of anyone else.'

Matilda leaned back in the sofa and looked into the distance. Her mind raced through her past cases. Yes, she had sent many murderers to prison and some would indeed be free now. However, she couldn't think of a single one of them who had the mental capacity to put so much research into finding these victims just to get back at her.

'Matilda, I finished reading the book about Carl Meagan this afternoon,' James said, sitting forward and crossing his fingers. 'Have you thought maybe the killer is targeting you because of Carl? By your own admission, you failed to find him. The book certainly paints a very bad picture of you. Technically, you're a potential victim for the killer.'

'Do you think the killer could be related to Carl's family?'

'I don't know the family. I can't answer that.'

'Philip and Sally Meagan are suffering. They want to know where their son is. They wouldn't put other families through the pain they're going through.'

'Do you know that for sure?'

Matilda thought for a long moment. 'I …'

'When was the last time you had any contact with Carl's parents?'

She blew out her cheeks. 'I can't remember.'

'Grief does strange things to some people. We never know how it's going to affect us until it happens.'

You don't need to tell me that. I'm the perfect example of a normally rational person falling apart at the seams when they've lost the only person they've ever loved.

Matilda shook her head. 'I'm sorry, I don't see Philip and Sally Meagan becoming serial killers to get at me. They wouldn't do that.'

'Matilda, I don't know the Meagan family. I don't know the case at all. I'm just telling you my opinion based on this case. Sometimes it's helpful to get an outsider's perspective. There's no way you'd think the Meagans capable of this crime whereas I have no qualms in putting their names into the hat.'

'No,' Matilda said firmly. 'No. I refuse to believe that.'

James shrugged. 'It wouldn't hurt to find out their alibis for the time of the murders.'

She took a deep breath. She felt sick. 'Do you think I could use your bathroom?'

'Sure. Upstairs, first on the left.'

'Thanks.'

Matilda couldn't leave the room fast enough. As much as she respected James's opinion and professional acumen, there was no way the Meagans were suspects in this case. She walked slowly up the stairs and entered the bathroom, locking the door behind her. She looked at her reflection in the mirror and rolled her eyes.

God I look old. Old and tired.

Matilda splashed her face with cold water. She could feel a headache coming on. Trying to remember every case she'd worked on, everyone who had ever wanted to torture her.

She patted her face dry with a very thick and luxurious towel and left the bathroom. On the wall was a framed picture of an old map of Scotland. Along the landing, the door to the master bedroom was ajar. She pushed it open with her foot and stuck her head inside. The bedroom was as neat and tidy as a hotel room. Nothing on the surfaces, nothing out of place. It was perfect. On the bedside cabinet was a paperback novel, *Messiah*, by Boris Starling. So James did read crime fiction. This made Matilda smile.

The next room along was a spare bedroom with two single beds in it. His daughters probably slept in here when they visited. It looked like it hadn't been used for months; it was cold and there was a fusty smell of dust.

The third bedroom was a box room James used as a study. There were filing cabinets along the back wall and a desk under the window with a laptop, desktop computer and a charging tablet. She turned to leave the room when she paused. On the desk was a hardback copy of *Carl*, by Sally Meagan. There were Post-It arrows sticking out of the top of various pages. Matilda opened it at random and saw James had highlighted or underlined certain passages. She frowned, placed the book on the desk and turned to leave the room.

On the back wall was a chart of all the victims in Matilda's hanging case. Staring at her were black-and-white photographs of Brian Appleby, Joe Lacey, and Katie Reaney. A map of Sheffield below marked the areas they lived in. A whiteboard offered information on the victims, details on hangings, including the best way for a person to die by hanging, and profiles on potential suspects. There was a colour photograph of the noose used to kill one of the victims. He'd commented on the thirteen turns in the rope. His notes were more detailed than the ones she had in her dining room at home. There was even a glossy photo of Matilda.

'Matilda, would you like another coffee?'

The call came from downstairs. The words didn't seem to register with her. Then she remembered where she was. Christian Brady's words about James possibly being the killer echoed through her head. She was stupid to have come here alone, especially without telling anyone.

'Oh, no thanks. I'd better be going home.'

Matilda wanted to leave the house quickly and be with someone she knew, someone she could trust. She ran down the stairs to find James waiting for her in the doorway of the living room.

'Everything OK?' he asked, smiling.

'Yes. Fine,' she replied, her eyes fixed firmly on the ground. 'I should be getting on. I promised Adele I'd pick up a takeaway. She'll be wondering where I am,' she lied.

'OK. Well, I'll probably see you tomorrow. I've been asked to pop in to see Valerie.'

'Oh, right,' she said, struggling to put on her shoes without rushing. 'Thanks for the coffee and the chat.'

'You're welcome. Any time.' James opened the door for her and let in a blast of cool night air.

'Goodnight then,' she said, practically running out of the house.

She didn't look back as she made her way down the drive, but she knew he was watching her from the doorway.

She climbed into her car, locked herself inside, and breathed a sigh of relief to be out of the house. Why did he feel the need to have so much information on the case? The thought sent an ice-cold shiver down her spine.

As she drove past, James was still standing in the doorway. He raised a hand to wave goodbye. She returned a painful smile. She was just turning the corner when she noticed the garden posts in his front garden and the rope used to link them. Was it twelve-millimetre polyhemp? She bloody hoped not.

Chapter Fifty-Two

Danny Hanson couldn't sleep. He'd spent most of the evening on the Sheffield forums reading people's comments on the killer. Since his double-page feature on the three victims and their pasts, anyone with a chequered history was panicking. Danny had made notes, potential interviewees he could contact to add background, on the off-chance there was a fourth victim.

***SheffGal80**: My brother spent three years in prison for armed robbery. Is that enough? Should we be worried?*

***SUFC2000**: Who did he rob? Did he get much?*

SheffGal80: *He did a few petrol stations in 2002.*

***SUFC2000**: A few and he only got 3yrs? What's his neck size? LOL*

***Oooooowls**: People get away with murder these days. This bloke is doing everyone a favour. If you can't do the time don't do the crime. I know a few people he can hang if he's running out of victims.*

***PinkJill**: My sister reckons she knows the killer. She used to date a bloke who was dead keen on hanging being brought back.*

BADGER76: *I knew Joe Lacey. He was a good bloke. His*

family are in bits. What he did was a mistake, and he paid for it. The law is there to punish people, to dish out the sentence, not for people to turn vigilante. The police do nothing. Even if this killer is caught he'll only get a few years. This country is a joke.

CaptainSheffield: *Anyone fancy a game of hangman?*

Danny had messaged a few people who he thought he could get some information out of. Some seemed genuinely frightened. Maybe this would deter people from committing crimes in the first place. Is this what the killer wanted?

He heard a noise outside of his bedroom door. He stopped what he was doing and looked at the gap underneath his door. There was a yellow light from the landing. The strip was broken by someone standing outside. Danny's heart skipped a beat. There was a knock.

'Danny, do you mind if I use some of your milk? I've run out.'

Danny swallowed. His paranoia was practically off the scale. Even in the relative safety of his own room he was scared of a shadow under the door or a creak of a floorboard. 'No, it's fine, Gill, go ahead.'

'Thanks. I'll replace it tomorrow.'

Danny watched as she moved away down the corridor. He went to check the door was locked before going back to bed.

It was gone midnight by the time Danny turned his laptop off. He could have spent the whole night scrolling through the message boards. Some of the arguments between people were interesting, especially the ones who thought the killer was doing Sheffield a favour. When he was studying to be a journalist he'd dreamed of a career at a daily national, getting scoops on political scandals and being on the front line with British troops in the Middle East. He didn't expect the excitement to come straight away, and not on a local paper that usually had more adverts than stories.

It took him a while to fall asleep. His mind refused to settle. He was just nodding off when his mobile started vibrating on his bedside table. He reached out from under the duvet, grabbed the phone and pulled it into the warmth of his cocoon. He looked at the display. Once again, the caller had withheld their number.

'Shit,' he said to himself. He watched the screen flash at him, felt the vibration in his clammy hand. He really didn't want to answer it. He pictured his attacker fleeing from the park. Why was he doing this? Yes, these people had committed crimes in the past, but they'd been to prison and were living normal lives. What gave him the right to act as an executioner?

The phone stopped ringing and Danny visibly relaxed. It started up again straight away.

'Fuck.'

He licked his lips, took a deep breath, and answered the phone.

'Hello?'

'Good morning, Mr Hanson. Gordon Berry is hanging around in between the train station and the bus station.'

The call ended before Danny could ask who Gordon Berry was and why his next victim was outside rather than in his house.

He threw the duvet back and jumped out of bed. He scrambled around for some clothes. It didn't matter whether they were clean or dirty, he just needed to get to the train station before anyone else found the body.

While driving through the quiet streets of Sheffield, Danny wondered whether he should call Matilda or wait until he'd checked it out for himself. It could be a hoax. He went over the phone call in his head; did it sound like the killer? He couldn't remember. Maybe this was a hoax. Matilda wouldn't appreciate being called out. He smiled grimly to himself.

There wasn't anywhere to park around the train station, so he pulled up on the pavement and flicked on the hazard lights. He slammed his car door closed behind him and looked at his watch: 12.45. There was very little traffic about and no people in the nearby vicinity. Suddenly, he felt afraid. Had he been set up *again*? Was he about to be jumped on and attacked? Or worse.

From the entrance of the train station there was a main road to cross then a covered walkway to the bus station. All the time Danny was crossing the street, his eyes were firmly fixed on the narrow walkway. Was there really a dead body in there? He hoped not. He'd never seen one before. He remembered his nan dying when he was eight years old. At the funeral, the coffin was open for people to say a final goodbye, but his mother wouldn't allow him to go up to her. While she was busy chatting with other mourners, he tiptoed close enough to see the edge of her face – she was white and looked as if she was sleeping. He didn't know what all the fuss had been about, the dead weren't scary at all.

At the entrance to the walkway, Danny composed himself. A steel and glass structure acted as protection from the elements for commuters going from the train station to the bus station. On one side was an abandoned building, on the other, a steep incline to the road. He took his phone out of his trouser pocket and turned on the torch. With shaking hands, he held it up and lit his way ahead. He took a deep breath. Pointing the phone left and right, he slowly walked deeper into the darkness. The sound of his heart pounded in his ears, along with the echoing footfall from his only pair of smart shoes. He was more than halfway through when a passing car turned into the next road, its headlights lighting up the whole tunnel. Danny squinted and turned his head to avoid the glare and came face to face with a hanging man. He gasped and fell backwards, dropping his phone. He was shaking, struggling to breathe. Sweat prickled on the back of his neck. He scrambled around in the dark for his phone without taking his eyes from the silhouette in front of him. He eventually found it and aimed its beam of light in front of him. There it was, the hanging body just like the killer had told him. There was one difference though: this time, there was no pillowcase covering the face. Danny saw, close up, in full technicolour, the effects of hanging on a human being.

'Fuck,' he uttered, his teeth chattering.

He unlocked his phone and quickly scrolled through the contact list until he came to Matilda's name. He pressed call and hoped she would hear it. He hoped she was close by. He didn't know how much longer he would be able to sit alone in the dark with a dead body.

'Danny?'

Matilda pulled up in her silver Ford Focus, the squealing brakes cutting through the quiet cold air. Adele, in the front passenger seat, followed her.

'Danny?' she called again for the journalist.

'I'm here,' came the faint, nervous reply from the tunnel.

As Matilda and Adele entered the walkway, Danny came running towards them. He looked pale, frightened, his eyes wide with shock.

'I'm sorry. I should have called you as soon as he rang, but I didn't know if it was a hoax or not. I didn't think you'd want me dragging you out of bed over nothing. I'm really sorry,' he waffled.

'It's OK,' Matilda said, holding him by the shoulders. 'Just calm down, breathe slowly and tell me what happened.'

Danny took a deep breath, but it didn't help. He was hysterical. 'I've been sick, I'm sorry,' he said, pointing behind him.

'That's all right, don't worry. This is Adele, she's a pathologist, she'll take care of you. Adele.'

'A pathologist?' he asked faintly.

Adele smiled. 'Come with me, Danny. We'll go and sit in the car.' She put her arm around him and led him away.

Matilda watched while they walked towards the vehicle. She had never been a fan of journalists, and while working on the Starling House case last year, she had found Danny to be arrogant and lack respect in his questions. Now, she felt sorry for him. It was never easy being among the dead, especially at a crime scene. It was something Danny was going to have to get used to, if he wanted a future in crime reporting.

Gordon Berry's eyes were wide and staring, his tongue protruding. From what light she could get from her phone, she could see evidence of rope burn marks around his neck and blood beneath his cracked fingernails. Matilda looked up at him with sadness. After seeing the evidence of a struggle at his house, she genuinely thought the killer had made a mistake. It had just been a setback. He made sure he succeeded in his task.

Chapter Fifty-Three

As soon as Valerie Masterson heard the news of a fourth body she had requested a meeting with Matilda first thing. She wanted Christian Brady and James Dalziel there too, but Matilda said she'd like to speak to her alone for now. Reluctantly, Valerie acquiesced.

Valerie stood behind her desk, arms folded, a look of steely determination on her face. Unusually for her, her desk was a mess of newspapers, both local and national.

Matilda slumped in the leather visitor's chair, visibly dejected. Now the national press had picked up the story it wasn't just the weight of South Yorkshire she had on her shoulders, it was the whole country. Since the slim and attractive Katie Reaney had been killed, the tabloids had splashed her all over the front pages. Once her past had been revealed and the motivation of the killer examined, journalists had arrived in Sheffield by the coachload, eager to find a new angle on the rare occurrence of a serial killer at large in the country.

'What the hell is going on, Matilda?'

'I wish I knew, ma'am,' Matilda sighed.

'That's not the answer I want to hear.'

'It's not the answer I want to give, but it's the truth. The killer is a very smart individual. He's left no forensics behind at the scenes and there have been no witnesses. All we've got is a tall, slim man with dark hair. Most of the blokes in the station answer to that description, let alone the half a million living in Sheffield.'

'This cannot be allowed to run and run, Matilda. Have you seen the newspapers this morning? I've had Kate Stephenson on the phone three times already. They've had an online poll and of the two thousand who answered, seventy-three per cent have no confidence in South Yorkshire Police. Seventy-three per cent, Matilda.'

Matilda put her head in her hands.

'And from where I'm standing, I'm one of them. You're not exactly exuding confidence right now,' she added. 'I'm keeping Christian Brady as acting DCI for the rest of this case. You can't do this on your own. Now do I need to bring someone else in?'

'No,' Matilda replied quietly.

'And what about you?' Valerie asked after studying Matilda's pained expression. 'Can't you cope, is that it?'

'Of course I can cope,' Matilda snapped.

'What about James Dalziel? He's supposed to be helping you put together a profile of this killer. Why didn't you want him here?'

Matilda pictured his spare room; the detailed information, the images he'd somehow managed to get hold of, the photograph of her. She knew his psychological insight was invaluable but was he really pointing them in the right direction, or was Matilda reading too much into this, like she did everything else.

'We don't need a psychologist—'

'Oh don't you?' Valerie interrupted. 'Would a psychic be more useful? James Dalziel is a highly respected criminal psychologist. He knows what he's talking about. Listen to him.'

Matilda was silent. Her eyes darted left and right as she contemplated the minefield she was currently in the middle of.

'What have you got against him?' Valerie asked.

'Nothing.'

'Are you sure?'

'Of course I am. I just …'

'Is it Ben Hales that's getting to you? Do you need more time off?'

'No I don't,' she replied firmly.

'Then what is it?' she snapped again. Matilda didn't reply. She looked past Valerie and out of the window at the bleak Sheffield skyline.

'Matilda,' Valerie leaned forward, 'I'm not pissing about now. I want this killer off the streets and in a cell as soon as possible. I've got the chief constable breathing down my neck. If you're no further forward by the end of the week, I'll have to bring in someone else. If that happens, we'll both be for the high jump. If we can't solve our own crimes, then we're fucked.'

Matilda looked up. It was rare for Valerie to swear.

'I'll have the killer caught by the end of the week,' Matilda said. Neither of them believed her.

The atmosphere in the incident room was heavy. There was no jollity, no banter, even Rory Fleming had his head down and he was usually the clown of the group.

Matilda walked to the front and slammed her hand down on Faith's desk. Everyone fell silent.

'No pissing about, no snide comments, no jokes, nothing. I want answers. We've done door-to-door with every victim, we've interviewed family, friends, colleagues, neighbours, postmen, milkmen and chimney sweeps, what are we missing?'

She looked out on a sea of blank faces. Nobody spoke. Nobody volunteered any information. Everything had already been said several times before.

'The killer is intelligent,' Matilda continued. 'No forensics, no evidence; he makes sure nobody sees him. What kind of person does that?'

'The invisible man,' Rory sniggered.

'One more wisecrack, Rory, and you'll be back in uniform by the end of the day.'

He looked hurt. He knew she wasn't joking.

'He's a man on a mission,' Faith said.

'OK. Let's start there. What kind of mission are we talking about?'

'He's saying these people haven't paid enough for their crimes, so he's taking the law into his own hands.'

'What kind of person thinks that way?'

'I don't know.'

'Come on, Faith, you're doing well.'

'Someone who's disillusioned with the law maybe.'

'So someone who has been a victim and not seen justice served?'

'Yes.'

'OK. I'll go with that. So, we're looking for a victim who believes the law isn't tough enough on criminals.'

'No offence,' Sian said, 'but that could be anyone. You only have to read the papers to see a story about a killer being given five years or prisoners living in luxury. People have had enough.'

'We're going around in circles here,' Matilda said. She felt tired, physically and mentally. 'Faith, you're good with the Internet. Have a look at forums where people have been spouting off about the law being easy for criminals. Anyone local, let me know.'

'I have been doing. There's loads of people who are pissed off with the levels of crime in this country. They're all saying the same thing: the courts don't care about the victims, prisoners using the Human Rights Act to their advantage, not giving a toss that they violated their victims' human rights,' she said.

'Is that you talking or the people in the forums?' Rory asked.

Faith didn't reply but gave him an evil look. 'What about the victims of unsolved crimes? If they think the police haven't worked hard enough to solve their case, maybe they've taken the law into their own hands.'

'And once they'd solved their own crime they got a taste for being a vigilante,' Scott continued Faith's idea.

'Does that really happen, though?' Rory asked. 'Once you've killed do you get a taste for it?'

'I don't know. Ask James Dalziel.'

'Right.' Matilda clapped her hands together. 'Faith, Scott, Rory, I want you all to look into the crimes our four victims have committed. Contact the relatives of their victims and get an alibi for the time of the murders.'

'We've already done that,' Rory said.

'Well do it again,' Matilda shouted. 'Kesinka, get a list of unsolved crimes, any complaints made to the police about their cases not being taken seriously, any complaints about individual officers. Christian, Sian, South Yorkshire Police has twenty-six unsolved murders on their books. Have a look at who might have a grievance towards the police for not solving the murders. Start with the most recent and go back. Where's Aaron?'

'He called this morning,' Sian said. 'Katrina gave birth by caesarean section earlier this morning. It's still touch and go.'

'Right, OK. Send him a text, tell him not to worry about coming to work any time soon. Ranjeet, get a team of uniforms together. Go back to every murder scene and knock on the doors of the neighbours. I know we've questioned them before, but I want them questioned again.'

'Yes, boss.'

'Rory, Scott, go to where Gordon Berry worked – where was it again?'

'KKE Engineering,' Faith answered.

'Go there, interview all of his colleagues. We need to know everything about him, what he was doing, his personal life, everything.'

'But you asked us to—'

'I'm not arguing with you, Rory,' Matilda almost exploded. 'Just do it.'

'Ma'am,' he said, looking dejected.

'Any questions? I didn't think so,' Matilda said quickly before anyone could ask anything. 'I don't want anyone in this incident room unless you have to be. I want a presence out on the street. Also, no talking to the press. They're swarming all over the city. Keep your mouths shut and do your job. That goes for every single one of you.'

Matilda turned away from the rapidly emptying room and entered her office, slamming the door closed behind her.

She could feel the pressure of the task weighing her down. Her vision was blurring. A panic attack was looming.

She slumped into her chair and closed her eyes. She was immediately transported back into her hallway and staring at Ben Hales hanging from her bannister. In her vision, he was very much alive. The rope was tight around his neck but he was looking right at her, his eyes burning into her soul, and smiling that annoying grin he often sported when he thought he had one over on her.

Matilda opened her eyes when a knock came on her door. It was Christian.

'Everything OK?' he asked.

'Not really. What can I do for you?'

Christian closed the door behind him and sat down. 'Remember when you asked me if there was anything bothering the team?'

'That seems like a lifetime ago,' she scoffed.

'I've overheard a few DCs talking. Brian Appleby was a paedophile, Katie Reaney was a child killer. The reason for the team seeming distracted out there is because of victim apathy.'

'You mean they don't care that a paedophile and a child killer have been murdered?'

'I don't know that for sure, just from what I've overheard.'

'Right,' Matilda said, standing up. She threw open the door to the main office and called everyone to attention. 'A paedophile, a hit-and-run killer and a child killer,' she said, pointing to the photographs on the murder board. 'Usually we have some sort of sympathy for a victim, but with these three, and now with Gordon Berry, I'm guessing there's little compassion around. Am I right?'

Matilda waited but nobody said anything. She looked at their blank faces. She knew Christian was right.

'Joe Lacey has three kids – Jason, Esme and Victoria. Katie Reaney has two, Jenson and Bobbi. They're all under ten. They've lost their parent. They're going to grow up wondering what happened to their parent. Don't do it for Brian, Joe, Katie, or Gordon, do it for their kids. Find the killer and bring them to justice.'

Matilda didn't wait for a response. She turned on her heel and went back into her office and slammed the door so hard behind her the entire wall shook. Christian was still sitting, waiting.

'Get photos of Lacey's and Reaney's kids, get them put up on the boards. I want everyone to see who they're doing this for.'

'Are you all right?' Christian asked.

'Do you want the truth, Christian? No, I'm not all right. There's a killer out there who's taunting me and I'm having to find him on my own because not one single detective here gives a fucking toss,' she shouted. Everyone in the incident room looked at her. She took a deep breath. 'Acting DCI Brady, you're in charge,' Matilda said. She picked up her jacket from the back of the chair and walked out of the office.

Chapter Fifty-Four

Matilda needed some time away from the station, not much, just half an hour or so to be on her own, to calm down from her emotional performance at the briefing.

She stormed out of the building, managing to avoid the barrage of press who had set up home by the front steps. Before she could work out a destination she found herself outside Costa in Orchard Square. The strong caffeine smell emanating from the building was calling to her. She ordered a large latte and asked for an extra shot of caffeine to be added. No, she didn't want to try their new blend for an extra twenty pence. No, she did not want any cakes or cookies.

Sitting in the corner, thinking she was alone with her thoughts, she began to relax as the strong coffee flowed through her veins. This was sheer bliss – until she looked up and saw the worried expression on the smooth face of Danny Hanson gawping down at her.

'Are you following me?' Matilda said.

'No, I'm not following you. I was already here. I saw you come in.'

'Oh.'

'Can I join you?'

'To be honest, Danny, I just wanted a few minutes to myself.'

'I can understand that. I'd really like to talk to you though.'

'If you're looking for a quote or something to put on the front pages, you've come to the wrong person.' It didn't take long for the effects of the caffeine to wear off. She could feel her hackles rising once more.

'I don't want to talk about that. This is more … personal.'

Matilda took a longer look at the young journalist. The worried expression ran deeper than his face. The way he held himself, the throbbing vein in his neck, the dark lines beneath his eyes. He was troubled. She nodded to the chair opposite.

'Thank you.' He gave a nervous smile, pulled the chair out and sat down. 'I've called in sick today. I don't think Kate was happy.'

'It's understandable.'

'When I decided I wanted to be a journalist, I didn't expect to be targeted personally, to have a sadistic killer calling me. This is frightening me,' he said, lowering his voice and looking around.

Matilda no longer saw an annoying young upstart sitting opposite her. She saw a terrified individual whose rose-tinted view of his ideal job had been destroyed. 'It's frightening me, too, and I've been in this job for a long time. Seeing a dead body, especially a murder victim, is not something you get used to. I don't think you should get used to it either. We need to have feelings in order to do our job properly. Now, you're just starting out. This is a highly unusual situation you've found yourself in. You may never face a story like this again.'

'I'm having trouble switching off. I'm not sleeping. Every time my phone rings, I worry it's him.'

Matilda shrugged. 'That's natural. There is nothing I can say to you to make you feel better.'

'I'd like you to tell me he's not going to come after me again.'

'I think he's going to come after one of us. I just have to make sure I get to him first.'

'What if you don't?'

'Then we're both screwed.' She took a long sip of her coffee. 'Hang on a minute, what do you mean "again"? Have you seen him?'

Danny looked down.

'Danny, what happened?'

'I had a phone call. I was told to go to Weston Park to meet someone who knew the killer. I went, and I was attacked.'

'Why didn't you call me?'

'I was chasing a story.' He shrugged.

Matilda shook her head. She could hardly chastise him. She had acted on impulse many times in the past. 'Did you get a good look at the killer?'

He paled as he remembered. 'Tall, slim ...'

'With dark hair?' Matilda finished the sentence for him.

'No. He had dark red hair, a big mess of it.'

Matilda frowned. 'You're sure?'

'Absolutely.'

'Was he very thin?'

'Yes. I think they call it geek-chic, don't they?'

'Why didn't you report this, Danny?'

He looked sheepish. He muttered something, but Matilda didn't hear. She asked him to repeat it. 'I told Kate. She told me not to say anything. She said if the killer saw the police were involved, he might stop calling.'

'Nice to see she has her staff's best interests at heart,' she replied with sarcasm.

'I don't think I'm cut out for this job.'

'Hang on a minute,' Matilda said, ignoring Danny. She took out her mobile and sent a text to Sian. She would have called, but she didn't want Danny overhearing the name of the person she suspected. Within seconds, her phone beeped an incoming text. God bless Sian Mills. She showed her phone to Danny. 'Is this the person who attacked you?'

'Possibly. I think so.'

'Bloody hell,' Matilda exclaimed, sitting back in her chair. Right from the start they'd had their eye on George Appleby and had let him go. They could have prevented three other people from being killed. He'd fooled everyone.

Sian finished reading through an email. She looked up and caught Faith Easter and Kesinka Rani deep in conversation. They were speaking in hushed tones, something they had both been doing a lot of lately. Sian didn't like that. It smacked of secrecy and segregation within the team. On the pretence of making a fresh coffee, she picked up her mug and went over to the drinks station.

'Isn't it a bit early to be talking about going on holiday together?' Kesinka asked.

'I thought that, but Steve said it would be nice to get away from being around other coppers. When we go out drinking there's always either a uniform he knows or a detective I know propping up the bar.'

'I can see that. Me and Ranjeet sometimes drive for miles to get a bite to eat so we won't be interrupted by someone from work. Coppers are so thick-skinned, aren't they? They won't let you have a meal in peace.'

'Thick-skinned or just plain thick, some of them.'

They both laughed.

'So where's he taking you then?' Kesinka asked.

'Not sure yet. He's looking into a few places.'

'So are things getting serious between you?'

'I'm not sure,' Faith replied, trying to hide her grin. 'I've been out with some losers in my time. Steve's different. For a start, he's gorgeous. Have you seen his smile? My God I could melt. Things have been great between us this week. You know I'm house-sitting for my aunt? Well, Steve's been staying over too. It's like living together. The thing is, though, he's the first bloke who I've actually looked forward to being with. Do you know what I mean?'

'Absolutely. I'm the same with Ranjeet. He's really shy, but he's so sweet.'

Steve entered the incident room. 'Is someone free to chat to Karen Lacey?' he called out to anyone. Faith immediately went red at the sight of her boyfriend and looked away.

'I'll talk to her,' Sian replied quickly before anyone could get a chance. She was standing by the kettle, empty mug in hand, listening to the two love-struck DCs and she could feel her blood sugar levels rising. So much for Matilda's talk about solving these crimes for the victim's children. There was definitely a degree of victim apathy in the incident room.

Steve filled Sian in as they walked down the stairs together. Joe Lacey's widow wanted to talk to someone and it couldn't wait.

Karen Lacey stood up as Sian entered the foyer. She'd lost weight since her husband had died; she looked drawn and tired.

'Karen, you wanted a word?' Sian asked.

'Yes. Is there somewhere private we can go?'

'Erm, yes I think so. Steve, are there any interview rooms free?' she asked the PC, who was back behind the front desk.

'Three and four are available.'

'Thanks. Could you bring us a couple of coffees too?'

'No problem.'

Sian led Karen into the interview room and told her to take a seat. It hadn't been used yet today. There was an underlying smell of cheap disinfectant and even cheaper coffee.

'This won't be recorded, will it?' Karen asked nervously, looking at the recording equipment.

'No. How are you coping?' Sian asked, sitting opposite her.

'I don't know. The kids are staying with my parents in Bakewell for a while. I need to sort out where we're going to live. We can't stay in that house.' Karen spoke quietly, tears welling in her eyes.

Sian gave her a sympathetic smile. A quiet knock came on the door and Steve entered with a tray of coffees. He placed them between the two and left without saying a word.

'Would you like anything to eat?'

'No thanks,' Karen replied, wrapping her bony fingers around the mug. She looked freezing cold despite the fact it was finally beginning to warm up outside.

After a long silence, Sian asked. 'Karen, what did you want to see me about?'

She cleared her throat. 'It's Joe. The papers are saying that whoever is going around killing people it's because they've committed crimes in the past. Is that right?'

'That's what we're assuming, yes.'

'And the reason he's doing it is because he doesn't think they've served long enough sentences. Right?'

'Again, we think so.'

'Oh God,' Karen cried.

Sian dug deep into her pocket and pulled out a screwed-up handkerchief. 'Here, take this. It's wrinkled, but it's clean.'

'Thanks,' she said, wiping her nose. 'The thing is, when Joe ran over Rebecca Branson twenty years ago, he wasn't driving.'

'What?'

'I was. I didn't have a licence. I was taking lessons, but I couldn't actually drive. Anyway, we'd been out all night at a New Year's Eve party and when we were going home the roads were really quiet. I said I'd drive. It would be good practice for me. I saw Rebecca run out between two parked cars. I got confused and instead of slamming my foot on the brake I pressed the accelerator. There was nothing I could do. She was over the bonnet before I could …' Karen broke down, her loud sobs drowned out her words.

'Take your time, Karen.' Sian leaned forward and placed a sympathetic hand on her arm.

'My dad was a magistrate at the time. My mum was a solicitor. Can you imagine what it would have looked like if their daughter had been convicted over a hit-and-run? Joe said he'd take the blame. It was his car. He'd say he was driving if anyone ever asked.'

'But he'd been drinking.'

'I know. He was sober, we both were, but we'd been drinking since lunchtime the day before. We stopped just after midnight though, but it was still in his blood. When he went to prison, Mum and Dad told me not to have anything to do with him, but I couldn't. I couldn't abandon him. Not just because he lied for me, but I did genuinely love him. I always have.'

'Does anybody else know about this?'

'No. It's always been mine and Joe's secret. He's died because of me. He was murdered because of what I did. What am I supposed to do?'

Sian sighed and leaned back in her seat. 'From a mother's point of view, I think you should go home and be the best mother you can be to your three children.'

'Shouldn't I go to prison?' she asked, wiping her nose.

Sian nodded. 'But what good would that do? What would happen to your kids? Karen, go home, look after your children, and forget you ever came here today.'

Karen sniffled and wiped her eyes. 'I needed to tell someone, you understand, don't you?'

'Yes, I do. Come on, I'll drive you home.'

Chapter Fifty-Five

Following her coffee with Danny Hanson, Matilda went back to the station. She had hoped she would feel refreshed after having some time alone. Unfortunately, that hadn't happened. She sneaked into her office and gently closed the door behind her. It was soon flung open by Christian.

'Adele's been trying to get hold of you. She said your phone kept going straight to voicemail.'

Matilda dug her iPhone out of her pocket and looked at the screen. 'The battery's died,' she said. She rooted around in her bottom drawer for a charger and plugged it in. 'Did she want anything in particular?'

'She's done the post-mortem on Gordon Berry. There is some severe bruising to his body that looks like he was beaten,' Christian said, reading from a notepad. 'The bruising is relatively fresh. She thinks it was done a day, maybe two, before he was killed.'

'That explains the disturbance at his house. Anything else?'

'Yes. There is a nice footprint on the back of his knees. She may be able to get the print of a shoe from it. No bruising though. She's found red dust in a head wound which she says is from a regular household brick. She seems to think he was attacked from behind, a swift kick to the back of the legs, smack on the head, and he's rendered unconscious. Then he's hanged.'

'Have her check the footprint found at the Lacey's house to see if it matches.'

'She's already checked.' He smiled. 'No match.'

'OK.' Matilda squeezed her eyes tightly shut and gripped the bridge of her nose. 'If he was attacked a day or so before he was killed, then that happened before he came to the station.'

'It would appear so.'

'What have his colleagues said about him?'

'Hang on. Rory, in here!' Christian shouted over his shoulder.

Rory came bounding into the office, a silly grin on his face.

'Tell the boss what Gordon Berry's colleagues said.'

'Well, Tuesday was Gordon's forty-seventh birthday. He and a few others went out for a drink straight from work. They were in the Banker's Draft all night, until just before midnight when they all went their separate ways.'

'Did Gordon go home alone?'

'Yes. He arranged to go out with a female co-worker for a meal on Friday, but on Tuesday he went home on his own.'

'How?'

'He walked. It wasn't far. A few of them said he was pretty pissed but he knew where he was going.'

'Was there anyone in the pub who he had a run-in with?'

'No. They were a small party. They had a few drinks and a laugh.'

'What about on Wednesday?'

'He didn't turn up for work on Wednesday.'

'Why not? Did he call in?' Matilda asked.

'No. They weren't surprised by all accounts. They assumed he had a massive hangover and was sleeping it off.'

'Did nobody think to go around to see how he was?'

'No.' Rory shrugged.

'KKE Engineering isn't far from Attercliffe. It wouldn't have taken five minutes for someone to check on him.'

'They just thought he was hungover.'

'So after he came to the station on Wednesday morning, where did he go until he was found hanged in the early hours of Thursday morning?'

Rory thought for a while. 'Maybe the killer was keeping him somewhere.'

'With his other victims he's hanged them in their homes. Why not take Gordon back to his house and kill him there?' Christian asked.

'I don't know.' Rory shrugged.

'I think the killer was following Gordon for the majority of the day and waited until he could strike. He'll have gone home from his night out and found the Hangman in his house. Gordon put up a fight and managed to get away. He obviously saw the face of his attacker, which is why the killer didn't take any chances when he found him again and murdered him as soon as possible. That's why he didn't cover his head with a pillowcase; because he didn't have one on him,' Matilda said, feeling things coming together at last.

'The killer followed him to the walkway between the bus station and train station, knocked him unconscious, then hanged him?' Christian said, trying to get everything straight in his head. 'Then he called Danny Hanson and told him where he was.'

'Exactly,' Matilda agreed.

'But when Gordon came into the station, why didn't he report anything? Why did he do a runner?' Rory asked.

Matilda was about to answer when she looked over Rory's shoulder into the incident room. DC Faith Easter was on the phone, handset wedged between her shoulder and head, frantically scribbling down on a notepad. DC Kesinka Rani was at the murder boards, a thoughtful look on her face. DC Ranjeet Deshwal was talking to a uniformed officer at the entrance to the room.

'Thanks, Rory,' Matilda said.

He glanced at the DI and DCI. They obviously wanted to discuss something without a lowly DC within earshot. He gave a half-hearted smile and left, closing the door behind him.

'Do you know what we've not given enough consideration?' Matilda asked Christian once the door was closed.

'What's that?'

'The possibility of two killers.'

'Are you serious?'

'We've got James Dalziel telling us the Hangman is a police officer, but I can't get my mind off it being a vigilante killing,' Matilda said, bridging her fingers.

'A police officer could be a vigilante.'

'Yes. So could someone who has been disgraced by the actions of his father.'

Christian thought for a moment. 'George Appleby?'

Matilda nodded.

'Why him?'

'He lured Danny Hanson to Weston Park and attacked him.'

'Why would he do that?'

'I've no idea. Maybe Danny was getting too close, too soon. Yes, the killer has been contacting Danny, feeding him information, but that's another element of his control. He's giving Danny what he wants him to know.'

'The thought of two people working together to kill others is frightening,' Christian said. 'It's beyond evil.'

'I know. Christian, we need to bring George in and formally interview him. If we can break him down, we might start getting somewhere. On their own, I can't see George Appleby or Danny Hanson being the killer. I can't even see anyone on our team being the killer, but when you put the two together, well, who knows?'

'Hang on, it doesn't make any sense,' Christian said, sitting up. 'If the Hangman has been feeding information to Danny to print, why attack him? And why leave himself to be identified? Why not kill Danny?'

Matilda frowned. She hadn't thought of any of that. 'But if George Appleby isn't the killer, why attack Danny in the first place?'

'Because … I don't know,' Christian struggled for an answer.

Matilda flopped back in her chair and let out a sigh. 'I'd almost convinced myself he was the killer, then. I knew I shouldn't have spoken to you about it.' She smiled. 'I still want him interviewed about the attack on Danny, though. And while you're at it, get his alibis for the murders too. He's too much of a loose cannon.'

'I'll have him brought in,' Christian said, heading for the door.

'Be hard on him. The time for pissing about has long gone. Oh, one more thing, keep this theory about two killers under your hat.'

Matilda spent the rest of the afternoon sitting at her desk nursing a headache. She had so many scenarios running around her mind.

When Matilda looked up from her desk she noticed the incident room was all but empty and it was dark outside. Another day had gone by and they were no closer to identifying a killer. They were, however, one day closer to ACC Masterson fulfilling her threat and bringing in someone new to oversee the case. She could certainly kiss goodbye to the Major Crimes Unit and the chance of promotion.

Matilda yawned. She should probably go home and get some sleep. If she stayed awake, however, she could achieve so much in the hours she would waste on sleep.

Chapter Fifty-Six

A shaking finger hovered over 'send'. Eventually, it was hit and the text message was sent to five people's mobile phones. Within seconds, across Sheffield, five people received the same message. They all looked at their phones with furrowed brows. They all had the same question: what the hell was going on?

'I thought you said you were definitely making a decision about the carpet tonight,' Stuart Mills said.

'I was,' Sian said, putting on her coat.

'Over breakfast, you said you were not going to bed tonight until you've finally chosen one.'

'I know.'

'So where are you going?'

'Out.'

'I can see that. Where?'

'Just out.'

'If I was paranoid I'd wonder if you were seeing another man.'

'As if I'd find another man as perfect as you.'

'Do you expect me to buy that?'

Sian thought for a moment. 'Yes.'

'So, I'm transparent. Just be careful, Sian,' Stuart said with worry in his voice.

'Scott, do you mind if I miss the gym tonight?' Rory asked as they left the station.

'No. I was going to say the same thing to you. I want to make a start on the packing. Now we've signed, we're going to start having to pay the bills. We may as well move in as soon as possible.'

'That's what I thought too.'

'Great minds think alike.' Scott smiled. 'See you in the morning.'

They both reversed their cars out of the car park carefully and made their way to the exit. Rory, in front, indicated left, so Scott indicated right.

'Please don't tell me you're going back out?' Jennifer Brady asked her husband.

'Yes. Sorry. I won't be long,' Christian replied, looking for his shoes.

'I thought Matilda was back at work now.'

'She is.'

'So why are you going out?'

'Because I … have to,' Christian replied, struggling to think of an excuse.

'But you haven't seen Zachery for days and you said you'd help Phoebe with her project.'

'It doesn't have to be in until Monday. I'll do it at the weekend.'

'But you promised,' Jennifer said, putting her head to one side and looking at her husband with her big brown eyes.

Christian went over to his wife and kissed her on the tip of her nose. 'I am a world expert in making robots out of cereal boxes and a roll of tin foil. It won't take me long at all.'

'Will you be coming back home tonight?'

'Of course I will,' he said with doubt in his voice.

'I love you DI Brady,' Jennifer called to her husband as he headed for the front door.

'Love you too, Mrs Brady.'

Adele sent her son a text:

Going out. Feed yourself.

Chapter Fifty-Seven

Matilda sat alone in a draughty wooden hut, with the lights off. She was surrounded by complete darkness. She should be frightened. Nobody knew she was here, anything could happen. Surprisingly, she felt buoyed by a sense of determination.

A car turned into the car park, its headlights shining on the windows, through the thin curtains, and briefly lighting up the whole room, before plunging it back into darkness.

A car door slammed closed. Heavy footfalls thumped on the wooden terrace outside. There was a knock, but the caller didn't wait to be invited in. The door swung open. 'Hello?' The voice was shaken, almost scared.

Matilda turned on a light. 'Sian, thanks for coming. Have a seat.'

'Matilda, what's going on? I thought I was being lured here by a serial killer.'

'Yet you came anyway.'

'Curiosity.'

'And all you did was call out a pathetic hello?'

'How would you address a serial killer?'

Matilda thought for a while before smiling. 'Good point. Besides, I texted you from my phone.'

'For all I knew the killer could have murdered you and used your phone to lure me here.'

'You've got a strange imagination, Sian.'

'It comes with the job,' Sian said. 'I've never been in here before.'

'No. Neither have I,' Matilda said, looking around the dimly lit function room in Bradway Bowling Club.

'Are you going to tell me why I've been dragged out of a nice warm house?'

'We'll wait for the others. Coffee?'

'Please. Who else is coming?'

'You'll see.'

Matilda went over to the counter and made them both strong coffees in large mugs. 'It's a shame you don't carry a snack bag around with you. I could just do with a bar of chocolate.'

'Are you all right? You seem a bit … preoccupied.'

'I'm OK,' she lied.

A car turned into the car park and lit up the clubhouse.

'Another lamb to the slaughter?' Sian asked.

Christian Brady, Adele Kean, and Rory Fleming joined Sian and Matilda. They all grabbed a chair and put it in a circle. The door opened, and Scott Andrews bounded in.

'You lying sod,' Rory began. 'You said you were going home to pack.'

'So did you,' Scott admonished.

Matilda interrupted. 'I'm sorry for the mysterious texts and that you've had to lie and make excuses to come here, but everything will be explained. Now, Scott, grab yourself a coffee and a chair and join us.'

Scott did as he was told. He sat next to Rory. The two new flatmates suddenly looked less certain of each other.

'Firstly, have any of you told anyone you were coming here?'

They all mumbled no.

'I didn't even know this place existed,' Rory said.

'That's good. We have Pat Campbell to thank for the choice of venue,' she said, referring to the retired detective sergeant who had helped Matilda out on a number of occasions since she'd left the force. 'Her husband is a treasurer. There was supposed to be a club meeting tonight, but Pat got them to cancel it.'

'What are we doing here?' Christian asked.

'South Yorkshire Police secret bowling league,' Rory said, laughing at his own joke. Nobody else did.

'Before I answer that,' Matilda swallowed, 'I also want to take this opportunity to apologize to you all. I've been very short and snappy with some of you, and I'm sorry. I think we can agree this case has affected all of us in ways we didn't expect. Now, the reason for this clandestine meeting is because I believe the killer is a serving police officer on our team.'

Matilda paused. She expected someone to jump to the defence of the team. She was shocked by the silence, but not completely surprised by it.

'James Dalziel has been saying for a while that the killer is a police officer. He emailed me a profile of the killer,' she said, digging her phone out of her pocket. The light from the screen lit up her face. She looked drawn, shattered. 'He thinks the murderer is suffering from Narcissistic Personality Disorder, which is why he's been contacting me and Danny Hanson. He has a grandiose sense of self-importance,' she said, reading from the email. 'He will feel superior, special, unique, or expect others to see him in this way. He'll have an inflated judgement of his own accomplishment and devalue the contributions of others.'

'Sorry,' Christian interrupted, 'but isn't that all hypothetic? Any of it can be found online, surely.'

'Christian, I know you're not a fan of criminal psychology.'

'It's not that. I just wonder if anyone has considered James Dalziel in all this.'

'You think James is the killer?' Adele asked.

'It wouldn't be the first time someone has abused their

position of power. I'm slightly concerned we're putting too much credence in what he says. We shouldn't take everything James says as gospel.'

'He does have a point, Christian,' Sian said. 'The killer is calling Danny Hanson, and you, Matilda. He obviously wants attention. To be acknowledged for the crimes without being caught. That is a level of narcissism. Isn't it?' she asked, looking around the circle at the doubting faces staring back at her.

'Yes, it is,' Matilda said. 'Let's put Christian's theory to the test, first.' She turned to the DI. 'Why would James Dalziel be doing this?'

'I don't know.' He shrugged. 'Why does anyone decide to kill? Maybe he's the one with this narcissistic disorder. Maybe he's fed up with lecturing a bunch of zombie teenagers.'

'Wouldn't he go on a shooting spree then?' Rory asked.

'All I'm saying,' Christian continued, 'is that if you want to commit a murder and not get caught, who better to do it than a criminal psychologist?'

'Also, you said something about an inflated judgement of his own achievements,' Sian said. 'James is divorced, he's separated from his children and he left his job in Scotland. He had the ideal life and now he's back to square one. Yet, from the outside, you wouldn't think so. Maybe he's looking at his own life with rose-tinted glasses.'

Matilda squeezed her eyes tightly shut. She immediately pictured the photograph of herself James had on his spare bedroom wall. She should say something, confide in those she trusted, but there was a little voice inside telling her to keep her cards closer to her chest than usual. Was the killer a police officer? Or was James the Hangman and telling Matilda the killer was an officer to play with her mind? *No wonder I'm getting so many headaches.*

'OK, but how is he getting his information about the victims, then?' Scott asked. 'Nobody knew Brian Appleby was in Sheffield.

Nobody knew Katie Reaney had changed her name from Naomi Parish. How did he find all that out without access to the PNC?'

'I don't know,' Sian replied thoughtfully.

'So we're back to the killer being a police officer,' Adele said.

'Why did you ask just us to be here, boss?' Scott asked.

Matilda opened her eyes. 'You're the only ones I can trust. We are the Murder Investigation Team, apart from Aaron who is otherwise engaged. I hand-picked you all. I know you.'

'You didn't hand-pick me,' Christian said.

'That's true. He's the killer,' Rory said, pointing at the DI and lightening the mood.

'But I know you. I trust you.'

'Erm,' Scott raised his hand slightly, 'why isn't Faith here?'

'Because I don't really know Faith. She was DI Hales's recruit. Not mine.'

Everyone looked uncomfortable. Matilda wasn't in the main incident room. Her office was offset from everyone else. They, however, all worked with Faith Easter on a daily basis. They knew her. They trusted her. They suddenly realized how serious this was.

Matilda saw dissent on their faces. 'I have nothing against Faith. She is an exemplary detective and has more than proved her worth over the years.'

'Just not enough to be included here,' Rory said, as an aside but loud enough for everyone to hear.

Matilda took a deep breath. 'The reason Faith isn't here is because of me and my paranoias. Like I said, Faith is a brilliant detective, but because I didn't pick her for the MIT, I'm reluctant to trust her one hundred per cent. Faith may be at ninety-nine per cent, but in my eyes that's still not enough.' Matilda looked into the middle of the circle. Her hands were shaking, and she could feel the growing sensation of a panic attack creeping up her back. 'It's down to me being a complete fuck up that I can't allow new people in.' Her voice was quivering. 'Everything that's happened to me over the last couple of years has messed with my head so much that I don't have room to trust anyone else.'

The room fell deathly silent. None of them, apart from Adele, had ever heard her speak so frankly about herself before.

They all stole brief glances at each other. They felt embarrassed by their boss's openness, yet at the same time, honoured she could trust them with her darkest confessions.

'Matilda,' Sian said quietly, 'no offence or anything, but do you think we should get the ACC to bring in someone else. If the killer is a colleague, then we're all too close to see it. A fresh pair of eyes may be needed.'

'I agree,' Scott said.

Matilda took a deep breath. 'We can solve this,' she said unconvincingly.

Once again, everyone exchanged worried glances.

Matilda continued. 'Now, I want to ask you all who you think the killer is. I've had Sian go through all the members of the team. Between us, we haven't been able to come up with anything. So, does anyone have any ideas?'

'I can't do this,' Scott suddenly said.

'Do what?'

'We work with these people every day. There has to be a degree of trust between each other. We have to have each other's backs, in case things kick off. Now you're asking us to choose one of them to be a killer. I can't. I'm sorry, I can't look at my colleagues in that way.'

Adele jumped to Matilda's defence. 'Scott, Matilda isn't asking you to choose someone. She's asking if you've noticed a change in anyone lately. Have any of your colleagues been acting differently, making furtive phone calls, a change in their personality?'

Matilda gave Adele a smile of thanks.

'I don't know,' Scott said, the pain of the situation etched on his face. 'I'm pleased you feel like you can trust me, but, if I start questioning my colleagues and wondering who they're phoning then, no offence boss, but I'm going to end up like you.'

Matilda looked at everyone in the group in turn. 'You're right, Scott. I'm sorry. To all of you, I'm sorry. I shouldn't have called you here like this. It wasn't fair. Go. All of you, go home, do whatever it is you do in the evenings. Have fun. Be with your families. I'm sorry.' Matilda was the first to break the circle. She went into the corner of the function room, her back to the group.

'I think we've all had a pretty hard day. Maybe we should knock it on the head and try and have a good night's sleep,' Christian said, standing up.

'Good idea,' Sian agreed.

Scott and Rory were the first to leave. They couldn't get out of the clubhouse fast enough.

Sian walked slowly over to Matilda and placed an arm around her shoulder. 'You should have opened up sooner, Mat. We're more than your colleagues, we're your friends.'

'I know,' Matilda said quietly through the tears.

'You know where I am if you need me. Any time.' Sian kissed her on the cheek then left, saying goodbye to Christian and Adele as she went.

'Boss,' Christian said, from a distance.

Matilda sniffled and turned around.

'This didn't go quite as planned, did it?' he asked.

'Not really.' She laughed. 'It was more like a group therapy session.'

'Leave it with me. I've had a few ideas. I'll speak to Scott and Rory in the morning.'

'Thanks, Christian. You're a good man.'

'That's why you trust me.' He smiled and left the room, closing the door firmly behind him.

'How do you feel?' Adele eventually asked.

'Empty.'

'At least your team know how you're feeling now.'

'I think I've lost them, especially Scott and Rory. Sian told me the other day that they all look up to me. Now they've found I'm completely messed up.'

'But you're not messed up and the team won't think anything less of you for admitting how you really feel. They'll look at you and see a woman who is achieving great things in the face of adversity.'

'Really?'

'Really. Everyone is on Team Darke. Now come on, I'm hungry and you're buying.'

Adele turned and walked out of the clubhouse leaving Matilda alone. She looked around her at the depth of the darkness she was suddenly encased in. *Darke by name, dark by nature.*

Chapter Fifty-Eight

'Morning ma'am, can I come in?'

Faith Easter entered Matilda's office. The young DC stood tall in her powerful-looking navy trouser suit and sensible-yet-stylish shoes. Gone was the severe ponytail, replaced by long straight dark hair to just below the shoulders. It gave her a softer image, yet Matilda knew her no-nonsense attitude lurked just below the surface.

'Of course you can, Faith, have a seat. What can I do for you?' Matilda gave her an unnecessarily large smile. 'Let me just clear off a few things,' she said, picking up files from the chair and dusting away crumbs and lint. 'There you go.'

You're overcompensating.

'It's you that wanted to see me,' Faith said, confused. 'Acting DCI Brady said so, anyway.'

'Yes, of course, sorry. I'd like you to bring in George Appleby. He attacked Danny Hanson, and I want a fresh face to interview him. Do you think you're up to it?'

'Yes, sure. Definitely,' she replied, a smile on her face.

Matilda smiled. 'Good. You and Kesinka bring him in, and I'll observe the formal interview.'

'Yes, ma'am,' Faith said. She left the room with a spring in her step.

Matilda watched her head for Kesinka. They shared a few words, then both grabbed their jackets and left the office. Matilda's eyes moved on to Ranjeet who was busy typing on his computer. He briefly looked up as Kesinka passed him and gave her a sweet smile. It was nice to see relationships developing. Not just romantically, but professionally too. Faith and Kesinka worked well together. Of course Faith was part of her team. What was she thinking by leaving her out last night?

Christian headed towards Scott and Rory carrying a tray with three large lattes on it. He placed it down gently on the table and sat next to Rory.

They were in Marmaduke's on Norfolk Row. It was an independent coffee shop, and was one of Christian's favourite places to visit on the rare occasion he had time to do so. He and his wife often had a bite to eat or just a coffee whenever the kids where off their hands.

'Are we having another secret meeting?' Rory said. 'Should we call each other 007 or something?'

'No. But I want you both to do something for me and I didn't want to talk about it in the office.'

'Last night when I said—' Scott began.

'Scott, forget about it,' Christian interrupted.

'I didn't mean that I didn't want to end up like Matilda. I just meant—'

'Scott, drop it. I know what you meant and so did Matilda. You were right. It wasn't fair to ask us to investigate our colleagues. However, we do need to rule people out. Now, I want you both to do me a favour.' He leaned forward so as not to be overheard, even though there was only an elderly couple in Marmaduke's with them.

George Appleby had decided to defy the gossip and return to

university. He had spent the previous evening worrying what everyone was going to say when he stepped into the lecture hall. In the end, it wasn't as bad as he had expected, mostly because everyone seemed to be ignoring him. He wasn't happy about that, but he could live with it. When two detectives entered the hall, and called his name, he wished for the ground to open up and swallow him whole. Why couldn't they just allow him to continue with his life without all this drama?

All eyes had been on him as he was led through the corridors of Sheffield Hallam University, flanked by two plain-clothed detectives, and out to a waiting pool car. He hadn't protested, but he kept thinking of the stories that would be spread about him now.

He accepted the offer of a cup of tea and sat in the interview room with his skeletal fingers firmly gripped around the plastic cup. His pale face looked scared, and he was constantly biting at his bottom lip. He had an oversized navy cardigan hanging on his skinny frame. He said he didn't want a solicitor present.

Kesinka started the recording and cautioned George Appleby, before she handed over to Faith. As promised, Matilda was in the observation room. She told Faith, through the earpiece, to start with Gordon Berry's murder and work backwards.

'George,' Faith began. She smiled at him, but he didn't reciprocate. 'Can you tell us where you were on the evening of Tuesday, 11th April?'

'I was at home,' he said softly.

'Can anyone verify that?'

'My housemates.'

'Which ones?'

'All of them.' He frowned.

'We went to your house this morning and spoke to two of your housemates. They said you weren't at home on Tuesday evening.' Faith looked down at her pad. 'You still hadn't come home at midnight when Anil and Anita went to bed.'

'Oh Tuesday? I thought you said Monday,' he lied unconvincingly. 'I was out.'

'I'm guessing that. Where?'

'At the pub.'

'Which one?' Faith asked, getting slightly annoyed at his short answers.

'Walkabout.'

'On your own?'

He hesitated. 'No. Well, yes, but, no. I went on my own, but I got chatting to some people at the bar.'

'Had you seen these people before?'

'No.'

'Did you get their names, or numbers?'

'No.'

'Would you recognize each other again?'

'Probably not.'

'So, really, you have no alibi for Tuesday night.'

'I do. I've just said, I was in Walkabout.'

'But you can't prove that.'

'I didn't think I'd have to,' he scoffed. 'I don't go out and make sure I always have people with me, so I can prove where I've been. Do you?'

'George, we will be pulling CCTV footage from Walkabout and the surrounding area,' Faith said.

'Good. That'll prove it then.' He folded his arms.

Faith glanced at the mirror Matilda was standing behind. She raised an eyebrow and hoped the boss would give her something to say back to George, but all she heard was silence. She took out a photograph from the file in front of her, a blown-up image of Gordon Berry, and placed it in front of George. 'Do you know this man?'

'No,' George replied, barely glancing at it.

'Would you like to look again?'

'No, I don't recognize him,' George said after an exaggerated stare. 'Who is he?'

'I'm glad you asked that. His name is Gordon Berry. He was found murdered yesterday morning.'

'So?'

'He was hanged. Just like your father was. Just like Joe Lacey was. Just like Katie Reaney was. You don't seem to have an alibi for the days and times any of those were killed either.'

'What are you saying?'

'I'm not saying anything.'

'You think I murdered them?' he asked, raising his voice. 'Do I look like a killer to you?'

'What does a killer look like, Mr Appleby?' Kesinka asked.

'I … well, I don't know, but not me.'

'How long are we going to play these games, Mr Appleby?'

'I can't believe this.' He leaned forward and slapped his hands down on the table. 'You drag me out of a lecture, parade me through university like I'm some sort of Jack the Ripper and then accuse me of murdering four people. You can't do this.'

'Mr Appleby, I can do whatever I want—'

'Steady,' Matilda said to Faith through her earpiece.

Faith started again. 'Until you provide us with a suitable alibi for your whereabouts we're going to have to consider you a suspect.'

'That's better,' Matilda said.

'Why would I kill them? I have no motive. I didn't even know these people.'

'There's your father.'

'One person,' he scoffed. 'And I hadn't seen him for years. Not since he got sent down. I had nothing to do with the man.'

'Do you expect us to believe that?'

'Yes I do because it's the truth. For fuck's sake,' George replied, getting flustered, 'are you grilling the other victims' relatives like this, or am I the only one?'

'You're very quick to temper, aren't you?' Kesinka asked. 'Do you have anger issues?'

'Jesus Christ! I can't believe this. No. I do not have anger issues. Well, I didn't until I met you two.'

'Ask him about Danny Hanson,' Matilda quickly said.

'Do you know Danny Hanson?' Faith asked.

George froze. For a second too long. 'Er … no. I don't think so.'

'Are you sure about that?'

'Er … yes.'

'Danny Hanson is a reporter on *The Star*. He's been covering the murders extensively. The whole of Sheffield knows all about your father because of Danny's journalism.'

George shrugged. 'So?'

'Danny Hanson was attacked by someone who matches your description,' Faith said.

'What? Tall and thin with messy hair? You were at the university, we all look like that.'

Faith opened a file and read from Danny's statement. '"Tall, thin, dark red unkempt hair, a slight southern accent". Do you often walk around Weston Park during the hours of darkness?'

George didn't reply. His eyes firmly fixed on the table.

'So what happened?' Kesinka asked. 'Was he too strong for you? Did you try to get the noose over his neck, but his big scarf and coat got in the way?'

'No.'

'Were you interrupted? Did you have to abandon your plan to kill him?'

'What are you talking about?' He flustered. 'There was no plan.'

'So it was a spontaneous thing then?'

'No. I—' He stopped himself.

'Go on,' Kesinka prompted.

'Fuck,' he uttered. 'I wasn't thinking straight. The story had just been printed about my dad, and I'd been getting taunts.'

'Taunts?' Kesinka asked.

'Yes. On Facebook and Twitter. People saying things about me.

My housemates have asked me to leave. My mum doesn't want to know me. It's like I'm on my own and everyone's against me,' he said. His face was a picture of angst. A tear escaped from his eye.

'Why did you strangle Danny Hanson?'

'I didn't strangle him.'

'You grabbed his scarf and tightened it around his neck.'

'I know what you're thinking. I tried to strangle him, so I must be behind the hangings. I'm not. Honestly. I grabbed his scarf because he was wearing one. I saw red. I'm sorry.'

'Do you have problems controlling your anger, Mr Appleby?' Kesinka asked.

'Good,' Matilda said.

'No,' he sniggered. 'You're taking this out of context.' George ran his fingers through his unruly hair anxiously. 'I was planning to talk to Danny, you know, ask him how he had the cheek to write those things and not to think of the consequences. But when I saw him, I just, I don't know, I—'

'Snapped,' Faith completed his sentence for him.

'Yes.'

'Did you snap with your father, Joe Lacey, Katie Reaney and Gordon Berry too?'

'No. You're not listening to me,' he said, his voice full of emotion. He was physically drained by the bombardment of questions.

'You're going around in circles. Stop the interview, give him a breather,' Matilda said.

'I tell you what, we'll stop here for a short break. Then, we'll restart, and you can tell us exactly where you were.'

'Interview terminated 11.47,' Kesinka Rani said, turning the recording off.

'You did good work in there, Faith,' Matilda said as they both joined her in the observation room. 'You need to rein in your …

excitement a tad,' she said with a sympathetic smile, trying to find the right word. 'Don't let your frustration affect your questioning.'

'OK,' she said, taking her boss's words on board.

Matilda looked past the DCs and into the interview room where George Appleby had his head in his arms on the table. 'Right, go and get yourself a cup of tea. Give him half an hour to stew then have another go. I'll be upstairs.'

'Ma'am,' Faith called her boss back, 'is he seriously a suspect?'

'No, I don't think so.'

'What about the attack on Danny Hanson?'

'Danny said he doesn't want to press charges, so we've no case. I would like to know his alibis for the killings though, just to put my mind at rest. Go and get yourselves that tea.'

Matilda watched as Faith and Kesinka headed in the direction of the canteen. How could she have possibly doubted those two?

Matilda left the room and headed for the stairwell. Once on her own, her mind went back to the clandestine meeting last night. Would Scott and Rory treat her any differently now? She nudged shoulders with a PC coming down the stairs. He dropped a few files. Matilda waved an apology. Deep in thought, she carried on and felt a prickly sensation creep up the back of her neck again.

Chapter Fifty-Nine

'Adele, what are you doing here?' Matilda asked as she entered the incident room to find Adele and Sian chatting over a coffee.

'I needed to get out of the office for a while. I've had Simon Browes on the phone to me all day.'

'Why?'

'Now that your serial case has made the national press, he's suddenly interested in it. The bloke's a glory hunter.'

'I hope he's not planning on talking to the press.'

'No, he wouldn't do that. He'd more likely write a paper on it and make sure he's mentioned more times than he should be.'

Matilda helped herself to a chunky KitKat from Sian's drawer. 'Why would anyone actively seek publicity? I can't stand it. It's like the killer, he's loving the newspapers writing stories about him. There are other ways of getting attention.'

'Yes. He could audition for *Big Brother*,' Sian sniggered. Her phone started ringing. She picked it up and turned away.

'You think that's what this is all about then? Attention seeking?' Adele asked.

'That's what narcissistic people do. They want us all to look at them, to see what they're doing. He's staging his murders. He's contacting the press to make sure they get the story.'

'Welcome to twenty-first century Britain. Everyone's life is in the public domain nowadays,' Adele said. 'Oh, by the way, my burglar's been caught.'

'Has he?'

'Yes. I had a call from a Sergeant Blumenthal who said a bloke had been arrested. He'd admitted a spate of burglaries around the city, including breaking into my house.'

'Nice to see someone in South Yorkshire Police is capable of solving a crime,' Matilda said, looking at the faces of four dead people on the murder boards.

'Oh my God,' Sian said. 'Ma'am, I've just had Karen Lacey's sister on the phone. She went round to Karen's house this morning – she's hanged herself.'

Matilda drove with Adele in the back and Sian in the front. They had been going for over ten minutes in a heavy silence when Sian shattered it with her revelation about Karen's secret visit the day before. She filled them both in on who the real killer of Rebecca Branson was and how she and Joe had covered it up for all these years.

'You should have told me, Sian,' Matilda said.

'I was going to come round last night, but you sent that text and we had that meeting and it just went by the by. I'm sorry. I told Karen to go home and be the best mum she could be to her kids. How stupid can you get? Her husband had been murdered because of something she'd done. I should have known this would happen.'

'Sian, don't blame yourself,' Adele said from the back seat. 'Nobody could have foreseen this.'

'If you want me to resign, boss, I will,' Sian said, gazing out of the window. The sun was trying to break through the heavy clouds hanging over Sheffield, but it still looked dark and dreary.

'Don't even think about it,' Matilda warned her.

Matilda pulled up outside the Lacey house. Selina Bridger was waiting for them on the doorstep. Her arms were wrapped tightly around her chest. She was an older version of Karen Lacey, with the same hairstyle and colour, and the same build. Her face had the haunted look of the recently bereaved, just as Karen's had when Matilda first met her. As soon as Selina saw Matilda and Sian climb out of the car, she hurried towards them.

'I didn't know whether to call for an ambulance or not, but I mean, she's dead, isn't she?' Selina waffled.

Sian held her by the shoulders. 'It's all right, Selina, calm down. Do you want to go back to your home and we'll come and see you in a bit?'

'No. I'm OK. I'll wait here.'

Matilda and Adele entered the house. It seemed like an age since they were both last here when Joe Lacey was found hanging in the garage. They made their away along the hallway. The house was cold, silent and unlived in. The stale Minion cake was still on the table in the dining room.

Matilda turned to the door leading to the garage and pushed it open. The cold hit her and she shuddered. The darkness surrounded her as she descended the steps, the sound of her shoes echoing around the room.

Adele fumbled for the light switch, eventually flicking it on. Their eyes adjusted. The Audi was still there. The shelves on either side were still stacked with paint tins, boxes of odds and ends that would never come in useful for anything. Children's bikes were propped up against the wall. And Karen Lacey was hanging from a beam on the ceiling.

'Jesus,' Matilda uttered.

Karen was hanging in the exact same position as her husband. The hook drilled into a beam on the ceiling. Karen was lifeless, the noose tight around her neck – thirteen twists in the rope – and there was a white pillowcase pulled over her head.

Adele came down the steps and had a good look at the body. 'Shit.'

'What is it?' Matilda asked.

'I think you'll find Karen Lacey was murdered.'

'What are you talking about?'

'She didn't take her own life. This is victim number five.'

Matilda turned to Adele. Horror etched into her face. The nightmare was getting worse.

Chapter Sixty

By the time the crime scene at Meersbrook had been processed and Karen Lacey had been cut down and taken to the mortuary, it was dark, and there was only one place Matilda wanted to go – back to the office. She needed to go through the files of the victims, to start from the beginning, even if that took all night.

'Boss, I was just leaving,' Faith said when she saw the DCI enter, looking shattered. 'Is it true about Karen Lacey?'

'I'm afraid so, yes.'

'Bloody hell. Those poor children. Anyway, I was going to put this on your desk. I didn't know if you were coming back or not. Me and Kesinka interviewed George Appleby on our own. I hope you don't mind.' She paused for Matilda to answer, but she didn't. 'Anyway, it didn't go on for too long. As soon as we opened the door, he started talking and we couldn't shut him up. It turns out George is struggling with his sexuality. He had a drunken kiss with a gay friend at Christmas, and he's not sure if he enjoyed it or not. He's been going online to find blokes, and he's been meeting them. He showed us all the messages he's been getting. I think we can rule him out.'

'OK,' Matilda said, only half listening.

'I told him to be careful and I've been on to the LGBT Police

Network. They gave me a few local groups who he can talk to. He's just a very worried and mixed-up lad. This business with his dad isn't going to help either, and his mother sounds like a complete cow by all accounts. I felt sorry for him in the end.'

'Thanks, Faith, I really appreciate what you've done today. You get off home. The traffic will be murder getting to Hillsborough soon.'

'I'm not staying at home at the moment. I'm house-sitting for my aunt while she's away. You know those old townhouses on Rocks Avenue? It's lovely having a place all to myself.'

'What?' Matilda asked, distracted.

'It doesn't matter. I'll see you in the morning.'

Faith turned and left Matilda's office. She picked up her mobile and coat from the back of her chair and headed for the exit. She turned to look at her boss. As much as she would love to be a DCI one day, she didn't want to sacrifice her family and her social life.

Matilda sat at her desk and went through the files of Brian Appleby, Joe Lacey, Katie Reaney, and Gordon Berry. Now there was Karen Lacey to add to the list. James Dalziel told her she already knew who the killer was, and she was starting to think he was right.

Matilda spent almost an hour wracking her brain. The only people she saw on a regular basis were those at work – detectives, uniformed officers, civilian staff, the ACC, SOCOs, Adele, members of the press. Outside of work, Matilda had no life. She didn't speak to her neighbours, she wasn't a member of a gym or any groups. There was nobody in her local supermarket who she was on first name terms with. If James Dalziel was right, if Matilda did know the killer, then it had to be a member of the police. If that was true, the repercussions were going to be massive.

'Adele it's me,' Matilda said into her phone. 'Have you done the PM on Karen Lacey yet?'

'Not yet. Why?'

'Are you sure she was murdered, and she didn't just hang herself over what happened to her husband?'

'Well, no, I'm not one hundred per cent. I just found it odd she would hang herself and put a pillowcase over her head.'

'She could have done that because she thought she should have been killed instead of her husband.'

'True. But if—'

Matilda had already hung up. She looked through her phone for another number and dialled. It went straight to voicemail. She decided against leaving a message and searched for another number.

'Kate, it's DCI Darke,' Matilda said to Kate Stephenson, editor of *The Star*.

'DCI Darke, nice to hear from you. Have you seen this evening's edition? We've got a profile on all of the victims so far, and I've managed to get hold of Paul Britton. You'll have heard of him, I'm guessing – the renowned criminal psychologist. He's written a lovely piece for us on serial killers. Our sales have jumped in the past couple of weeks.' The glee in her voice was unmistakable.

'Great. Fingers crossed the Hangman will be bigger than the Yorkshire Ripper and it's staff bonuses all round.'

'There's no need to be flippant. Was there something you wanted?'

'Yes. I'm trying to get in touch with Danny Hanson, but his phone seems to be switched off.'

'Yes, bless him. He's feeling the strain. I told him to take a couple of days' leave. He doesn't seem to have the staying power when it comes to pressure. We may have to let him go.'

'You're all heart, Kate.'

'I'm running a business here, not a convalescent home. If you want to be a successful journalist, you leave your emotions at the door.'

Matilda rolled her eyes. 'Could you give me Danny's home address?'

'I'm not sure about that. Is this something I should be privy to?'

'No. Just a private discussion between me and your young reporter.'

Reluctantly, Kate told her where Danny lived. The DCI ended the call while Kate was mid-sentence, trying once more to pump Matilda for information.

Matilda knew the area where Danny Hanson lived. The traffic wasn't on her side and she was caught up in a tailback that added an extra thirty minutes to the journey.

When she finally arrived, the door was answered by a bedraggled-looking young woman in her early twenties. She was dressed in a long pink dressing gown and novelty slippers.

'Do you have to bang so loud? Some of us work shifts,' she said by way of a greeting.

Matilda showed her warrant card. 'DCI Matilda Darke, South Yorkshire Police. I'd like to speak to Danny, please.'

'Well, he's not here,' she said.

'I've been told he is.'

'He'll be at work. He spends a lot of time at the paper.'

'His editor has given him a couple of days off. She says he's at home.'

'Well, you're welcome to check for yourself,' she said, standing to one side to allow Matilda to enter. 'He's in the attic. Mind the loose carpet on the first few stairs.'

Matilda took the steps two at a time and wasn't even breathless when she reached Danny's bedroom door. Maybe she should consider a full marathon next.

She knocked on the door and waited. There was no reply. She banged again, louder.

'I'm asleep,' Danny shouted from inside the room.

'So am I. It's DCI Darke, Danny, open up.'

'Shit,' Matilda heard him say under his breath. She decided not to take it personally.

The door was unlocked and opened. The smell hit Matilda straight away. Stale air and sweat. She walked in and edged carefully around the boxes.

'Is this where you live?' she asked, noticing the damp patches on the wall, the mould around the Velux window, the threadbare carpets, mass-produced furniture and lack of curtains.

'Yes. What's wrong with it?'

'Nothing,' she lied.

'We can't all be earning a DCI's wage. Do you have any idea how much student debt you carry with you these days? Yes, I've got a full-time job, but try getting a mortgage when the banks see how much you earn compared with how much you pay out. Once they've stopped laughing it's "thanks for your interest, Mr Hanson, but not at the moment",' he said, almost snapping.

'I'm sorry,' Matilda replied. 'Your housemate seems nice, anyway.'

'The blonde or the brunette?'

'The blonde.'

'Gina. She's a bitch. All smiles to your face then once you're out of the room she's pulling you to bits.' He sat on the bed with his head in his hands.

Matilda studied him. His hair was a mess, stubble was trying to come through in patches. His T-shirt was wrinkled and torn. This wasn't how a young professional should be living, not even a journalist.

'Couldn't you move back home with your parents?' Matilda suggested.

'I'd love to, if there were any jobs going. I'm lucky I got this one. Lucky,' he sniggered, looking around his room. 'Journalism's dead practically. I doubt I'll reach retirement age in this business. Mind you, there probably won't be a retirement age once I get to my seventies. Thank you very much, Labour. Or is it the Conservatives I should blame? Difficult to tell these days.'

'Danny, can you focus for me, I need to ask you something,' Matilda said, perching on the edge of his bed.

'Has there been another body?'

'We think so.'

'Who?'

'Before I tell you, have you received any more calls from the killer?'

He shrugged. 'No idea. I've turned my phone off. I'm actually frightened of answering it, can you believe that?'

Yes I can.

'Can you turn it back on for me, please?'

Frowning, Danny opened the top drawer of his bedside table and pulled out his iPhone with the cracked screen. He switched it on and waited for it to come to life. He tapped in his passcode. They both sat, staring at the outdated phone. The screen went blank. Matilda sighed. The killer hadn't made contact. Karen Lacey's death was suicide, not murder. Suddenly, the screen lit up signalling voicemails and texts.

'What do you want me to do?' Danny's voice was shaking. It had been more than a day since he'd turned off his phone. He was dreading listening to the messages. What if the Hangman realized the phone wasn't on and threatened him in some way? What if he'd threatened his family?

'Listen to the voicemails. Put it on speaker.'

'Shit,' he muttered.

Danny held out the phone in his clammy left hand and listened to the robotic voice telling him he had three new messages. The first was from his mother asking if he was coming home for his sister's birthday next weekend. The second was from Kate Stephenson asking for his password on his computer as they needed to get some information he'd been working on.

She's all heart.

The third wasn't a message at all. A couple of seconds of breathing then the caller hung up. Matilda wondered if the killer had contacted Danny and decided against leaving a message.

'What about the texts?' Matilda asked.

Danny flicked through them. There were seven unread. Mostly from friends and colleagues. He opened the last one then held up the phone to show Matilda. It was from a number not stored in his phone.

Oops, my bad!

'What does that mean?' Matilda asked.

'It means he's made a mistake. Has he?'

Matilda shook her head and looked down. 'I'm afraid he did. But he's just made up for it.'

George Appleby was in the bath. The door was closed but not locked. He lay back in the hot deep water. There was nothing about himself he liked – his oversized feet, his red hair, his sunken eyes. He was ugly.

He picked up his phone and swiped a wet finger across the screen. He looked at his text messages. He hadn't received any in days. He had sent his mother six messages in the past twenty-four hours. She had read them all but hadn't replied. He had finally managed to get through to his sister, who seemed to be shagging her way around Europe. She wanted their mother's version of what happened, confirming, then made an excuse to end the call. There was no querying about him, his health, his studies, or how he was coping. She was selfish. She was definitely their mother's daughter.

Nobody would speak to him. Nobody would listen to him. Even his so-called housemates wanted him out. There were people George could speak to at the university, counsellors, lecturers, but George didn't want that. He knew his conversation would be private, but how private is private? He couldn't stand any more humiliation.

This was a nightmare. When his father was first arrested, and word had got out about him being a paedophile, George's life had changed. He had been constantly bullied at school, and it didn't matter where he moved, the gossip followed him. He begged and pleaded with his mother to be homeschooled, but she refused, told him to get used to it. She hardened overnight, turned from sympathetic to a hard-faced, unemotional bitch. That was the only way to describe her. George often felt like he had lost two parents.

He looked at his phone one more time, before dropping it on to the towel on the floor. Screw it. Screw his family. Screw his housemates wanting him to leave. Screw the university. Screw the police. Screw Sheffield and screw life.

He leaned over the bath and picked up the razor blade he'd bought that morning. Holding it firmly in his right hand he pointed it towards a bulging vein on his left wrist. George had looked on the Internet for the best, and quickest, way to kill yourself by slashing your wrists.

He decided not to look. He had never liked the sight of blood. He rested the blade on his left wrist and closed his eyes tightly shut. As it dug deep into his skin and the blood started to flow, he felt himself relax. His whole body began to float and rapidly weaken. He quickly swapped the blade to his left hand and cut open his right wrist. The release was orgasmic.

George Appleby, nineteen years old, felt a smile spread across his face as his life ebbed away from him.

Chapter Sixty-One

'THE HUNT FOR THE HANGMAN CONTINUES

Sheffield residents are living in fear as a serial killer claimed his fifth victim yesterday…

STEEL CITY KILLER CLAIMS VICTIM No. 5

The Hangman of Sheffield has struck again as a fifth victim was found in the leafy suburb of Meersbrook…

HANGMAN'S REIGN CONTINUES

A serial killer dubbed 'The Hangman' has claimed a fifth victim in Sheffield, England as police begin to lose control of the situation…

LIVING IN FEAR

Sheffield residents tell of their fears as the killings continue…

POLICE CLUELESS

> South Yorkshire Police are coming under intense pressure to replace DCI Matilda Darke as the serial killer plaguing the Steel City claims a fifth victim…'

ACC Valerie Masterson scrolled through the email sent to her by the chief constable. Snippets from online news agencies, national and international newspapers. She closed the email. She couldn't read on. This was a nightmare. Her mobile rang, and she recognized the number of the chief constable. He hardly ever called her on her mobile. This was not going to be a good conversation. She took a deep breath, smiled, and answered the phone.

'Martin, how are you?'

'I'm fine,' he replied, stressing the 'I'm'. 'Yourself?'

How could she answer that? 'I'm coping.'

'Really? The press doesn't seem to think so. I'm assuming you've read my email.'

'I have, yes.'

'You have five murder victims on your hands, Valerie. Not to mention twenty-six unsolved murders within South Yorkshire. Do I have to place South Yorkshire Police under special measures?'

Valerie paled. 'No, absolutely not, sir. The press has blown this out of all proportion.'

'So you don't have five victims?'

'We have—'

'In that case, whether they've written the truth or a pack of lies, you still have five victims and no hint of a suspect,' the chief constable interrupted.

'I wouldn't say that, sir.'

'Wouldn't you? So, you do have a suspect?'

Valerie ran her fingers through her grey hair, firmly pulling at it. 'We are pursuing several lines of enquiries.'

'You're not giving a bloody press conference, Valerie, you're talking to me. The sooner we get a Major Crime Unit with a new team set up in South Yorkshire the better.'

'You're bringing in a new team?'

'Surely you didn't think we'd recruit from within? You really do need to read the papers more, Valerie.'

The line went dead. Valerie stared at her phone and leaned back in her chair.

The morning briefing went on longer than usual as Faith, Kesinka and Ranjeet took everyone through their interviews with Karen Lacey's neighbours. This time they asked about the neighbours themselves. Did they get on with the Laceys? What was their relationship like? How did they feel when they found out what Joe Lacey had been convicted for in 1997?

Interviews with Gordon Berry's colleagues and family were still ongoing and being processed. As was tracking down everyone identifiable from the Banker's Draft CCTV footage on the night of Gordon's birthday celebrations.

It was no longer victim apathy the detectives seemed to be suffering from. It was complete apathy in general. There were so many people to interview, and all the questions were exactly the same.

The look of defeat was on every face as, once again, Christian Brady took everyone through each victim in the incident room. What had they missed? By lunchtime, everyone felt like they had done a full day's work; their patience was wearing thin.

There was a knock on Matilda's door. She looked up to see Sian on the other side and beckoned her in. There was laughter in the background.

'What's the joke?'

'Scott and Rory are watching *Innuendo Bingo* online. Don't ask,' she replied, rolling her eyes. Sian closed the door behind her and sat down. 'I'm afraid I've got some bad news.'

'I don't think I can handle any more, Sian.'

'George Appleby killed himself yesterday.'

'What?'

'His housemates found him in the bath last night. He cut his wrists.'

Matilda's face turned white. 'Oh my God!' *Did we push him too hard?*

'He left a note. It wasn't addressed to anyone in particular. It stated that he couldn't go on living with who his family was. He felt isolated and alone and thought it would be better for everyone if he was dead.'

'That is tragic,' Matilda said, looking genuinely sorry.

'I know. Students have a hard time at university, people don't realize that. Poor sod.'

A burst of hysterical laughter from outside jolted them back to the present. People are being murdered. People are killing themselves. People are dealing with anxiety and anguish and bottling up their emotions, but for others, life went on.

By the end of the day, Matilda was resting her head on her desk in her tiny, messy office. She was staring blankly out of the windows into the incident room.

Scott and Rory were having a private conversation by text, even though their desks were within spitting distance of each other. Matilda frowned as she watched the intense drama play out. Eventually, Rory stood up and went over to DI Brady's office. Matilda shrugged. Knowing Rory and Scott they were probably discussing who was having the bigger bedroom in their flat.

A few minutes later, Christian tapped on the glass. 'Mind if I interrupt?'

'No, come on in.'

He closed the door behind him and sat in front of Matilda's desk. He spoke in quiet tones, barely above a whisper. 'I've had Rory and Scott working on a little job for the past day or so. It's to do with when Gordon Berry came into the station.'

‘Go on,’ Matilda said, rubbing the spot on the back of her head that still hurt slightly.

‘There are a few cameras in the foyer, but none of them show a good view of the office behind the front desk. Rory and Scott have been going over the footage and they’ve finally found a decent angle. They know who Gordon Berry saw when he came into the station.’

‘Who?’ Matilda said, sitting up. She could feel the energy return to her tired body.

Christian reached into his inside jacket pocket and took out a folded-up photograph. He unfolded it and handed it across to Matilda.

‘Is this it?’

‘It’s not the best photograph, I grant you. Don’t forget, those cameras have been there for many years and technology has come along so far since—’

‘This is pathetic. All we can get from this is he’s tall, got dark hair, wears a uniform and—’ She stopped, squinted, and held the photograph closer to her eyes.

‘What is it?’

‘Have you got a magnifying glass?’

‘Not personally. Hang on.’ Christian opened the door and asked Sian. Obviously, she had one. Sian was equipped for most eventualities.

Matilda went over to the window, angled the photo to catch the light and studied it through the magnifying glass.

‘I know who the Hangman is,’ she said, looking up at Christian and Sian.

Chapter Sixty-Two

A full half an hour passed as Matilda contemplated her next move. She sat at her desk in silence, mulling over the entire case. She should have seen it sooner. This was no ordinary killer she could walk up to and arrest. She would have to be smart. She needed a plan. Picking up the receiver, she pressed an extension button and waited for a reply.

'DS Mills. CID,' Sian said, answering her phone.

'Sian, it's Matilda. Don't look up. Don't move.'

Sian sat frozen at her desk. Around her, colleagues and friends, went about their business. Sian took a risk and glanced up. Straight ahead, Matilda sat at her desk in her office with the door closed. They made eye contact.

'What's going on?' Sian said quietly.

'You need to act like you're having a normal conversation. Just carry on doing whatever it is you were doing before I rang.'

Sian leaned down and picked out a packet of Maltesers from her desk. She opened them and shovelled a few into her mouth.

'Really? That's what you were doing?'

'What? I'm hungry.'

Matilda rolled her eyes. 'Fair enough. Now, Sian, when Karen Lacey came to see you, who was around?'

'Everyone. I was in the incident room when the call came through. Rory and Scott were talking about their flat. Faith and Kesinka were discussing their boyfriends. Christian was in his office.'

'Anyone else?'

'Ranjeet was doing something with the photocopier.'

'Who called you to say Karen had come to see you?'

'Oh, nobody. Steve came in and asked if anyone was available to talk to her. She hadn't come to see me specifically.'

'OK. Was there anyone who could have overheard your conversation with Karen?'

'No. We went into an interview room.'

'Which one?'

'Three I think. Why?'

'And three doesn't have an observation room overlooking it, so you couldn't have been overheard that way.'

'No. What's going on?' Sian asked, concerned. Despite trying to appear nonchalant, she was looking straight at Matilda now.

'I think you've just confirmed who our killer is.'

Matilda came off the phone to Sian and was about to make another call, when Sian came into the office with a black coffee and a Bounty.

'Are you going to tell me who it is?' Sian asked.

Matilda handed her the photograph and the magnifying glass. 'Don't look at the fuzzy man, look at the desk. What's on top of the red folder?'

Sian squeezed her eyes together as she tried to focus. The penny suddenly dropped. 'Jesus Christ! You can't be serious, surely?'

'I'm afraid I am,' Matilda said. She had a similar expression to Sian.

'Should we be scared?'

'I'm doing everything possible to keep everyone safe. I need to get the killer away from the station, so I can confront them.'

'How are you going to do that?'

'Right now, I've absolutely no idea.'

'What do you want me to do?'

'I know it's difficult, but you need to be as normal as possible. Act like nothing has changed.'

'Shit,' she said under her breath. 'I'm going to need a deeper snack drawer.'

Matilda watched Sian leave and go back to her desk. Kesinka called her over. She went, but she wasn't the usual chatty Sian everyone knew and loved. She stood by Kesinka's desk, arms folded firmly across her chest. While Kes was talking, Sian's eyes wandered suspiciously around the room, watching the people she had worked alongside for years. Suddenly, they didn't look so friendly anymore.

It didn't seem to matter what subterfuge Matilda tried to put into place, she couldn't seem to get her chief suspect out of the station without raising suspicion. In the end, she made the decision to wait until the end of the day and everybody started to go home. It was a long and agonizing wait. It was tempting to storm out of her office and slap the cuffs on him, drag him into an interview room and beat him into submission. For practical reasons, that wasn't possible. She kept going back to the statements James Dalziel and the other criminal psychologists she'd been in touch with had given her. A killer of this kind, a man suffering with such delusions, a narcissist, wouldn't come quietly. He'd want to go out in a blaze of glory, and he'd take as many people with him as he could.

There was no chance Matilda was going to risk her team, or anyone in the station for that matter. It had to be her, and the Hangman, nobody else. If she was cornered and he decided on a murder/suicide, then so be it. All she had left was her house, and Ben Hales had destroyed that for her.

'Sian, have you heard from Aaron?' Matilda asked from the doorway of her office as people were leaving for the day.

'Yes. Katrina's back home. Mother and baby are doing fine.'

'Good. Before you rush off, do you want to talk about having a whip-round or something?'

'Sure.'

Matilda waited until Sian had closed the door behind her before informing her of the real reason for getting her in the office.

'So are you clear on what I want you to do?'

'Unfortunately, yes I am.'

'I know it's not going to be easy, but it's the only way. Take Scott with you. I've got Rory heading for Batemoor.'

'What are you going to do?'

Matilda thought for a while. 'I think I'm going to be winging it.'

Sian and Scott drove in silence through rush-hour traffic. The atmosphere was heavy, as they knew what task lay ahead once they had reached their destination. With every red light they reached, they simultaneously breathed a sigh of relief. An extra few seconds added to their journey was most welcome.

'Shit!' Scott suddenly said. 'I've just remembered something.'

'What?' Sian snapped.

'Faith isn't staying at home at the moment. She mentioned something about house-sitting for a relative.'

'Oh bloody hell, Scott,' Sian said, fishing out her mobile phone. 'Why didn't you say so earlier?'

'I forgot.'

'Boss, it's me,' Sian said into her phone. 'Scott has remembered that Faith isn't staying at home. She's house-sitting.'

The realization dawned on Matilda too. 'Of course she is. She told me too. I was only half listening. Ask Scott if he can remember where.'

Sian relayed the message. 'He says not, but it's a big townhouse just outside the city centre.'

'That doesn't exactly narrow it down. Hang on.' There was a pause. 'Yes … I … Rocks Road. I remember because I thought she was talking about Rocky Road,' Matilda gave a nervous laugh. 'I'm not far. I'll divert. You two double-back and meet me there.'

'Will do.' Sian hung up. 'Turn around when you can and head for Rocks Road.'

'Sorry,' Scott said. He wore a heavy frown of guilt.

'Not a good start, is it? I've got a bad feeling about this.'

Rory drove at speed up Meadowhead. He'd finally broken free of the evening traffic on Chesterfield Road. He wished he was in a squad car; he could have used the blues and twos.

He went straight ahead at Meadowhead roundabout, causing three cars to beep at him and a white van to swerve. In Rory's defence, he was in the right in the tussle with the white van man. He didn't slow down when he reached the turn-off to Batemoor and entered the housing estate at fifty miles per hour.

As he approached his destination, he slowed down. Matilda had told him not to draw attention to himself, to make it look like he was visiting a friend or a relative, like this wasn't an ambush. He slowed to twenty miles per hour and felt like a kerb crawler as he crept along the roads at a snail's pace.

Up ahead, he saw the house and quickly found a suitable place to park. He climbed out of the car and took his time straightening his jacket, as if people's lives weren't in any danger.

He knocked on the green door and waited. Took a step back and looked up at the ground-floor maisonette. It was in complete darkness. He knocked again, more urgently now.

'He's not in.' A woman approached the block pushing a double buggy with a further two small children either side of her.

'Do you know when he'll be back?'

'No. He left over a week ago carrying a few bags. He told my Roger he was going away for a bit. House-sitting, I think he said.'

'Did he say where?'

'No.' She unlocked her door and went into her own home, slamming it closed behind her.

'Bollocks,' Rory said to himself. He headed to his car, mobile phone clamped to his ear.

Matilda pulled up outside a row of new-builds. Townhouses on three floors. They looked smart, welcoming, and homely.

It was dark. The solar-powered street lights weren't very powerful and didn't provide much light for the road. There was a fine drizzle falling and the breeze had picked up too. As Matilda stepped out of her car she looked around her. An elderly woman was walking an elderly dog, both wrapped up against the elements. She stared up at the houses. Most had lights on. Families sitting down to an evening meal or watching television. Children doing their homework. Behind each of these front doors, lives were continuing as normal. Behind one of them, Matilda had no idea what to expect.

Matilda recognized the car parked outside number 9 and walked slowly towards the house. The windows were dark. Despite the car on the drive, it appeared nobody was home.

She rang the bell and waited. There was no reply. She leaned into the doorway and rang again, listening for any sound of movement from within. There was nothing. She tried the handle and found the door was unlocked.

'Shit,' she mumbled. She remembered when she knocked on Gordon Berry's door and it opened. She hoped there wasn't going to be a similar scene of carnage here.

Matilda pushed the door slowly open and stepped into the hallway. It was cold and dark. She closed the door behind her. She didn't want to turn on the light for fear of alerting someone. There were three doors ahead of her, all closed. She noticed an underlying smell of newness – new carpet, new decorating. Then she heard something.

Matilda stopped in her tracks. It was faint, but definitely there. Breathing. Shallow breaths. Whimpering.

A light was switched on. The hallway and staircase were suddenly illuminated. Matilda looked up and saw Faith Easter standing at the top of the stairs. Crying. Her hands tied at the wrists, her legs at the ankles. She had a gag around her mouth, breathing was difficult. Attached to the bannister in front of her was a rope. The other end had been tied into a noose tightened around Faith's neck.

'Faith?' Matilda asked quietly. 'Oh my God. Don't move.'

'I'm sorry, boss,' she struggled to speak through the gag. Her words were barely audible.

'Stay calm.'

Faith's eyes kept darting to the left then back on Matilda. She was signalling. He was beside her, out of view.

'Why don't you come out into the open, Steve,' Matilda said aloud.

There was the sound of slow, sarcastic applauding as PC Steve Harrison stepped out from the shadows behind Faith and rested his arms on the bannister. He was still dressed in uniform.

'You finally twigged on, did you?' he asked. 'It took you bloody long enough. DCI Matilda Darke, head of the Murder Investigation Team, in charge of the entire CID. Talk about punching above your weight. I thought I was going to have to go on killing people forever.'

'Why are you doing this, Steve?'

'Why? You mean the great DCI Darke doesn't know?'

'I know you've tried to get into CID twice. You've failed the National Investigators' Exam twice. I know you've had several run-ins with your sergeants. Been called up on your lack of commitment on many occasions.'

Steve was shaking his head. 'No. You've got it all wrong. I am committed. *Fully* committed to my job. It's people like you who don't want me to succeed. If your face doesn't fit, if you're not prepared to brown-nose, if you show evidence of using your own initiative, you're not welcome.'

'That is rubbish, Steve,' Matilda said, glancing from Steve to a petrified Faith beside him.

'Oh come on. I've seen you being all pally with the ACC. There isn't a day goes by but you're not in her office having coffee. And what about DI Brady and DS Mills? Talk about suck-ups. And don't get me started on Scott and Rory. What the fuck are they even doing in CID?' With each name he spat out, his anger grew. This was a long campaign he had been waging. He'd been full of resentment and hatred for so long that it was finally bubbling to the surface. Just like it did with Ben Hales.

'Steve, if you're feeling disillusioned about the police force, there are people you can talk to.'

He laughed bitterly.

'Tell me about Brian Appleby,' Matilda asked. She wanted to keep Steve talking for as long as possible, at least until Sian and Scott turned up. If Steve Harrison really was a narcissist he would welcome relishing in his crimes.

He smirked. 'You've seen the CCTV footage?'

'We have.'

'I had the desk to myself. In walks Brian Appleby, all confidence and swagger, designer clothes, then he just comes straight out with it: "I'm a paedophile from Essex", like it's the most natural thing in the world. I went through the motions but didn't log his information. I kept it up here,' he said, tapping his temple. 'Then I had an idea.'

'You decided to execute him.'

'I was doing the world a favour. Getting rid of a pervert. You know, I was only planning to kill him. It was the way the filthy nonce came into the station like he didn't have a care in the world.'

'So why did you kill the others?'

'You,' he replied, his voice lowered.

'Me?'

'When you arrived at Brian Appleby's house I'd found out that morning that I failed my National Investigators' Exam. I was feeling pretty pissed off. Then you turned up. You showed me your warrant card, you took the forensic suit from me and you just walked inside. You didn't give me a second glance. I was nobody, a nothing. Then the way you spoke to that journalist, Danny Hanson, everything seemed to fall into place. He was another one, just like me, a lowly on the first rung of the career ladder, doing everything he could to catch a break and you swotted him like a fly. Once you're at the top, you don't give a fuck about the people on the bottom.'

'So you continued killing because I ignored you?'

'It wasn't just then. You've ignored me every time you've seen me. Outside the hospital room, where that paedo got beaten up. I even mentioned it was my birthday. At Joe Lacey's house. Did you even know I was there?'

Matilda looked at the ground.

'You didn't, did you? It's us in uniform that do all the legwork, the shit nobody else wants to do and you don't even acknowledge it. When you bumped into me on the stairs and I dropped some files, you didn't apologize. If it's not affecting Matilda then Matilda doesn't want to know,' he spat.

'Steve, you're reading far too much into this,' Matilda tried to assuage his anger.

'Am I?' he shouted.

Matilda listened for the sound of a speeding car, for Sian and Scott to come bounding into the house, but there was nothing. How much longer could she keep him talking?

'How did you know Katie Reaney was going to be in the house on her own that night?' she asked.

'I didn't. I'd been watching her for months. She should really have been victim number two, but I could never find a time to catch her alone. I think she was my favourite kill.' He gave a warm smile that lit up his whole face. He may blame Matilda for starting him off on his murder spree, but, at the end of the day, he'd enjoyed every single moment.

'How did you put the noose into my bag at the half-marathon?' Matilda asked. She edged herself closer to the stairs.

'Really? You're asking me that? It was me who handed you your fucking pack,' he said, venom in his voice. 'You didn't see me? You didn't fucking see me? You really are the most self-centred woman I've ever met.'

'Steve, I understand that you're pissed off, but your argument is with me, not Faith. Why does she have to be here? I thought you two were in a relationship.'

'She thinks we are,' he said, nodding in her direction. 'I wanted information about the case and she was happy to give it, providing I shagged her every once in a while. Still, we have to suffer to get what we want, don't we?'

Faith's tears were uncontrollable.

'She loves you, Steve,' Matilda said softly, hoping the prospect of a positive in all this would win him over.

'Does she?' He shrugged. 'You see, she's another one. She was hand-picked by DI Hales to go into the MIT when you were off boo-hooing over your husband. She had the prime opportunity to make something of herself, of her career, and what happened? She couldn't handle the pressure. Like Scott and Rory, she doesn't deserve to be in CID. All three of them should be in uniform.'

'How did you find out about Joe Lacey, Gordon Berry, and Katie Reaney?'

'When you're ignored it's easy to do research on the PNC and Internet forums when you should be working.'

'You made a mistake with Joe Lacey though.'

'Yes I did. When Karen was confessing to Sian I couldn't believe it. You see, Sian's another one. She likes to think she's everybody's friend, but when you wear a uniform, you're easily overlooked. I walked into that interview room with a tray of coffee and she didn't notice the recording device. Completely oblivious.'

'Did you really have to kill Karen Lacey?'

'What kind of a question is that? Of course I did. She allowed someone to serve her sentence for her. When I went to see her I think she was actually pleased. She didn't struggle at all. I'm sure she would have thanked me if she could.'

'Gordon Berry overpowered you though, didn't he?'

Steve shrugged it off. 'I think being pissed probably gave him more confidence. You should have seen his face when he came into the station.' He grinned. 'He nearly shat himself.'

'How did you find Gordon again after he'd done a runner?'

'It was easier than you think. I phoned him. I put on an accent. Told him we knew who he was from CCTV and asked if he wanted protection. He jumped at the chance. I arranged to meet him. Unfortunately, he clocked me and did a runner. I soon caught up with him though, at the bus station. I enjoyed the chase, actually. You see, that's another example, when Gordon sent you flying, it was me who picked you up. Did you thank me? No. Did you notice it was me?'

Matilda didn't reply.

'Answer me, you bitch!'

'No. I didn't,' Matilda said quietly.

'Because you don't see. You don't notice what is going on right under your fucking nose unless it directly affects you. I've heard people talking about you. Matilda's in the toilets crying again. Matilda's in torment about Carl Meagan. Matilda's still grieving for her dead husband. For fuck's sake, Matilda, get over it.'

'You have no idea—' Matilda started, struggling to keep a handle on her emotions.

'I have every idea,' he shouted above her. 'Don't stand there and think just because you're a higher rank you can silence me.

I have the upper hand now. I'm in charge. By the time I'm finished you'll either be dead or in a fucking mental asylum.'

From his back pocket, he took out a white pillowcase and pulled it down over Faith's head. He smiled at Matilda.

'Steve, no,' Matilda began.

He bent down and grabbed Faith by the legs. He lifted her up and threw her over the bannister. She tried to scream but the gag was too tight. Matilda ran forward to catch her before the rope around her neck tightened.

Chapter Sixty-Three

'Get out of the way, you gormless bastard.'

DC Rory Fleming screamed out of the driver's window at a lorry reversing from a side road at a snail's pace. The driver of the lorry leaned out of his cab and casually gave Rory the middle finger. Rory reached into his pocket for his warrant card and flashed it.

'Reverse or I'll arrest you for assaulting a police officer.'

Valuable minutes were lost while the driver wasted time reversing. He wasn't going to give the hurried detective what he wanted easily.

'About bloody time,' Rory cursed under his breath as he was able to mount the pavement and continue his journey towards the city centre.

He was on the wrong side of town and the traffic was still heavy with people making their way home from work. He'd called Christian at the station to ask where Faith was staying. Rory knew where he was heading; he just had no idea whether or not he would get there in time.

He broke the speed limit on Woodseats Road, almost colliding with a single-decker bus who refused to move for him. When he turned right onto Abbeydale Road and saw the length of the tailback, he almost screamed. He slammed on the brakes and slapped his hands hard against the steering wheel, inventing a few new swear words.

Sian and Scott had also been caught in traffic on the opposite side of the city, as they made their way from Hillsborough to the city centre. Eventually, fearful for Matilda and Faith, Scott mounted the pavement and drove round two buses and a fleet of cars. He blocked out the bad language and the horns from impatient road users. He ignored the red light, slamming his foot down on the accelerator. Sian, in the front passenger seat, shut her eyes tightly and held on to the dashboard for dear life.

'My God, Scott, what are you trying to do?' Sian said when she dared to open them again. 'You're going to get us killed.'

'I've been on the advanced driver's course. I know exactly what I'm doing,' he said as he swung the steering wheel right, taking a tight corner at forty miles per hour.

'Are you sure? I would like to get home in one piece tonight.'

'You will.'

'An alive piece.'

As they left the city centre, the traffic seemed to disperse, and the road ahead was quiet. Scott slowed to a more respectable speed and entered a housing development.

'There,' Sian called out.

'Where?'

'That's Matilda's car.'

'I can't park here,' Scott said.

'Then just pull over. Shit, there's Steve Harrison.'

Sian was out of the car before Scott had brought it to a complete stop. She reached into her back pocket for her telescopic baton and flicked it to its full length.

'Steve,' she shouted.

Steve Harrison stopped and turned at the call of his name. He saw Sian running towards him, baton held aloft.

'I don't think so, Sian.' He smiled.

At six-foot tall, Steve was powerfully built and had a good six inches on Sian. As Sian reached him, he dodged the baton, raised his left arm and punched her in the face, knocking her off her feet onto a parked car. Her head smacked against the bonnet and she slumped to the ground. He turned and ran.

'Jesus Christ, Sian, are you all right?' Scott said, running over and crouching beside her.

Sian was dazed. Her jaw was numb, and she could feel her lip swelling.

'That bastard's loosened my teeth,' she mumbled through the pain.

'Come here,' he tried to help her up.

'No. I'm all right. Go after him.'

'What about you?'

'I'm fine. Just go.'

'You're sure?'

'Scott, just get after him, will you?' She tried to scream through the pain in her jaw.

Scott turned and sprinted off in Steve's direction. It wasn't long before he had him in his sights. Two of South Yorkshire Police's fastest runners were now locked in a battle of the fittest.

Sian struggled to her feet. Put a hand to her mouth and it came away covered in blood. She felt wobbly but managed to get out of the road. She saw Faith's car in the driveway and used it to support her as she headed for the front door. Pushing it open she went inside. When she saw what was in front of her, she completely forgot about her own pain.

'Oh my God!'

Chapter Sixty-Four

To the people of Sheffield making their way to bus and tram stops after a long day at work, the sight of a man in a fitted grey suit chasing a uniformed police officer looked strange, though not entirely unusual. This was Sheffield, after all. They quickly stood to one side as Steve barged his way through, sending people tumbling to the floor. Scott, the more respectable of the two police officers, sidestepped and jumped over obstacles. Unfortunately, this was slowing him down. The gap between them was lengthening.

Steve had been faster in the half-marathon, too. The sense of urgency wasn't the same, however. Scott remembered keeping his eyes forward during the race. He had been fine for Steve to finish before him. As Scott had caught his breath by the finishing line, he had seen Steve looking at him. Leaning against the railings, head held high, he'd had one hand on his hip, the other holding a water bottle. He'd smiled at him. It was more a smirk. That had annoyed Scott more than anything.

Now, the rematch was on. The conditions were not ideal, and both weren't wearing the correct gear. Scott's shoes were expensive Ted Baker Chelsea boots that were not designed for running in. As he pounded the hard streets of central Sheffield, he could feel the stiff leather cutting into him once again. His feet felt wet.

Was it sweat or blood? He was dreading finding out. Why did his suit have to be fitted too? Yes it showed off his athletic frame, but it was not good for running in. The seam in his trousers was straining with each leap. He could feel the fabric tighten around his thighs. He would make a point of dressing for comfort from now on, not for style.

They ran down the High Street and across Fitzalan Square and down Commercial Street. As Scott had to slow for a double-decker bus, he looked up and saw Steve standing at the tram stop.

'Stop that man,' Steve shouted. 'He's a killer. He's the Sheffield Hangman!' He pointed towards Scott.

Scott looked around at the frozen public who stared at him with expressions of worry, anger and fear. Who would they believe? A young man in a suit or a young man in a police uniform. Eventually, a huge bear of a man in a high-visibility jacket stepped forward.

'You bastard.' He grabbed Scott by the shoulders then pulled his arms back. 'I've got him, mate,' he called to Steve. 'You want to cuff him?'

'Let go of me.' Scott panicked as more people gathered to stop him from wriggling free. 'I'm a police officer. I'm a detective. Let me go.'

'You're not going anywhere. Murdering scum,' the man shouted into Scott's ear. He could smell the warm rancid breath of a smoker as he abused him with vitriol.

Others stepped forward, grabbing for him, pulling him down to the ground. Scott tried not to lose sight of Steve in the growing crowd. His last image of Steve was of him smiling before turning and walking calmly away, hands in his pockets and his head held high.

'I'm a detective,' Scott screamed. 'I'm a detective with South Yorkshire—' He couldn't finish his plea as a steel toecapped boot hit him hard in the stomach.

'Matilda,' Sian said from the doorway.

'Oh, Sian, thank God,' Matilda cried breathlessly. 'I'm not sure how much longer I'm going to be able to hold on. Go upstairs and untie the rope.'

'What?'

'Now. Quickly.'

Matilda's voice was shaking. She had her arms wrapped tightly around Faith's legs. She was standing on the tips of her toes, struggling to keep Faith aloft and the pressure of the noose off her neck.

'Matilda,' Sian said, calmly.

Matilda turned her head and stared into the blank wide eyes of her DS.

'Matilda, you can let go now,' Sian said.

The tears were streaming down Matilda's face. 'I can't. If I let go, she'll die. Sian, run upstairs and cut the rope, untie the rope, whatever, just do something. I can't hold her for much longer.'

Sian placed her hand on Matilda's shoulder. Her voice shook. 'You can let go,' she struggled to speak through the tears. 'Matilda, you can let go. She's gone.'

Matilda gasped for breath. The tears continued to fall. 'I can't,' she mouthed. 'If I let go, she's going to die.'

Sian slowly prised Matilda's arms from around Faith's legs and pulled her boss into a tight embrace. Matilda fell into Sian's arms and they both collapsed to the floor, wailing in agony at the death of Detective Constable Faith Easter.

Chapter Sixty-Five

Scott rolled over to protect his body from the blows. As he did so, his warrant card fell out of his inside pocket. The kicks stopped, and he saw the sky again as the crowd stepped back.

'Shit, he *is* a copper,' he heard someone say.

Slowly, through the pain, he picked himself up. He looked down at his scuffed shoes and torn suit. He wiped his nose with his sleeve and saw the smear of blood on the grey fabric. His suit was definitely ruined now. He glanced around at the group who only moments ago had been baying for his blood but were now shocked at their own behaviour. They couldn't look him in the eye.

Scott bent down and picked up his warrant card. He took several deep breaths, before slowly walking away. The crowd parted in silence.

He felt dazed. He could have been killed. That thought made him sway and he steadied himself against the old Yorkshire Bank building. Around him, life went on as normal. Trams stopped to pick up passengers, buses noisily made their way up the incline of Commercial Street, workers chatted as they headed for home. All the sounds mingled into one undetectable white noise as Scott's head swam.

He looked back at the faces of the crowd who had ambushed him. They all seemed shocked, saddened, sorry by what they found themselves to be capable of. They all knew where it would have led. This is what Steve Harrison had turned people into.

He felt a vibration in his back pocket. He reached for his phone and tried to focus on the cracked screen. Rory was calling.

'Yes,' he answered, trying to sound as normal as possible.

'Scott, where the hell are you?' Rory was shouting into his phone, struggling to be heard over the sound of racing traffic in the background.

Scott cleared his throat and swallowed his emotions. 'I'm … I'm just up from Ponds Forge. Where are you?'

'What are you doing there?'

'I'm going after—' Scott stopped talking as he caught something in the distance.

'You're what? I didn't get that,' Rory shouted.

'It's Steve,' Scott said. 'I can see him. He's—'

'He's what? Scott, what's going on?'

'He's waiting for me.'

'What are you talking about?'

'Rory, you need to get over here.'

Scott ended the call and returned the phone back to his pocket. He slowly walked down Commercial Street and over the bridge where the tram went on its way to Meadowhall.

Standing in the middle of the bridge was Steve Harrison. He could have run. He had the perfect opportunity to make his getaway. By the time Scott had been found, he could have been long gone, out of Sheffield, heading for the nearest airport. So why was he standing still in the middle of the bridge?

Scott didn't rush. He ached so much he couldn't have rushed even if he had wanted to. Steve showed no sign of running away, even when Scott was close enough for them to have a conversation without having to shout.

They stood on the bridge facing each other. Below, speeding

traffic of the multi-lane parkway continued as normal – buses, cars, vans, lorries – all of them ignorant of the stand-off taking place above.

'You've taken a bit of a beating,' Steve sniggered.

'I could have been killed,' Scott said.

'Would I have been able to take credit for that?' he asked with a smile.

'Why have you done all this?' Scott asked.

'I've already had this conversation with Matilda.'

'I need to take you in, Steve.'

'You'll have to catch me first,' he replied, turning and walking away, further up the bridge.

'Why haven't you run?' Scott asked, confused.

'Where's the fun in that?' Steve shouted over the sound of fast-moving traffic below.

Scott waited until Steve had left the bridge and was close to the tram intersection. The last thing he wanted was to end up going over the railings and onto the parkway below. As soon as Steve was clear, Scott picked up the pace and ran towards him. With a final burst of speed, he rugby-tackled him to the ground.

Steve immediately tried to break free. He elbowed Scott in the stomach, hit him in the face. Scott cried in pain and tried to maintain his dominant position on Steve. But it wasn't easy, and soon Steve managed to wriggle free. He stood up.

'You're pathetic, Scott. You do all this running and think you're so fit, but it's all for show. All style and no substance.' He kicked Scott in the stomach, looked down on the stricken DC and smiled.

Below, Rory was speeding along Sheaf Street. As Ponds Forge International Sports Centre came into view he started to quickly look around him for any sign of Scott or Steve. Nothing. As he approached the Park Square roundabout he saw Steve standing on the bridge.

'Shit,' he uttered to himself. He was in the wrong lane and

already at the junction. There was no way he could get to them by car, and there was no place for him to pull up and jump out.

He drove into the centre of the roundabout, indicating right, and began circling.

Scott was curled up in the foetal position, his arms wrapped around his body for protection, his face contorted in pain. Steve had been relentless in his attack on his fellow officer. But now he was smiling down at him with his hand held out. Scott looked confused and shook his head.

'I'm offering you a lifeline, you moron. Take it,' Steve said.

Scott realized he had no choice. Reluctantly, he held out his own. Steve grabbed him and pulled him to his feet.

'I couldn't have you just die here. Where would be the fun in that?'

Before he knew what was happening, Scott saw the evil in Steve's eyes. He pitched forward, pushed Scott hard and into the path of a tram approaching from behind.

'Fuck it,' Rory said aloud, making up his mind.

He threw the steering wheel left and cut across two lanes on the roundabout. Ignoring the beeping horns, he slammed his foot down on the accelerator and shot up Commercial Street. He looked behind and saw no trams coming down the bridge. It may be dark, but the street lights would show there was a car on the tracks; they'd see him in plenty of time to stop, wouldn't they?

He made an illegal U-turn at the traffic lights and headed for the bridge. He saw Steve up ahead, on his own. Where the hell was Scott? Rory turned left, mounted the pavement and slowed down to ten miles per hour. It was enough to knock Steve off his feet, but not enough to cause him permanent injury.

Before Steve realized there was a car behind him, he was on the bonnet. Rory slammed on the brakes, and Steve rolled off, falling to the ground.

Rory jumped out of the car and ran around to the front. Steve was moaning in pain.

'Where is he?' Rory screamed. 'Where's Scott? What have you done to him?' He grabbed Steve by the collar and shook him hard.

Steve looked up and smiled.

'You bastard,' Rory exploded, punching him in the face. He felt his nose crack beneath his knuckles. Reaching into his back pocket, Rory took out his handcuffs and dragged Steve over to the nearest tram stop where he cuffed him to the railings. 'When I find out what you've done to him I'll fucking kill you,' Rory spat in his face.

He turned and ran up Commercial Street and along the bridge. There was a stationary tram on the tracks. People had alighted and were gathered around, glaring down at the ground.

'Oh, Jesus, no,' Rory said. He whipped out his warrant card as he approached. 'Police!' he screamed.

The crowd began to disperse, and Rory saw the unconscious body of his colleague, friend, and flatmate, Scott Andrews.

Epilogue

Monday, 15 May 2017

Adele pulled up outside Matilda's house. Summer had arrived early. The sky was blue and the clouds were white and wispy. There was a slight breeze, but it was bright and warm.

She walked down the drive and knocked on the front door, only to find it unlocked. She pushed the door open and stepped inside.

'Matilda?' she called out, a hint of worry in her voice.

'In the kitchen,' came the reply.

Adele closed the door firmly behind her before heading to the kitchen. 'Did you know your front door was … Oh! Sorry, I didn't realize you had company,' she said as she noticed a man in a cheap navy suit sitting at the breakfast table with a mug of coffee in his hand.

'Adele, this is Mr Chappell. He's brought the brochures round.'

'Wow, that was quick,' Adele said, taken aback.

'We don't waste time,' Mr Chappell flashed his well-practised estate agent smile. 'I'll let you get off. Enjoy your holiday. If there are any issues, give me a call when you get back.'

He said his goodbyes, flashed his fake smile once again to Adele, then showed himself out.

Adele picked up one of the brochures. 'They take good photos, I'll give them that. They always seem to make houses look gorgeous.'

'Cheeky sod, my house is gorgeous.'

'It won't be your house for much longer.'

'No,' Matilda replied, sadly, taking a longing gaze around the kitchen.

'Are you sure you're doing the right thing, Mat?'

'Yes.' Her answer lacked confidence. 'Anyway, let's not dwell on all that now. There's a plane at Manchester Airport that has two seats in first class with our names on them.'

'You're right,' Adele beamed. 'I'm so excited. I can't remember the last time I had a holiday.'

'Me neither.' She could; it was with James, but she had already cried over her husband this morning, so she tried to put it to the back of her mind.

'Right then.' Adele clapped her hands together. 'Actually, I think I might just run to the loo again. I'm so excited.' She smiled then trotted off to the downstairs toilet.

Matilda's eyes dropped to the brochure advertising her house for sale. The board wasn't going to go up in the front garden until she returned from holiday. She looked around her dream kitchen, as if seeing it all one last time. She knew she was making the right decision. It just didn't feel right.

Her eyes fell on the open door leading into the hallway. As promised, her parents had redecorated, changed the furniture and the curtains. It was completely different, but she still couldn't get the image of Ben's dead body out of her mind. That was what he had hoped to achieve. And he had succeeded.

Reluctantly, Matilda had listened to advice from Adele, Valerie and Sian, and phoned her former therapist, Dr Sheila Warminster. Once she had told her everything that had happened since their final session several months previously, Sheila had booked her in for an appointment straight away.

It felt different to all the other therapy sessions Matilda had. This time, she was in the driving seat. She opened up and spoke for the entire hour. Sheila had cancelled her next appointment and they talked more. Matilda mentioned everything: Faith's murder and the subsequent nightmares that had followed. Blaming herself for not seeing PC Steve Harrison as the killer sooner, Scott's brutal attack, his weeks in hospital. Fortunately, Steve had pushed Scott into the side of the speeding tram. He hadn't been hit full-on, more of a glancing blow. As he fell to the ground, he had banged his head on the concrete which rendered him unconscious. He spent three days in Intensive Care before he was moved to a ward. He was back at work within a week of being discharged. Now Ben Hales hanging himself in Matilda's house was her biggest problem.

'I can't get it out of my mind,' Matilda had told Sheila. 'Whenever I leave the lounge or the kitchen. Whenever I come downstairs or in from the garage or the front door, I see him hanging there. I've redecorated, scrubbed and scrubbed, but he won't disappear. I can still *smell* him.'

'Have you considered moving house?' Sheila had asked.

Yes, she had. Many times. However, she had always thrown the suggestion away. It wasn't an option, not until someone else had said it out loud, then it made perfect sense. She should move. Although James built the house from the foundations up and it was their dream house, it was stopping her from moving on. She loved James with every fibre of her being. However, he was gone, and she needed to come to terms with that.

She had left the session feeling like a huge weight had been lifted from her. On her way home, she stopped at Abbey Lane Cemetery to pay a visit to James. As she tidied up his grave and laid a bunch of red roses she knew he would hate, she told him of her plans. Then went home with her head held high. Full of determination and plans.

'What are you thinking about?' Adele asked coming back into the kitchen.

Matilda jumped. 'What? Oh nothing, just new starts.'

'New starts all round,' Adele said.

'Sorry?' Matilda asked.

'The Major Crimes Unit. It's in today's paper. A new unit dealing with serious crime and cold cases to be headed by Detective Chief Inspector Matilda Darke.'

'Oh that.'

'Yes, that. Valerie was singing your praises.'

'God knows why, I didn't do anything.'

'You caught a serial killer, Matilda.'

'Rory caught him,' she corrected her.

'You identified him as the killer. The papers said he's hoping to plead insanity.'

'Yes, that got thrown out straight away. He's sane all right. He knew exactly what he was doing. He'll never be released from prison,' Matilda said, looking past her friend and into the garden, or somewhere far far away in the distance.

'Have you chosen your team for the new unit?'

'Not yet. I'm waiting until after the memorial for Faith.'

'Poor girl.'

'I keep going over it in my head. I caught her. I know I did.'

Adele didn't tell her it would have been better if Matilda hadn't caught her. A straight drop would have snapped her neck, and she would have died almost instantly. Instead, Matilda held her while Faith slowly choked to death. She didn't need to know that, however.

'There were too many factors for you to have saved her,' Adele said. 'Has James Dalziel been in touch?' she asked, changing the subject.

'Yes. He came round last week to see if I was all right. He

brought me some flowers. I apologized for thinking he was the killer, and he admitted that he was attracted to me.' She blushed. 'That's why he had my photo in his study.'

'Ooh,' Adele teased.

'Don't get your hopes up, Adele. He's moving back up to Scotland.'

'Oh. How do you feel about that?'

Matilda laughed. 'Adele, I don't know what you've got in your mind, but there was never anything going on with me and James. Even if I wanted to pursue anything, I wouldn't with a man obviously on the rebound. Now, come on, that plane won't wait for us.'

An excitable smile spread across Adele's face. 'Monaco isn't going to know what's hit it when we land.'

Matilda left the house, closed the door and locked it. From inside she heard the landline ringing.

'Leave it,' Adele said. 'Unless you're looking to claim back PPI?'

Matilda smiled, and they headed for Adele's car.

The phone continued to ring. Eventually, the answer machine picked up the call.

'Hello, you've reached Matilda Darke. I'm sorry I can't take your call at the moment. Please leave a message after the tone and I'll get back to you as soon as I can. Bye.'

The wait for the beep was a long one.

There was a pause before the caller left their message. 'Matilda? It's … it's Sally Meagan. I'm probably the last person you were ever expecting to hear from, but I need some help and I don't know who else to turn to. The thing is, I've received a phone call from a solicitor this morning. Apparently, before he died, DI Ben Hales had been looking into Carl's disappearance. He says he's found him. He knows where Carl is. Could you give me a call please?'

Acknowledgements

It sometimes seems unfair that my name appears on the front of the book when I have received so much help and advice from such wonderful people. However, in the spirit of a BAFTA winner's acceptance speech, I would like to tearfully thank the following people:

My agent, Tom Witcomb for his feedback on my work. I'm privileged to have a hands-on agent who strives to make me work harder to make each book the best one yet. Thank you also to everyone at Blake Friedmann.

My editor, Finn Cotton, has been a great support. Thank you for your hard work and encouraging emails. To everyone at Killer Reads and Harper Collins, particularly Sarah Hodgson, a huge thank you. To my copy editor, Janette Currie, for correcting my errors (fewer than the last book, thankfully). To the designers of the cover, my thanks and my apologies.

Fellow writer, Neil Spring. Writing can be a very lonely process. It helps to have someone in your corner you can turn to for support, advice, and to use as a sounding board. I'm grateful to have Neil for all those things. He's a mighty fine writer too.

Claire Green at the National Digital Autopsy Service, pathologist Philip Lumb, and all the staff at the Medico-Legal Centre in Sheffield for their advice, showing me around the post-mortem suite, and making sure my work is as accurate as possible. Thank you to Simon Browes for answering all my medical questions. I hope nobody ever reads our text conversations about hangings and stabbings. Chillingly gruesome. A massive thank you to 'Mr Tibbs' for everything concerning police procedure. Any factual errors in this book are all mine and for the purposes of fiction. Don't blame the experts.

A special shout out to my mum who mentions my books to most people she meets and for baking the best cakes ever. To my sister, Donna, for running the Sheffield half-marathon so I didn't have to. To Jonas, Chris, Kevin, and Max, a manly hug and a big slap on the back, except for Max, he gets snuggles. To Debbie and Katie for the fun meals at possibly the worst pub in Sheffield.

Finally, a big thank you to the readers, bloggers, and reviewers, especially the ones who have been with Matilda from the beginning.